BATTLE FOR QUADRANT 8304

EUGENE WEAVER

by Eugene Weaver / First Edition

ISBN: (Paperback) 979-8-9886578-6-6
ISBN: (KDP) 979-8-9886578-7-3
Eugene Weaver
North Canton, Ohio 44720
Edited by Staci Frenes
Cover design and interior design by Rafael Andres

For my family, Joani, Lucas and Hudson Weaver,
who wanted me to continue writing the fantasy
and science fiction novels I started way back
in 1986 when I was 12 years old.

Contents

PROLOGUE

THE FIRST ESCAPE

Jake Riley lay back in bed, Elise resting her head on his bare chest. He calmly stroked her golden blond hair lovingly. They both were silent after the lovemaking, enjoying the afterglow.

Elise broke the silence. "I know you're probably still mad at me, but you do know you have to do this, right?"

Silence fell again across Jake Riley's room on the second level of the Command Center on Mining Complex VI as he continued to stroke her hair. He had fallen in love with this fellow resistance fighter, but he knew this was the right move. Neither of them was safe. Not only was the complex overrun with a virus, appropriately called the Rot, but Levon Gonidec's war machine back on their home world of Troria was in full swing. It was only a matter of time before he and Elise would be rounded up like so many countless others and put to death. Railara, the farthest planet in the quadrant from Troria, was their only hope. The solar system's only hope.

Avoiding her question, Jake responded, "It's all set up. I leave in the morning. You're the new acting commander until the skeleton crew is relieved after the last Kernadium shipment is picked up. We'll intercept the Trorian transport freighter and get you the hell out of here. Chris agreed to stay back and look after you, not that you need it. Petrino was also informed by command that he was to remain as well. So, he's going to be even more unpleasant than normal. I believe he chose Sonia Bonnel to stay behind as his assistant. But we both know he did that just to get to her."

Nodding slightly, Elise pressed into Jake. She loved him. Strong, handsome, and most importantly, a leader. Something her planet was in dire need of. She had forced him to agree to the Railarian government's proposed rescue. They needed someone on the inside, someone who had worked on one of Alnorix Mining Organization's cloning facilities and had insider knowledge on how best to take down the evil dictator, Levon Gonidec back on Troria.

Jake continued, "Once I'm enroute to Troria, an 'accident' is going to be reported. The ship is going to be pulverized by a stray asteroid, but I'm prepared, as are my assailants. If all goes as planned, I'll be fine. Suspect for sure, but what's one man to Levon's seemingly indestructible forces? They'll chalk it up to another dead Alnorix employee. One that may or may not have been spying on them. You, however, have *got* to watch yourself. They suspect me and I'm positive you're on their list as well. I just wish you could go along with me tomorrow!"

"You know I can't do that. It would be signing the death warrants for Chris and Sonia. Hell, even Petrino. As deplorable as that man is, he's a cog in the machine and is just as expendable as the rest of us in the grand scheme of things," Elise replied.

Nodding, Jake added, "Whatever you do, Elise, while I'm gone, do not put anything past Petrino. Play your cards right and we'll soon be reunited. Keep as much of this as possible from Chris and Sonia, they have enough to worry about. We're almost there. Soon we'll all be off this damned moon."

"Sonia respects you, Jake, we all do. Which is why you must go. I know you think it should be me but this is our chance. This is a chance for all of Troria. You have what it takes to see this through, to bring down Levon Gonidec and his regime. With the help of Railara's president, Gideon Novare, I know in my heart that good will prevail. Somehow."

Elise looked up at Jake, staring into his eyes with her beautiful green eyes. She moved forward, pressing her soft lips against his. He kissed her back, passionately. She slid the thin blanket off of her naked body and climbed on top of him once more.

CHAPTER 1

CAN OUR QUADRANT SURVIVE THIS?

Sitting inside the small transport shuttle the following morning, Jake Riley ran a hand through his hair and looked out at Mining Complex VI. He couldn't believe he was leaving Elise Bennet behind, but this was bigger than both of them. The madman on his home world had to be stopped. If not, the entire solar system was in jeopardy of falling into his hands. Railara, the farthest planet in quadrant 8304 from Troria, was also only planet that stood a fighting chance of helping bring down the regime on Troria, and he would be the man to lead the change.

The transport shuttle took off, the other employees on Moon 002 having departed on another shuttle. It was just Jake and the android assigned to transport him safely back to Troria where we would be "debriefed" upon arrival, which was code for interrogated then murdered.

He was quite glad he had been singled out to travel by himself, rather than in a large transport shuttle with nearly thirty people, which could have spelled disaster and the loss of many lives. This way, the rescue attempt by the Railarians would be much easier. On the ship, it would only be him and the appointed android pilot.

He made sure to bring his suit and oxygen tank. Looking down at it in his lap as the small, rectangular shuttle powered up its thrusters, he thought, *I might be doing a spacewalk in this thing. I suppose there's a first time for everything.*

The ship took off, dust from the nearly dead moon kicking up around them. It lifted into the air above the five buildings that made up Mining Complex VI. In the distance, the tall Poule plants where the Kernadium was harvested shook from the vibrations of the engines.

Staring down at the Command Center, Jake thought of his love inside, looking up at him. "I hope to see you soon, Elise," he whispered.

The ship blasted out of the dull, orange-colored atmosphere of Moon 002, up into the vastness of space where rescue from the clutches of the evil Gonidec awaited.

Elise Bennet looked out the top floor window of the Command Center. She already missed Jake Riley, a true born leader if she had ever met one. "Safe travels, my love. Know that I believe in you, and I believe in our mission, a solar system free of tyranny."

Levon Gonidec sat in his office inside the capital building of Troria. A thin, tall man with black hair combed over his head and piercing dark eyes that complimented his tanned skin, he was as attractive as he was ruthlessly evil, something he had used to his advantage over the years in his rise to power. At one time he was the person everyone wanted to be around. He oozed confidence, which had garnered him increasingly more attention from the right people. Mainly, the Alnorix Mining Organization, which would later play an integral part in putting him in power.

He wore his well-tailored and official military garb, complete with medals for achievements both unearned and unwarranted. He typically wore this when preparing to address his people, which he was about to do, knowing the fear it stirred in them. The people of this planet knew the military was at his beckon call, and this suit reminded them of just how close each of them was to imprisonment—or worse, death by any number of cruel and terrifying methods if disobedience to the rule of law he set forth was discovered.

The event would be broadcast all over the planet. His words were law and his mercy was minimal, reserved only for those most loyal to him and the regime he had built over the years. He had made his military a mighty force to be reckoned with. His puppet company, the Alnorix Mining Organization, or the AMO as it was known throughout the quadrant, was beyond profitable, and he had sunk much of its resources into his own protection, amassing an enormous fleet of ships at the ready to attack the remaining holdouts in quadrant 8304, followed by those in surrounding quadrants. The military and Alnorix Mining worked in tandem, as one large empire.

Today, Gonidec was filled with rage. Rage he intended to take out on his people and those supporting a free quadrant. Railara, the planet he had wanted most since taking power, was rich in Kernadium and soon to be his for the taking. But he knew he had to act. The time for deliberations was over. Any more hesitation would show weakness. He had put his military on alert and would soon lay out his plan of attack. All opposed would be deemed enemies of the state and dealt with accordingly.

"We're ready for you, sir," a woman said, peeking her head into the office.

He nodded in reply, shooting her an icy stare, then stood to his feet and made his way to the door leading to his own private broadcast station. Once behind the podium, he gave the nod. A green light in front of him lit up as he began his speech.

"People of Troria, I, your leader, Levon Gonidec, come to you this evening with grave news. We are under attack. Data has been stolen. The second moon on Treon III has been all but destroyed. Two of our own fleet have been lost along with numerous crew members. I have wanted nothing but peace. Since taking over this role, peace and prosperity have been my ultimate goals for all."

He paused, his icy stare piercing the screen in front of him. He continued, "A small group of terrorists have seen fit to disrupt our way of life. To steal from us. Kill our people.

And I shall no longer stand by watching this happen, not to our great and mighty world, and the planets where the AMO have employed many of our loyal citizens.

"Railara, our enemy, seeks to stop progress. They themselves sit on Kernadium but would have us suffer by ceasing all mining off-world. These elites cannot continue in their attempt to police this quadrant. They would have us stop production of life-sustaining means on planets devoid of any substantial life. Even now, they amass their military forces, claiming their own weapons of destruction are to be used as a deterrent. A deterrent against us! They mean to stunt our progress and cripple us as a nation! If we sit idly by, we, the free people of Troria, are doomed."

He paused again for dramatic effect. "No longer will we simply *talk* of war. War is upon us and we must answer accordingly. To do this, we will meet them on their own turf. I alone will protect our world and our resources, crushing the enemy. They will try and they will fail. Our way of life must remain. Our way of life must be spread throughout this quadrant and beyond. And so, now, the true might of my regime will move forward. We are undeterred. And I urge all to stand with me. Stand for our strong world and your strong leader. We will fight and we will win! Those that are not with me are against me!"

Another pause to let this statement sink in before the transmission was then cut.

In a small apartment room not far away, Corinna Bonnel, a frail woman whose heart was continuing to worsen, shuddered in her seat, watching the transmission. Her mind went to her dear daughter Sonia and her eyes welled up with tears. Quietly she said to herself, “Can our quadrant survive this?” as her tears spilled forth.

CHAPTER 2

THE RISE OF LEVON GONIDEC

At almost nine years old, Levon Gonidec knew he lived in poverty and abuse, and was old enough to know right from wrong. His father, a brutal man, continually beat his mother who was frail and never fought back for herself or her son. Levon had almost no feelings for either of them, seeing them both as weak in their own ways.

His dad Glenn, a large, overweight brutish man with a thick mustache and messy, greasy black hair, reeked of alcohol and smoke. One eventful morning, he walked into their small kitchen, noticing the rice and dried meat cooking for dinner, which is what they usually ate. It was all they could afford. His father worked odd jobs around Troria, but his recent failing health got him turned away lately from even the most menial jobs, such as washing the transportation shuttles around town. This in turn made him more hostile toward the two of them.

Smelling the pungent, gamey meat sizzling in the pan he walked over, picked it up, and threw it into the sink. His mother Wendy whimpered out a protest at the meager amount of food now resting in their sink instead of their empty stomachs. "Please Glenn, this is all we have!"

Slapping Wendy across the face, Glenn shouted back, "Shut up! I give you Marks to go to the store to buy food and this is the shit you attempt to serve me. You trying to kill me? Is that what you're trying to do? Kill the boy while you're at it!"

"No, please, it's all we can afford!" Wendy tried to explain.

"So, you're saying I can't provide for you, is that it?" Glenn yelled then shoved Wendy back against the stove. She attempted to shield herself from Glenn's fist but was unable to do so. His closed fist smashed against her cheek. She lost her balance and, in the process of trying not to fall, grabbed hold of the stovetop. Her hand landed squarely on top of the still lit, blazing hot burner, still lit.

Screaming in agony, Wendy went down onto her back, hitting her head against the side of their small kitchen table. Burnt skin from her frail hand stuck to the oven burner and sizzled. Young Levon screamed in terror while Glenn, taken aback by the turn of events, simply stood over his wife who was knocked out from the hard blow to her temple. Along with her extensive burns, she would need medical attention. That meant Marks. Marks they didn't have.

Blood flowed from the gash the table's edge had caused, and even at this young age, Levon knew this was more than a simple bump on the head. This was life-threatening.

Rushing over on his hands and knees to his mother, Levon reached for her as Glenn kicked him across the face with his hard, dirt-covered black boot, sending the boy sailing backwards as if he were little more than a rag doll.

"You stay away from her, you little shit. Everything was fine around here until she decided to have you. Not my choice, hers. And here we are. No money, living in this dump, and this bitch coddles you every chance she gets!"

Levon didn't say anything, just held his hand to his bruised face. White hot anger flowed through his veins. He hated his father. So much so, he played out his fantasies of murdering the man by killing small animals around their poverty-stricken neighborhood of Ash City with its rampant prostitution, drugs and violence. His favorite method was cutting the stomachs open while the small creatures howled in pain.

The pool of blood from her temple grew larger. His mother wasn't moving. Her hand, a grotesque mix of chard black and bright red meat still sizzling.

His father approached her, berating her. "Come on, get up, it's not that bad. Your hand is your own fault. What were you thinking grabbing hold of a hot stove? Stupid! And that's just a bump on your head. Come on, get the hell up!" He tried to sound nonchalant, but his tone revealed otherwise;

this was serious. If she was dead, he would be blamed. Then what? Prison in this godforsaken city was a death sentence.

Glenn got down to one knee and pushed the dead woman's shoulder. Wendy slumped over, her eyes open and already glazing over. "Oh shit!" he exclaimed, realizing she was indeed, dead.

While bending over her, Glenn hadn't noticed young Levon Gonidec stand to his feet and pick up the long, dirty knife. It was the one his mother had used to cut up the only meat they could afford to feed the fat piece of shit kneeling over her dead body.

Glenn glanced back to see the boy standing behind him right before the six-inch blade plunged into his left eye socket. There was a small pause as he tried to blink but his eyelid wouldn't close over the blade.

He fell backwards onto the floor, on top of Wendy. His feet began to convulse as the knife piercing his brain disrupted his motor skills. He urinated on himself.

Levon moved over of the man, watching as the blood began seeping out of the slit-open eyeball, running down his cheek and mixing with the blood of his dead mother below him. laying below Glenn. Trying to protest, the man was unable to speak. He couldn't talk and his only movements were involuntary twitches. His pants became warm and wet with the expanding alcohol laced urine.

Bending down, Levon took hold of the knife with both hands and pushed as hard as he could, sending the blade deeper into his skull, slicing through brains. He pushed and twisted harder yet until the knife would move no further.

A steady stream of blood now pumped out of his gouged eye. Glenn felt his body slipping into darkness. His lungs filled with stomach fluids and half-digested food that now choked the small bit of life he had left out of him. The last thing the dying man saw out of his remaining good eye was his son and murderer staring down at him, emotionless.

Levon stood to his feet. Through sheer chance, both were dead, lying in a pool of their own blood. He was free.

Instinctively, Levon knew what to do. He wiped his prints off of the knife and lifted his dead mother's hand, placing it around the knife. She had stabbed his father through the eye, he fell on her, burning her hand and knocking her head against the table. End of story. The police wouldn't look twice at this open-and-shut case of two lowlifes that were better off dead.

Levon would leave town. He wasn't even sure if anyone knew he existed. No schooling other than what his mom had attempted to teach him. His school had been and would continue to be, the cold, dirty, and violent streets of Ash City. A city in which he would escape. He was going to be somebody. Even at barely nine years old, he knew great things were in store for him. He just had to seize the moment. Which is exactly what he did in that small, grimy kitchen.

As the years ticked by, Levon became even more street smart, making friends with the right people and never, ever showing fear. He made friends with a local crime boss, Lizzy McCoy, who had his hands in a little bit of everything illegal in Ash City. Prostitution and drugs were his main source of income. He took a liking to the young and hungry Levon, making him a Marks runner. As the Marks piled up and Levon gained more of Lizzy's trust, the jobs got bigger.

At sixteen, Levon was selling drugs himself, but his favorite job was pimping—both men and women. The people he prostituted were like all people that were weak or needy, and he despised them. Women and children especially irritated him.

He was tall for his age and his outgoing and confident demeanor made him appear much older, as did his muscular form. His tan smooth skin, slick black hair, dark eyes, and toned body were alluring to people, which he used to his advantage.

Lizzy was gunned down one night in a drug deal gone bad, leaving Levon, at age nineteen, to assume power. Everything was falling into place. He was amassing foot soldiers, people that were loyal to him, would die for him. He quickly cleaned out the rest of the small-time dealers in Ash City, making it his own. The police were well taken care of and with it came protection. They liked the young, handsome man who made their lives easier. Drug dealing, gambling, and prostitution were all but legalized and crime seemed to plummet.

Nearby cities got wind of the young man who had cleaned up the city by himself. People that crossed Levon soon were never heard from again. Rumors swirled that bodies were being cut into pieces and burnt to ash in Ash City. The Marks rolled in and with them, more notoriety. Soon, his hold on the city extended farther, his henchmen making short work of neighboring cities gangs if they didn't fall in line, pledging their allegiance to Gonidec alone.

In his twenties, Levon continued growing, expanding. He was untouchable. Around the planet, in the crime world, his name was on top. What he said went unquestioned. He wanted a new drug manufactured. Done. He wanted to create his own small fleet of off-world ships. Done. He could have anyone and anything, but what he soon aspired to was leader. Leader of Troria.

He legitimized himself in his early thirties while still silencing any and all opposition by brutal force. He appeared on more and more holographic shows broadcast throughout Troria, becoming a household name. His dashing and charming demeaner endeared himself to a good portion of the planet. Half of them feared him and what he was capable of while the other half hung on his every word, no matter how insane he sounded. In their eyes, he could do no wrong.

Setting his sights on politics, he wanted to rule with unchecked power. He'd prove to his dead scumbag dad what he was really capable of. Once he was in power and ruled Troria, he would take over all of quadrant 8304 and become Grand Emperor over all of the planets, a title he would give himself. Sex, drugs, and alcohol were fine, but they eventually wore off. Unlimited power was his continual drug of choice.

He ran for president while still in his thirties and easily won. It was no surprise to anyone. He made sure he would win through voter intimidation—threats of violence from his mob and lies that he himself would perpetrate every chance he got. The media seemed to eat it up and publicized his every word. And if that hadn't worked, he'd fudge the numbers. His rule was inevitable.

People turned on each other. No one seemed to know what to believe was actual truth. Right was wrong and wrong was right. The Marks he spent on lavish homes and vehicles were quickly replaced by his seemingly countless supporters willing to give what they had to help his cause. To rid the planet of boring politicians and usher in a new era of true law and order. Only the strongest would survive. No help would come to the weak. Weakness was a virus Gonidec and his regime would squash.

Alnorix Mining Organization was an upstart business that saw the potential to make billions of Marks by coming alongside Levon Gonidec and his campaign, knowing that half of the planet were terrified of the man. This gamble paid off. He was elected and his first order of business was the creation of mining complexes across the solar system. He promised numerous jobs, another lie, as clones were created in their place. Cheap to make and disposable. Levon was good at devising ways to dispose of the bodies. He had perfected it throughout his years as a high-level drug dealer.

No communication was allowed between planets and the nearest mining complexes that were built—another show of force and unmitigated power. Talks were had by the leaders of all planets, but none wanted to face Levon Gonidec's wrath. So, he was left alone.

However, small patches of resistance began to spring up in cities across Troria. Leaders in the resistance came forward with plans to take down the Gonidec empire, but they would need first-hand information on the mining complex conditions. The resistance's only hope was the other planets in the solar system banding together.

Railara became the prime candidate for leading the push-back against the tyranny Levon Gonidec sought to achieve. With the help of Railara and several other planets like Veaphus and Druthea, covertly, people were put in place on the mining complexes throughout quadrant 8304 and information was gathered. All damning and crucial in uniting the planets in the quadrant together and moving forward with the hopes of taking Levon Gonidec out.

Frequently in his speeches, Gonidec uttered the words, "They must be dealt with! They don't want us to mine what is rightfully ours! They don't want us to live freely! *They!* It's them against us and our way of life!" It was drilled into the people of Troria, though the majority of them read through the lies.

Levon Gonidec's plan of a solar system bowing before him was all-too alluring. The pieces were falling into place. War was about to be waged.

Standing under a small overhang inside the prison compound to avoid the soft rain falling from the dreary clouds overhead, Nicholas Mohr, the heavyset, gruff forty-nine-year-old head of all the mining facilities, looked at Gonidec from the corner of his eye. They were standing in front of fifty *enemies of the state* inside a large open-air space with four walls on all sides. All fifty people had their hands bound behind their backs.

Men, women, and several teenagers as young as twelve stood in rows of ten. Many had been severely beaten to avoid any attempts at a revolt. The youngest were softly crying, knowing what was to come, with no one to lean on for support.

Omar Botto stood on the other side of Gonidec, his right-hand man who carried out numerous evil deeds, and who enjoyed keeping everyone around him in a perpetual state of terror. Few people were trusted in Gonidec's inner circle quite like Botto.

A brutal man, at forty-nine years old he was tall and imposing with a greying head of closely-cropped hair and piercing brown eyes. He was muscular and used his strength to break people often. He took on the jobs that most others, even in a regime such as Gonidec's, would rather steer clear of. He had no qualms about following out orders to the "t". If that meant the murder of man, woman, or even child, he would do it with no questions asked. Because of that ruthlessness, he had risen up the ranks quickly, becoming one of Levon Gonidec's most trusted insiders.

Gonidec spoke coldly, staring straight ahead of him. "Mohr, you are to go to Moon 002 and take care of your little 'problem' who seems to have gotten himself into trouble with some stolen information about our facilities here. See to it you dispose of him but bring that *thing* he's created back to me. We have use for it here. Destroy any files he has on the mining facilities and my military installations. That son of a bitch thinks he can blackmail me? He's a cog in my machine that's overdue to be liquidated. His time is up. The same applies to that woman, what's her name?"

"You're referring to one Elise Bennet, sir," Nic Mohr responded. "Dr. Petrino thinks he has a free ride and that he's invaluable with his clone experimenting knowledge, he'll be expecting me. I've got it all set up. My android pilot and I are leaving first thing tomorrow in my *Deimos*. Extraction is all set for the doctor and his files. As for the woman, she will be dealt with along the rest of the skeleton crew there. No witnesses." He paused, then added, "I intend to inflict great pain on that traitorous spy. I trusted her for the job up on Moon 002. That *bitch.* We still don't know the whereabouts of the previous commander, Jake Riley, another potential spy. When he was shipped off, his ship vanished. All signs point to an asteroid collision with the debris left behind. I question that, however."

Ignoring him, Botto said, "Sabotage has been set up as well on Moon 002. If all goes as planned, there shouldn't be a soul left by the time we arrive for the final Kernadium pickup, sir. Moon 002 will soon be a thing of the past. We've harvested all of the Kernadium we can and with the Rot overrunning the place, it's time to cut our losses. I wish we could just nuke the moon from orbit, but too many planets in the quadrant, if you know what I mean."

"Yes, well that won't be a problem soon. The Gonidec Regime will rule this solar system and all planets that don't comply will fall," Gonidec said. "Railara's Kernadium, all of it, will belong to me. Both of you, see to it that you don't fail in your tasks." Levon paused, looking at the soaking wet and cold prisoners in front of them who had been standing for several hours, awaiting their inevitable demise.

"Let's get on with this, I'm getting cold. All of you have been found guilty of spying against the sovereign nation of Troria. Some of you are family members of the guilty. I want you to know their efforts were in vain and you, too, will pay the price for their terrorist activities," Levon announced icily.

Filip Marsa, a high-ranking lieutenant standing near the soldiers lined up directly in front of the prisoners, was to carry out the unenviable task today. Something he had been made to do more times than he could remember. He looked at the leader of Troria for the nod which came immediately upon locking eyes with the tall and handsome Gonidec.

"Soldiers, prepare to fire on my mark!" Filip Marsa shouted.

A row of ten soldiers raised their Defender II rifles to their shoulders and aimed at the defenseless prisoners. A woman fainted and fell to the wet concrete below. Another person, a boy who had just turned twelve, shouted out for his fallen mother several rows up from him.

"We will be avenged! Mark my words! You will fall, Levon Gonidec!" a man in the front row said defiantly. He was covered in bruises, his arm twisted behind his back in a way that could only have been broken. He spat in Gonidec's direction.

This made Levon smile thinly. He enjoyed this defiance in the face of death, not like the rest of these pathetic things. It gave him that much more of a thrill when they were dispatched. He won. They lost. That's the way it had always been.

"Fire!" Lieutenant Filip Marsa yelled.

Laser fire seared through the air, piercing the front row, dropping them to the ground. One laser connected with the defiant man's head, and he fell instantly. The soldiers continued to fire as each row dropped to the ground. Men, women, and children, all reduced to lifeless corpses in seconds. Several attempted to run but had nowhere to go and were quickly shot in the back. In less than thirty seconds, the massacre was over. Fifty souls lay dead on the grey concrete that was quickly turning red.

Filip Marsa turned to look at the murderers behind him, but they had already left the crime scene, leaving him to clean up the death that surrounded him. He clenched his teeth angrily, glaring in the direction where the leader of Troria had stood. He turned toward Levon Gonidec's sprawling fortress, built on the backs of the hard-working people of Troria. Hate filled his eyes as he thought of countless people, his own family included, that had lost their lives since Gonidec's rise to power.

"Come on! All of you, clean up time. All bodies are to be immediately sent to the incinerators; you have your orders now *move*!"

CHAPTER 3

WHO AM I?

Open your eyes. He sat up in bed screaming, sweat covering his face, his dark brown hair wet and clinging to his forehead. He felt something slimy fall from the top of his head, sliding down over his chest and onto his lap. He grabbed hold of it—it felt like slippery, soaked-through, wet sheets—and scanned the dark room. It was empty, or at least sounded so. His nakedness made him feel all the more vulnerable. *Where am I? What is happening?*

It wasn't just quiet, it was the lack of any sound at all, as if the room had been wrapped in sound-deadening material. He couldn't see his hand in front of him; he would have to search the room blind. *Am I actually blind? I don't remember being blind.*

He suddenly became aware of something jammed down his throat and he started to gag. Quickly, he grabbed hold of the tube that seemed to be dangling from above, and pulled it out, feeling it move from his stomach to his throat then out his mouth. He spit up bile and coughed it out.

He ran his shaking hands over his wet face then down to his chest and arms. IVs were stuck into both arms. He quickly pulled them out and felt liquid splash against his arms. His mind processed these feelings along with questions: *Blood? What is blood? His brain immediately supplied the answer: Blood is a specialized body fluid. It has four main components: plasma, red blood cells, white blood cells, and platelets. Blood has many different functions, including transporting oxygen and nutrients to the lungs and tissues.*

Am I covered in blood?

Upon pulling the IV cords he quickly realized they were attached to something above his head, mounted to the wall or ceiling. Grasping both IVs, he gave them a hard tug and they immediately recoiled from his pull, shooting up and out of his wet hands, startling him as he looked up in vain, hoping to see something that gave him an idea of where he was.

The IVs were gone now. Just him and the bed. As if an internal computer were processing these thoughts, his mind said: *Get up! Move!*

He pulled the rest of what he assumed were sweat-covered sheets from his unclothed body—*Who took my clothes off?*—and carefully swung his left leg out of the small, single-occupant bed and dropped it to the floor. It was cold to his touch. He dropped his right foot to the floor beside his left then contemplated what to do next.

I don't know how large this room is. I don't know where the hell I am! I don't know who the hell I am! What's my name? He shook his head, then pushed himself to stand onto his two bare feet, immediately raising both of his hands in front of him to safely ascertain where the walls were. If there were indeed walls in this place.

Opening his mouth, he moved his lips and spoke aloud in a broken language that was both foreign and familiar to him. "It…is…so…hot…in…here! Hello?" *I can speak, how do I know how to form words?* There was no response, and there wasn't an echo, so he assumed he was inside a small, enclosed area. He moved forward, dragging his feet as he went, not trusting his surroundings or his own feet for that matter.

He shouted, "Come on!" then paused. "Come on!" he shouted again, still getting used to using his mouth and forming words. In frustration, he attempted to reach any sort of structure his outstretched fingers could touch. The fear was almost more than he could bear. He didn't know who he was or where he was, but he kept moving forward slowly.

"It is so hot…someone, anybody? Help…me! Please!"

He was beginning to panic as a feeling of claustrophobia swept over his exposed and sweaty body. His feet shuffled a bit faster as he frantically searched for a wall. His outstretched hands hit something solid.

Quickly, he began sliding his hands along it, trying to find a corner or better yet, a door. He was moving to the left when he hit a corner. He spoke again in this strange language that seemed to be downloading into his brain at a pace too rapid for his thoughts to keep up with. "Okay, we're getting somewhere. I'm in a room, now I need to find a light source."

Continuing to run his hands along the wall, he found what he was looking for. A small rectangular shape that was nearly flush with the wall. He felt around it, trying to find a switch or a knob of some sort that he could flip on. His finger found what he was looking for and clicked upwards. Fluorescent lights flashed on harshly above him, illuminating the room.

He saw the bed back against the far wall, a simple, white, rectangular structure with a thin mattress that appeared to be bolted to the floor. *Why bolt a bed to the floor?* And the sheets. Except they weren't sheets. They resembled a clear sheet of plastic with a hole ripped through it. *That's what fell off of my head. I was encased in that,* he thought with a shudder.

The walls were white, as was the small slab that had held him when he was out cold, most likely from whatever was in the IVs. Blood and sweat smears covered the sheets. He looked down at the tiny holes in his arms where the needles had recently been pulled out, seeing a line of drying blood down to his hands. He glanced up to where he assumed the IVs had retracted to and noticed a shiny metal plate on the wall behind the bed with small medical instruments and smaller light sources attached.

Images flashed inside his head, planting themselves deep into his subconscious. Medical instruments. Lights.

The tube that had been in his mouth was attached to a circular ceiling mount. *So, they stuff the tube down my throat from there. Lovely.*

He glanced around the rest of the room. A door beside the wall outlet had no handle. *Shit!* Above the light switch was a keypad with buttons numbering zero to nine in rows of three. *Numbers, I know these numbers.* "How the hell should I know the code to this door?" he said angrily as he attempted to opened it, then moved back, scanning the remainder of the room.

The lights hurt his eyes with their intense brightness, the heat stifling in the sealed-off room. He could breathe, though, so there must be ventilation.

On the wall facing his bed was the thin outline of what appeared to be another door. He quickly walked toward it and began looking it over. There was no handle, so he tried to slide it open. No luck. Next, he pushed against the outline with both hands and the entire panel gave way, moving backward roughly one inch before the door slid over to the right completely. "Pocket door, this is called a *pocket door*."

He shook his head, his brain felt scrambled. Numbers, words, thoughts, images, all random, pressing onto his brain in an instant and attempting to organize themselves. It was becoming easier for him to articulate words and thoughts.

He stepped forward into the dark space and immediately lights clicked on. *Must have tripped a sensor or something* he thought as he stepped further into the now illuminated opening.

It was sparse inside the narrow closet, with numerous compartments but only a few items in them. "Clothes, please... let there be clothes," he said, frighteningly aware of his nakedness as he inspected the compartments. He wasn't sure how he knew he needed to cover his naked body. His eyes moved quickly back and forth in an attempt to grasp all of the bits of information that seemed to be flying at him in rapid succession.

He quickly grabbed a pair of black boxer briefs and matching socks, putting them on before looking over anything else. Tan cargo pants he pulled from the open compartment beneath the undergarment's cubby and slid them on. Perfect fit. *These must be my clothes* he thought as he pulled a gray T-shirt from another compartment and pulled it over his head.

"Now to figure a way out of this box!" he exclaimed, glad to be clothed.

Scanning the other compartments, he searched for anything that might jog his memory. His name, or better yet, the code to the keypad that hopefully opened the other door to his current prison cell.

A manila folder lay on the top shelf. He pulled it off and opened it, scanning its contents. *How did I learn to read?*

On the first page, scribbled in ink, he read, "Clone #572: Subject named *Michael* appears to be coming along nicely and has reached full physical maturity. A strong one judging from his muscle mass. Basic motor skills and cognitive awareness activated. Recommend detailed memory implant on 10, September 3123. Suggested possible work detail for subject: hard labor in mining complex, security detail at complex entrance and/or potentially compromised areas of research facility. Subject can begin its functions immediately upon activation."

"Michael, my name's Michael. I'm a…clone? I have no memory, but I can think for myself, I can talk, I can feel. Think, damnit!" *You have to remember something, anything! I know what a clone is, but how?*

Frustrated and frightened by this new realization, the man quickly scanned the rest of the page. The name Dr. Anthony Petrino was scribbled in the bottom right-hand corner near a small emblem of a drilling machine with the words *Alnorix Mining Organization* beside it.

Sliding the paper to the back, he looked at the next sheet in the folder. Diagnostics and medical charts. Heart rate, blood pressure, skeletal growth, five senses, all documented. He flipped through the rest of the pages containing more information on his own progress. Hair growth rate, sexual organ functions, muscle mass, all appearing to be optimal. Age: thirty-three years, upon completion of incubation period.

He rifled through the stack further and came upon a picture of a man lying on a bed exactly like the one in the room, a clear film covering him, IVs connected to his arms and a feeding tube jammed down his throat. Caucasian. Brown hair hung loosely from his head, with chiseled facial features and upper torso. He reached up and felt the hair on his head. This was him.

"What's the date? What the hell is the date? How the bloody hell do I get out of this fucking room!?" Michael yelled as he quicky flipped through the remaining pages in the file. Talking was becoming more fluid with every word, though it still felt awkward and choppy.

The last page in the folder appeared to have information on his room: "#55, located on level three of this facility, temperature at 85 degrees for final incubation period, after which outer embryotic film will be removed to keep specimen in womb-like state until final memory implant." The page was dated August 28, 3123.

He set the folder back down in the compartment and headed over to the keypad on the wall. Studying it, he thought for a bit, his eyes moving back and forth. Thoughts were once more being pushed into his brain. He was getting used to the information dumps implanting themselves inside his head so he simply waited until it subsided then pressed the numbers 0910 followed by the enter button. Nothing. He tried 3123, followed by the enter button. Nothing.

"Room fifty-five, okay, here goes."

He punched 55 into the keypad. Nothing. Shaking his head in frustration he quickly tried again, this time entering 0055 and hitting enter. There was a hissing sound as the door slid back into the wall.

For a few seconds he stood in the doorway, instinctively feeling defenseless. *I need a weapon.* Michael glanced back inside the room and quickly went back to the closet where he recalled there being a rod to hang clothes on. He grabbed hold of it and pulled, easily breaking it free of its loose constraints.

Holding it in both hands, he inspected his new source of what his mind told him was protection. It was roughly fifty inches long and hollow inside, made of what felt like a durable metal. He instinctively swung the rod in the air as it made a swishing sound.

"I think this should work. Not sure how I know that. Not sure how I know anything," Michael said frustrated, looking down at the rod in his hands.

What am I protecting myself from? He felt vulnerable and utterly alone, his mind rapidly implanting thoughts and images of dangers possibly lurking outside the claustrophobic room he was evidently just born in.

He looked toward the darkness past the open door. Cold dread filled his brain as he forced himself to walk to the door once again.

CHAPTER 4

NOT ALONE

Michael entered the hallway. The lights from the small room he had just exited illuminated his immediate surroundings, but beyond that it grew darker. Only small baseboard lights lit the path directly in front of and behind him.

"I'm on level three. I assume I need to head to level one. But then what?" Michael stuttered to himself as he began to make his way forward into the looming near-darkness.

The wide walkway was a dull gray, the ceiling roughly ten feet high, he guessed, as he stared up at it then back down to the rows of doors exactly like the one he had just exited.

He turned to see how far he had walked. Judging by the light that was still visible behind him, he guessed around sixty feet. He turned back to face the front once more, clothing rod in hand. *Am I going in the right direction? Shit. Maybe I should double back and go the other way.*

His mind computed that it was significantly cooler outside of his room. He attributed this to the probability that he was indeed a clone and the room needed to be kept warm for proper incubation to complete his birthing process.

"Are there more like me behind all of these doors?" Michael wondered aloud, not trusting his surroundings and how quiet it was. He approached a door marked 47 with a keypad like the one in his room mounted beside it.

"What the hell, let's see what we've got here," Michael said as his new fingers awkwardly pushed 0047 on the keypad then hit enter. The door hissed and slid back into the wall revealing a dark room. He felt around the inside of the door and clicked on the harsh fluorescent lights revealing a room identical to his own.

His eyes immediately went to the birthing container. There was something inside, completely covered by the now familiar, clear, filmy substance. Keeping his clothing rod in front of him, he made his way into the room to get a closer look.

Michael peered down at the half-developed form inside the clear film with IVs in both arms and feeding tube jammed down its throat. This particular clone was little more than a skeleton with exposed internal organs. One eyeball in its left eye socket, the other empty. Pink brain matter could be seen through parts of the exposed skull, as well as veins pumping blood to a heart that sent it to other exposed body parts.

"Female. This one is female. How do I know what male and female are?" Michael exclaimed, puzzled at his new mind working so fast at gathering and imprinting data. He stared at what his brain told him were mammary glands on its chest, then touched the thin amniotic sack, causing it to jiggle slightly. He set his rod down against the birthing container and quickly made his way to the closet, hoping to get more information on this partially developed clone, and more insight into his own cloning.

Pushing against the panel as he had done in his own room, he felt the closet door move backwards lightly then slide into the wall. Lights clicked on above him, illuminating an identical closet to the one he had just discovered in his own room.

He found a similar manila folder, pulled the files out of the compartment, and moved back into the room where the clone fetus lay so he could examine it while reading over the notes.

"Clone #469: Subject named *Lara*, gestation period taking longer than expected, suggest increasing the vitamin dosage to four times daily instead of the current three. If subject is not ready by the recommended detailed memory implant on 5, November 3123, it will be destroyed due to cloning insemination process not taking hold optimally. Suggested use, food sustenance for labor force on Mining Complex VI as long as no internal rotting has occurred. Thus far, no detections of Rot present in host."

It was signed by a Dr. Kevin Bradley. As with the first page on his own file, he saw the drilling logo with the words *Alnorix Mining Organization* next to it.

Michael's eyes widened with revulsion. "Food? We eat the rejects?"

Quickly flipping to the last page, Michael saw that the date marked on the sheet read August 5, 3123. Not bothering to put the folder back where he found it this time, he sensed a new sensation programming itself into his brain. Anger—he knew that's what it was without knowing how he knew it—surged through him upon reading how these clones were tossed aside if the development stage didn't take. Literally ground up into food for those that had come full term.

He instinctively tossed the folder on the floor, picked up his rod, and turned to leave the room. His anger quickly morphed into a brand-new sensation, sadness. Sorrow for this lifeless being, seemingly tossed aside like useless garbage. Out of a subconscious respect for her, Michael turned the light back off and entered the code once more, sealing the door closed behind him.

Again, the long and quiet hallway. He moved forward, scanning the numbers of the doors as he went. They were counting down. Several doors were open and dark. He entered room 43, peering inside after flipping on the light. Empty except for the clear film that looked to be dry now. "Someone else survived, I guess. But where are they?"

The room next door was also empty. He glanced in then quickly turned the light back off and moved on. At the next room, he punched 0040 onto the keypad and the door slid back and into the wall.

The odor of rotten meat hit his nose immediately as he reached for the light switch and clicked it on. Inside the 85-degree room, he felt a new sensation, smell, programming itself while he scanned his new surroundings. He put his arm to his nose in an attempt to mask some of the smell, but it did little to alleviate the rancid, foul odor. Wanting to turn and flee the room, his curiosity got the best of him and he moved forward instead, toward the amniotic sack.

Inside the clear film lay the remains of a partially-developed skeleton with chunks of muscle around it. Organs seeped out of the stomach and chest cavity, rotting in a pool of green and red liquid surrounding the corpse. The IVs and feeding tube dangled above, having eventually fallen out as the body continued to decay.

The jawbone had slid off the rest of the barely-formed skull, and whatever liquids had been inside the body now lay in a thin pool along with the organs. He wretched at the grotesque display of death sprawled out on the birthing container. Bits of undigested food from the feeding tube and bile spewed to the floor, making the scene in the room even worse.

Michael wiped his mouth and knew he needed to get out of the room, but not before grabbing the medical chart in the closet. He would make it quick. He ran to the closet, pushing the sliding door back and rushing in as the lights clicked on. He wasted no time, grabbing the files and running out of the room. He quickly entered 0040 and the door sealed shut along with the rotting specimen inside.

Moving away from the door where the stench was still lingering, he began looking at the files in the hopes of gaining more insight as to where he was and what was going on here. Wherever *here* was.

The handwriting looked the same as on his own pages. "Dr. Petrino. A human. He is a human, and we are not." His brain processed and stored this data as he read on.

"Clone #206: Subject named *Seth* shows extreme signs of malnutrition from the infection. Feeding tube not taking well to the host's stomach due to internal alien growth. Several more dark green rotting lesions spotted on lower intestines. Recommend ceasing incubation before more resources are spent. Body to be incinerated."

He flipped to the last page, looking it over and saw the date, August 28, 3123. His brain did the math, processing this new information. *Two weeks before I was supposed to have a memory implant. Which I assume didn't happen.* Michael puzzled at the path of horror he was encountering down this long hallway.

He stuffed the first page into his pocket, wanting to hang on to it as proof of what was taking place in this hallway of horrors. He dropped the rest of the folder on the floor haphazardly, still trying to make sense of the madness of his existence thus far.

Suddenly, Michael felt a severe pounding blast through his head, bringing him to his knees. He grabbed his head with both hands, grimacing at the throbbing jolts running through his body.

In his mind's eye, he saw himself as a boy, kicking a ball around in a yard with several other boys, all of them about ten years old, judging by their height. It was warm outside, the yard large, with trees surrounding the neatly-mowed property. He heard a female voice in the distance calling, "Michael, time to come in for supper!" and he knew it was his mother.

The old two-story house where a pretty but tired looking blond woman stood on the front porch with her hands on her hips had seen better days. His mother was wearing an apron and a yellow dress.

"Aw, Mom! Why now? I'm having fun with…"

"Michael, don't give me that attitude, come in now! Or when we talk to Papa later this evening, we'll have to mention this bit of not obeying. This is the second time I've asked! You remember what he told you before he left for planet Geatune 7, right?" she hollered back as he continued running around the yard with his friends.

"Okay, okay, I'm coming! Sorry guys, gotta run. See ya tomorrow!"

A sandy-blond-haired boy closest to him yelled back, "You're so lucky your dad can work off-world! See you tomorrow, Mikey!"

"Papa will want to say hi when we call tonight. He's been working really hard up there. He misses you," his mothing said softly as she ruffled his hair when he got to the top of the steps leading into the house.

The vision disappeared, and the pounding in Michael's head subsided. He looked around the deserted hallway once more. All was quiet. No more kids yelling and playing in his head.

"What is happening to me!? Where is everyone? What made me wake up? Damnit!" Michael tried to shake the vivid memory from his head. He felt immense love for his mother already, but wasn't entirely sure if she even existed.

He heard something and quickly glanced up, looking down the dark hallway from which he had just come. It sounded like something hitting a wall.

"Hello?" Michael called out, peering at the desolate corridor. Silence followed. He looked back at the doorway in front of him. He had made it to the end of the hallway to what he perceived was an exit. But what if that noise was someone like him? Stuck inside their room, not yet figuring out the closet and the codes on the wall. It could be someone in need of help or, better yet, someone who could help him figure things out.

Fear once more etched itself into his thoughts. He was learning so many new sensations and how rapidly they could jump from one to another. One second fear, the next puzzlement, the next revulsion.

Turning toward the sound, which seemed to be sporadic, Michael headed back down the hallway gripping his iron bar tightly in both hands. The unease he felt in this long, dimly lit hallway was palpable.

"Hello?" he called out again and was immediately met with another thud, this time much closer. Whatever, or whoever, was down there was close. He stopped at room 51 and put his ear to the door, listening.

Slowly, he raised his hand and gently tapped the door. A pause, then, thump, thump. "Can you hear me?" Michael called out apprehensively. "Call out if you can hear me!" he nearly shouted but was met with silence.

Michael contemplated his next move. *Do I enter the code and see what's in there or try to get the hell out of here?* "Come on, Michael, just open the damn door."

He raised his finger and slowly punched in 0051 then hesitated over the enter button. His head began pounding again as another memory came, searing itself into his brain. Grabbing the sides of his head, Michael closed his eyes and immediately saw a teenager of about fourteen. He had long, brown bushy hair and the beginnings of muscles on his arms, though nothing like the biceps on the grizzled man beside him. He was working with the much older man whose baseball hat covered most of his graying long hair. They were in a garage near the same house from the previous vision.

Above the garage, the sky was clear and blue. In the distance, a planet hovered in the sky with rings around it. In the daylight it was difficult to make out the color of this unnamed planet, but it had an orange hue that complimented the rings around it. On the opposite end of the sky were three distant stars that served as the planet's light source. A small spacecraft shot silently across the beautiful blue sky in the distance.

The boy and the bearded man worked on an engine hoisted up by a large chain. Beside it sat an *Arden Transport Cruiser*, or as they were known on planet Sibunia, ATC's. Used to fly short distances and not able to breach the atmosphere, it was all Michael Astier's family could afford. As they continued to reassemble the engine, the boy looked at the man who was adjusting a rubber belt on the engine in front of him.

"Dad, have you ever been to Trunah?"

The man continued to tighten up the belt until it was secure. He wiped the engine grease off of his strong hands on a rag and replied in a gentle, deep voice, "Well, son, you know I've been all over the galaxy. Been to numerous planets, but Trunah? Nope. Never been. That's one for you to discover on your own when you're of age. You still want to get into the mining business, huh?"

"Yes, Dad! I want to travel the galaxy. I'm going to be strong like you someday, you know I will. Miners always get the tough jobs on distant planets, and I know I can do it!" younger Michael replied back excitedly.

Nodding his approval, the man grinned as he peered at his son through his squinty hardened eyes. Eyes that told his son, *I love you and I'm proud of you.*

Snapping back from this vision, Michael stumbled backward with his hands still on his pounding head. Both of these visions caused sharp and immediate pain that subsided quickly once they ended. Other memories seemed to be swimming in his subconscious as well now, from his past as a young boy and teenager. These few were the most vivid, as if his brain were a large, heated pot with various ingredients being dumped into it and stirred at random. These new memories, and the force with which they arrived, gave him a new sensation: pain.

He stood alone once more in the desolate, dim hallway. The thumping on the other side of door 51 had ceased. *Was that just in my head? Like these visions of my past? A past that seems to be imprinting itself periodically,* Michael thought, confused as he weighed out his options.

Once more, he raised his finger toward the enter button. *Push it!* his continually programming mind commanded. This time, he pushed it without hesitating.

CHAPTER 5

TENSIONS RISE IN BUILDING A

Dr. Petrino glanced at his watch as he paced the Command Center room located in the main building at Mining Complex VI of the AMO on the small moon of planet Treon III. There were ten mining complexes in this solar system, quadrant 8304. On each of them, employees harvested Kernadium from cactus-like structures known as Poule Plants which, in their prime, were purple with swathes of crimson red throughout their trunks.

This building, known as *building A,* easily identifiable as Command Center in large block letters near the top of the oval-shaped gray structure, was the central hub where all of the human staff coexisted and communicated with headquarters. Tensions were nearing the boiling point inside.

"So, you think you're actually going to get the coms back up and running?" Dr. Petrino asked in his usual aggressive and agitated tone, something the rest of the small group of people were used to at this point. The tall, skinny, man in his mid-forties took the round glasses from his pasty face and wiped them on his lab coat. His pale skin appeared greasier than usual due to the many hours of sleep he had lost recently.

He ran his hands over his thinning hair, once pale blond and now sprinkled with white throughout. He walked to the large window overlooking the planet's surface. Wind howled, visibly blowing dirt and debris across the landscape.

Large rock formations littered the desolate area. They ranged in color based on how heavily they had been mined, but most were dark gray to nearly black, matching the color of the rocky terrain. Once mining was complete, the once beautiful Poule plants took on the appearance of rocks, eventually crumbling to dust and blowing away with the harsh weather conditions of the moon—yet another result of the heavy mining done on each of the Alnorix mining locations.

Working at her computer was Sonia Bonnel, thirty-two, who had been at the mining complex since graduating from Otheania University on Troria with a degree in biotechnology, specializing in cloning animals. She was somewhat short in stature with curly brown hair she continually brushed out of her face. She felt as though her time on Moon 002 had aged her far more than she would have liked. No love life, shifts lasting some days up to eighteen hours, with few friends to speak of. But she had learned back on Troria it was best to keep your mouth shut if you want to survive.

Troria, her home planet, had quickly devolved into a cesspool of violence and despair thanks to Gonidec and the AMO. A police state where good people quickly learned to look the other way and keep their mouths shut or else face imprisonment or death. The wealthy got far wealthier, so those in power remained in power and craved it more. Until finally, the planet became a place where a little more than the top ten percent ruled the other ninety.

Sonia herself felt destined to a life of servanthood to the higher-ups. Anything to save her mother, Corrina Bonnel, who was sixty-five years old and in dire need of heart surgery, which didn't come cheap. Even her current five-year long job stationed on Mining Complex VI would barely cover it. Such was life on Troria for the have-nots.

She pushed her dark-rimmed glasses up as sat hunched over her monitor in the corner of the large room, now sparse as it had been decided by those in power back on Troria to shut down the facility due to the outbreak of the clone rot that had begun springing up one month earlier.

Most personnel had left on the transport shuttles that had arrived earlier, and all that was left to keep the small complex operational was commanding officer, Elise Bennet, Dr. Petrino, his assistant, Sonia, and a tough black man by the name of Christopher Berger, one of the security guards who had unfortunately been chosen to stay on for a bit longer while his friends would be relocated to bigger, better, and potentially much more prosperous work. Even at the relatively young age of thirty, Chris showed the stress of working at Mining

Complex VI on his face, though this didn't keep him from his strict workout routine every morning in the exercise room the AMO provided to all of its employees.

"I can't get anything to work here," Sonia said grimly as she looked back at her computer that was nearly useless in its current state. "I mean, we've shut down all vitals on the remaining clones per headquarters orders but without the coms up, we're blind here. Unless we want to go door-to-door and do it manually. And I for one do not want to get the Rot. None of us are equipped for that."

Chris cracked his knuckles as he walked over to where Sonia sat, looking down at her computer monitor displaying their oxygen levels. "Where we at with oxygen? I mean, we don't know what caused this total system failure and com link break, but the most important thing now is our air. We're looking at, what, roughly a three-day evac time for them to get the last transport shuttle over here from Alnorix? By my estimations, and yours, Sonia, we have maybe, *maybe* two days left of oxygen unless we get the generator back online or figure another workaround."

Sonia replied bitterly, "Unless one of you plans on strapping on an oxygen tank and mining suit and heading over to the generator facility and seeing what the hell is going on, I am happy to listen to any and all options, because I'm fresh out."

Sonia knew Chris was tired. Tired of the low pay for hard work on this now drained small moon orbiting Treon III. The muscular black man had arrived two years ago in good spirits and made friends quickly. Soon after, he saw what was really going on inside the facility and how the mining was accomplished with clone slave labor. They were seen as expendable in the rapidly deteriorating climates of any planets and moons where Kernadium was harvested. The process decimated the environment, as the Poule plants, once dead, depleted the soil of any and all nutrients.

"He should go!" Dr. Petrino shouted as he turned from the window to look at the frustrated man in the disheveled company uniform. "You're the security guard, Chris. It falls on you! Last time I checked, I outrank you, got it?"

"Hey, that's what we have those damn clones for!" Chris replied, glaring at Dr. Petrino. "I have literally no idea how to run that generator. I was never trained. None of us were! Those greedy bastards back at headquarters shipped every non-clone off-world, our superiors included. Who's even in charge here?"

"I am." A voice sounded from the doorway.

Dr. Petrino, Sonia, and Chris all turned as Elise Bennet walked through the door. Tall and slender, her blond hair pulled back into a tight ponytail, even now in these final days of Mining Complex VI, she held her head high, kept her dress attire professional and had an air of confidence. Something Dr. Petrino hated. A woman in power.

"Ah yes, the great Miss Bennet. Back once more for another update, I'm assuming. Well, here it is: we're stuck on this dead rock and we're running out of air. Other than that, we're doing great in here!" Petrino all but shouted in frustration at the beautiful and intimidating woman who entered the room.

Elise looked at him, unmoved and unaffected. She walked across the room as Chris and Sonia awkwardly watched the stand-off unfolding. Once she got to the wiry doctor, she stood in front of him, far too close. She knew this made him extremely uncomfortable.

"You will address me as commander. Just as you were instructed by the previous commander Jake Riley's orders before he left for Troria for re-assignment. Do I make myself perfectly clear, doctor?" Elise said calmly but with authority.

Petrino quickly looked away, averting his eyes and nodding his head sharply. Then, in frustration, he turned back to look out the window and the strong winds outside.

"Commander, the remaining clones are infected, dead, or dying, and now we have an unknown generator power outage. Hell, I'm just glad we still have lights and electricity. All other life sustaining functions are gone," Chris reported, trying to control his tone. He disliked the arrogant Dr. Petrino to the point of hatred but knew he was only days away from never seeing the greasy-faced man again. The sight of Elise calmed his nerves.

"I'm going out to attempt repairs to the generator," Elise said firmly, looking at all three of the remaining employees. "I have enough knowledge of its layout that I think I might be able to figure it out. If that fails, I'm going to go to the cloning facility."

Sonia piped up, alarmed. "Why? The place is disease-ridden. If any clones remain alive, they might figure out how to get out of their rooms. This evac happened too fast! We're just assuming cutting off life support took care of them. Who knows what you'll find out there!"

"Cutting their life support is something I strongly disagreed with, but that's another conversation, one I hope to have with my superiors when we get off this dead rock. We have a transport arriving in three days with two days of air left here. If I can't get the generator back up and running, we might be able to divert emergency backup from the cloning facility to the Command Center. Also, I've got this." Elise raised her Alnorix issued sidearm, aptly named Defender I, a small but powerful laser emitting weapon.

Chris and the rest of the security team had Defender II's, rifles based off of the handgun, firing essentially the same laser blast but with one major difference: it had two barrels, one on top of the other. The top barrel emitted an explosive red laser blast outward while the bottom barrel produced a short burst of intense flames. This was ideal for the harsh worlds they were stationed on, both for safety purposes and emergencies.

Several of the planets the mining facilities inhabited had indigenous life that ranged from potentially dangerous to outright deadly. All of them, however, were frightened of fire, so Defender II's came equipped with a flame barrel that required connection to a small tank on the bottom of the rifle that carried a small amount of Kernadium.

Chris cleared his throat before speaking, "Yeah but we were specifically told to avoid the contaminated area. You willing to break protocol? I mean, that Rot stuff is highly contagious if you come into close physical contact. They're not going to let you board the transport, you know that, right? They're gonna see that someone opened the outer door that's been sealed off."

Elise replied, "Look, you all are my responsibility so if it means three of us four getting off this rock then so be it. We've more or less let all sixty of our clones in current incubation die and I'm not about to finish the rest of this small band off just yet. We aren't going to make it three days. We all know that. If anyone has any better suggestions, I'm all ears." She shifted her eyes from Chris to Sonia to Dr. Petrino who quickly glanced at her then back down to the floor.

Shaking his head in resignation, Chris mumbled, "Okay, I'm coming with you."

Elise nodded her approval, glad for another set of hands, especially Chris Berger's since Jake was now gone. She knew Chris had all but checked out of this unpleasant job, but she still trusted that at the end of the day, he would do the right thing, what was necessary to get the job done, and hopefully, go home safely.

"Sonia, keep the com open, we may not be able to communicate with anything off-world, but we can still communicate with each other," Elise said calm but firmly. "Chris and I will keep our headsets on inside the mining suites. Dr. Petrino, if we do end up having to get inside the cloning facility, be ready to supply us with various passwords and anything else we may need. I don't want to be stuck behind a sealed door. Got it?"

"Yes," came the short reply from Petrino, who didn't bother looking over to see Elise and Chris leave the Command Center as the door slid shut silently behind them.

"I hate that woman," Petrino spat out, glaring over at Sonia, the only person left who had to listen to his constant complaining. "I hate being here. Why couldn't I have left along with the rest of the doctors and clone reproduction staff? Bradley and Sarah got to leave, and I'm stuck here on this hellhole. I have seniority! Troria may be a hellhole, too, but nothing is this bad."

"How does it feel to have literally no friends?" Sonia responded quietly without looking up from her computer monitor as she continued trying to figure out what the generator failure and severed coms off-world.

Petrino raised his eyebrows and quickly pointed a long, bony index finger at her, shouting, "You're one to talk! Your lack of any real relationships whatsoever here made you an easy choice to stay behind! News flash, honey, Mr. Nicholas Mohr himself, head of operations across all AMO facilities, asked me for several names of qualified backup staff to stick around until the last transport came back to pick us up. And I gave him your name, immediately! See, it doesn't pay to undermine me like you've been doing for the three years you've been here. Especially that incident in the rec room, remember? So, we get to endure each other just a little bit longer, alright?"

Sonia glared at him, trying to keep her cool as she brushed a bit of unkept curly hair out of her face and pushed her glasses back up on the bridge of her nose. She knew he was still her superior, even if normal protocols were devolving around them, and he would certainly throw that in her face if she wasn't careful.

Petrino enjoyed getting the best of his enemies, which he had considered Sonia and Chris for years now. "Shit rolls downhill, sweetie," he mumbled just loud enough for Sonia to hear as he thought bitterly of how much Dr. Kevin Bradley and Dr. Sarah Baudet despised him.

"Please don't call me honey or sweetie. Grrr! I hate this! I hate this moon!" Sonia shouted in frustration as she ran her hands through her curly hair, stood up and headed toward the door.

Petrino liked getting under people's skin, especially staff he outranked, which was now just Sonia and Chris. But since there was no one else to protect him and keep the peace here, now that the rest of the security detail had left the godforsaken moon, he kept out of Chris's way. He needed him.

But it was Elise he hated most of all, even if he was infatuated with her. She was too attractive. Whenever she was in the room, he tried to avert his eyes from her chest pushing through the tight, white shirts she always wore. Her attractive slim figure complimented by tight, light-brown cargo pants issued by the AMO, her full lips, her smell. She always smelled *good*, and he hated that it drew him all the more to fantasize about her. He would often angrily masturbate to thoughts of her in the privacy of his tiny quarters. He was jealous of her attractiveness, her confidence, how people immediately gravitated to her when she was first transferred to Moon 002.

He wished it would have been Elise instead of Jake that had left with the previous transport, but Jake had seniority. He had been there for the full five years, much like Dr. Petrino himself.

He had tolerated Jake, maybe even considered him a sort of friend. At least Jake attempted to treat him with a small hint of dignity and showed signs of being a decent leader here at Mining Colony VI. After all, Petrino was little more than a meat harvester. Harvesting clones for hard labor, at least ninety percent of them. None of which lasted more than one year in these conditions or elsewhere in the mining territories.

The same could be said for humans, which is one reason the clones were created. They were like batteries, used until drained. Given fond memories of childhood through implants. Made to feel as though they were less than one year from retirement from the mining industry and looking at a large payout and a nice place to live out the rest of their days in early retirement. Ninety percent of them had to work out amid the Poule plants, harvesting liquid Kernadium sent back to Troria for fuel for the numerous means of transportation on the planet, as well as other industries.

He had to play his cards right. If so, he could get out of this whole mess safe and sound. However, the fear of Levon Gonidec loomed large in the back of Petrino's mind. He knew where he fell on the food chain when it came to the Gonidec regime and its ties with the AMO, and it was low.

Due to the current ruling body of government, the military on Troria was large and growing rapidly, much to the dismay of every other planet in the quadrant. Larger military forces meant bigger and stronger artillery and the means to transport them. Which meant more fuel consumption. The rate at which Gonidec's government was using up the sparse Poule plants on their own planet was unsustainable. So, the decision was made to quietly create cloning facilities off-world at the ten locations in quadrant 8304 and harvest the planets dry.

Snapping back to the present, he saw Sonia get up and move to the door and shouted, "Where the hell do you think you're going?"

To pee. I have to piss, is that okay? Want to come watch? I'm guessing it'll get your mind off of Elise's tits for a second, Sonia thought bitterly, wishing she could stand up to the pathetic bully in a doctor's lab coat as she hung her head and walked out of the Command Center, the door sliding shut behind her, nearly catching her white lab coat in the process. On her way out, she mumbled to herself, "I hate my life."

Sonia kept her head down often and was good at her job, sickening as it was. She didn't ask questions, knowing her place within the company and as a citizen of Troria. She hated how things had taken such a downward spiral on Troria, but her sick mother back on her home world kept her submissive: she needed this job and its pay for her mom's survival. Healthcare on Troria was non-existent for low-income individuals. While she hated her job, her love for her mother exceeded her discomfort.

"Fucking *bitch*!" Petrino shouted in the empty room. Unlike the truly beautiful Elise, Sonia was little more than average and just seemed to blend in. Easily avoidable. *Barely human,* he would think sometimes when she passed him in the hallways during work shifts. He often forgot she was incredibly intelligent, graduating with high marks in her class before being stationed at Mining Complex VI.

"Clones have more personality than you do, you flat-chested, boring piece of wall dressing! You're expendable. You all are!" Petrino shouted once more into the empty space. He looked around, needing to calm himself. "Where are my cigarettes?"

He brushed papers off of a nearby desk, finding his half-smoked pack of Scarlet Lights and pulling one out. He jammed the rest of the pack into his lab coat's chest pocket and lit it with a nearby lighter.

He breathed in the nicotine, relishing one of the few joys he had left on Moon 002. One of the few joys in his life, period. Sucking down the cigarette, he turned again to look out over the desolate landscape of Treon III's dead moon. The moon that he had helped ravage, leading close to five hundred clones to their death by their mere creation on the formidable moon. Something he continually shoved to the back of his mind. *They're clones, they're not people.*

He took another drag of the Scarlet Light, blowing the smoke out against the window, making the already dreary exterior look even worse. *Hell. I'm in hell, but I'm getting out of here.*

CHAPTER 6

MINING COMPLEX VI

The success of Mining Complex VI was proof that docile clones were better than forced clones. Mining Complex VI, on Treon III's Moon 002, the smallest and first of AMO's ten facilities across the solar system in quadrant 8304 during its prime, had a total of twenty employees overseeing its population of sixty clones. The clones were manufactured and harvested in the Clone Replication Facility, or *Building B*, closely situated beside the Command Center and Human Living Quarters.

The manufacturing process, done by the three doctors on staff and a few assistants, took place in the main lab located on level one. Synthetically grown eggs were transported from Troria then fertilized with lab-created, mutated, engineered sperm. The mixture had ensured a speedy incubation and gestation period, usually no longer than several months. However, this process was also highly volatile and resulted in numerous casualties.

The doctors and assistants kept close watch over the incubation stages inside each of the sixty rooms in the Clone Replication Facility. Keeping the newly-formed fetuses on a healthy diet of growth hormones and stimulants ensured that they grew to adulthood at an extremely accelerated rate. It also ensured maximum profitability for the AMO for their property, much of which trickled into Levon Gonidec's personal accounts.

The process of new clones "arriving" was easy for the doctors and their assistants as well as a security guard or two to implement. When the clone was ready for service, they were kept unconscious once removed from the amniotic sack, then cleaned and dressed and taken to an office in the Command Center through an underground walkway beneath the planet's surface that only the human staff were made aware of. Once seated, they would be awakened by a quick injection to the neck only to be told they had dozed off in the waiting area after the long flight over, just as the doctors had programed them to think.

From that point on, they were given a debriefing, typically by the commanding officer on duty, followed by a tour of the facilities making them feel at home, then shortly thereafter, put to work. Building D was the housing location of the rotating staff of clones, simply marked, Living Quarters. Each floor housed twenty clones, one per room. The building had a cafeteria, workout room and recreation center located on the top floor, and each room had a small bathroom. Intermixed with the clones were several humans making sure peace was kept. These people were almost always stationed at the cafeteria and were assigned cleaning duties inside, leaving the hard labor to the clones outside on the hostile moon.

And hard labor it was. Clones worked in eight-hour shifts around the clock, twenty-four hours a day. Moon 002 had perpetual dim light, never fully dark, never fully light. The Poule plants thrived in the dim light from the distant star in quadrant 8304. The low light, coupled with high winds, ensured the large, thick plants continued to slowly produce Kernadium from the deep reserve under the rocky soil. At the core of the few planets and moons that could produce such plants contained specific minerals conducive to the production of the Kernadium.

Clones on mining duty outside wore specially made and inexpensively constructed mining suits with oxygen tanks. They suffered immense back pain and constant headaches from the long hours breathing in recycled air.

Each miner was issued a large drill connected via a hose to a cart with barrels. The task was simple, continuous drilling into the Poule, cacti-shaped plants at their red- colored base. The long drill-shaped syringe slowly sucked out the thick green liquid which was stored in building E, temperature controlled and watched over by several security guards at all times. Later the barrels were taken off-world back to Troria where the Kernadium would then be distilled and made into the fuel that powered nearly all vehicles both on the ground as well as in the air.

Several of the clones whose vitals produced the highest results in terms of physical fitness and health were awarded jobs such as security detail and, in some cases, even kitchen duties serving humans.

The lifespan of all clones, however, was severely diminished. A one-year, life-limiter DNA implanted into nearly all of the clones upon fertilization, coupled with the dangers of mining for Kernadium, kept the mortality rate at nearly one year per clone. The Kernadium was extremely toxic and, even with the inexpensive mining suits and gear, prolonged exposure meant certain death. Any human caught reversing the lifespan limiter was punished with either incarceration or, it had been whispered, execution.

All of the clones were given memory implants leading right up to their arrival on each of the ten mining colonies, ensuring they all had something to remember, live for, and look forward to—returning to their loved ones back on Troria or another nearby planet. Large sums of Marks, the currency on Troria, were dangled in front of them. Usually enough to retire early and live out the rest of their days peacefully.

However, none of the clones actually made it off of the mining planets. A transport shuttle flew in regularly, taking sick and injured clones, along with those that had lasted the full year and were still in relatively good health, to a predetermined location on uninhabited worlds where they were quickly disposed of.

Most of the staff, except for the three doctors, were unaware of exactly what happened after these clones boarded the shuttles. Several security guards onboard from Troria were tasked with the unpleasant job of disposing of the used-up AMO's property. This process began as soon as the clones boarded the large, boxy transport shuttle with a "sleeping sedative for the long journey home." The pills were little more than cyanide capsules; once ingested, the clones' fate was sealed within minutes of leaving the mining facilities.

After the killing pills had done their job, the bodies were dumped into a man-made crater, a small amount of Kernadium poured onto the pile of corpses, and then lit on fire. Nothing remained due to the sheer intensity with which they burned. Kernadium was extremely flammable and would continue to burn until nothing was left but ashes that quickly blew away. Because there were no remains, no attempts were made to cover the burn piles.

Since the operation began, there had never been talk among the clones of what was actually happening. Typically, the brain functions of most were reduced to that of worker bees, save for some that were given significantly better implants due to their better developed bodies. Michael Astier was one such case. His anatomy had been monitored closely and he was determined to be a fine *specimen*, and therefore administered higher quality memories and more sophisticated brain functioning capacity, ensuring he would perform his job at a higher level until his time was up. Primarily, that of security on Moon 002.

At times, a clone with a growth defect such as a foot or hand deformity was left to grow inside the birthing container strictly as a food source for the rest of the clones. A quick needle to the heart ended their life once they were grown enough to feed a large quantity. The kitchen in the Command Center had a large station for humans to cook the food provided by their home world, while a separate section was used for the grounding up and processing of clones for consumption.

The humans knew to some extent what went on in the mining complex, and while no one enjoyed this particular line of work, they all signed up for it, willing to look the other way, even if they hated what was taking place. Most of them. There had been rumblings within the corporation that sympathizers to the cause of cloning brutality and euthanasia were emerging. Therefore, the human labor force experienced a high turnaround: a rotating group of new employees eager to make decent pay would be shuttled off-world to the mining complexes spread throughout the solar system in quadrant 8304 in an attempt to keep morale up and insubordination low.

Stringent screening processes had been set up on Troria for the human labor force hoping to land jobs off-world as life on Troria grew worse every year that Levon Gonidec was in power. Jobs were scarce and primarily went to the most affluent of citizens unless one planned to enlist in their continually growing military force. The planet had been run by Levon Gonidec's authoritarian government for nearly seven years and counting and under its rule, the cloning process had been green lit quickly to maximize profits and line the pockets of those in charge along with strengthening the Trorian military through the continual Kernadium liquid harvesting.

Because the rather inexpensive practice of cloning was passed into law on Troria for purposes of safely harvesting Kernadium on other planets, the only thing the AMO had to worry about was insubordination from within. Their employees were screened well. Only on rare occasions was it required that human personnel be taken immediately off duty due to their inability to carry out the difficult task of clone harvesting and destruction.

The people of Troria were given little information about the goings-on across the various planets in the solar system harvesting Kernadium. All they knew was that it was a glowing success. The Kernadium was good for business back home, keeping most transportation vehicles and their military filled up on fuel. The shameful means by which it was harvested though, was another story. Some had turned a blind eye to what seemed to be a shady collaboration between the planet's authoritarian government and the AMO, knowing it would do no good other than get them or their families killed. But there were some, a small group that was growing, that sought to take down Levon Gonidec's regime one way or another.

One such person was Jake Riley, previous Commanding officer on Mining Complex VI, who had recently left on one of the transport shuttles as the company had begun its process of shutting down the site and moving on. Leaving behind Elise Bennet in charge, much to his dismay over a woman he was rapidly falling in love with. They both knew the future of the entire solar system could fall on the courageous few that chose not to turn a blind eye to what was happening.

This was how it had been for five years on Moon 002. The docile clones on Mining Complex VI had seemed a success in the short term. Everything was going well. An end date was coming soon due to the planet being recently drained of its entire Kernadium liquid. Only one more warehouse-load of barrels remained in storage that would be taken along with the remaining humans once the transport freighter arrived.

However, only several short days before the last transport was to arrive, the generator located in the Generator and Main Server Room, Building C, beside the Clone Replication Facility, failed, compromising the complex in numerous ways, foremost of which was loss of breathable air. The entire facility had been scheduled to be closed down permanently after the final Kernadium haul was picked up by one of AMO's transport freighters, but the spread of Rot throughout the clones made things even more difficult for the skeleton crew to navigate around.

After numerous attempts to keep the virus under control, disposing of the infected, the deadly disease took over the Cloning Replication Facility and the Clone Living Quarters. Shortly thereafter, communications were lost days before the clone known as Michael Astier awakened prematurely inside his embryotic sack in the Clone Replication Facility.

CHAPTER 7

MICHAEL MAKES A FRIEND

The door to room 51 slid open as light hit Michael's eyes. His brain told him to protect himself so he raised the clothing rod above his head, ready to strike at any dangerous foe that might have been preparing for an attack.

Precious seconds passed. No one came out of the open door. Michael, still alert to any danger, kept his rod in front of him, ready. Then, from around the corner of the opened door, a young girl stepped out.

Dumbstruck at the sight of this young, frail, fair-skinned girl, Michael cocked his head to one side and immediately let his guard down. This gave the girl the opportunity she needed. She leapt out of the room and landed on top of the stunned Michael as he dropped to the ground, both fighting for the rod.

No sooner had they collided with the floor than Michael began regaining his defensive composure. Grabbing the nearly five-foot-tall girl that couldn't have weighed more than seventy-five pounds, he tossed her off of him before she had a chance to pry the rod out of his strong hands.

As soon as she hit the floor, she bounded back up, her blond hair flopping over her porcelain-smooth face, which she brushed back impatiently and took off running toward the front of the hallway.

"Hey, wait!" Michael yelled, standing back up, his mind urging him to chase after her. He easily caught up to the girl who wore a pink tank top, white spandex pants, and a pair of white sneakers. She had reached the front of the hallway where the outline of what Michael had assumed would be the exit was, frantically searching for a way out.

Michael's mind quickly imprinted the size of the child. She was much weaker than him and thus of no discernable threat. Reaching her, he lowered the rod so he wouldn't appear threatening to the obviously terrified girl. Speaking in a calm voice as he caught his breath, he said, "Look, hang on, my name is Michael. I just woke up in room fifty-five a little while ago. I'm not going to hurt you, okay? I just want to know your name. Do you know your name?"

The frightened girl stared at him then back at the door with a keypad and flat square panel flush with the wall beside it, weighing out her options, which weren't many. She turned back to Michael, her green eyes wide, and let her guard down slightly as she said meekly, "I think my name is Olivia. At least that was what the folder I found in my room said. I'm not sure how or when I learned to read, but I can. I'm scared, mister!"

"I know, I am too," Michael responded in a composed and collected tone. "But you're safe with me, for now." His mind deduced this was the correct course of action so as not to frighten the girl any more than she obviously was. *Children can become frightened easily. They usually cease being as frightened in the later teenage years.*

"Resourceful girl. Good job. My name is Michael Astier, or that's the name the doctors gave me. From what I have ascertained, I was created here. Do you know if you're a…clone?"

"I woke up inside a slippery wet film. It was dark and there were things in my arms and throat. They hurt when I pulled them out. I was so scared. I had to search the dark room to find a light!" Olivia shifted her eyes from the floor to Michael then over to the door.

Nodding, Michael replied, "Yes, same here. Exactly the same predicament I found myself in earlier. You're dressed, did you find the closet, I assume?"

"Yes. I just picked the ones on top of the pile," Olivia said as she looked down at the clothes she was wearing and shrugged. She reached into a pocket and pulled out a folded piece of paper and a small flat device with a screen on it. "Oh, and I found a file that had my name—Olivia Petrino, it says here, and age, eleven years old. It also says, 'test subject already has limited memory implants and full growth to happen gradually at later date. No life limiting DNA implanted. DNA acquired from human doner. Doctor will take full ownership off-world September 15, 3123.'"

She held both out to Michael who recognized the last name she read immediately from his own files: Dr. Petrino. He took the paper and what appeared to be a video monitor. He looked at the notes. Everything she said was true. The doctor's name wasn't anywhere on the sheet, but he recognized the handwriting.

No life-limiting DNA implanted? Michael wondered what that meant as he continued looking over the sheet in his hand. A sick feeling crept through him but he needed to deal with more pressing matters at the moment.

"It looks like this Dr. Petrino has taken it upon himself to give you his last name. I believe he's the guy that created me as well. Good chance a great number of the rooms here have his signature on the files inside. Do you remember anything at all? Before this?" Michael was curious about this strange new person who had literally leapt into his life and had apparently been birthed at around the same time as he was.

"I know how to talk. I know fear. I knew I had to get dressed to cover myself. And the tube in my throat felt bad. But I have no memories. Every now and then my head hurts and I know new things. Like, that thing I gave you can be watched, moving pictures appear on it," Olivia responded softly, looking up at Michael.

Michael sensed she was getting more comfortable with him already and was glad his processing skills were continuing to evolve. He handed the paper and the small video device hack to her and said, "We need to figure a way out of here, Olivia. Let's take a look at that door, shall we?"

They turned to the door as Michael spoke again. "This keypad is like the ones in the rooms, which have codes corresponding to their numbers, but I have no idea what the code could be."

Olivia nodded in reply as they both looked over the black square flush with the wall. Michael raised his hand and touched the screen. It flashed on with a thin green line around the base.

"Please place right hand on security scanner for clearance," a robotic voice said. Michael looked at his hand, his mind processing what he had been instructed to do. He moved the rod to his left hand, raised his right hand and placed it against the illuminated screen.

"Access denied. Please place right hand on security scanner for clearance," the voice said once more.

Michael looked over at Olivia and was about to tell her to give it a try when the pounding in his head came back with a vengeance. He dropped the rod to the ground and belt over in pain as he clenched the sides of his head.

His father, now much older and in a frail state, put his arms around his son. They stood over the open grave with onlookers surrounding them as a man dressed in black read words from a book in front of the casket. The man spoke calmly and with genuine sympathy in his voice. "And in closing, Suzannah Mary Astier, survived by her beloved husband Kenneth M. Astier and loving son Michael Nathan Astier, will be remembered best for her warm smile, kind heart, and her continued service to those in most need in our community. May she rest in peace."

The scene shifted and shook in Michael's mind. People moved forward at a fast rate of speed as if something in his head was fast forwarding the entire landscape. It stopped. Now in his twenties, he and his dad stood alone by the fresh mound of dirt covering the gravesite in the cemetery. On the horizon, the same planet glowed above the heavens from deep space. Neither said anything for a short period, silently paying their final respects to their lost mother and loving, faithful wife.

"Dad, why her? What are you going to do without Mama? I can't leave for academy. I'll be over five hours away from you! How are you going to do it, Dad?" He looked over at the grimacing older man, now with some of his muscle mass gone, hunched over with a face that had seen much sorrow.

Kenneth looked over at his son, cleared his throat, and in his gruff, thick voice replied, "Son, I don't know why these things happen. But when your mom got sick, I made do as you finished up college. I'll be okay. I'll manage knowing that you're making something of yourself. You're like me, strong-willed, tough, and you aren't a coward. You're going to do great things. I know you will."

"But Dad, my profession will likely take me off-world! What if you need me? I've trained hard to be a miner. It's in our blood, but family is more important. You're more important to me than a career!" Michael cried out as bitter tears ran down his face.

Sighing, Kenneth put his hand on his son's shoulder and nodded, "You're right, family is important. But this is your life. You've got one shot at it. You've trained hard, you're tough. My best days are behind me but knowing you're following in your old man's footsteps is proof I did something right with the life I was given. I'm not gonna let you squander all you've learned by staying in this small dead-end town. There are planets to explore, and you'll be the best. I know you will, son. I can see it in your eyes."

The old man put his arm around his son. They stood close together as a gentle rain began to fall, looking out over rolling green hills filled with trees and roads that led out of this small town where Michael had spent his youth. He had dreamed of one day being a miner like his dad, a man he was proud to call father. A man who had loved him and his mama, had provided for them both on his meager salary as a miner himself, paving the way for better things for his well-educated son.

A sound caught their attention as they looked up to see a large, sleek metallic gray spacecraft blasting through the atmosphere on its way to continue searching for the planet's much-needed Kernadium.

"Are you okay? Hey, Mr. Michael? What happened? What's going on?" Olivia asked frantically as she put her hand on Michael's shoulder.

He hadn't fully come back from the deep childhood memory implant that continued to swirl around in his brain. In the foggy darkness of his closed eyes, Michael wondered if these memories could actually be real. They felt so real they couldn't be made up. He could still faintly smell the rain, the grass. They were vivid parts of his being, his existence.

Snapping out of the vision, Michael stood upright, shaking his head. He looked around and saw the thin blond girl beside him looking confused and frightened with her hands over her mouth, as if suppressing a scream.

"I guess that's how us clones get implanted with memories," Michael said, giving his head one more shake. "That one was a doozy. I believe this is all supposed to happen when we're still on those tables in our rooms, not fully conscious. I assume it's a slow-releasing implant. I can tell you with the utmost certainty, it's not pleasant, but it sounds like you won't have to go through that."

"I just have thoughts zap into my head. I haven't experienced anything like that though. Not yet. I hope I don't, it looks like it hurts. I was really scared!"

Nodding, Michael replied grimly, "It does. Not just physically but psychologically as well. If you understand what that means. Hell, I'm just figuring out what all of this means myself."

She shook her head at him puzzled, imploring with her eyes for him to say more.

Michael tried to explain further. "The physical pain is an instant pounding in my head, but on top of that, intense emotions are being stamped into my subconscious. I just experienced the death of my mom. I loved her and already have vivid memories of her as a child, a teenager, and into my twenties. It *feels* real. I don't know. It's hard to describe. For all I know, these are memories flooding back into my mind and I've been unconscious for some time. The paperwork in my room, however, flies in the face of that theory. From what I'm seeing in this place, my brain is telling me to not trust anything, including these memories. I wish I had more answers for you, but I'm about as lost as you are."

He paused and looked at the innocent girl in front of him. Newly born, probably going through early-stage puberty, and trying to understand what these intense feelings mean. And himself a newborn, unsure of what was real and what was made-up in his own still growing and evolving mind.

He hoped to meet this Dr. Petrino. There were a few things he wanted to discuss with this man he didn't know but his brain told him he already didn't like. This man who seemed to be playing creator and destroyer. His mind went to Olivia's words, *life limiting DNA,* and he shuddered at the thought once more.

He saw Olivia was at a loss for words, her eyes darting from him to the empty hallway to the door, processing everything that was happening in rapid succession. "Let's see if you have any better luck with the door than I did, Olivia. Give it a try. Put your right hand against that panel there and we'll see what happens."

Nodding, she cautiously took a step forward, slowly raising her hand and placing it against the panel.

"Access granted," the robotic voice said through a speaker system above as the door slid open.

"Your prints worked and mine didn't," Michael said while his mind worked out this new information, instructing him about the basics of DNA. "I'm guessing yours are an identical match to Petrino's or this scanner somehow reads something called DNA," he mused, glancing over at the wide-eyed girl standing beside him.

Michael peered into the room, Olivia quickly following, looking over his shoulder to see what lay ahead. Directly in front of them was an elevator, to the left, two machines filled with various snack foods and beverages for purchase. *Elevator, vending machines, okay, I know what these are.*

They cautiously crept into the room as Olivia pointed to the other side of the room opposite the vending machines. "Look, stairs!" she whispered to Michael.

They both walked over to the elevator. A sign beside the doors read, *Please ensure proper protective equipment and oxygen tanks are activated before exiting cloning facility on level one. Our employees' safety is important to the Alnorix Mining Organization.*

"Why do I find that hard to believe?" Michael smirked as he walked over to the elevator while Olivia headed toward the food and drink selections in the vending machines. The room was small enough that she felt safe leaving the side of the tall, muscular stranger who, so far, was her only means of protection in this lonely and frightening new world.

The double-doored elevator had one button on the side to gain entry. Michael pressed it and waited for the sound of gears turning. What he heard instead made him freeze where he stood. Olivia immediately looked up with eyes wide and ran to his side, both hearing the high-pitched, piercing scream below them echoing up from the elevator shaft.

They slowly backed away from the elevator toward the door that had remained open. Neither saw the figure standing just outside the door, shrouded in darkness.

CHAPTER 8

GENERATOR SABOTAGE

Jake Riley sat across from Gideon Novare at his presidential round table on Railara. Jake scratched his short beard, looking impatient and agitated as the older man spoke.

"Jake, with all you've done for us here on Railara in our fight against Levon Gonidec's regime on Troria, I know you don't want to hear this, but there is much more work to be done. His fleet is advancing. If we don't do anything, the other planets in the quadrant will follow suit and sit by with their hands tied behind their backs. They're looking to us for leadership ever since Gonidec took over and started building his infernal Mining Complexes across the quadrant."

The regal-looking man with graying hair eyed Jake. He knew the history Jake had while running operations on Mining Complex VI. About his love affair with Dr. Elise Bennet whose safety he had great concern for, as she was one of a handful of people left back on Moon 002. Among them, Dr. Petrino.

"We need to act!" Jake replied angrily. "I want to get those remaining on Moon 002 off of that disease-riddled deathtrap before it's too late!"

Nodding, Gideon tugged at his jacket and cleared his throat, knowing how sensitive a subject this was. "I agree. And soon they will be out of there. But for now, we need to keep out of that place and stay off Gonidec's radar. They're scheduled to leave in a few short days. Until then, we need to think about what plans we have to set into motion for taking out Gonidec himself. It won't be easy, but this war will cost millions upon millions of lives throughout the quadrant if we don't play our cards right. And that means keeping quiet. Not pushing his buttons. His military is vast and deadly. But we've got people on Troria ready and waiting. And when the time is right, we'll strike. Silently."

"But when?" Jake nearly shouted, restraining himself in front of the president of Railara. He sat back in his seat in the room overlooking the beautiful capital city of Aphus and shook his head, replying grimly, "I know I shouldn't put the needs of a few people over the entire quadrant, but I don't trust Petrino." And truth be told, he missed Elise, though he couldn't bring himself to admit something so personal to the president of Railara.

Gideon Novare nodded his understanding. He knew the man sitting across from him was in love with a woman who was stuck on the hostile Moon 002 along with several other unlucky souls.

Ignoring Jake's question, as he himself wasn't sure of the answer just yet, he stood up. "If you'll excuse me, I have some paperwork to fill out."

Jake got to his feet, shaking hands with Novare before he left the room quietly, his mind turbulent. Fearing for his love back on Mining Complex VI. Fearing for what was to come with Gonidec's war that was imminent.

He knew his part to play would come soon, he knew what would be required of him, but he wasn't sure how it was going to succeed. It was a one-in-a-million chance, the plan they had cooked up, and even then, there was much to hash out and little time to do so.

He thought of Elise for the millionth time. Of the love that had been simmering in his heart over his time on Moon 002. His mind drifted to their quiet talks about work that inevitably led to talks about their pasts. About their future desires. They had become good friends. And then, lovers.

They had the same ultimate goal as well: taking down the AMO and more importantly, the Gonidec regime back on their home planet of Troria.

Elise and Chris headed down in the elevator to the ground level of the Command Center.

The top floor, level four, where they'd just come from and where Petrino and Sonia still were, had numerous windows overlooking the surrounding buildings. Rows of computers, now mostly inactive, were set up around the various permanently installed metal desks. Communication to all parts of the mining facility took place here, including a full set of security cameras which were currently offline.

Level three held the kitchen, cafeteria, and recreational activities with several pool tables, a dart board, and several arcade games, all old and barely working at this point.

Level two housed the rotating staff of twenty humans from Troria. Each had a small but adequate living space, significantly larger than the sixty clones' quarters. The sparse rooms consisted of a single bed and a bathroom with a sink, shower and toilet crammed in a tiny space. A mini-kitchen provided space for those that wanted to eat in their rooms, and a couch with a small projection device for entertainment purposes mounted directly overhead onto the opposite white wall made up the "living room."

The first level was mainly for show. Offices were set up to give the new "arrivals" of clones their briefing, but the offices were also used for the rotating staff coming and going. The elevator connected all of these levels for quick and easy access.

There was also a stairwell that was rarely used, and an underground walkway that connected to the Clone Replication Facility as well as the Generator and Server building. No walkway connected the clones living space to any other part of the mining complex for safety and secrecy reasons. The more clones could be kept in the dark on what was really happening across all the mining complexes across the solar system, the better.

Elise and Chris exited the elevator once the doors slid open on level one. With the outbreak of Rot, both had weapons at the ready. They would need to put on mining suits with oxygen tanks to work on the generator, though. The generator room was used so rarely the AMO had decided none of the generator buildings across the ten planets would have breathable air, requiring their employees to suit up in order to do any service maintenance on the equipment. Another cost-cutting method implemented throughout all of the mining facilities.

They made their way to the door to the underground walkway, located inconspicuously in a far corner, away from prying eyes. "We'll need to get our suits and oxygen hooked up," Chris said in a tired tone that was obvious to Elise.

Smirking, Elise looked over at him. "I know, Chris."

She bit her tongue. She wanted to tell him this was his job, to help his commanding officer in what was officially a pretty dire situation. She was confident Chris respected her, at least enough to do what was required of him. But once the rest of the staff was shipped out with full pay and he had been relegated to stay behind with Petrino, his demeanor took a turn for the worse.

She knew he had seen horrible things on a nearly daily basis here that had numbed him. He was a good guy hired to do a shitty job at the ass end of the solar system by a truly reprehensible government. All to line the pockets of the bigwigs at AMO and the powerful dictator, Levon Gonidec back on Troria. He knew it and she knew it. The entire staff of twenty had known it. Such was life on Troria and its mining facilities.

Elise had heard whispers about what went on in this place before signing up for the job on Moon 002, back on Troria getting her training. Things she fully intended to deal with later. Her primary reason for pushing for this job in the first place was to figure out a way to bring about the end of cloning as a means of profit, and if possible, to bring about the fall of Levon Gonidec's regime back on Troria. Her home world was no longer capitalistic. It was now a full-on dictatorship. Witnessing first-hand what was happening across all of the mining complexes throughout the galaxy was at the very least, a start to what she hoped would be a solution to the Gonidec problem that plagued quadrant 8304.

At the door, Elise pushed her hand against the unlocking scanner as the robotic quickly voice stated, "Access granted."

The door slid open, and they walked through, Elise leading the way. Small service lights lined the long hallway walls as they quickly made their way inside. Building A was the main hub to the other buildings accessible via tunnel. Small signs marked the two different accessible destinations above the entrances: *Building B: Clone Replication Facility and Building C: Generator / Server Room.*

"I wonder if we could get power re-routed to just one primary location. Hole up there and wait for the cavalry," Chris pondered as they walked the hallway toward the generator room.

"Maybe, we'll have to see when we get there. This is all recent, so not sure what we're up against. I'd rather not have to go to the Replication facility or their living quarters with the Rot virus essentially out of control in both locations. Even with the clones deceased, the threat of infection for humans is as high as if it were inside of us," Elise replied grimly as they continued to walk.

Thinking on this for a second, Chris said, "Yeah, well, the two doctors' assistants and the toughest security dude here, Dex Scott, weren't so lucky, were they? Leah and Carley didn't deserve what happened to them. God, they looked terrible. At least they got out of here and can hopefully get help back on Troria."

Elise glanced over at him, contemplating how to respond to his surprisingly positive outlook on their futures before speaking. "I'm not so sure how lucky they were. Did you see them board the last transport out of here? I saw them in the clone facility in isolation. But I never saw them leave."

"What are you saying, Commander?" Chris replied in a lower tone, his eyes shifting over to her.

Rolling her head from side to side, Elise calmly replied, "I'm saying, I didn't see them leave. I was quickly put in charge by Jake Riley before he left, orders from the higher ups. But it all happened so fast—the Rot spreading after attempts to quarantine had failed, and the decision to abandon this place and leave behind this skeleton crew. To do what—tie up loose ends and make sure the remaining Kernadium is safe and secure before back-up, in these conditions? Then sealing off the Replication Facility and Clone Living Quarters...it was a lot. And I never actually saw Dex, Carley and Leah leave."

They walked in silence a bit farther before Chris finally spoke. "I've seen some shit, Elise. I mean, *I've seen some shit* here over the course of two years. I kept my head down and my mouth shut. Wanting to get my time in, get back home, and get paid. This job…and forgive me for speaking to my superior like this but, this job *sucks*. Life on Troria sucks, sure. But less so than here."

Nodding in agreement, Elise said, "I know, Chris. When I signed up for training back on Troria I hadn't expected this. I mean, I know things are tough all around, we all need to get paid. Anyway, let's just get the generator back up long enough to get us through the last transport out of here."

Chris looked at her, gauging her reaction. "For what it's worth, I used to voice my opinion. Especially to Commander Riley back when I started. Dude was cool as fuck. But I could tell pretty quick that I just needed to bury that shit. Which I did. But everyone knows where everyone stands. I mean, this place isn't exactly huge. And me? I hope there comes a time when I can expose these corrupt motherfu…" he trailed off, realizing he was speaking to his commanding officer.

Elise smiled, then chuckled a bit, which caught Chris slightly off guard. She added, still chuckling, "I hear you. I don't think anyone, even the higher ups, my superiors at AMO, think what goes on here is particularly ethical. It's business."

"So, you and Jake Riley. You guys seemed pretty chummy toward the end, before he was reassigned and you were left in charge of this dump." Chris wished he had kept his mouth shut as he glanced over at Elise who had slowed her walk.

"So that's the gossip, huh? Whose sleeping with who on this desolate rock?" Elise shot back almost comically, but her mind was elsewhere. *I miss you so, Jake Riley. And I can't communicate with you, so please be okay!*

"Well, you know, what the hell else is there to do around here? Work and screw. Rinse, repeat." Chris said with a grin.

"Keep wondering, Chris. Normally a question like that to a superior officer would get your ass written up, but under the circumstances, let's just leave it up in the air, shall we?" Elise said firmly, wanting to get off the topic of Jake Riley.

Chris nodded, not as tense now as he had been back up in the Command Center. More than likely because he was no longer in the same room as the sleazy Dr. Petrino.

As they got closer to the entry to the Generator building, Elise thought about the real reason why she had taken the training and got the job. She would see to it that she got as much information about what happened here back to the movement that was slowly taking hold on her home world.

The rebellion against their corrupt government, against the people that had green lit this constant killing machine known as AMO, consisted of a new group of resistance fighters and government officials sympathetic to the cause. The cause of protecting these planets against their continued Kernadium extraction, thus ensuring they were little more than shells floating in space, funding the ever-growing Gonidec military force. But most importantly, the resistance group wanted to stop the production and wholesale murder of clones. In Elise's eyes, they were just as human as she was.

"That Dr. Petrino. I don't trust him. He's all sorts of shady. I've seen things. And I've heard things. From other assistants. Hell, from Sonia herself. They call him the *pervert god.* You wanna know why?"

"I've seen the way he looks at me. I think I can figure it out," Elise said frigidly.

"It's not just that. It's not just how he lewdly stares at... women. It's the god part that gives me the absolute willies about him. He's messing with DNA," Chris said under his breath, as if to himself.

"Time to suit up. We're here," Elise said, too preoccupied with the present task to ask Chris to elaborate further. She eyed the grouping of lockers against the wall as they reached the door leading into the Generator and Server room building.

"I bet if we need to, we could collect all of the suits and oxygen tanks to use until the last transport arrives," Chris suggested. "There's four of us, we'd have to check their levels. With the generator currently down, we won't be able to fill them up back at the Command Center, but it might give us enough time."

Elise nodded. "That's an idea."

They each grabbed an orange suit from a locker and slipped them on over their clothes, then pulled out the thin rectangular tanks against the backs of the lockers. The tanks had enough air to last several hours before needing to be filled back up. It was inconvenient and cost cutting as well as dangerous for the clones that used them. Several had perished due to insufficient oxygen in their tanks.

Once the oxygen tanks were connected and the helmets fastened, they opened the sliding door leading into the generator room. The building consisted of two large rooms: one housed the generator that powered every main function on the facility grounds, and the other held the computer server where all data was stored for running and maintaining every building. The generator worked in tandem with the server room. With the generator down, most every other function was down other than emergency lighting.

They approached the generator, currently silent instead of humming in its usual way, a large square with black plated paneling that nearly filled the entire room. On the front numerous operation buttons and switches and digital readouts were lifeless.

Elise breathed inside her uncomfortable suit and helmet, thinking of the clones that wore them for at least eight hours a day. If they could get to those suits, they would easily have enough oxygen; however, they were all in the sealed-off Clone Living Quarters in building D.

Standing beside her, Chris peered into the terminal. What they saw made them glance at each other with eyes wide then slowly back away from the large opening.

"Come on, we need to get out of here. There's no fixing that. It's done. That's no accident," Elise said grimly, peering inside the sabotaged machinery that was smashed to bits. Accessing her com inside her helmet, thankfully not connected to the generator in any way, Elise then buzzed the Command Center. "Sonia, come in."

After a slight pause her voice came through both Elise and Chris's headsets. "Sonia here, how's it going?"

"The generator is gone. Sabotaged. We're going to check out the server room, hang tight," Elise replied.

A heavy sigh came through their coms. "Sabotaged? What do you mean? What are we gonna do now? We need to get oxygen!"

"We're going to take it easy. We're going to check out the server room, like I said. Then we're going to head back and figure out our next plan of action, got it? Elise out."

Silence followed for a few seconds before Sonia replied quietly, "Okay, be safe, both of you."

Once the com went silent once more, Chris said quietly, "I think Sonia and I are on the same page, we're both sick of this rock. She's been here a hell of a long time."

Elise nodded as they backed away from the ripped-out wiring and smashed buttons and switches.

"That's not the only thing destroyed. Look," Chris said pointing to a grouping of thick cords on the floor that led to the server room. All severed.

Looking toward the server room, Elise motioned for Chris to follow.

"We *really* need to get the hell out of here!" Chris shouted inside his helmet.

"We need to figure out who, or what sabotaged this," Elise replied, trying to not sound frightened.

"Son of a bitch," Chris mumbled, knowing she was right but hating the feeling of growing dread that had crept into the pit of his stomach.

They approached the server room door, each holding their respective weapons tightly. Rows of circuit boards lined the smaller room as the door opened. They walked forward even more cautiously than their entry into the generator room, weapons raised.

It was quiet. No hum of computer systems. They began to make their way through the rows as Chris whispered, "Dead. Everything is dead."

Numerous circuit boards had been pulled out and were smashed on the ground. Deliberately.

"I think it's time to get back to the Command Center," Elise said in a controlled tone. "Let's grab the suits on our way back." She wished Jake were here with them. She pushed him out of her mind. She was in charge here.

"I hear that. Good thing elevators are all run separately from either of these trashed rooms. And the backup battery lighting system. Otherwise, we'd be totally screwed," Chris replied anxiously, his eyes darting back and forth as they backed out of the server room into the generator room once more.

They stopped as they heard a sound coming from just outside, swiveling around at the same time, guns raised to see where the noise came from.

In the doorway stood Carley Branch, assistant to Dr. Kevin Bradley, her once brown hair had nearly all fallen out, her left ear missing, and her eyes crusted over with green puss, one of which was also missing. In its place was a ghastly green substance hanging from the socket, slowly dripping to the floor. Her nose had slid off her face, with more of the green puss leaking from the hole left behind.

Her white lab coat was covered in blood and more of the green substance that looked like liquified moss but was in fact the highly infectious Rot. What was left of her shirt under the lab coat was torn through, revealing a caved-in chest that oozed the green puss. What used to be Carley Branch was now a grotesque monstrosity of slime and Rot.

Elise and Chris raised their guns to fire at the infected creature. From behind Carley, another figure, even worse looking, leapt forward at them. Outside the generator room, Carley closed the sliding door, trapping the infected clone inside with Chris and Elise, then left, heading back through the tunnel toward the Command Center.

Elise and Chris realized they had been locked in with a living-dead clone and turned their weapons on it. Wearing typical clone-issued tan cargo pants with a white T-shirt, the top of his head had caved in, a clear sign of advanced infection, and a mixture of sickly green Rot, thick blood, and brain matter ran down his face. Glazed eyes and a left arm that revealed exposed bone with thick, green slime dripping down onto the hand convinced them that whatever had once been alive was now a corpse shell. Only the infection kept it going, looking for more warm flesh to infect and spread to, seeking to ingest every part of the host body and then expand.

It opened its mouth and let out a guttural rasp as more of the putrid, thick green liquid oozed out, lunging at them at a much faster speed they expected.

Elise was the first to open fire. Holding her Defender I pistol outstretched in front of her with both hands, she pulled the narrow trigger as dark red streams of laser burst forth angerly at the approaching monstrosity.

The infected man dodged the oncoming fire, as if the Rot was in self-preservation mode. Elise's laser fire connected with the back wall close to the exit as she kept firing. Lines of laser fire erupted beside her as well. Chris had brought his Defender II up to his shoulder and pulled the trigger.

The creature jumped toward them again just as it reached striking distance. Elise and Chris's weapons each made contact at the same time, sending it flying backwards through the air at the close-range impact. It landed several feet back from them with a new hole in its chest. Another laser blast sending its already sickly left arm several feet behind the creature, what was left of it.

The man writhed around on the ground, gurgling noises coming from its open mouth that continued to spew green Rot. Its eyes rolled back into the skull showing nothing but their whites. It attempted to get back up and continue its pursuit as Elise and Chris cautiously made their way over to it while keeping their distance. Both of then peered down at the large hole in its chest. Green and red liquid flowing out of it.

"Man, I am not getting paid enough for this shit!" Chris exclaimed, looking down in disgust.

"Come on, we need to put this thing out of its misery," Elise replied, trying to not show her revulsion as well.

"What we need to do is burn it. That's the only way to kill the virus," Chris said.

"First things first," she replied, aiming the Defender I at the clone's head. It was still writhing on the ground, unable to stand, sliding around in a pool of its own blood and Rot.

Elise pulled the trigger. At this close of range, the laser blast completely destroyed its head, thick green slime pouring out of the now exposed stump. A small bit splattering onto Elise's mining suit helmet and gloves caused her to flinch instinctively.

The man's limbs and torso still moved, though much slower now that its head was in small pieces all over the floor.

"Like I said, we've got to burn it," Chris said grimly as he clicked a small switch on the side of his Defender II down and quickly pressed the trigger once more. A burst of flames erupted out of the bottom barrel, immediately engulfing the writhing headless abomination on the ground.

Soon the twisting limbs ceased to move at all. Charred flesh and bones lay sizzling in a pile as smoke rose from the remains.

Elise and Chris wasted no time in running past it toward the closed door leading into the tunnel and back to the Command Center. The door, however, was now locked from the outside.

"Sonia, come in. We've got problems. Plural."

CHAPTER 9

HAND-TO-HAND COMBAT

While Elise and Chris were dealing with their first run-in with the Rot, Michael and Olivia were backing away from what sounded like a low guttural roar from below the rising elevator. As the sound grew louder, they realized whatever was causing it was on the approaching lift.

A ding echoed in the small room and the door slid open revealing what had once been a cloned human but was now little more than a walking monstrosity. No facial features remained, and green slime covered nearly all of a naked body with a hole in its stomach dripping green, slime-covered entrails. The Rot had eaten the flesh from its head, leaving only a skull with white eyes and an open mouth that was moaning in pain and anger as it lurched forward toward the stunned Michael and terrified Olivia.

The girl immediately screamed at the creature in front of her as Michael instinctively grabbed hold of her arm to run. Turning, they both saw the shadowed figure approaching from behind them. With its prey now in full view, the thing lunged forward toward them at full speed.

Michael's eyes widened in terror as he suddenly realized he had seconds before this other creature made contact with them. His mind imprinted more data: *Fight this off, protect the child!* Not hesitating, he pushed Olivia to the side, away from the slime creature in the elevator, took the metal bar into both of his hands and ran at whatever was approaching him.

They met in the middle of the hallway, Michael attempting to bring the bar down onto the head of another clone, a woman, also naked and showing lesions on its body with green puss and slime oozing out of them. However, not near to the extent of the thing in the elevator, which Michael's brain quickly surmised must have been in a more advanced state of decomposition.

The bar connected with the clone's neck sending it stumbling over to the side of the hallway. Stunned at the hard blow, it howled in pain and anger as it dropped to the ground, fresh green and red liquid seeping from the fresh wound on its neck. It pulled at its long hair, yanking thick clumps out at a time and revealing a greenish growth underneath.

"Olivia! Get to the closest room with an open door and close it behind you! Room forty-three, go now!" Michael yelled without turning to look at her, hearing her footsteps running in that direction.

Behind him, the slime-covered being in the elevator lurched closer as the infected clone woman scrambled to her feet again.

Olivia yelled out, “Michael, come on! Get in here!”

“Close that door and do not open it until I tell you, Olivia!” he yelled back angrily, pointing in her direction, hoping she would obey. *Children obey firm commands from parental figures* his mind imprinted. He heard her start to cry as the door slid shut.

Time to take care of this. I’m not letting them get me and I sure as hell won’t be letting them get the girl he thought as he brought the bar up once more into a fighting position, glaring at his opposition.

The woman was now on her feet, fresh green slime and blood oozing down her bare chest. She opened her mouth, screaming in anger, eyes rolled back into her head, and lunged at Michael. But he was ready. Swinging the bar as hard as he could, he connected with her already damaged neck. It snapped, sending her head completely sideways as she stumbled backwards once more.

The elevator creature had nearly reached Michael. Spinning around, he poked the hideous being in its face and the metal rod easily pushed through its head, coming out the other side. Tainted green brains spilled out of the fresh opening.

Revolted at the sight, Michael grimaced and quickly pulled the rod out of its head, sending brain matter and dark green slime spewing on either side of the fresh holes. It moaned loudly, opening its mouth wider as its bottom jawbone stretched the thin skin around it, tearing it open until it fell off, sliding down its body and landing on the floor.

Without hesitating, Michael swung the rod as hard as he could, connecting with the side of the creature, easily knocking its head off at the neck and it smacked against a door close by before sliding to the ground. The headless creature stumbled a bit then fell backwards, hitting the floor with a splat and all but exploding at the impact to its soft body made almost entirely of green, mucus-like substance.

He was learning quickly how to kill. He turned back toward the still approaching woman, whose head was now completely sideways, gravity continuing to pull it down farther past its broken neck. Green slime oozed out of her open mouth. The whites of her eyes looked blindly at him.

She screamed once more, with difficulty, and fluids gurgled in her broken windpipe. He raised the bar, about ready to strike, when his head began to pound.

"Not now, please, no!" Michael shouted as darkness took over.

Images flashed inside his mind. Rigorous training. Lifting weights in the gym. Getting stronger for his mission off-world. Preparing to be a spacecraft pilot and miner, like his father before him. He would make them both proud—his dearly departed and much missed mama and his dad. He was being trained in self-defense, hand-to-hand combat. He wanted to not just be better than his classmates at the training academy but the best. To prove he was up to any challenge, like his father had always been.

Olivia, meanwhile, had obeyed Michael and immediately ran to the room's closet, dismayed to find no metal clothing rod. Instead, she found several shiny metal objects that appeared to be surgical instruments. She scanned the assortment, none of which looked like they would do any significant damage, except for one. It had an open handle and a curved blade roughly thirteen inches in length with sharp little points across it. *A bone saw.* Staring at it, her mind imprinted the information at a rapid pace, even at the young, tender age of eleven.

Holding it tightly in her hand, she ran back to the door, entered the code, 0042 and hit enter, just as Michael had done. The door slid open and she saw Michael landing on the ground, clinging to the rod but obviously having another memory implant.

Olivia swallowed hard and ran toward the repugnant, naked woman. Head sideways, green and red fluids running out of her open neck wound and mouth, she stood over Michael as he grimaced on the floor in pain, eyes tightly shut.

The clone woman, unable to move her head, swiveled her body toward the girl and began to reach out her bony arms toward her. Olivia, however, was faster. She slammed the bone saw down onto the woman's outstretched arm, easily slicing the soft, rotting limb off at the elbow. The severed arm fell to the ground as green puss immediately began oozing out of the stump. The woman instinctively raised her remaining hand to the stump where her arm had just been. Green rot instantly seeping through her fingers onto the floor.

Caught off guard, the woman stumbled backward as Olivia took another swing at her with the bone saw but missed as the blade sliced through empty air.

Michael returned from this latest memory implant, his head pounding and everything blurred. He shook his head as his surroundings came back into focus. Near his face, green puss lay in pools from the monster exploding when it hit the ground. The smell hit his nose as his eyes fell on a severed arm with more of the green slime oozing from it. He winced at the rancid, decaying meat smell.

He heard a guttural scream and looked up to find Olivia swinging a small hand saw, a bone saw, at the now armless naked clone woman hobbling toward her.

Michael got to his feet, grabbing the rod tightly in his hand, and crept up behind the rotting figure at the same time Olivia saw him. The clone, sensing the man had risen, attempted to turn around but it was too late. The metal rod smashed against the back of her head, sinking deep into her skull and dropping her face first to the ground.

Running to where Olivia stood trembling, he looked at her with soft eyes and as calmly as he could asked, "Are you okay? I know I told you to stay put, but thanks for saving my ass there."

She looked up at him, eyes wide with terror, trying to grasp everything that had been coming at them in such a short amount of time. Looking back down to the woman whose brains were just bashed in, she saw the clone was still moving.

Arms and legs slowly flailing back and forth as if desperately trying to stand back up.

Keeping her eyes on the living-dead creature on the ground, she said, "I couldn't leave you out here with these… whatever they are. You helped me and now I help you. Please, let's not separate again, okay?"

Michael shot her a brief thin smile and nodded. He sighed, looking over the gore-strewn floor and walls. "Well, now we know what we're up against. We've got to get out of this building. There's bound to be more of them, and I'm not sure how contagious this stuff is…yet."

"Where does it come from? Gross, it smells awful!" Olivia replied, wrinkling her nose at the putrid smell that filled the hallway.

Michael contemplated not sharing what he knew about the Rot virus with the young girl but thought it best she should know to defend herself in case he wasn't around.

"This disease eats away from the inside, I know that much. Rot is what it's called. I read it on another clone's doctor analysis sheet. It makes the insides almost like jelly, easy to push through with a blunt, or sharp instrument. I think the virus, or whatever it is, slowly turns the internal organs and bones into thick green mush before taking over the mind and controlling its victim. Eventually leaving the infected nothing more than a pile of that green…stuff."

"What are we going to do with her?" Olivia asked softly, staring down at the pitiful naked squirming body at their feet.

"We've only seen what's on one level in this place. I fear there's more. One way or another, we've got to get out of this building," Michael replied, determined to find a way to safety, or a way out of their current predicament at least.

To their complete surprise, the nearly decapitated clone spoke. "You humans come here. Drain the planet. Leave it dead. But you won't kill us, not all of us."

Michael moved in toward her, gripping the bar tightly in his hands. Olivia followed behind him, gripping the bone saw, holding it close to her chest firmly.

"What?" was all Michael could muster, repulsed at the sight in front of him, yet curious to find out more about this disease. Or possibly an exit strategy.

They both bent down, close enough to hear her but far enough away that she would be incapable of grabbing hold of either of them.

Through garbled and guttural groans, the clone mumbled something unintelligible, thick green puss oozing from her mouth.

They both watched as the creature before them continued to writhe, wondering if it felt any pain at this point in its mutation.

"Cover your eyes, Olivia," Michael said as they both stood up. He raised the metal bar high above his head and brought it down as hard as he could on top of the already heavy damaged head of the woman. The poor creature's tainted green-colored brains spilled out of the freshly made cavity. It continued to twitch and move but made no attempt to stand back up.

"How can it still move?" Olivia asked, peeking through her hands covering her face.

"Whatever that thick green liquid is, it takes over the host completely. Apparently even after death. Let's get back to the elevator," Michael replied quietly as he shook his head in disgust.

They turned from the unsightly mess in the hallway and headed back to the elevator. Michael pressed the button again and the door slid open quickly, letting out a pool of green slime from the creature that had come up on it.

"Gross," Olivia said, wrinkling her nose.

"Come on," Michael replied as they walked into the elevator, trying to avoid the slime.

He looked over the buttons and was about to hit level one when he heard a banging noise above them where a large, square emergency hatch in the middle of the ceiling had been ripped out. Michael and Olivia both looked up, startled.

Two more Rot-controlled clones were attempting to claw their way inside the elevator to get at the fresh, untainted host bodies below. One was a beefy blond-haired man with one eye missing, green puss oozing out. The other was thin with matted-down hair thick with green slime and dark red blood. The sickly ooze dripped to the floor as they fought with each other to gain access to the new, untainted organisms below.

Olivia screamed in terror as Michael put his hand against her, moving her behind him. The door to the elevator closed and Michael began frantically pressing the open button just as the larger of the two infected creatures shoved the smaller one down into the elevator where it landed with a loud thud next to Olivia.

She continued to scream as the second man jumped down, feet first, onto the elevator floor, landing on top of the squishy body below. Unlike the other infected bodies they had thus far had the misfortune of meeting, this one was large and significantly more threatening. He was a well-built man, obviously in peak physical shape before the Rot got to him. Other than the infected eye, he looked relatively unscathed. In his blue work pants, black boots, and no shirt, his exposed muscles rippled, and the veins under the skin revealed a thin light green color running through them. Rot.

"Are we ever going to get off this damn floor?" Michael shouted in frustration. The door opened. He quickly pushed Olivia out and followed her, glancing back at the belt on the shirtless muscle-bound man where several items were attached. One looked like a small communication device of some sort. *A means of communication,* his mind imprinted.

The lumbering, beastly man began moving forward toward them, the veins in his neck popping out with thin drops of green rot running out of them. The door to the elevator slid shut before him just as he reached his prey.

"He's going to open that door in a few seconds! Take the stairs, now!" Michael said as he pointed to the stairwell. Olivia nodded and they ran to the door, opened it, and headed inside, closing it behind them just as they heart the ding of the elevator door opening.

The shirtless man stepped into the room, breathing hard as he looked around the empty area he had foggy memories of. *Vending machines.* He had purchased many snacks and drinks from both of them. His eyes continued searching. *Stairwell.* He glared at the door. In his Rot-infected state, one overriding primal need raged inside of him: *find more hosts.*

CHAPTER 10

DR. PETRINO'S SECRETS

"So, now what? Generator and server room are both fucked! What's Elise's next big plan?" Dr. Petrino said, not expecting an answer from Sonia, the only other person in the Command Center.

Sonia knew time was of the essence in helping her commanding officer get out of the room she was trapped inside with Chris. *Confidence, Sonia, you know what needs to be done.*

She ignored Dr. Petrino as she continued her communications with Elise and Chris. "I'm going to walk you through how to bypass the door lock mechanism from inside."

On the other end, Elise replied, "Good, I'm not sure where Carley is headed next, but it might be your way."

With a furrowed brow, Sonia replied, "Things seem to be going from bad to worse. But I'm going to get you out of that room, hang tight."

Elise nodded on the other end of the com. "Thanks Sonia, I knew you could do it."

She turned to Chris, thinking aloud. "Dex Scott and Leah Lowe must still be here as well, not taken off-world like we were led to believe. So, at the very least, three Rot-infected people could be loose in the tunnel system, along with who knows how many clones. The infected clones seem to mindlessly claw, scratch, and bite anything not infected. How will humans react after significant Rot exposure?"

Chris shrugged. "This mess just keeps escalating. First, the Kernadium is all harvested from this rock and then Rot infects the clones. Then the corporation bails, leaving behind a skeleton crew to watch over their last precious warehouse full of Kernadium. Now, we end up in the sabotaged Generator and Server room running out of air. I think that covers about everything."

"Let's just get this door open, shall we?" Elise said, ignoring Chris's unhelpful rant.

Sonia came back on the com. "So, here's what you need to do, pop off the surrounding metal piece around the screen in front of you. If you can't find anything to wedge in there, a few hard cracks with the butt of your Defender should do the trick."

Elise looked around then over at Chris who gave her an approving nod. Taking the butt of her gun, she began hitting the edge of the encasing around the screen. After several tries, it came loose. One more hard jab from the Defender and the outer housing fell uselessly to the floor.

"Got it."

"Good, there should be two wires under the exposed screen, a blue one and a red one. Pull them out as far as you can and they should each pop out of their ports," Sonia said. She glanced up to see that Dr. Petrino had come over to stand behind her. Gross, she thought.

Immediately sensing her revulsion, he smirked and took a step closer and continued to peer over her shoulder.

"I've got 'em," Elise came back quickly.

Trying not to appear bothered by the stale cigarette smoke wafting over her, Sonia kept going. "Now it should be as easy as swapping them. Plug the red into the blue outlet and blue into the red. This will give you hand print access from inside once more, bypassing the security lock."

Taking both wires in her hands Elise eyed the ports they needed to go into and started the process.

"Wait, wait, wait! I forgot to tell you! Do not under any circumstances, touch the exposed wires to each other! Severe shock. Good chance of instant death and it will also fry the circuits," Sonia said frantically.

Elise froze. The wires were within a centimeter of touching as she was adjusting them in her hands. "Thanks for the heads up," she said with some sarcasm.

"Stupid woman," Dr. Petrino said coldly from behind her.

Sonia shot him a look of fury before blurting out, "Dr. Petrino, do you really care if any of us lives or dies? I'm trying to help here and that smoke is distracting." *And nasty smelling, just like you!* she wanted to add, but held her tongue.

"I *care* because I want us to find a solution as well, I'll have you know!" he threw back at her, quickly looking down at the old watch on his wrist then up at the sky, outside of the Command Center.

"What's out there that's so important? And why are you always looking at your watch? We aren't going anywhere," Sonia said, noticing his restless demeaner. She continually had to remind herself that this man was her superior, but even with her typically quiet and meek disposition she was completely fed up with the doctor, letting her disdain for him show more and more in this rapidly deteriorating situation they all faced.

Taking a second for his rebuttal, he clapped back, "I'm checking my watch to see how much time we have left and to see if the last transport out of here might be early. You deal with stress your way; I'll deal with it mine."

She didn't respond, only shaking her head and trying to get back to helping Elise on the other end.

Elise, meanwhile, was having difficulty inserting the wires into the new housing. "I have to take off these damn gloves. I can't get a good enough grip," she said.

"Oh, hell no. Elise, no gloves means no oxygen. You've got to keep them on!" Chris said, shaking his head in protest.

"Well, you got a better idea? They can't touch each other, and I can't get a good enough grasp on them. You want the job?" Elise shot back, tilting her head to one side.

"Damnit Elise, fine. But you need to make this fast."

Nodding, she twisted her gloves counterclockwise a half turn. They hissed as oxygen was extinguished from her entire suit. She had taken a large gulp of air before doing so, but now time was of the essence as she held her breath tightly.

"You got it yet?" Sonia said, startling Elise who almost extinguished the breath of air she had been holding.

Chris quickly responded, "Hang on, Sonia!"

Silence followed on the com. Elise tried not to shake as she cautiously inserted the blue wire into the red outlet. Then, carefully she did the same for the red wire, clicking it securely into the blue outlet.

"She's got it!" Chris said to Sonia as he blew out a sigh of relief.

"Put your hand on the screen," Sonia said quickly.

Elise quickly put her hand on the flat panel and the door slid open. She didn't wait for Chris and quickly ran in, with him following close behind. Once inside the hallway, she immediately slammed her exposed hand against the panel and the door slid shut once more.

Letting out the huge breath that was burning her throat, Elise sucked in the fresh air. "Good job, Sonia! Under normal circumstances that shouldn't have been difficult, but considering what we're up against, that was quite unpleasant."

In the Command Center, Dr. Petrino bent down beside Sonia and said loudly into the com, "So how exactly are we going to survive here with less than two days' worth of oxygen left?

Ignoring the question, Elise replied, "We're heading back to the Command Center and regrouping. I have a few ideas."

"Are you absolutely positive the generator is gone?" Dr. Petrino grumbled.

"Feel free to come down here and inspect it yourself," Chris began angrily, but Elise put her hand on his arm and shook her head, wanting everyone to keep their cool. She hoped there was still time to find a solution.

The com went silent. Sonia looked up at the squirmy, uncomfortable man still standing over her and asked in as condescending a tone as she could muster, "Is there anything else, doctor?"

He pulled out another cigarette, lit it and took a drag, blowing it in her direction as he walked away, back to the window looking out over the desolate planet. A planet where days blended together due to the constant dim light casting a depressing reddish haze with dust continually swirling.

Wiping his greasy face with his free hand, Petrino's mind went to his time spent in college getting his doctorate degree in medicine. No one liked him. He had tried but failed every attempt at human connection. His grades reflected his isolation as he poured his time solely into medicine—specifically, the advancements in cloning technology.

No, he didn't have friends, but that hadn't always been the case. He was smart and excelled in nearly every subject, from high school all the way through graduating from Otheania University on Troria. In college, he had had numerous acquaintances he got along with well, even several lovers. However, his interest in cloning technology grew substantially once the AMO grew in prominence. He delved into more advanced research, experimenting with various animals and human hybrids.

His misdeeds went undiscovered, and he continued down the path of questionable biotechnology and cloning. He became more and more reclusive, shunning his family, now long since dead. He let himself go, lost a lot of hair, and took up smoking. The friends he did have abandoned him after he snapped at them one too many times.

He also sided with many of Levon Gonidec's policies, further alienating himself from people. Seeking an opportunity to experiment undisturbed with a regime such as Gonidec's, he had learned that the AMO was beginning to look at off-world mining for extracting the thick dark green Kernadium from Poule plants. He decided that Moon 002 could be a place for him to thrive. And to experiment relatively undisturbed.

He signed up to be one of the first to arrive. Shortly after getting settled in, he once more found himself with no friends, other than commander Jake Riley, who treated him with some decency. Dr. Kevin Bradley and Dr. Sarah Baudet always seemed to be watching Petrino closely, and for good reason. Things went missing from time to time. Small surgical items, things he could easily stash away and use on his own time for a big project he kept secret.

Once Elise Bennet came along, Petrino became even more reclusive, after an attempt at flirting with her had failed miserably. Flirting used to be something he excelled in during his college years, but those days were over. Now he was awkward and most everyone in the complex found him utterly creepy.

Several of the staff witnessed an uncomfortable conversation in the rec room after their shifts had ended one evening nearly six months ago. As usual, Petrino had been sitting unnoticed and ignored at the bar. After one too many scotches, something he was not used to, the alcohol gave him enough liquid courage to approach the always stunning Elise who was spending a bit of down time with several office staff and Jake Riley at a nearby table.

He had glanced over to where they all sat, laughing and enjoying themselves

The staff would on occasion get a bit dressed up when lounging at the rec room, perhaps to make it feel like a "night out on the town." Tonight was one such night. The rec room was packed with everyone off-duty. Petrino had gotten up and stumbled over to where they all sat, coming to an abrupt stop in front of the table, swaying slightly as he stood in place. He looked at Elise, who was out of her work clothes and wearing a particularly form-fitting, low slung white dress. She looked stunningly beautiful with her bright green eyes and perfectly groomed long blond hair.

He locked eyes with her and began stammering, "So, what say we get out of here. I could show you around the cloning facility. You'd, um, you'd be surprised at what I have, what we have achieved in cloning technology lately. We can determine even quicker if a clone is destined for the feeding trough or if..."

Jake cleared his throat as Dr. Sarah Baudet, who was also sitting at the table quickly piped up, "Doctor, you're drunk. Show a little dignity. Please. If you want to sit down with us and have a conversation, feel free, but if you're just going to ogle over Elise here and discuss things that are, shall we say, a bit inappropriate, then I suggest you head back to your room and sleep it off."

Petrino's face instantly turned red. Elise looked down at her drink as she crossed her legs and her arms, feeling his eyes falling over her. Dr. Sarah and the rest of the table sat in silence looking up at him.

"Sit there and make fun of me. The attractive table thinks they're better than everyone else!" he nearly shouted as spittle flew from his mouth.

Christopher Berger, also at the table, set his drink down and in his deep voice said, "Hey, Dr. Petrino, relax there, buddy. We're not making fun of you. We're just chillin', alright?"

Noticing the growing attention around the table from other patrons in the large rec room, Jake motioned for Chris to stand down with a wave of his hand as he pushed his chair back and stood to his feet. Jake was a handsome man. Light beard, brown hair combed over his head, soft but firm voice. He put a hand on Petrino's shoulder.

"Come on, let's get you a cup of coffee. I'll hang with you at the bar. What do you say, Anthony?" Jake asked in as kind voice as he could muster as he tried to diffuse the situation. He glanced at Elise who gave him a quick smile.

Staring at the table, now even more self-conscious than before, Petrino brushed off Jake's arm and glanced at him. Even in his drunken state, he could tell Jake was trying to do the right thing. Finally, he nodded in agreement, not before glaring over at Chris.

They both turned to walk away when Sonia Bonnel, who was usually shy, blurted out just loud enough for Petrino to hear, "And that is what I've had to deal with for the past three years."

"Hey, fuck you, lady! I'm your superior and don't ever forget that! Your ass belongs to me!" Petrino yelled as he turned around, beet red in the face, glaring at her.

Jake quickly took him by the arm and led him out of the rec room. He could tell by the pressure of the grip Jake was done messing around. Better Jake than Chris, he'd thought.

Once they made their way out of the rec room, Petrino shook himself free of Jake's grip.

Jake exclaimed, "You know, I have half a notion to bust your ass for that, Petrino! I'm looking out for you here! Me! You've got no friends because of shit like that! You can't do that. Come on, man. You're a doctor dealing with highly volatile cloning for a huge mining corporation. Use your head! You've got people that report to you directly! Sonia Bonnel is one of them!" He tried to control the volume of his voice.

"It's bullshit. It's all bullshit. They sit in there all high and mighty," Petrino began to say through a haze of single malt scotch and stale tobacco breath.

Jake raised his hand in protest, stopping him, and exclaimed, “You’re a doctor. And once this is all over and we’re off this rock, you’re going to be wealthy enough to do whatever the hell you want to do back on Troria. You know that? But if you keep pulling stunts like that, you’re going to be written up again. I’m tired of giving out these worthless warnings!”

“I see the way you both look at each other. Of course, she would have to go for someone like you! I mean, come on. Handsome fella, they all go for guys like you.”

“I’m not going to respond to that. Grow up, Petrino. Seriously, you’re a doctor for crying out loud. And a good one. Use your head, man!” Jake retorted growing angrier.

He took a breath. “Last chance. Another write-up and you can kiss any bonus goodbye. Hell, you can kiss any further career back home goodbye. You’ve been here too long to throw it all away! I’m doing you a favor here, buddy. Get sobered up. Drinking doesn’t suit you. Tomorrow, apologize personally to everyone that was at that table. I’ll give you a list if you don’t remember.”

Shaking his head, Petrino started to argue.

“That’s an order from your commanding officer. Go get some sleep, Petrino.” Jake turned and walked back into the rec room leaving Petrino standing alone by the door.

He could hear the table laughing. *They’re laughing at me*, he thought as he turned around and headed back to his room.

At the last minute, just as he was approaching his own room, he decided to walk a bit farther. To Elise’s room. Because there were only three doctors on staff, they were given an emergency security access key. Something none of the staff were aware of and something the doctors had all but forgotten about as they were never used. A little-known fact about the keys, but something Petrino was keenly aware of, was that they left no traces of entry and no records were recorded onto the servers.

He looked both ways in the empty hallway. It was quiet. Most people were at the rec room party and those that were not were either working their shift or sound asleep. The party on level three would go on for several more hours at least. He raised the security access key to the handprint reader. It lit up red as he quietly said, "Emergency access code 483759."

The door to Elise's room slid open quietly. He stepped through the open door and it slid shut behind him. *Get in and get out*. This was something he had planned to do for several months but this latest incident upstairs, coupled with the alcohol, had finally set the plan into motion.

Careful to not disrupt anything, he clicked the light on by using his card. He wanted no fingerprints left behind. He headed toward the bathroom. Her room was like all the others except it smelled wonderful, like her. Small touches throughout the room made it her own, and just being there made him become aroused. *Quick, get what you need then leave!*

In the bathroom, he glanced at the shower and immediately pushed thoughts of her naked body out of his mind, trying to stay focused. As carefully as he could, with the tips of his fingers, he pulled several strands of her blond hair from the brush sitting on the sink. He pulled out a small bag he had in this pocket. It had once housed a new syringe and he hadn't discarded the bag it had come in.

Opening the sealable bag, he dropped the hair strands inside. He was about to leave when he looked at her waste basket beside the toilet. Reaching in, he pulled out a crumpled-up tissue with several drops of dried blood on it. He couldn't believe his luck. *Nosebleed. I've seen her get them sometimes due to the thin, dry air.* He stuffed the blood dotted tissue into the bag as well, sealed it, and quietly left the room.

He breathed in the smell of the room from memory as he walked quickly back to his own room when he heard laughing. He got to his room and placed his hand on the handprint reader as the laughing grew nearer. His door slid open.

Elise and several people from the rec room party, Sonia included, rounded the corner. He nearly leapt into his room as they looked up, seeing his door slide shut. He heard them walk past as well as muffled laughing. His heart raced.

Almost caught! He would have been sent off-world on the next transport and surely been excommunicated from the doctor's association back on Troria. She could have even pressed charges. *I could have seen jail time! What the hell, Petrino?* He clenched his chest in fright and his eyes darted back and forth nervously.

Then he pulled out the small bag with the beautiful strands of blond hair and the blood dotted tissue. "This is why I risked all of that. Right here."

He smiled as he stared at the contents of the bag and pondered this wonderful turn of events.

CHAPTER 11

STAIRWELL GETAWAY

Michael and Olivia quietly closed the stairwell door behind them and immediately began heading down the steps, careful not to make too much noise. Thus far, the building they were trapped in had been a house of horrors with infected people lurking in the shadows.

They had to make their way down to level one if they were to even attempt escaping this building. When they reached level two, they heard the door above them open and looked up to see the giant shirtless man glaring down at them.

"Olivia! Run, go!" Michael yelled when he heard the man's boots begin descending the steps.

They began running down the stairs, the giant man's boots on the thick metal stairs continuing to echo through the tomb-like stairwell. When they reached level one, Michael burst through the door, pulling Olivia along with him and slamming the door shut behind him.

Scanning this new room, Michael pointed and exclaimed, "There! Another door!"

They ran to the door with a handprint scanner beside it. "Must lead somewhere! Better than being open targets here." He motioned for Olivia scan her hand.

"But Michael, we need to hide!" Olivia exclaimed.

The stairwell door burst open as the large, shirtless, one-eyed man barged in, the whites of his remaining eye bearing down on them.

Raising his metal rod in front of him, Michael motioned for Olivia to stay near the door as the beastly man moved slowly closer, stalking him. *He senses I have a weapon. He still has reasoning.*

Once more, Michael saw the small, rectangular device clipped to the man's belt. His mind processed it like a machine, instructing him to get to it. It reminded him of the small foreign device Olivia had in her back pocket. If *we get out of this, we need to see what's on that thing,* he thought as he prepared to fight the giant.

The man opened his mouth and green mucus spilled out, dripping down his chin. Michael charged toward him, but the infected beast grabbed hold of the rod, pulling it out of his hands and throwing it aside.

Grabbing Michael by the shirt, he lifted him up off of the ground. *Vulnerable locations on man...groin! Kick him in the groin!* Michael pulled back his dangling foot and kicked him as hard as he could in the groin. This seemed to have the effect he was hoping for, as the man dropped him to the ground and roared in anger and pain. *He still has feeling. Good,* Michael thought as he scrambled away from him on all fours.

"Michael, here!" Olivia shouted from behind. He glanced back to see Olivia had opened the door and was now sliding the bone saw across the floor in his direction.

Sharp edge, cuts through flesh his mind processed quickly. He didn't hesitate, grabbing the bone saw, turning around, and immediately bringing it down between the man's first and second toe, plunging the blade through the bone nearly back to the base of his right foot.

The man screamed in anger and pain as Michael furiously sawed at the foot until the blade cut through completely, hitting the floor beneath. Blood gurgled up through the large cut, giving Michael enough time to stand to his feet, still clinging tightly to the now blood-covered bone saw. Small amounts of the green puss remained on the blade, much less than the other creatures they had thus far encountered.

Michael took the precious seconds he had while the man lay in agony on the floor to grab hold of the small device clipped to his belt, causing the injured giant to strike out with a closed fist, connecting with Michael's jaw and sending him flying backwards onto the ground.

Olivia screamed. "Get up, Michael!" She grabbed hold of his arm and tugged at it.

Michael pulled himself up as the angry infected man attempted to charge at them, but his right foot split down the middle, making him fall down face first. A cracking sound of skull hitting steel echoed through the room when his face made contact with the hard flooring. He quickly attempted to stand back up as blood gushed out of his now busted nose. The green slime and fresh blood covered his exposed, muscular chest, making him all the more menacing in appearance.

The man roared in anger. The Rot that infected his body was making him progressively more violent and aggressive as it searched for new hosts to infect and spread to. *It could sense the blood inside warm bodies, not caring if the host was human or clone, it was all the same to the virus. Infect, grow, and multiply.* The man's brain was quickly deteriorating to its most basic animal instincts as the Rot took total control of all his functions.

Michael resisted the urge to nurse his throbbing jaw with his hand, his mind processing the new sensations of pain and calculating when to fight or flight. He had the device from the man's belt and the bone saw. There was no more time to grab the metal bar that now lay in the corner of the room.

The man slid forward on the bloody floor reaching out toward Michael, who took the opportunity to swing the bone saw at the man's outstretched hand, severing it completely from his body. Thick green fluid oozed out of the stump on his arm, right above his wrist.

Michael backed up and took one more look at the injured, muscular man who looked back at them with his one eye turned up into his head. Then he spoke in a slow garbled voice, as if blood and slime were blocking his vocal cords, "You won't leave this place alive, clone bastard."

"We'll just see about that," Michael retorted grimly. "Come on, we've got to move!" he shouted as they ran through the opened door.

Olivia once more slammed her hand against the handprint reader and the door slid shut behind them.

The monster of a man who was now relegated to one working foot managed to stand. The pain he had felt when an infected clone had bitten his eye out in a surprise attack was slowly subsiding. Even his destroyed foot and stump where his right hand used to be, while painful, seemed to already be dulling. He looked at the foot that was split in two, the bone and gristle exposed as thick blood mixed with a green-colored puss oozed out. His busted nose leaked the same mixture of green slimy puss and blood.

These injuries ceased bothering him. His mind had been slipping ever since the Rot took hold and began working its way through his body, wrapping itself around organs, entering into his blood stream and changing his DNA. It was killing the human part of him as well as destroying his pain threshold, until he would soon be nothing but a gelatinous mass whose only aim was to spread to new host bodies.

He contemplated hobbling over to the door his prey had just escaped through. *The second time they've escaped me. It will be their last.*

Instead of following the underground walkway, he would bring in reinforcements. The one-time security guard for AMO picked up his severed hand and placed it on the handprint reader leading into the lab on level one. The door slid open and he peered inside. The entire room had a red hue due to the emergency lighting.

The main lab was where most of the initial incubation occurred. Once the synthetic host eggs of the clones were fertilized and had proven to take hold, they were then left to begin their growth inside tiny incubation containers small enough for an infant. The clones were in a vulnerable state through the first month of fertilization and growth. The doctors' assistants' care and watchfulness played a large part in their very early development.

Once they had reached twenty pounds or thirty inches in length, whichever came first, they were transferred to their own room on levels two and three. There, they had IVs injected into their arms and feeding tubes inserted down their still growing throats to provide the needed nutrients for further growth for the remaining months until they reached full maturity and were able to receive memory implants. Then they were delivered by one of the three doctors or their assistants on staff. The amniotic sack was sliced open and they were cleaned and washed thoroughly and given several immunization shots.

The lab was circular with numerous small incubation containers that were easily accessible to the staff of doctors and assistants. Surgical equipment surrounded the containers as well as incubation lights to keep the fetuses warm through the early stages of growth.

This area was also a place where clones unfit for work duties for any number of reasons, primarily growth defects, were sent to be euthanized if they had survived long enough in the amniotic sack in their own rooms on levels two and three. It was here that the bodies were sliced up to better transport to the clone kitchen prep area on level three in the Command Center.

The giant man, previously known as security guard Dex Scott, who had once been the official muscle at Mining Complex VI, stood in the doorway. He opened his blood covered mouth and let out another bellowing yell, his own version of a call to arms.

Numerous groans and shrieks echoed in reply through the dimly lit room as shadowy figures stood to their feet and made their way forward.

Michael and Olivia stood in the underground walkway looking at the signs above two passageways reading *Command Center and Generator / Server Room.*

"We're in the Clone Replication Facility now. The Command Center sounds like where we need to be heading. What do you think?" Michael asked.

"I think you're right. Whatever we do, I think we best do it quickly. That scary man doesn't look like he's going to stop coming for us until he's dead. Or, more dead I guess," Olivia responded shakily.

Comfort the child, she is scared, Michael's mind told him. He was learning as he went how best to deal with friendly as well as hostile individuals. Luckily, he hadn't had another sharp memory implant that caused him to black out. "Olivia, I'm sorry you've had to see these things. I'm going to do my best to get you somewhere safe." He put his hand on her shoulder as she gave him a brief, if forced, smile.

"Come on, let's get going. If that beast gets through this door, which he likely will, he won't know which direction we went. That's a small bit of good news," Michael added as they began walking quickly down the quiet, dimly lit walkway toward the Command Center roughly eight hundred yards away through the winding tunnel.

Michael pulled out the device he had grabbed off of the man's belt and looked it over. Again, his mind processed the new data rapidly, the information burning itself into his brain. "I don't know what this is. I just know I had to get it off that man, but why?" Michael said dourly just as the throbbing in his head returned.

"Oh shit, not again! Olivia, I'm having another memory implant, if he comes through that door, ru…"

He felt the shuttle in which he was sitting lower to the ground. The ship itself was nothing special. Similar ones could be seen in the skies over Troria. Both Alnorix Mining and the current administration's military used nearly identical vessels for transporting goods in space. Goods and people, of course. The ships themselves were narrow and rectangular in shape. Large boosters on the back shot the shuttles through space to their destinations, fueled by the very substance he would be mining for, the valuable and highly prized Kernadium.

The flight to Moon 002 had been uneventful. He hardly remembered it. Once they landed in the designated area where all Alnorix transports docked, he would be led to the Command Center where he would be briefed on how things operated at this facility as well as receive his official job duties.

Michael stretched his muscular arms from the long flight to Moon 002. He thought of his dad, his friends back home. He would see them all again once his job was complete. His primary goal was to do the best job he could once he arrived on Moon 002, orbiting the planet Treon III in the 8304 quadrant. *I've done it! I'm working off-world! My training has paid off!* He had spent his whole life leading up to this moment.

He was proud to be working for such a successful company. They had supplied jobs to people like him for years now, giving them an opportunity to grow in the company, which is what he hoped to do. He was fairly certain he would get a security job or possibly even shift manager but hoped to do a bit of physical labor on the planet's surface at Mining Complex VI. He was doing a good thing for his home world. For his dad, for his deceased mother and for himself. He would be leaving his mark on society. During the flight he made small talk with several other transports to Moon 002. All excited for their new job opportunities. Michael stared out the window, watching stars pass by in the distance as Moon 002 near the planet Treon III loomed larger and larger.

Once they landed, he and the other fresh workers quickly disembarked and were taken to a waiting room in the Command Center. Michael sat, waiting for his turn for the official arrival interview. As he looked at his flying companions, all of their faces seemed to be masked or blurred out. As if he wasn't meant to fully see their facial features. He was sure there were both men and women on board the flight. *Right?* They all had appeared excited to be joining the team on Mining Complex VI.

When it was finally his turn, Michael sat down in a seat facing his superior, a well-dressed woman who gave him the guidelines for work on Moon 002. He would be security detail for the living quarters, along with pulling shifts periodically for tired or worn-out miners working the Poule plants. He was informed that the work was hard, but the pay would more than compensate for his time spent. Only a one-year commitment.

He was then given a set of clothes, keys, paperwork to fill out and a communications device that he was to carry at all times while on duty so his foreman could reach him. Although the woman behind the desk whose name eluded him was attractive, he hadn't had much time for the opposite sex growing up. Hadn't even been that interested in them, his career was of utmost importance. Relationships could come later.

The attractive woman finished up going through the process of life on Moon 002 on Mining Complex VI and he was dismissed. On his way out of the office, he began to shake, his shoulders seemed to be moving on their own accord. Something hit him on his face. But there was nothing in front of him. Another hard crack across his cheek. *What is happening?*

Olivia shook him once more, pushing on his shoulders, and was about to slap him on the face once more as she yelled, "Michael, please! Wake up! Now!"

Michael grabbed her wrist, stopping the blow from connecting once more. Olivia froze, wide-eyed.

"I'm back, thanks for the help!" he exclaimed getting to his feet and shaking his head, trying to reorient himself to the present.

They both began walking quickly as Olivia asked innocently, "Did it hurt you again?"

"I think I'm near the end of it, at least it led me up to this place we're in. I must admit, I'm not sure what is real and what isn't. I know how I got here, and I know it happened. I can feel it. And I miss my parents. I wish I could talk to my dad, to believe he really existed, but I just don't know. I know where I woke up and what I did to get to where we both are now, but it doesn't line up with the memories that are burned into my subconscious. And yes. It hurt. But I'm starting to think that pain is okay. It makes me feel," Michael paused, then finished his thought, "alive."

As they walked down the long, winding tunnel toward the Command Center, Michael thought of various parts of his life. Birthday parties on Troria. His favorite foods. His pet peeves. His allergies. *Were they all designed in a lab to make his short stint on Moon 002 feel more real? To make him a better worker? A harder worker? All for nothing, only death?* He didn't want to believe it. For his sanity, he couldn't. He was more than just a random few strands of DNA whipped together in a lab by some guy named Dr. Petrino. So was this innocent child walking beside him.

Sighing heavily, Olivia broke the silence, “I’m sorry.”

Michael smiled at this kind-hearted young girl. She had no harsh implants like he had, just basic knowledge that an eleven-year-old would know at this point in her lifespan. She was a clean slate that had suddenly found out she had likely been manufactured here. And she felt bad for *him*? “Olivia, it’s time for us to figure out if it’s just us on this rock or if we have help. I’d very much like to meet this Dr. Petrino. He seemed to be playing God around here. I’m assuming with both of us. Let’s see if we can meet our maker.”

He looked at the communicator in his hand. He now knew the official name of it, after his last implant. These devices were known as Communication Transmitters. This was its fifth iteration developed by the AMO, so they were currently called CT5’s.

“I think this is for talking to others. I know it is,” Michael said, stunned at his sudden knowledge of the small device.

Looking this one over in his hand, he saw, engraved on the side the name Dex Scott. *That beast’s name is, or was, Dex Scott.* Olivia peered over his shoulder at it then up at him. “Well, let’s see if we can get anyone on that thing,” Michael said hopefully.

He looked at the small device with a speaker in the center and green and red buttons on the side, working through how it functioned. He cleared his throat and raised the CT5 to his lips and pushed the green button.

CHAPTER 12

A NEW ALLIANCE

Outside of the generator room, Elise and Chris noticed the oxygen tanks in the remaining lockers were gone along with the mining suits. "Looks like Carley, or what used to be Carley, wants to take away our remaining oxygen," Elise said morosely. "She must still have some thought processes left after being infected."

Chris added, "She knows where all of the remaining oxygen tanks are here. So do Dex and Leah. Not sure what state they're in but they could make an already grim situation worse."

They turned off their oxygen tanks, removed their helmets, and checked to see how much they had burned through while inside the generator room. "Shit, we've got under one hour left in these tanks. Can you believe this was the best that the AMO could do with providing acceptable oxygen for the clones here?" Elise said bitterly as she quickly pulled the front zipper enclosure down and slid easily out of her mining suit.

"It's no surprise," Chris replied. "The suits are cheap ass, I wouldn't trust these things with my life, unless I absolutely had to. But I'm not a clone programmed to not give a shit and keep on busting ass for the man until I drop dead. And these tanks, they barely pass quality control, two hours is the absolute minimum allowed. This stuff is manufactured as inexpensively and quicky as possible back home. Easy to discard, just like the people that have to wear them."

"Come on, let's keep moving," Elise said, pushing the anger and contempt down inside. For now.

They stuffed their mining suits, oxygen tanks, and retractable helmets into the lockers and continued through the walkway, heading back to the Command Center.

"So, what's plan B? Or I guess at this point, plan E or F?" Chris asked with a smirk.

"Survive until we get back to the Command Center. That's the current goal," Elise replied with a determined look.

Both kept their Defenders at the ready, knowing Carley and any number of infected clones could be lurking in the dimly lit walkways. Time was of the essence.

When Chris's CT5 clicked on, they both froze, looking down at the communication transmitter. These devices were only used between the security staff, usually to joke with each other or let each other know their whereabouts during shift changes.

"Please don't let this be Dex. Please let him not be one of those..." Chris said shakily.

"Answer it," Elise replied quickly, cutting him off.

Chris pulled the CT5 from his belt and turned it on.

"Again, I repeat, my name is Michael Astier and I'm here with a girl named Olivia. We're here in an underground walkway. We need help. Come in. Anyone!" Michael's voice echoed through the device that crackled with static at the poor reception.

Elise looked over at Chris with eyes wide. "What...the... hell," she murmured in surprise.

"Um, hello. This is acting chief of security, Christopher Berger. Who am I speaking with again? And where did you get your communication transmitter?"

After a brief pause, the crackly voice came back on. "My name is Michael Astier. I guess I'm a—clone. That's what the folder in my room said. We need help. The guy I took this off of is coming after us. I assume there are more, judging from the number of run-ins we've been having."

Elise held out her hand. Chris looked at her gravely and handed the CT5 over. She clicked it on and replied to the voice on the other end. "Michael, listen to me closely. Are you or your companion showing any signs of infection?"

"Considering I was just born a few hours ago, I think I'm fine. I can't speak for Olivia here but I'm fairly certain she's alright. Look—can you help us or not?" Michael fired back impatiently.

Nodding, Elise responded quickly, "Yes. We need to get you to the Command Center building with us. The infected aren't the only thing we have to worry about. Where are you?"

"We just left the Clone Replication Facility, according to the signs. It's fucked. Like, you really don't want to go that way. A gigantic half-dead man missing one eye and now a foot is in there and he's pissed and I'm fairly certain he's going to find a way through. We're heading toward the Command Center building. Is that your current location?" Michael shot back quickly.

"You're heading in the right direction. Keep on that path. And hurry. The walkway isn't safe either. We just ran into several in the building where our generator is located. Got one of the infected but one got away. Probably in here with us now. Go, hurry!" Elise said hastily, then added, "We'll be waiting for you close to the entrance to the Command Center. Can't miss it, just don't deviate from the path. There are several security checkpoint station access rooms along the way, avoid them."

"Alright, we're on it. See you both soon. Michael out."

The CT5 went silent. "Come on, let's keep heading back; hopefully we'll intercept them along the way," Elise said hastily as she took off down the long hallway.

Chris joined her, saying what they were both thinking. "It's Dex. He's here, along with Carley and I'm sure Leah as well. They never left. And two of them are hunting us. This just keeps getting better and better."

In the distance, Elise and Chris heard screaming. "They're coming through the door from the Replication Facility. They must be using their handprints, going from building to building and bringing along other infected clones with them!" Elise exclaimed, both running with weapons in hand.

They rounded a turn in the walkway and didn't see the two strangers heading their way. Nearly colliding with the man and young girl, Elise and Chris quickly raised their Defenders out in front of them.

"Stop right there! Let's see the hands! And put that saw on the ground!" Chris shouted as he shakily pointed his Defender II at Michael's head.

Weapons that fire. I know these devices. They're deadly. Michael's brain calculated rapidly for him as he raised his hands in the air. "Easy! We're the ones you just talked to. We need help! You can hear those things, right? They're heading this way and they're pissed!"

Elise could see Chris's nervous, pent-up anger coming to a head and she put her hand on his arm and spoke calmly. "Hold on, let's take it easy. We've got the guns, they don't. If they were infected, he wouldn't be talking coherently like his is. And he's right, whatever's down that walkway is heading toward us. We've got to go right now."

"Look, I'll give you the damn bone saw, just get us the hell out of here!" Michael shouted frantically. Olivia cowered behind him, not wanting to show her face. Her mind raced, calculating the situation, imprinting what was happening and how to respond. It told her to stay close to safety, and that was Michael.

Looking at the bone saw in Michael's hand, then over at Elise whose impatience was evident, Chris nodded hastily and they turned in the direction of the Command Center.

The shrieks grew louder behind them. Olivia ran beside Michael who was directly behind Elise and Chris. The walkway tunnel had several winding curves which slightly blocked one's view for a few brief seconds, built this way to ensure structural rigidity on the continually shifting landscape due to the Poule plant harvesting nearby.

The door came into view as they rounded the last bend in the walkway. None of the four looked up to see Carley Branch hanging from the light fixtures above, the Rot coursing through her twisted, contorted and decomposing body, keenly aware of the sound of their feet echoing underneath her.

Elise noticed a small pool of thick green liquid on the ground and her eyes widened as she looked up toward the ceiling, but it was too late. The rotted corpse of Carley Branch dropped from the light fixture, landing on Chris who hadn't seen either the Rot on the ground or the descending figure.

Too quickly for any of them to register, Carley took advantage of the few seconds of surprise to bite into Chris's exposed throat with all of her remaining jaw strength. Her teeth dug into his flesh, breaking the skin and biting through his Adam's apple and larynx. She pulled back, ripping Chris's throat wide open as bits of green Rot dripped from her mouth.

Chris's Defender II slid out of his grasp and out of reach of Michael or Elise. Michael pushed Olivia away as Elise yelled in anger and surprise at the situation that was now clearly out of their control.

From behind them, a group of infected clones made their way toward them in the shadows with a loud chorus of painful moans, arms outstretched, advancing at an alarmingly rapid speed. The survivors had one minute, maybe less, to get to the door of the Command Center.

On the ground, Chris writhed in pain and horror, unable to gasp a breath of air and choking on his own blood. Elise tried frantically to pull Carley off of him as Michael quickly came to her aid, grabbing Carley's other arm and flinging the raving mad infected woman off of Chris.

She smashed against the side of the wall, further injuring her soft body as most of her internal organs spilled out of the large open wound in her stomach from the impact. But still she kept coming. Opening her mouth, green Rot and bloody remnants of Chris's throat flowed out as she attempted a scream blocked by the gurgling fluids trapped in her throat.

Elise took the small window of opportunity and raised her Defender, aiming it at Carley's walking corpse lunging forward, pulling the trigger at point blank range in the center of her forehead. Carley's head exploded, sending brains and green Rot backwards. The headless body slumped over, still twitching.

"Come on, we have to go! Grab his arms!" Michael shouted, pointing down at Chris who was still squirming, holding onto his throat as his blood drained out in a pool on the cold floor. Death shock had set in as he coughed up a mouthful of thick blood, spilling all over his face.

"Go, now...get the hell out of here," Chris sputtered as his body grew limp.

Elise looked frantically at Chris, then back at the host of the living dead, infected with the green Rot, now near enough to make out facial features. She motioned for Michael and Olivia to run and hollered, "Damnit, he's gone! We have to go, now!"

All three of them took off, covering the last stretch toward the door.

Pick up the weapon, you know how to use it! You're a security guard here, remember? Michael's brain computed as he swooped down and grabbed the dropped Defender II from the ground.

Elise put her hand against the scanner as the door slid open and they all quickly ran inside. She was about to turn around to close it but Olivia, the last through, instinctively placed her hand on the scanner and the door slid shut behind them.

Elise stared at the girl who raised her green eyes to meet hers. There was a small pause before Michael shouted, "The big one is hurt but he's on his way too. I cut off his hand but that might not stop him. Can we seal this door shut from inside?"

Elise looked at Michael, snapping back to the issue at hand. Before she had a chance to reply there was pounding at the door.

"Come on! Please hurry! That's the big scary man again!" Olivia wailed, staring at the door in terror.

Elise saw the panic in the girl's eyes. Eyes that reminded her of her much younger self. She reached past Michael and Olivia and accessed the security emergency lock function inside the office area. The door would remain sealed unless there was another Rot mutation inside unbeknownst to her.

"That'll keep us safe in here for now," Elise told her two new companions.

Michael nodded and was about to say something, but Elise hurried past them through the offices on the ground level. He and Olivia immediately followed.

Michael recognized the offices in the large, open room from his latest implant.

With the Defender II in hand, he gave the bone saw back to Olivia. Everyone needed some form of protection here and that would have to do for now.

She took it without a word, not wanting the murderous object her mind told her she needed in this dangerous place.

At the elevator, Elise pushed the button and then got in, motioning for Michael and Olivia to follow. The elevator whirred to life, quickly raising them up until a *ding* signified their arrival at level four where, this time, no ghouls waited for them.

In the Command Center, Sonia sat at her computer monitor while Petrino stood at the large window overlooking the immediate exterior. He turned to look when the three entered the room.

"What the hell," Petrino said, stunned.

Sonia slowly stood up from her seat, pushing her glasses up to get a better look at their guests before asking, "Who are they, and where is Chris?"

Elise, Michael, and Olivia, exhausted from the last several hours that felt like days, stood in the doorway for a few seconds before Elise broke the silence. "This is Michael, and this is Olivia. Chris is dead."

Scanning the room, Michael's brain processed what was happening. *These new people may have answers.* Without missing a beat, Michael stated, "We have some questions that need answering."

Standing by the window, Petrino pulled his cigarettes out, drawing one from the pack. His hand shook almost uncontrollably as he raised it and put it between his lips.

Outside, at the entrance to the Command Center building, Dex had arrived at the sealed door. He hobbled forward while infected clones around him moved out of his way to let him pass. He held out his severed right hand, placing it against the handprint reader. The door remained shut.

The Rot-infected Dex tossed the hand aside and turned to look at the group of mindless infected clone zombies, all in various states of decay and infection.

He limped over to the nearest one, a thin clone whose head was covered in green mucus, his bottom jaw completely gone. Numerous dark green boils under the skin showed through his tattered T-shirt. Dex grabbed him then opened his mouth wide until the top of his head cracked loose and fell backward, touching the back of his neck. Out of his exposed windpipe erupted thick, green, vein-like tentacles covered in green puss, wrapping around the clone zombie who offered no resistance.

The vein tentacles entered the clone's eye sockets and mouth, pushing their way inside the man's cranium and down his throat. Thick torrents of green Rot were sucked out of the host's body and into the huge man. Once drained, the clone was little more than a skeleton with a thin film of skin covering the cartilage that had once been bones. Dex's tentacles pulled out of the clone and dropped it to the ground. The Rot pulsed through his body as he reached for the next one and did the same.

His muscles stretched and pulsed. He was growing, and healing. His back hardening. He continued to drink the Rot from the living dead clones surrounding him.

CHAPTER 13

ORIGIN OF THE ROT

Leah Lowe had been busy since being infected. She could sense things; she knew Carley would no longer be able to carry out her duty, which was to collect all of the oxygen tanks and take them to Building E, the Kernadium storage facility, so Leah had taken over for her. The green Rot had destroyed her insides and was slowly eating all of her, taking control of every aspect of her being. She was dead, but still active for now, until the Rot completely took over her body, rendering her little more than a thick pile of the green jelly-like substance.

Dex, Carley, and Leah had been left behind, sealed off in the Clone Replication Facility with the rest of the infected clones to be dealt with when the final transport shuttle arrived later, eliminating all evidence of what happened to the clones on Moon 002. A needle to the heart had been administered, killing them quickly. But they weren't fully dead.

As the Rot took over their bodies, flowing freely through their bloodstreams and pushing into their organs and bones, they were revived. For a short time, they would be under its control, to do its bidding. And for Leah, that meant collecting the oxygen tanks. The Rot craved uninfected hosts, primarily, but it was also destructive by nature. It wanted to seek out and assimilate, and then destroy what the warm-bodied hosts had built.

The infected no longer breathed, so leaving the buildings had no effect on their slowly rotting bodies. This advantage gave them an upper hand over the non-infected personnel inside Mining Complex VI. Once the Generator and Server room had been taken out, the next step would be the total destruction of the facility.

No one was sure exactly how the Rot virus began. It was theorized that some of it slipped into the Clone Living Quarters on the boots of one of the clones. Only Leah knew exactly how it had all started—with the smallest insects buried deep in the planet's harsh landscape. The small creatures fed off of the Poule plant, connected to their roots. While they fed on the thick green Kernadium juice, they in turn injected small amounts of the green substance back into the plants, keeping them alive. As the plants were slowly drained, the tiny parasites either died off or crawled to the surface in an attempt to find another food source.

Invisible to the naked eye, these tiny creatures had oval-shaped bodies with over one hundred legs and two sharp pincers which they used to dig into the Poule plants. Their mouths were lined with sharp teeth and opened over the entirety of its body, ingesting large quantities of Kernadium. Though rarely used, the tiny insectoids had hard shell-like wings enabling them to fly from one part of the plant to another quickly. Breeding took place deep underground and as they grew, they came up searching for the Poule plant's roots. Once it was time to mate, they would head back down, the males dying off once impregnating the female hosts, and then eaten.

This was how it had been for millions of years until the humans arrived with their drills and their clones to mine the planet's resources of its nutrients.

One of the many unrecognizable clones, during one of the many forgettable shifts outside on the planet's surface, had drilled slightly too close to the ground. The vibration and depth brought several of the microscopic beings to the surface where they were stepped on by the clone. At the end of his shift, the clone took off his helmet, suit, and boots in the decontamination room in the Clone Living Quarters. The boots, covered in the tiny, microscopic insectoids, sat atop the suit.

When another clone took the mining suits to the wash cyclers, the insectoids easily jumped from the suit to human flesh, some of them spreading their wings and flying into the man's ear. Through the canal, tympanic membrane, and down the eustachian tube, they burrowed deep into the unwittingly infected clone, their pincers digging and ingesting red and white blood cells, which they soon developed a taste for.

As they fed, they shed bits of their bodies, their DNA mixing with the clone's.

Soon, the man began to feel ill as tiny particles of thick, green mucus, microscopic at first, grew and expanded inside his body. Feeling sluggish and delirious, he was taken to the Replication Facility by a visibly annoyed security guard. A large, brutish man that few, if any, clones liked being around due to his seemingly endless contempt for all of the miners.

When the doctors examined him, they assumed he was little more than a malfunctioning clone showing developmental abnormalities. However, that theory changed quickly once the green liquid took over the body, and the clone began exhibiting animal behavior his programming couldn't account for. Communications were sent back to the AMO headquarters but the concerns were brushed off. Doctors were told to *keep them posted* on any further adverse developments but, as it was a clone, there was nothing to worry about. *Just burn it* was the typical response.

Dr. Kevin Bradley, however, wanted to conduct more research in case this became a widespread health crisis in Mining Complex VI. Leah Lowe and Carley Branch were on duty with Dr. Kevin Bradley, when, after a week of continual observation, the clone began to show aggressive tendencies and needed to be restrained. He was also beginning to give off a foul odor similar to rotting meat. Several days and numerous tests later revealed that the disease ravaging his body was in fact contagious and the deteriorating and non-responsive clone needed to be destroyed.

A quick needle to the heart would finish the clone off quickly and painlessly. The assistants prepped the body for liquidation by way of needle then fire, loosening the restraints for transport offsite to be incinerated. As Dr. Bradley prepped the needle, Leah was arranging the restraint straps on him when the clone opened his eyes. Carley, standing over him, noticed only the whites were visible.

"Leah, his eyes!" she called out, drawing the attention of Dr. Bradley as well.

As Carley glanced down at the clone's eyes, he lashed out at her hand, biting down onto her index finger, which she quickly pulled back when the clone nipped the tip of it. Dr. Bradley and Carley moved to secure the straps once more as the clone spat at Leah, the saliva landing on her face. Though a face mask covered her mouth, she was unaware that small particles of the tainted saliva had landed in her left eye.

The women were excused from the room as Dr. Bradley contacted HQ and was informed immediately to dispose of the clone. A quick injection of the death liquid into the man's heart didn't work, he continued to struggle with his restraints, and Dr. Bradley realized how grave their situation was—a virus that could survive death.

The decision was quickly made to burn the body in the location where all deceased, worn out, or expired clones were taken, nearly five miles away, to the burn pit located inside a crater out of sight from the mining complex.

Before burning, the clone was to be dissected by Dr. Bradley, with the help of Dr. Fiona Ewart, the most outgoing of the three doctors, a perky redhead nearing the end of her tenure, ready to get back to life, such as it was, back on Troria.

Dr. Petrino would perform the autopsy. The stench was unbearable for all present. Green puss and slime had taken over ninety percent of the host's body. Bones had become little more than thick green cartilage. Even with the face masks, gloves, and other protective gear, all three were nervous about the possibility of infection.

Once the deed was done, the body parts were quickly bagged and boxed up and taken to the burn pit via the single moon rover named the Big Boy, a six-wheeled vehicle designed by the Trorian military that worked quite well on all of the mining complexes for its hauling capabilities. The vehicle was located inside the Kernadium storage facility.

The task of running the box of remains to the burn pit fell to security guard Christopher Berger. The rest of the remains on the operating table were washed down the drain once the body was gone, the surgical instruments left in the wash tub for a nameless clone to take care of. It is theorized that this unsanitary method was how the virus spread through the community of clones so quickly. But no one was certain just how it took off. Some of the human staff thought it was possible the clone meat was tainted and the rest of them had eaten the Rot meat.

Leah and Dex had been sleeping together on and off for the past year, mainly out of sheer boredom. Neither cared for the other in any way other than instant gratification. Leah would go so far as to say she hated the mean-spirited, aggressive man, but the sex was hot while it lasted. The night she had gotten a small bit of the infected clone's saliva in her eye, she had sex with Dex. Unprotected sex.

As it would soon be determined by the doctors at Mining Complex VI that the virus was transmitted through the transference of bodily fluids, not yet airborne, things quickly spiraled out of control. Within one week, more clones fell ill along with Dex, Leah, and Carley whose finger had indeed been nipped by the infected clone's teeth. Once several clones began showing symptoms, they became aggressive, biting their fellow clones. Some of the infected took longer to display any symptoms, others only several days.

At the two-week mark after the initial infection, it was determined that everyone should pull out of Moon 002 and cease all operations. The clone population would soon be depleted, as numerous reports of bites and scratches were being documented. The humans grew scared to stay and work and, since the Kernadium was almost completely extracted, transport shuttles began arriving from Troria to pick up as many containers as possible while relieving all but a skeleton crew of duty, much to everyone's pleasure. Everyone except Elise, Chris, Sonia, and Dr. Petrino.

Dr. Bradley and Dr. Fiona were relieved to get away, not just from the Rot but also from Petrino, who was acting more strangely than ever. In the days leading up to their departure, they noticed him spending increasing amounts of time in room 51. When they asked him about it, he shrugged and said he would rather stay in the Clone Replication facility with his work than with the rest of the assholes in the Command Center.

Even while numerous clones were still healthy and not yet showing symptoms, AMO unanimously decided the entire clone population should be sealed off and left to fend for itself until the final freighter returned to transport the remaining skeleton crew and Kernadium. At that point the buildings were to be razed, killing off every living and dead thing left inside, which was scheduled to happen in under three days. However, thanks to the Rot-infected Dex, Carley, and Leah, the oxygen would run out before then. And then, the remaining highly-flammable Kernadium would be waiting for the arriving freighter that would never make it off-world—if their plan worked.

When the Rot virus assimilated with the humans it infected, they were able to continue using some of their brain functions, making them far more dangerous than the infected clones. They were able to plan and carry out devious tasks until the Rot virus twisted itself throughout their host bodies to the point that what had once been human was no more, and all that remained were liquifying masses of green disease.

Nearly all of the clones produced for the AMO were simply worker drones whose sole purpose was to harvest Kernadium. They had thoughts and minds of their own but on the most basic level. Eat, work, sleep, repeat until they expired. They were docile and had been designed in labs to cause as few problems as possible, making them easy to control. Like a herd of animals, they were docile, obedient, and submissive, doing what they were produced to do, then eliminated.

Due to their lack of high brain functions, the Rot infected most of the clones differently than their human counterparts. They were reduced to nearly mindless animals who's only thought process was to attack and spread the disease further. The Rot needed to assimilate, its sole purpose growing and expanding while killing off anything inside its host that resembled individual self-preservation. The clones were easy prey for the Rot virus and were quite literally, the perfect specimens for it to spread through quickly and effortlessly.

The few clones that were manufactured for guard duty and had more responsibility were programmed with higher brain functions and more knowledge, complete with a perfectly crafted history. Michael Astier was one such individual.

But Michael Astier was even further removed from the other clones on Moon 002. When the generator had been destroyed, he had miraculously awakened early and become self-aware before his memory implants had taken hold. Unmonitored and in his final stages of incubation, he was untampered with. No restrictions had been put on this clone. The only surviving fully manufactured clone on Moon 002 where this killing-machine Rot was taking over, he was a true anomaly.

CHAPTER 14

I WANT ANSWERS

Dr. Petrino was doing his best to avoid eye contact with not just Elise, but his pet project as well. Focusing on the cigarette between his lips, he pulled long drags, exhaling the cloud of smoke upward then glancing at his watch.

"You want to put that out? We're running out of oxygen, and we've got a young girl here with us now as well," Elise said angrily, glaring at Petrino.

He stared at her, then glanced over at Olivia. *His* Olivia. For a moment, he allowed himself the indulgence of admiring her newly alive presence, astonished at what he had created. She was perfection, exactly what he had envisioned as he had secretly watched her grow and take shape during incubation. She was the exact replica of a younger Elise, fulfilling his wildest dreams while making a mockery of the one in which she was modelled after. *I truly am a god!* A slight grin formed across Petrino's face for a brief second.

He shook his head to clear it then nodded quickly and extinguished his cigarette in the ashtray on the desk in front of him. "Chris is dead? What the hell happened out there?" he barked, his eyes shifting to his watch almost out of habit now. He felt a line of sweat beading up on his forehead.

Elise looked at Petrino. "Yes, he is. And we're all going to be dead soon too if we don't figure out a game plan. There's a host of those things down on level one behind the walkway exit just waiting to get inside. Carley was one of them, I blew her head off. I assume Leah Lowe is still here and from what these two have told us, Dex Scott is out there too."

Michael pulled the piece of paper he had been carrying since finding it earlier on level three inside the Clone Replication Facility. He cleared his throat and read, "Clone #206: Subject named *Seth* shows extreme signs of malnutrition from the infection. Feeding tube not taking well to the host's stomach due to internal alien growth. Several more rotting lesions spotted on lower intestines. Recommend ceasing incubation before more resources are spent. Body to be incinerated. Signed Dr. Petrino. August 28, 3123."

The room fell silent. Elise looked at him intently, as did Sonia and the doctor.

Time to find out what's going on here, Michael thought. He turned to Petrino, the one who had signed this and so many other such reports. "I'm a clone, aren't I? At least, I think I am. I have a lifetime's worth of memories up here, but I woke up a few hours ago naked on a table with shit stuck in my arms and down my throat. I read the reports in the closet," he said angrily, gripping the Defender II in his hands.

"Should he have that gun?" Petrino asked, glancing down at the weapon nervously.

"He's fine. Yes, Michael. You are a clone. I wish we had more time to fill you in but that is something we're incredibly short on at the moment," Elise replied, tilting her head to the side then nodding in frustration. "The generator's down, the servers are fried. We have less than forty-eight hours of oxygen left in here then we're going to suffocate unless we find a way off this planet or a breathable air supply. Oh, and fend off a horde of infected clones that are literally right outside the door."

"What's the story with the girl here?" Sonia asked as she walked toward her, looking her over.

"I'd like to know that myself," Elise added, looking at the pretty young blond girl then quickly over to Petrino, who immediately averted his eyes.

It was silent in the room for several seconds before Olivia reached into her pocket, pulled out her own folded piece of paper and read its contents aloud. "'Test subject already having limited memory implants and full growth to happen gradually at later date. No life limiting DNA implanted. DNA acquired from human donor. Doctor will take ownership off-world September 15, 3123. Signed Dr. Petrino.' What am I? Who am I?" She held the paper up in front of her then fell silent, sadness and confusion crossing her young face.

Trying to process this new, unexpected information, all eyes fell on Dr. Petrino. He looked up and cleared his throat, attempting to form some sort of an explanation as to this girl standing in front of them. He then nervously began stammering, "So, as you all know, we experiment here on Moon 002 and all of the Alnorix mining facilities. We were given free range to work on DNA cloning technology. So, I took it upon myself to um, well, to see what I could do with prolonging life. As you can see here, this girl will grow and have a chance at a long and bright future. You see, when—"

"Why does this child look exactly like me when I was her age? That's what I'm trying to figure out. I'm really, and I do mean *really*, fucking curious about that, so please, go on," Elise fired back, glaring at the pathetic, greasy man.

Petrino stared at Elise, not sure how to respond. Sonia, meanwhile, had approached the blond-haired girl, looking at her closely, as though inspecting her. My property he thought as a jolt of anger shot through him, further flustering him.

"Well, I needed DNA. Something other than the synthetic DNA used for our one-year clones here." He glanced nervously at Michael who looked angry. *Typical, everyone is always against me. It never fails!* He felt perspiration trickling down his face and quickly wiped it off, not wanting them to see how nervous he was.

Elise took her eyes off of the continually squirming doctor and stared at Olivia, immediately feeling a deep sense of compassion for the girl. She had barely become conscious and was thrown into a no-win situation, between the infected clones outside and whatever was going on in here.

She cleared her throat and bent down slightly to meet the girl's innocent eyes. "Olivia, look, I'm not going to tell you it's going to be all right. We aren't out of this yet. Not by a long shot. But I promise that I will do my best to get us out of here to safety and bring to justice those that deserve it."

Olivia replied softly, "Thank you, Miss Elise. I'm glad I'm safe in here with you and Michael…and you too, Miss curly-haired lady."

The suddenness and innocence of the comment immediately endeared Sonia to the young girl, and she smiled at her and responded, "My name is Sonia. Sonia Bonnel."

Olivia gave her a shy smile and said quietly, "I like your curly hair."

Sonia returned the smile. Already, she wanted to protect this child from the evil man across the room. She glanced at the admittedly attractive, for a clone at least, Michael. She pushed her glasses up her nose and said somewhat boldly for her, "You both should get something to eat and drink. And clean up. Make sure you don't have any of that—disease on you." Elise obviously had her hands full, so it fell to her.

"Good idea, Sonia," Elise said, breaking Sonia's watchful gaze on Michael. "Why don't you take them down to level three and get them some food? There are a few washrooms where they can get cleaned up too. We'll meet you down there in a bit. I would like to speak with Dr. Petrino alone." Her tone was calm but her grim facial expression showed otherwise.

"Come on, sweetie, let's get you some food. I'm sure there's some ready-made sandwiches down there. And pie with ice cream. You'll love it," Sonia said, glancing over at Michael, the tall and handsome clone. She'd never thought about them much. They were mass produced for a job, a product. Sure, she didn't like the way they were treated, but they were still a manufactured item. This one, though, immediately seemed so…human.

Nodding, Michael replied, "Thanks. Thanks to both of you. Sorry about your friend. I'm still trying to process everything—about me. About one-year lifespans…" He raised the gun. "What do you want me to do with this?"

Elise already liked him. Honorable. Doing what needed to be done. Protecting the girl. And he looked as though he didn't trust Petrino either. All positive qualities in her mind.

"I assume your memory implants have you trained in firearms handling? If so, keep it. We only have two of them currently. Top barrel is laser fire. Bottom is fire. Take them down with the laser then torch. That's the only way to be sure. Got it?" Elise said, confident in this man's abilities with a weapon already.

Inspecting the gun, Michael responded, "You are correct. I do know how to handle this weapon. I learned it in my basic training."

"That's right. Memory implant. We're going to talk more about this but right now, time is of the essence. Make sure Olivia and Sonia are safe and I'll see you soon," Elise said, turning to face Petrino.

Michael and Olivia followed Sonia out of the room while Elise calmly approached Petrino, who quickly took a step back. On their way out, he had noticed a black device in Olivia's back pocket. His eyes widened when he realized what the device was and where she had surely gotten it.

"Now, hold on. We're running out of air. We don't have time for this. We shouldn't split up!" he stuttered, putting his hand on a nearby desk to stabilize himself. He hated that he was intimidated like this. Intimidated *by this woman!*

"What is she?" Elise asked firmly, keeping her eyes locked on his. Her hand still held the Defender I.

"Look, I was angry. You know, you...you could have been nicer to me! You and all your friends. Remember that night when I tried to talk to you in the rec room? Huh? Remember that? You all made fun of me! You made me feel stupid. But I'm not stupid! I'm a doctor. I can give and take life!"

"We both know how that night went. After Jake walked out with you, I defended you, Petrino. I felt bad for you. I understand how hard it can be to be an outsider," she began, but was cut off.

"You know *nothing!* You with your looks. Walking around here in those, those tight clothes of yours! Every man, and woman for that matter, desires *you!* You think you understand? How could you possibly understand? Please, do tell. You get assigned here for a commander position and have been cruising right along. No worries. You get by solely on your looks, lady!" he spat out at her.

"You don't know me, Petrino. Where I come from. What I'm about. And it's going to stay that way. See, I don't trust you. At all. I tried to be your friend. *Friend.* But that wasn't good enough. I've seen how you look at me. I've seen how you look at every woman here, so I want some answers," Elise retorted, continuing to keep her eyes locked on his until he broke her gaze, choosing to look guiltily down at the floor in front of him.

Silence fell across the Command Center. Neither spoke but Petrino knew she was still waiting on an answer.

He cleared his throat, a habit he picked up primarily due to his constant smoking. "The party night in the rec room. After I left. I went to your room. I used my security access key to get inside. I took a few hair particles and a…um…a tissue with several drops of blood on it from your waste basket. I know you get nosebleeds from the lousy atmosphere and stale air here."

Elise stared at him. Hatred filled her heart for this pathetic man. Her one small private place in this depressing steel building had been violated. She had been violated. Elise chose to keep silent, wanting the man in front of her to keep talking.

He continued nervously, pinned to the floor by her stare, her silence. "Taking your DNA from your hair follicles and blood, I created Olivia. Similar to how the rest of the clones are made. In the lab. Advanced somatic-cell nuclear transfer fertilization. I was careful, of course. Taking the utmost caution to get it right. She is, for all practical purposes, you. Grown in our amniotic sacks in the Clone Replication Facility under my strictest private supervision."

Watching her warily, he continued, "Unlike the rest of the clones, I was able to manipulate the DNA, avoiding the typical age limit and without a significant memory implant. Other than the basic set of intelligence features we give them, she can be her own person, Elise! Build her own memories. She has your brain when you were her age. I have created a whole new life, an exact human replica ready for further imprinting."

"What were you planning on doing with her? How were you going to sneak her off-world back to Troria?" Elise shot back.

"Until I got drafted to stay behind on this hellhole and everything went to shit, she was going to go along with me in hibernation status on a transportable incubation container. I had her marked as a specimen that would have been fully covered. It was all set up. Take her back to Troria. And then I would raise her."

"Raise her for *what?*" she shouted, realizing what he had intended to do. She was to be his. He couldn't have the real one so might as well make one of his own. One that he could groom. And eventually…

Her eyes told him she had seen through his facade. He stammered, "I've always wanted to be a father. But I know I never would have. I'll be good to her!"

"You, Petrino, will be brought to justice is what will be happening to you. Breaking and entering. Illegal use of corporate property. Illegal cloning methods. Kidnapping. Possible sex with a minor! Shall I go on?" Elise yelled at him.

"Hey, hey! No! Nope. You can't say that. And you can't prove it. Just let me be! What harm is it to you? Huh? If we make it out of here alive, which is highly doubtful now, you'll get another well-paying job. You'll be fine. And I'll go to another job that I hate where people hate me! But with her, I have something to live for, see? I created new life!" Petrino was pleading now, trying to justify his actions as sweat dripped down the sides of his face.

Elise moved closer to him, glaring at the pathetic man in front of her. "I knew I smelled stale cigarette breath in my room that night. I chalked it up to having too much to drink and our interaction with you earlier in the evening. You're disgusting. And you won't get away with it. Mark my—"

She was cut off by a sharp pain in her abdomen. She looked down to see a scalpel blade plunged into her abdomen as Petrino's hand left the blade's grip. He stepped back, looking horrified at what he had just done, staring down at the wound that was now beginning to seep red. His eyes lifted to meet hers.

"What did you!" Elise stammered as she began to raise her Defender I up in retaliation and defense.

He lunged forward to grab it by its barrel and tripped over himself, falling on top of her in the process. They fell to the floor with a loud thud.

Elise's white shirt now had a circle of crimson red growing outward from the scalpel still sticking inside of her.

Petrino fought for control of the Defender I as Elise cried out in pain.

"Give me the gun, Elise, damn you!"

Elise knew she had precious little time. She had to free herself and gain the upper hand in this now life-threatening situation. She pulled the trigger on the Defender, blasting past him and hitting the wall above, hoping to get their attention on the floor below.

The sound of the blast distracted Petrino enough for Elise to pull out from under him. Seeing her slip away, he tried to pull the gun from her once more.

Now fighting for her life, Elise clutched the Defender in her left hand and swung upward with all of her might, connecting with Petrino's jaw, driving the top and bottom rows of his teeth together. He recoiled in pain and let go of her for a second to put his hand to his chin.

Elise screamed in pain pulling her right knee in to her injured stomach as Petrino again lunged forward, landing on top of her, this time grabbing hold of the scalpel and pulling it out as fresh blood seeped from the deep cut, further spreading out over her shirt. He raised the scalpel once more over his head, preparing to bring it down, this time into her heart. With all of her might, Elise kicked him away, sending him careening backwards, hitting the window overlooking the landscape outside.

Raising the Defender to eye level, she was about to pull the trigger but was unable to, realizing it would break the window, sucking out the remaining oxygen inside the Command Center. He took advantage of this brief pause to run away, clinging tightly to his only defense, the large scalpel covered in Elise's blood.

The pain in Elise's abdomen was increasing. She was certain shock would set in soon. She had to kill this man or at least incapacitate him, and soon. She saw him heading toward the door and began firing, causing him to duck down behind several desks close to the exit.

Try to leave through that door, motherfucker, and I'll blow your head off! Elise tried to push the pain out of her mind, glancing over toward the exit where Petrino was certain to attempt an escape.

Once more, silence filled the Command Center. Small bits of debris floated through the stagnant air following the laser blasts.

"What now?" Petrino yelled from behind the desk.

"What now? I kill you. That's *what now,*" Elise barked, grimacing at the pain.

"I can't let that happen, Elise. I've worked too hard. I'm leaving this godforsaken planet and I'm taking Olivia with me. One way or another. I've got a contingency plan. Unlike the rest of you, I think ahead. I plan accordingly." He stared at the blood-covered scalpel in his hand.

Elise breathed heavily, trying to think. An exact clone of herself was alive and in the building. To calm her nerves, she focused on Jake, her love. He was back on Railara, safe and planning the eventual takedown of one Levon Gonidec. *Jake, I wish you were here. I sure could use your help right now!*

CHAPTER 15

FROM BAD TO WORSE

Jake walked with chancellor Mya Brant down a long hallway inside one of the many military facilities on Railara's capital, Aphus. They were heading to another meeting with President Gideon Novare. Much was being discussed with the advancing of Gonidec's military activity throughout the quadrant.

"I can't reach Elise anymore," Jake said. "I have no way of communicating. I fear the worst, especially with Petrino still there as well. It's just her and a couple of other staff and I don't like it." His calm tone masked his grave concern for the woman he had fallen in love with over the years, a partner in the resistance back on Troria.

He knew Chris could hold his own but Sonia, while nice enough, seemed shy and soft spoken, averting her eyes when spoken to directly. Stuck there with Dr. Petrino, who despised her, and Elise, and any woman for that matter.

He hated having to put Elise in charge and leave but those were his orders, and he had to follow them in order to keep their true intentions quiet for as long as possible. And now she was cut off.

"I'm sorry, Jake. I truly am. We simply cannot send a Railarian ship of any kind to Moon 002 without drawing attention. As bad as things are now, it would make them worse. We *must* think of the big picture and that's taking Levon Gonidec out," the well-dressed Mya Brant replied.

They rounded a corner and entered Gideon Novare's private meeting space, greeting one another with a brief nod before taking a seat across the desk from Railara's leader. Jake knew what was at stake. He knew what lay ahead for them all if the mission they were planning failed. The fate of the entire solar system was resting on them. He grimaced to himself. *Give me the courage I need to continue on with this. Give Elise and all those still stuck on that moon courage as well.*

Novare jumped right into the situation at hand, without any preamble. He knew Jake was up to speed on the resistance and Gonidec's tyranny—not just on Troria but throughout the quadrant.

"Our planets might be on opposite ends of quadrant 8304 but close enough for war. That's for sure. And War seems imminent, Jake. AMO is draining planets of Kernadium and they're getting stronger. Railara's clock is ticking. We need to do something, or we'll eventually be taken over."

"Agreed, sir, but what?" Jake responded, knowing the answer already but wanting to hear it come from the leader of Railara's mouth.

"Bring them down. They want our Kernadium, our planet is swimming in the stuff. Gonidec's been salivating at the prospect of taking the planet over for years. But they need a larger military. And they've been getting it thanks to AMO, it's big business, mining. Big business means big payouts. That includes the black market. Illegal sales of the harvested Kernadium as well as clone slaves for large sums of Marks."

Jake nodded; he knew all of this already. "Look, when I joined the resistance movement back on Troria, I figured I would only get so far. A cog in the wheel, likely to get killed along the way. But here I am, free and safe, while my people are dying in huge numbers on Troria, and countless clones are being produced then murdered. Pardon me for saying so, sir, but why the hell has it taken so long to act?"

"Our government has been attempting to partner with other planets in the quadrant, but war is a son of a bitch. More innocent people die than the ones responsible. So, we've all been dragging our feet as the years have ticked by, and I deeply regret that now."

They both fell silent. President Novare gave a glance and a slight nod toward Chancellor Mya Brant who cleared her throat. "We have a plan to take out Gonidec but a lot of things need to fall into place."

"Go on, I'm listening," Jake Riley replied.

Sonia led Michael and Olivia down to level three, and after quickly scoping out the area, making sure everything looked safe, they sat down at a table in the rec room. The space was bland and corporate, like the rest of the building. A makeshift bar against the wall in the center of the room with tables spread throughout the room suggested a restaurant or lounge, but mostly it resembled every other drab corporate space owned by AMO.

Michael and Olivia had quickly taken turns in the washroom, splashing a bit of water on their faces—a new experience for both of them, which felt deliciously refreshing.

"Do you think we can see what's on this thing?" Olivia asked, pulling the small handheld video recorder out of her pocket and looking it over.

Michael asked to take a look at it as Sonia came back with a plate of sandwiches and several pieces of pie. "Dig in. Your first official meal since, well, since you were born! The meat is a processed protein-based substance. It'll fill you up, which is the goal here. Low quality for high productivity." She set them down in front of Michael and Olivia then pushed her dark-rimmed glasses up on her nose and gave them a slightly awkward smile.

Olivia took a bite of one of the sandwiches and grimaced at the flavor. Or lack thereof.

Sonia chuckled. "That's how I reacted the first time I tasted the *meat* here. Heavily processed stuff. Saves AMO precious Marks back home. Marks is what our currency is called..." she trailed off, not wanting to ramble.

Michael choked down several bites of his sandwich, his mind processing this human being, Sonia. Unassuming. She had a quiet, natural beauty about her. Her curly brown hair continually falling onto her face, which she brushed away, light freckles dotting her cheeks. Her dark rimmed glasses complimented her facial features. *Attractive, kindhearted, good natured. Sad.*

"Thank you, Sonia. Thanks for helping us out," Michael said with genuine appreciation in his voice. He felt sure of himself now, speaking to these new humans, sounding just like them.

His kindness made her instantly blush as she once again pushed her hair out of her face and quickly looked over to Olivia. "Try the pie. That I can actually vouch for."

Olivia took a bite of pie along with a cold white substance Sonia told her was ice cream. Immediately her face lit up. "Yum! Now this is good!"

Sonia smiled warmly at her. She hadn't seen an actual eleven-year-old girl in years. So pretty and so innocent. *Hardly a clone at all* she thought.

"Do you have any kids of your own, Sonia?" Michael asked, noticing Sonia watching the girl as he too took a bite of the pie, raising his eyebrows at the pleasant taste hitting his mouth.

"No, my mom is my only family. My career has never lent itself to relationships and kids. After getting a degree in

Biotechnology, I jumped headfirst into the business. And here I am. Three years on this rock and I might die here now," she said grimly before seeing Olivia look up at her with sad eyes.

"I mean, we're going to do everything we can to get out of here. Help is on the way, we just need to find more oxygen to last us long enough for the last transport to arrive. There's got to be a way," Sonia added. *I am sitting across from two clones, having a conversation. This is a first!*

"My memory implant tells me that there must be a way. We just have to figure it out, I guess that's how they wired me, still figuring it all out actually," Michael said in his calm and smooth voice.

Sonia smiled once more. These people were literally just born into a nightmare situation, yet both had more positive vibes than nearly every human employee she had worked with in her three years on Moon 002.

Michael picked up the video device and asked Sonia, "So what's this?"

Sonia's eyes grew wide. "Oh wow, that's one of the doctor's personal logs. If you found it in your room, it must be from Dr. Petrino."

"Well, should we listen to it, or watch it? Whatever this thing does," Michael replied curiously.

"May I see it?" Sonia reached her hand across the table toward Michael.

Glancing down at her outstretched hand, he contemplated giving the device to her. *She can be trusted* his mind continued telling him as he handed it over.

Sonia clicked it on. A screen appeared displaying a collection of thumbnail images of Dr. Petrino's face with various titles assigned to each one. She pressed the first thumbnail and the image enlarged, filling the screen as the video came to life.

"This is Dr. Petrino with the first of several log entries detailing my daughter's progress. I've taken the utmost precaution in harvesting the proper DNA as well as fine tuning the outcome for a perfect match. Once this is done, I will have the perfect creation to imprint with memories as I see fit. She'll start, however, with a clean slate."

Pausing the video image, Sonia looked at both Michael and Olivia, who shared her expression of horror at this bit of information. No one said anything, Michael and Sonia looking over at the frightened and confused girl sitting at the table with them.

She clicked play on the video image and they continued watching the screen intently as the doctor talked about his break-in into Elise's room, his theft of her hair and blood sample, and how he intended to hide his creation from the rest of the doctors and assistants.

Each video was just a few minutes in length, and after the first one, the updates consisted of basic information on Olivia's growth, his hatred for the staff at Mining Complex VI, and how he couldn't wait to be back on Troria with his *new bride.*

All three had stopped eating as they watched on in disgust at the doctor's plan.

Sonia stopped the video, shaking her head in disgust. "We don't need to watch the rest."

"Please! Play the last one! How does this end?" Olivia cried out, even more frightened in a situation that continued to get worse.

Sonia's heart broke for the innocence in front of her. *A clone with feelings.* Obviously hurt and scared, the poor girl had been brought to life by a sick and perverted man with a god complex for his own fantasies, things that had been hinted at in the videos. "Olivia, I don't think that's such a good idea."

Looking over at Michael, Olivia hung her head and said, "Please, for both of us. We were both born, or created I guess, into a lie. We already know Michael can only live a year. I was born to be with that scary man one level up but I don't know anything else about my life. Please?" she pleaded again.

Sonia looked solemnly at Olivia then Michael. He nodded in agreement before adding, "With what she's already been through, she deserves to see how those log entries end. Go ahead."

Sonia pressed the last entry on the screen, and once more Dr. Petrino's face came alive in front of them, this time disheveled and smoking a cigarette. "So, things have taken a turn for the worse. The Rot has spread throughout the clone population in just a few short weeks, and AMO is completely pulling out. I'm entering data onto my personal logs regarding numerous experiments taking place here by myself under headquarters' instructions. Including my personal specimen having a baked-in immunity to the Rot."

At this, the three exchanged relieved looks, continuing to listen attentively.

He took a drag on his cigarette, blew the smoke out and continued. "I trust I will be selected to leave this rotten hell-hole with most of the remaining crew. I've been told a skeleton crew will be left behind to make sure nothing happens to the remaining Kernadium and keep things operational. The infected clones have now all been sealed off in their living quarters. They'll kill each other off quickly while not infecting anyone else. Screw 'em. Any clones still in their incubation tables will be left there to fend for themselves. Some might wake up but they shouldn't last long. I have only one concern. Getting Olivia off Moon 002—with me. Everyone else is expendable. In fact, it's preferable they all perish. That will make it easier to transport Olivia off-world with the least amount of questioning."

He took a long drag then put his cigarette out into an ash tray just off screen then continued. "I'm happy to report, though, that Olivia has been implanted with extensive knowledge of the inner workings of not just Alnorix Mining but also Gonidec's regime and his plan for this quadrant and how he plans to implement it."

Olivia shook her head, covering her mouth with her hand in shock, unable to look away from this evil man's face.

There was a pause and a jump in the video. Dr. Petrino came back on. "I was selected to stay. Son of a bitch! Nicholas Mohr himself begged me, in his own asshole-ish way. Made me pick a skeleton crew. Good news is I get safe passage with my cargo as long as one Miss Elise Bennet doesn't make it off Moon 002. Seems she's been quietly sending back information to certain groups back home looking to take down AMO and Gonidec. Typical, that bitch."

The continued watching in horror as Petrino's scheme played out on the screen in front of them.

"I plan to take out the Generator and Server room. Kill off the oxygen. Act none the wiser, act concerned. Act frustrated. Then wait for secure pick-up on September 14 at three AM. Think while I'm at it I might give Leah, Carley, and Dex free reign of the place. Just to make it a little more interesting for Sonia, Chris, and Elise. Have fun, you three! Especially if you attempt to fix that generator. Of course, I'll be permanently deleting these messages once I'm safe, but boy does it feel good to unload here."

He paused again before continuing, "And Nicholas Mohr, this is for you. The contents of this video recorder will most certainly make their way to people you really don't want to see getting their hands on it. It will bring your boss's regime and AMO down. Trust me. I've made sure it will get distributed off-world, Railara, to be exact. You know who I'm talking about. If the Railaran's get this, it's war across the quadrant that I know you cannot afford to lose. And you know as well as I do the current regime on Troria will crumble with a united quadrant against them. Gonidec will give me free passage with the girl and my video recorder. I'm in control, I call the shots here! Dr. Petrino, out."

The transmission ended.

Sonia sat back in her seat and tossed the handheld device onto the table, running her hands through her curly hair. All three of them were quiet for a few seconds, digesting the grim information.

"Why would he say all of that to a screen? For us to find?" Olivia asked, breaking the silence.

Sonia sighed and responded to the very perceptive question. "Because he planned on taking it with him. Documentation. There's a lot of information on here, not just his video logs. This thing has detailed information on disposal of clones. Harvesting of the Poule planets. Gonidec's military plans that he managed to get his hands on. You name it, it's in here. This is his insurance policy. The man has no friends. Is driven by fear and revenge, and he spewed it all out on this thing. And… apparently, he's implanted detailed and sensitive information about Levon Gonidec inside of you. Which makes you a target. The good news is you seem to be immune to the Rot."

Just as Sonia finished her sentence, there was a loud boom from above, the unmistakable sound of gunfire.

Michael stood first. "We have to get back up there. Now!"

Sonia jumped to her feet, Olivia joining them as they took off running toward the exit.

In the Command Center Elise kept her Defender I trained on the exit. She had him dead to rights if he attempted to flee. She glanced over to where he was hiding, seeing a small plume of smoke rising from where he crouched.

Petrino had pulled out his lighter and lit a stack of papers, spreading them out across the floor. He hastily took off his lab coat, igniting it as well and placing it on top of the desk he crouched behind. The lab coat quickly engulfed in flames and spread across the desk, igniting more papers and scorching the computing equipment. Soon the entire front of the office was filled with smoke as flames continued to spread.

Elise inhaled the smoke, coughing harshly, the deep stab wound inside of her abdomen searing with pain.

Petrino made a run for the exit, keeping low in the cloud of increasing smoke.

The door slid open and Elise saw light piercing through from the other side. She quickly opened fire once again and heard a shout of pain and surprise.

Her Defender I made contact with Petrino's upper thigh, blasting through the rear and out the front of the leg. He screamed in pain at the sudden and intense bolt of fire, exiting the room and hobbling over to the elevator where he pressed the button and waited, panting.

His mind went to Olivia. What was he going to do with her? She had awakened too soon. A miscalculation on his end with the generator and server shutdown. He didn't even have his video recorder, left in the closet of her room. No matter, they would all be dead and he could extract the data remotely if necessary.

His plan was going to hell. His leg throbbed with pain. Luckily, it was a clean wound and the Defender's laser fire had essentially cauterized the wound as it passed through. He still had the blood-covered scalpel, which he had tucked into a belt loop during his skirmish with Elise. He looked at his watch, midnight. Three hours until the extraction. He needed to get to the *Big Boy*.

He hobbled inside the elevator and hit the level one button on the wall. The elevator hummed as it began its trek down, then stopped on level three. The door chimed and slid open to reveal Michael, Sonia, and Olivia, who stood closest to the door.

She didn't see it coming. Petrino lunged forward, pulling the scalpel out, grabbing hold of the frightened girl. He quickly brought it up to her throat, pressing hard enough to draw blood.

Olivia screamed out in pain. Michael raised the Defender II and aimed but couldn't get a clean shot with the girl directly in front of Petrino, who was clearly using her as a shield.

Sonia held her hands out and shouted, "Doctor, no! She's a young girl! Please!"

"She's my *young* girl, to do with as I please. So back away from the door. Time is running out up in the Command Center, see the blood on this scalpel? I'll do it again! You know I will!" Dr. Petrino shouted, grimacing through the intense pain in his leg.

"Please, someone, help me!" Olivia shouted meekly, which only made Petrino tighten his grip. The door slid shut, leaving Michael and Sonia alone on the third level.

"Damnit!" Michael shouted, slamming his fist against the closed elevator door.

"Come on, we've got to get to Elise! He's not going to kill Olivia. At least not yet. He's injured, so that'll slow him down, and where the hell can he even go? If those things are outside level one in the walkway, he's stuck!" Sonia rattled off, frazzled at this turn of events. She was a doctor's assistant, not a fighter.

She turned and ran to the stairwell, Michael following her up to level three.

Immediately the two of them saw smoke coming from the room as an alarm bell rang. They ran forward, getting hit with smoke and water from the extinguisher system above.

Take charge, you are trained in this. Michael quickly took the initiative, yelling to Sonia, "You stay here, I'll be right back!" He handed her the Defender II and ran into the burning room.

He scanned the smoke-filled room, coughing as he searched for life. He finally called out, "Elise! Are you in here?!"

He heard coughing and charged forward, trying to see through the haze of smoke in the room. In front of him lay Elise. A pool of blood covered her shirt and was now seeping onto the ground. He looked closer to see the wound Petrino's scalpel had made to her abdomen, his mind processing what he was seeing. *Doesn't look fatal but needs to be treated or she will lose too much blood.*

"Elise, can you move?" he asked as calmly as he could.

She nodded slightly, grimacing in pain.

"Hang on to me, ready?" Michael asked but didn't wait for a response as he scooped the wounded woman up in his strong, muscular arms.

Michael grimaced at the deteriorating state of the Command Center. He surmised that the unsatisfactory emergency sprinkler system would be unable to keep up with the growing flames, and that the lack of adequate ventilation would cause the entire floor to fill with smoke and carbon monoxide quickly.

Running out of the burning room, he headed over to where Sonia waited. She slung the Defender II over her shoulder and raised her hands to her mouth when she saw Elise.

"Elise! No! What happened? We shouldn't have left you alone with that monster! I never would have thought him capable of this."

"We need to get off of this floor and get her somewhere safe and tend to this wound. I don't think it's fatal as long as we stop the bleeding quickly." Michael gave Sonia an urgent look as smoke continued to billow out of the room.

"She needs to get to the Clone Replication Facility, that's where the medical equipment is. But that might as well be on another planet. My room on level two in this building—I have a med kit there and a Surface Sealer. Not sure how much good it will do or how long it will hold but it'll stop the bleeding at least. Let's go! We need to take the stairs, that elevator could shut down at any time with the fire!"

Sonia quickly took off as Michael followed, carrying Elise in his arms and carefully making his way down to the living quarters on level two.

The doorway to level two swung open and Sonia and Michael burst through with Elise, who was moaning in pain. *Reassure this injured woman.* "Stay with me, Elise, come on!" Michael said to her in his arms.

Leading the way to her room, Sonia kept the gun outstretched. Her minor training in firearms consisted in only the most basic knowledge, enough to get her by. Once at her room, she placed her hand on the scanner and the door slid open. Michael went first with Sonia right behind them.

Back at the elevator, the door slid open to the ground floor and Petrino pushed Olivia out, knife still at her throat. "What are you going to do with me? I won't go with you! I'd rather die!" she wailed as he continued pushing her into the office area.

"I created you and I can just as easily dispose of you. See the blood on this knife? Yeah, that's your DNA and that's Elise's DNA on there. I can make another one of you. You're disposable, do you hear me?"

Tears ran down Olivia's face as she nodded. *If only I had kept the bone saw,* she thought as he pushed her further into the office.

"Where are we going?" Olivia stuttered as she shuffled forward.

Petrino pushed her to a desk with a name plate marked *Human Resources Director.* He hastily pushed the center drawer open, revealing a Defender I pistol. Quickly pulling the scalpel away from Olivia's throat, he grabbed the gun and raised it up to her temple.

"So, here's the deal," he said in a near panicked state, his leg throbbing from continuous use after the laser blast. "I'm getting a med kit and you're going to help me. My leg needs tending to for the next part of our journey off this planet, which is happening tonight. I need it bandaged and I need some pain killers."

Olivia fell silent, sheer terror filling her watery eyes as he pushed her toward the far wall where a clearly marked med kit hung.

"Time for you to play doctor with Papa, Olivia. But first, hand over that video recorder," he said coldly, biting through the pain.

CHAPTER 16

BUILDING A IS LOST

Looking at her mother in her frail state, Sonia whispered sadly, "Mama, I don't know what else to do. You need the surgery and the only way I can make that happen is take this job. I know it's five years but the Marks I make will pay for the heart surgery you desperately need."

Corrina Bonnel responded in a gravely, tired voice, "Sonia, honey, you realize the dangers of working off-world for the AMO? My life is not worth that. You need to live your life! You're twenty-seven, unmarried and you don't have the slightest prospect. You've received a good education and got a degree in Biotechnology. That's such a huge accomplishment. Can't you find something here?"

Shaking her head in frustration, with tears in her eyes, she answered, "We've been through this. This is my opportunity. You're right. I have no significant other, no children. I have you and that's all I need! I'll keep my head down like I always do. Blend in. Do the time and get paid. You just have to hang on for me, okay?"

"I love you, my dear Sonia. You're such a good person. But you know that cloning technology at AMO comes directly from Levon Gonidec. It's inhuman! We've both heard the rumors!" Her grey hair hung over her weary eyes as she sat in her rocking chair in their small apartment in the heart of Troria.

Sonia shook her head in disagreement. "But Mom, they aren't *human*. Their brains aren't as developed like ours. They're like a battery. One year and they're recycled, so I'm told. They don't have a soul, they're just a product. I don't like it either but it's a necessary evil, I guess you could say. What they do, and what I will do, will save your life. We need this! The people of Troria need this. It's creating jobs and I'm one of the lucky few who got selected!"

Her mother, looking her in the eye, said calmly but firmly, "You remember your pet Gerican when you were ten years old? You named him Brak. That loveable little animal wasn't human either. Maybe it has a soul, maybe not. But when old Brak died, you were beside yourself, inconsolable. Would you call Brak a battery, something to be recycled after a year like those poor souls being created across this solar system all in the name of profit?"

"They don't have souls, Mom. It's not the same. Brak was an animal, clones are peo...." she stopped herself and realized her mother had a point. A point she didn't want to think about right now. She needed to stay focused on the goal: do the work, get paid, help her mother.

Sonia looked into Michael's eyes, looking for reassurance that she was doing the right thing. The strangeness of the situation flooded her for a moment. *He was a clone; she was trusting a clone.*

Holding a pair of scissors in her hand, she said, "Elise, I'm sorry I have to do this,"

and began cutting the shirt open down the middle. She pulled back, revealing a completely blood-covered chest and stomach.

"You've lost a lot of blood, but it isn't fatal. I've got to get you closed up," she said as calmly as she could.

Michael knelt beside her, examining the wound and the blood that continued trickling out of the slice in her abdomen. Sonia put a towel against it, and Elise groaned in pain. "Ouch, damnit, that hurts!" she said, grimacing.

"Sorry! Can you grab some water, Michael? I have some numbing medication in my bag over there," Sonia said as she pointed to the items in question.

Michael quickly got them, handing the water and the bag to Sonia who ripped it open, spilling the contents out onto the floor until she found what she was looking for. She picked up a small syringe and plunged it into Elise's neck. She then tilted the water bottle into Elise's open mouth. "Good, drink. That shot will numb the pain somewhat."

"Where's Olivia?" Elise murmured softly.

Michael and Sonia looked gravely at each other before Sonia spoke. "She's been taken by Dr. Petrino. I'm not sure how he plans on getting out of this building. He doesn't have oxygen and those things are outside the door. But, currently, she's with him."

Elise perked up a bit as the numbing agent slowly began kicking in. "I have the emergency lock activated down there but if he unlocks it, which he is more than capable of doing, we're all stuck. There's some mining suits and oxygen tanks down there as well. If he really wants out, he's going to get out." She looked down at her wound. "So, how bad is it?"

"I'm going to seal you up. Even with the shot, it's going to hurt, but we can't wait," Sonia said, lifting up a small device that had come from her bag.

"Do it. I'm not going to bleed out on this fucking rock, at least not here like this. I can still be of use, especially dealing with Petrino. We've got some unfinished business, he and I," Elise said shakily as she began feeling the effects of the morphine.

Sonia knew, at this point, it was up to her to see this through. The little girl somewhere below needed them. All of them. She smiled at Elise. "That's the boss I know and love. Michael, find something for her to bite down on," Sonia said as she turned the handheld emergency Surface Sealer, a small device doctors' assistants used to quickly seal up torn suits and torn clones. Many suffered deep cuts when dealing with the elements out on the moon's surface. The Surface Sealer stitched the cut-up clones quickly with relative efficiency.

Michael came back with a small, folded towel from the washroom, handing it to Sonia. "That'll do," she said, rolling it up and lifted it to Elise's mouth.

"Sorry I was short with you earlier, Sonia. Back in the generator room. You didn't deserve that," Elise said softly.

Sonia smiled down at her. She respected the hell out of Elise Bennet, and this was her chance to do something meaningful. Not just assist in creating disposable clone worker drones.

"I don't know all of the memory implants and knowledge you've got stored up there, Michael, but you're going to need to help me out with this," Sonia said, looking at the man across from her.

"I'm ready. Tell me what to do," Michael said, having calculated the risks and what appeared to be a non-lethal wound.

"Hold her down, here we go," Sonia said as she wiped beads of sweat from her brow in the hot room.

Crouching down, Michael gently put both of his hands against her shoulders. Elise bit down hard on the towel and Sonia got to work, pressing the tiny red trigger on the handle of the Surface Sealer as a thin gray paste flowed from a small hole on the top of the device.

Sonia pushed further down inside the cut and Elise screamed in pain, struggling against Michael's arms. The paste would seep down through the cut and seal off the non-vital organ, the liver in this case. Sonia continued pumping the thick liquid into Elise's open wound until it overflowed out of the entry point.

"Done," Sonia said, pulling the device back away from Elise.

Michael gently let go of her arms then looked down at her. "I think she may have just passed out," he said quietly.

Sonia whispered softly. "She'll be okay, for now. If that sealant busts, I can't do that again. She needs surgery, but under the circumstances, this will have to do. She'll have a hell of a scar if it doesn't break, but I've gotta tell you, without proper rest, it will break open. This isn't a fix-all. I think the tip of that blade pierced her kidney, but the wound could certainly have been much worse."

"Sonia, I've got to go get Olivia. Now. Whatever that doctor is planning, we have to stop him," Michael said, picking up the Defender II that was propped against the bed.

"I'm coming along," Elise said through her pain.

Both Sonia and Michael looked over at her. She was awake but in obvious pain. "Elise, you can't, the sealant will burst! You just said you're not dying on this rock, you've got to stay put for a bit, we'll be back!" Sonia replied anxiously. She wanted to panic. She had never been so out of her element. *Keep it together, Sonia.*

Elise tried to sit up and groaned in pain, lying back down. "Shit, *shit*! Okay, Sonia, go with him. Just don't forget about me back here. The fire is contained on level four for now. Not sure how soon or if it will spread to the lower levels but rescuing Olivia is priority one, not me."

Sonia began to protest but Elise raised her hand, "That's an order from your commanding officer. Go."

Putting the water bottle into Elise's outstretched hand, Sonia stood to her feet and looked over at Michael. "You heard the commander, let's go get Olivia. And try to figure out what he's planning on doing at three AM, then come back here to get Elise. Time is not on our side."

Michael nodded as Elise said quietly, "You continually amaze me, Sonia. Thanks again for helping me here."

Sonia squeezed her hand, then took off toward the stairs, leaving Elise behind as she laid her head back onto the pillow.

Meanwhile, on the ground level, Olivia had been walked through how to bandage up the wound on the doctor's leg as well as administer medication to numb the pain, a Defender I trained on her the entire time.

Petrino was now in possession of the video recorder, his meal ticket and insurance policy, along with the young blond Elise clone.

Olivia glanced at the scalpel stuck in his belt with Elise's blood smeared on it. Her fragile, young impressionable mind learned quickly, imprinting the awful things done to her by the very man that created her. She was filled with not only terror but the huge weight of deep sadness.

"They're going to come and help me, and you will pay for what you're doing. It's not right. Do you like being a bad person?" she said quietly, glancing up at him, her beautiful green eyes piercing him.

Petrino didn't hesitate, winding up and hitting the girl on the side of the head with the metal weapon in his hand. Olivia flinched at the sudden burst of pain, bringing her hand up to the fresh wound. She pulled her hand away and looked at drops of blood, fighting back tears. *Don't let him see you cry. Be strong like Michael!*

She had been alive for half of a day, yet she already knew what terror and hatred were. She hated this man. Even more than the creatures on the other side of the door that wanted to kill them. They were infected with a mutating alien virus. This man was simply evil.

"I gave you life. You should be thanking me. You can't even get infected with the Rot! But of course, that's not how it goes. No thanks. No acknowledging my accomplishments," he spat out at the injured girl.

Olivia rubbed her injured head. "From the little I know of you, I'd rather never have been born. Or however you created me. It's sick. You're sick!"

Petrino raised the Defender I at her face, his eyes filled with rage, finger on the trigger. They both stared at each other until he finally broke away from their locked eyes, looking at the door leading to the underground walkway. He shook his head, "Nope, no good. Gotta get outside now."

Olivia shook her head fiercely, knowing it was dangerous out there.

He got to his feet. "Get up. See the door over there? It leads outside. Not the walkway. Outside. We can do this two ways. Option one, you calmly and quietly put on the mining suit and oxygen tank hanging by the door then we both leave this building and make our way to the Kernadium storage facility. Option two, you don't get an oxygen tank and we'll see how long you can hold your breath. My guess is roughly one minute. Then you'll attempt to breath in this moon's atmosphere, which will cause your head to expand and then explode. If you think that little cut on your head is bad, you haven't breathed in Moon 002's atmosphere yet."

Olivia looked at him, horrified at her creator, her bottom lip trembling.

"Well, what will it be? Option A or option B? Time's a wasting."

"A."

"Good choice. You might be worth salvaging yet. Nothing that a mind sweep back on Troria wouldn't take care of. They can do wonders on clones. You'll find out. Or actually, you won't." He grinned at his wit.

Olivia quietly moved forward with Petrino hobbling close behind, Defender I aimed at her. *Soon this will be all over and I will be on the shuttle with my property heading back to Troria.*

At the set of lockers located near the door, Olivia opened several and found mining suites and oxygen tanks inside. She quietly put one on and zipped it up without looking at her captor, then she reached for an oxygen tank and puzzled over how to put it on.

"Let's go, hurry up! Shuttle's going to be here soon," Petrino called out, motioning with his gun.

A loud thud echoed throughout the offices. They turned in surprise toward the direction it had come from, the stairwell door in the far corner. Another loud thud. Then another.

The reinforced metal door was buckling under the immense pressure of whatever was smashing into it on the other side.

Eyes wide in terror, Petrino shouted, "Come on! Put your damn helmet on!"

He was sliding into his own mining suit and zipping it up, awkwardly trying to hold onto the Defender I as he went through the cumbersome process. Just as he pulled out an oxygen tank, Olivia gathered up all the willpower and strength she could muster and reached out, grabbing the video recorder from his back pocket. Quickly turning and slapping her hand on the door to the decontamination room, she ran through quickly, placing her hand once more on the scanner to close it behind her.

Petrino instantly dropped the oxygen tank and opened fire but the door had slid shut behind her. He screamed in anger, "Shit! Get back here, you little bitch! Give me back my video recorder!"

The emergency stairwell door burst open as Michael and Sonia rushed in, Michael in the lead, Defender II outstretched.

Petrino quickly bent down to grab the oxygen tank and screamed at the pain in his leg as he pulled up and slung it over his back.

"Stop!" Michael yelled out.

Petrino wasted no time, opening fire on Michael as he headed toward the depressurization room where Olivia had escaped minutes earlier.

Michael immediately returned fire in his direction while dodging the blasts from Petrino's gun.

As the shooting continued inside the large room, a loud roar emanated from the walkway where the door had blown off its hinges and enormous green, slimy tentacles grabbed hold of the busted door frame. Pushing itself through the door frame into the room was an all-new species of animal, mutated from various clone DNA into one singular entity. It was massive, not resembling anything human, a gelatinous mass of green puss and slime.

Petrino took the opportunity to quickly click into his oxygen tank and lock in his helmet as he opened the depressurization chamber and hobbled inside, closing the door behind him. As the door slid shut, he caught a glimpse of what was pushing itself into the room. It was hideous and huge.

Shaking it off, he saw that Olivia had already run outside and wasted no time. He walked over to the door leading out to the moon's surface and hit *open*.

Meanwhile, inside the offices, the creature had fully emerged from the doorway, a large jellyfish-like shape-shifting pile of green blubber. Green puss continued to spill out its orifices, the long tentacles leaving behind a trail of slime. Inside the creature's torso floated visible mutated organs and body parts of dead clones.

The being was attempting to mutate into a large human-shaped organism but hadn't achieved it yet. Arms and legs, human in shape, were trying to form then quickly dissolving and turning back into jelly. In time, it would fully resemble a clone. A very large clone, its head nearly touching the ten-foot-high ceiling.

It moved forward, toward Sonia and Michael. A mouth-like structure near the creature's base split open, revealing rows of both flat and pointed teeth. Dex's head and part of its spinal cord slithered out of the wide mouth, sticking to the creature's body. It slid upwards, the spinal cord cutting through the outer membrane of the being like it was thick jelly. The head came to a stop halfway up the outer torso of the jellyfish substance.

"You," it gurgled slowly, one white eye looking at Michael. The jellyfish being slid forward, knocking over desks and chairs as it moved. Sonia recoiled in disgust at the monstrosity moving toward them.

Processes and calculations flew through Michael's brain. This was new territory, even with advanced memory and learning implants. Michael opened fire with the Defender II. The laser blasts entered the creature but did little to slow it down. The Dex head bellowed out angrily as several of the tentacles latched onto nearby chairs, wrapping around them. Picking the chairs up, the creature flung them toward Michael and Sonia who jumped out of the way as the chairs crashed to the floor nearby.

"Fire! Use the fire!" Sonia called out pointing at the bottom barrel of the gun.

Michael aimed the Defender II once more, this time at the tentacles that had slithered dangerously close to them and continued to move forward.

He pulled the trigger, blasting out fire that connected with the writhing green appendages. They instantly caught fire and pulled back into the creature that was continuing to mutate as it slid forward. Dex's head also pulled back into the being's gelatinous insides.

Michael aimed at it again, about to pull the trigger, when another head pushed its way out of the mouth, spinal cord still attached. Christopher Berger's distorted, mutating face peered down at them.

"We...live...still," it said in a guttural, broken, and barely audible tone as it wiggled against the large mass of green mucus.

"Shoot it! Shoot it Michael!" Sonia screamed, pointing at the Chris head attached to his spinal cord.

Michael pulled the trigger, sending flames cascading forward, hitting the decapitated Chris head in the face. It shrieked and recoiled quickly as Michael moved forward, continuing to push it back.

Tentacles moved out yet again, grabbing a desk and several chairs and launching them at Sonia and Michael, who leapt out of the way but not quickly enough. A chair connected with Sonia's back, the force knocking her to the ground and causing her to cry out in pain.

Michael rushed to her and bent down as the creature began moving forward again. "Are you okay, Sonia?"

Shaking her dazed head, she replied, "Yes, but we won't be for long!"

Michael helped her up to her feet, both looking back to the mutating Rot creation. The fire had spread over its body, as the microscopic particles of green Rot contained fragments of highly flammable Kernadium. Numerous appendages and continuously altering organs caught fire inside the gelatinous mass causing it to slowly expand.

The jellyfish-like, mutating creature spun around, trying to shake the fire off. Chunks of green mucus, engulfed in flames, flew through the air, landing on nearby furniture and causing it to ignite instantly.

The water reserve had been depleted with the fire up in the Commend Center, so the flames spread quickly up the walls, onto the ceiling.

The elevator dinged and the door opened. Elise staggered out, holding her Defender I, opening fire on the creature across the room.

"Elise!" Sonia cried at the sight of her injured friend and commander. Michael looked up to see her trudging forward while continually blasting at the creature now fully engulfed in flames.

The sound of numerous screams echoed from the monster, as if the ingested clones were crying out in pain. It continued to flail its tentacles as the fire spread wherever it moved.

Rushing to Elise just as she began dropping to the ground, Sonia wrapped her arm around her, pulling her forward as Michael took hold of Elise's free arm. Together, all three of them stumbled toward the exit leading out to the planet's surface.

Michael and Sonia quickly began pulling one of the remaining mining suits onto Elise then themselves. Sonia stole a glance at Michael, still stunned she was stuck in this situation with a clone as her backup. Never a leader of any sort, she was now thrust into that very role with a little girl in need of rescue.

Michael caught her eye and gave her the briefest smile.

"I thought I told you to stay put," Sonia told Elise as they strapped on the oxygen tanks and grabbed the helmets.

"What? And miss out on all this fun? Never," Elise said with a grin, grimacing at her still fresh abdominal wound.

The creature rampaged through the offices, but slowing down with the continual fire that engulfed it, causing massive smoke throughout the level. "We have to get out of here now! That thing seems to be explanding!" Sonia ordered, hitting her hand against the hand scanner.

The door slid open and together they helped Elise out with them to the decontamination room, closing the door behind them. Petrino hadn't shut the outside door and the lack of oxygen hit them all at the same time as they struggled with their helmets and oxygen tanks.

They got settled, breathing in the air for a few seconds, until a loud thud knocked on the door. The creature had made its way over to them, still on fire. "Come on. We've got to move!" Michael yelled out inside his helmet.

The three of them trudged out onto the planet's surface through the opened decontamination room exit while the creature was expanding like a balloon being blown up. Its Rot-mutated insides swelled to their limit as fire engulfed it entirely. Then, with a loud, messy pop, it exploded. The wall of the lowest level of the Command Center building blasted outward. Fire erupted as chunks of the creature exploded throughout the floor, sending tiny particles of Kernadium throughout the entire area, igniting everything in its path.

The blast from the exploding clone Rot creature knocked the three survivors onto the ground outside on the moon's surface. Michael was the first to look up to see fire shooting out of windows on all of the floors of the Command Center building. Black smoke poured out and hung in the air, shrouding the building in an eerie black haze.

"Building's lost, we have to move, where's Olivia?" Elise said weakly, staring up at the ongoing destruction, holding her wounded side.

CHAPTER 17

RUBBLE

"Come in, Elise! Anyone! Can anyone hear me?" Jake shouted into his com, seated in a shuttle heading toward the large, shiny disc above Railara's atmosphere, Space Station Infinitum. He was met with silence. Shaking his head he thought for a bit, looking out at the looming space station in space.

He clicked on his com once more while piloting the small shuttle. "This is Jake Riley. Requesting authorization for communication with Lieutenant Filip Marsa of the Trorian military."

After a brief pause, a voice on the other end said, "Access granted. Please wait."

Jake sat back in his seat and ran his hands over his tired face. So many meetings. So much worry for the essentially stranded individuals back on Moon 002 about the constant threat of war reaching Railara. Terrorist attacks, death. These things haunted his thoughts constantly.

"This is Filip Marsa," a gravelly voice responded.

"Filip, Jake Riley here. We may have to push the timeline back. Moon 002 has really messed with the plan," Jake said grimly.

A pause, then, "You may be right. I know for a fact there are two Trorian vessels heading toward Moon 002. Any sign of a Railarian ship with one more Kernadium shipment awaiting pick-up will be seen as an act of war on your end. Sit tight. We need to let things die down on Mining Complex VI," Filip responded.

"I know, it's just…" Jake started.

"Jake, I know. I know Elise Bennet is still there. But we cannot fuck this up. Too much is at stake. Not just on our planet and yours, the entire quadrant. We need to cut the head off of the snake. It's the only way. Otherwise, it will be millions upon millions, and then..." Filip paused.

Looking at his com, Jake nervously asked, "Filip? You still there?"

"I must go," Filip replied in a near whisper. "If I'm found out it won't just be my death, it will be my entire extended family's as well. You know I've already lost my brother and several other relatives."

"Okay, be safe. I hope to see you soon, my friend," Jake responded, his ship now docking at Space Station *Infinitum.*

The com went silent. "Hang in there, Filip," Jake said quietly. But his mind was equally on the souls stuck on Moon 002 and the looming Trorian ships he now knew were on approach.

Olivia had been on the move, doing everything she could to get away from her captor while holding onto his precious video recorder. Her young mind had surmised that due to his injured leg, he would be slowed down significantly but no less dangerous. She had to continue moving if she had any chance of escape. But to where?

Moving toward the first building she saw, she assumed it was the one she and Michael had originally come from. *No use trying to get inside this one.* Still, the building would give her a small bit of protection from her pursuer instead of being out in the open, at least for a little while until she could figure out her next move.

Petrino was armed and running out of time. Three AM loomed large on his mind. He had mere hours to find his prey and get to his ride then off of this hellish planet in one piece.

Hobbling out toward the Clone Replication Center, he saw the outline of a person up ahead and hoped it was her and not one of the infected clones, specifically Leah Lowe. He glanced back to see three people in mining suits exit the Command Center.

"Son of a bitch!" he said out loud, realizing Michael and Sonia had survived, as had Elise.

Glancing back, Olivia saw Petrino continuing toward her. Changing course, she decided to make her way into the tall Poule plants out past the Clone Living Quarters instead. It would be a bit farther but she wasn't sure what other options she had.

"I see you out there," Petrino said grimly as he squinted into the distance, watching her small shape moving past the buildings toward the Poule plants. He, too, changed direction and headed toward the Kernadium storage facility where the *Big Boy* was fueled up, ready and waiting to be driven to the extraction point.

Michael and Sonia moved forward at a much slower pace than they had hoped for, but Elise was in bad shape.

"Guys, go on, I'll catch up. Get to the Kernadium storage facility. That's where the *Big Boy* is stored. He's planning on going off-world. With Olivia if he can."

"We're not leaving you!" Sonia replied as she held onto Elise's arm.

"What's the *Big Boy?*" Michael asked.

"It's our moon rover," Elise said into her helmets com system. "Used for things I would not like to discuss right now. Regardless, I'm fairly certain that's the game plan. You have to get to it. He's hurt and likely moving slowly, so go! I'm slowing you down! I'll catch up, I'm not down for the count just yet."

"Elise, we are not leaving you! Do you understand me?" Sonia shouted into her com, looking over at Elise. "I've been a ghost here on Moon 002 for three years! You've been one of the only people who's been nice to me. Hell, you even got me to come hang out in the lounge, remember? We almost lost you back there and we sure as *hell* aren't going to leave you behind again!"

A slight smile pursed Elise's lips before she replied, "Thank you, Sonia."

"I'm with Sonia. We stay together. We beat that thing inside the Command Center building, so injured or not, we're going to stick together and see this through. Olivia needs us. All of us!" Michael added before sensing a heavy vibration in his suit. He along with Sonia and Elise turned toward where they had just come from.

Another loud explosion had rocked the Command Center. Elise looked in horror to see the building cave in on itself, crumbling to rubble. Dust and debris shot outward from the implosion, moving toward all three of them.

"Run!" Elise cried out as smoke and destruction rained upwards and outwards.

The swell of debris engulfed Elise, Michael and Sonia as they began to run, seeing nothing in front of them but black smoke and dust. It looked like night had fallen for the first time across Moon 002.

Petrino heard the explosion as well and turned to see the destruction unfolding behind him. The large building had collapsed. The Command Center building lay in ruin. Smoke and fire had engulfed the area.

"That fire is going to spread through the walkway to the other areas. I've got to get out of here!" he muttered, hobbling faster as he was now nearly to the Kernadium storage facility where a large landing space had been erected for the transports to easily land and take off.

Olivia reached the edge of the Poule plants, nearly all of them black from being mined to death. They loomed large and ominous, roughly one hundred fifty to some nearly reaching three hundred feet high. Thick at the base all the way to their tops, large needles jutted out from high up on the plants as a defense against the elements on Moon 002. The needles rarely affected the harvesting of the Kernadium. Only on occasion was a clone's mining suit accidently punctured by a stray low growing needle.

The numerous arms on the Poule plants jutting outward looked all the more ominous caked in black death. They seemed to be falling inward and leaning significantly as more of the Kernadium was harvested from them. Even the ground beneath the plants was devoid of nutrients with the dead roots of the plants showing through. Eventually, they would fall to the ground or simply crumble where they stood. The dead plants needed to be extracted and removed from the harvesting area by the clones. Yet another dangerous and physically taxing job for the overworked clones with an already short life span.

Olivia continually turned to see where her pursuer was. She had lost sight of him which she knew didn't make him any less dangerous, even with his injury. He was armed with a deadly weapon and completely out of his mind. Her only hope now was that her new friends were alive somewhere and would find her and save her. She feared the worst, however, seeing the building crumble to the ground.

Tears streamed down her face as she made her way into the Poule plant area of Mining Complex VI. It appeared to be vast, and this heavily covered region filled with death made her feel more alone than ever. Olivia stopped before getting too far into the harvesting area and looked out toward the buildings which were now covered in a shroud of dust from the Command Center's collapse. She could only make out silhouettes.

She hesitated speaking aloud inside the mining suit for fear that her voice would be picked up by the doctor, so she remained quiet. She crouched down to a sitting position, not knowing what her next move would be.

Petrino, meanwhile, had made his way to the Kernadium storage facility. Before entering he looked back once more to see he hadn't been followed. However, with the dust and debris it would be nearly impossible to find him anyway. He noticed something else; it appeared that smoke was now wafting out of the Clone Replication Facility.

The fire was spreading quickly. *Luckily there's no walkway leading over to this building, or I'd really be up shit creek.* The AMO wouldn't look too fondly on their last batch of Kernadium going up in flames, he guessed. By his calculations, they would be back in time to pick this haul up, then it was *Bye-bye, Moon 002.* Now he needed to find Olivia and the video recorder. He estimated ninety minutes before his transport arrived to get them out of there.

He entered the building, glad it was safe from the fires that now appeared to be spreading. Lines of yellow barrels slapped with explosive insignia warning labels signifying the highly volatile liquid contained within sat on large pallets for easy loading and unloading. Roughly half of what the building held when operations were in full swing and the liquid was being harvested from healthy Poule planets. This was the last remaining Kernadium but it was enough to warrant one more trip from Troria to retrieve.

Noticing a pile of oxygen tanks close to the Kernadium barrels, he stopped in his tracks and looked around the large warehouse, hearing a moaning sound coming from near several of the barrels. He was about to keep moving, sensing imminent danger when a walking corpse stumbled out from behind a pallet of Kernadium.

It was Leah Lowe. Or what was left of her—a mass of green jelly Rot. Her only discernable features were a drooping face and hair pasted down with the thick green slime that covered her nearly exposed skull. What once had been an attractive young woman was now a barely recognizable gelatinous walking corpse.

Petrino looked on in horror at the hideous being in front of him. "Stay back! You hear me?" The walking corpse slowly made its way forward, as if not hearing him at all.

In a barely recognizable voice, the creature muttered, "Kill…me."

He had been responsible for setting the infected Dex, Leah, and Carley loose earlier and now this pitiful creature was all that remained. He tilted his head, looking at her, raised his Defender then hesitated. He looked over at the numerous Kernadium barrels; if those tanks were to explode, the whole building would go up in a ball of fire and him with it.

"Not today, honey," he shot out sarcastically then hobbled off toward the awaiting *Big Boy.*

He kept moving, looking over his shoulder as he went to make sure the Leah creature wasn't following him. She was in too bad a condition and had pathetically slumped over onto the floor. In the corner of the warehouse was a separate garage. He hobbled over to it. Every step he took was painful, even with the meds coursing through his system. *Not to worry, this will all be behind me soon. Get the Big Boy, get Olivia, get to the extraction point.*

He pressed the garage door leading into the Big Boy's parking space and with the whirl of gears, it opened up. He was thankful the Kernadium storage facility was on its own backup generator due to the highly flammable and valuable contents of the building.

He stared up at the six-wheeled moon rover, an impressive sight to behold considering the corners that had been cut in the development of the facility on Moon 002. The thick, steel-plated *Big Boy* had been developed by the military higher-ups on Troria to easily plow through strongholds of resistance fighters back on his home world as well as traverse over rough terrain. The lines of the dark grey *Big Boy* sloped low and wide, all six tires huge and thick and able to run over nearly anything, even intense heat. This particular model had the insignia *BB645* painted in red on its side along with the official AMO logo next to it.

"Time to get out of here. Time's wasting," Petrino mumbled as he made his way to the side. "Shit!" he cursed, looking at the several narrow steps that led to the driver's seat of the beast in front of him. Carefully, he holstered his Defender I then lifted his right leg to the first step. "Easy, I can do this," he said, the first step causing blistering pain through his left leg all the way up his side. He slipped and fell backwards onto the ground, landing on his injured leg. Screaming in pain, he rocked back and forth on the ground in agony.

Michael felt around on the ground in front of him, attempting to get his bearings after being knocked forward from the impact of the building behind him crashing to the ground. His mind immediately went to his companions.

"Sonia, Elise, come in!" he said as he squinted to see in front of him to no avail.

He was met with static on the other end. He pushed himself to stand up to his feet, grateful he hadn't dropped his Defender II when he fell forward. Raising it to his face, he looked through the scope and clicked, switching to night vision.

Moving forward, he saw a form lying on the ground. He hurried over to the figure and crouched down to see Sonia.

He gently rolled her over so she was facing him and shook her by her shoulders.

"Sonia, come on! You still with me?" he said into his com.

Slowly her eyes opened, blinking. "What's going on?"

"The building collapsed. We've got to find Elise," Michael said anxiously as his eyes searched the dirty wind swirling around them.

She stood to her feet, taking hold of his arm for stability, looking around for any sign of her friend and commander. "Look, over there! That's her!"

Elise had been knocked to the ground as well. Upon a quick inspection, Sonia's demeanor turned grave. "This is bad, Michael. Her helmet is cracked!" she muttered in dismay at the thin, jagged line running through the visor on the cheaply assembled helmet the AMO had provided for them. "It's only a matter of time before it implodes. We've got to get her another helmet or she'll die!"

"Elise, can you hear us? Wake up! We've got to move!" Michael shouted as he looked at her closed eyes behind the cracked helmet visor.

Elise's eyes blinked then slowly opened. Quickly realizing her visor was cracked, she put her gloved hands to her face. "This is bad."

"Yeah, we saw. Commander, we've got to move," Sonia replied.

Slowly standing to her feet, she began moving forward with the help of Michael and Sonia.

"Good, you've still got your gun," Michael exclaimed as he looked down at Elise's Defender I.

Gritting her teeth through the pain she said, "That fire's going to spread to the other buildings through the walkway. This whole mining complex is going down. Our main objective now is to help that little girl out there. Got it?"

Michael and Sonia nodded, moving away from the debris toward the Kernadium storage facility in the distance. On the rocky surface below, they felt another vibration and heard a thumping noise.

"Now what?" Sonia exclaimed.

They looked over to see the Clone Living Quarters looming large through the slightly thinning dust. It stood ominously quiet now, almost menacing. Elise shuddered at the thought of the dead clones left there to die, Rot infecting all levels inside the building.

"Come on, let's keep moving," Elise said.

Another thump and another vibration were followed by what sounded like a dull and muffled roar coming from inside the towering structure they were passing.

Michael grimaced. "There's something in that building. And whatever it is, it sounds like it could be even larger than the mutation we destroyed earlier."

CHAPTER 18

UNSTABLE GROUND

"Who were you speaking with, Lieutenant Marsa?" Levon Gonidec himself stood in front of the grizzled old man in his finest military garb, his hand outstretched.

He's getting more paranoid, which means he's getting more reckless, Filip thought, pulling out his communicator and handing it to Levon. Whenever he wanted to make a statement, he wore his official military uniform and it typically meant someone, or some ones were about to die.

"Mr. Gonidec, sir, I was just," Filip began.

"Quiet. I don't have the time or patience for this. Must I always have to listen in on conversations? I feel your eyes on me, Lieutenant. I know you hate me," Gonidec said smugly.

"Sir, I do not hate you," he lied.

Ignoring him, Gonidec looked over the communicator and lifted it in front of him, pushing it forward toward Filip's face.

"You know I can run search logs on these things, right? It's time consuming and a pain in my ass but I can and I will."

"Feel free, sir. I was simply communicating with my men the rest of this afternoon's agenda. Another state sponsored execution. This time only five individuals accused of being Railarian spies," Filip replied, trying to hide his contempt.

"Oh, not accused. Found guilty! There is a difference, my dear Lieutenant. Your brother was found guilty. I would hate to see anything else happen to your family. I want to trust you, Marsa. But trust is a hard thing to come by these days." He paused, then added for full effect, "So, the question remains, can I trust you?"

"Absolutely, sir. Please feel free to run a search on my communicator," Filip responded quickly.

Gonidec thought for a bit then handed the communicator back to his Lieutenant, "No, I don't think I will. Because I am feeling trustworthy right now. Especially considering what you are about to carry out for me. I trust these five will burn quite well?"

"Yes, sir. They will all burn to death per your orders," Filip responded. This time unable to mask his anger and sadness.

"Don't worry, Filip, my friend. Someday this will all be over. War will have ended and there will be peace throughout this quadrant. And if you play your cards right, you could possibly have one of the planets to yourself! Can you imagine? President and Leader Filip Marsa! That could be you! But if you ever cross me, it will be you that burns, along with everyone you've ever known. Do I make myself clear?"

"Absolutely, sir. You have nothing to worry about, sir!" Filip shouted.

Satisfied that he had made his point, Levon Gonidec moved forward to the awaiting prisoners about to be burned alive with the help of several soldiers carrying out Lieutenant Filip's command.

Filip Marsa followed the leader of Troria to the prisoners, pocketing his communicator that, if indeed had been scanned, would have blown the entire operation and certainly led to his quick and painful death along with the poor souls he now stared down at. *When will this nightmare end?*

"Soldiers, take your positions!" Lieutenant Marsa shouted.

Inside the clones' living quarters, the monster had been assembling itself. For several days the remaining clone population had been dying off. The Rot had spread quickly throughout the levels once the building was infected then subsequently quarantined off. Their fate was sealed, literally.

The bodies piled up gradually as the highly flammable green puss oozed across walls and floors in seemingly endless quantities from the living-dead clones. The entire building was now overrun. A cesspool of disease and violence, every square foot smelled of rotting meat.

Some had chosen to take their own lives in their tiny living quarters, unaware that even death couldn't keep the Rot away. Doors opened, the living dead entered, and every single body was quickly assimilated.

Gradually, the mass of walking death began to meld together. Veins filled with the green puss from the stronger clones wrapped around the weaker, ingesting them and growing. The many became the few then became the one. And the one, much like the other large mutation that had attacked the Command Center earlier, wanted out. The hive mind that controlled it had devised a way out of the securely locked outer doors.

The flammable and now highly explosive Kernadium-infused green Rot virus that coursed through its veins and was smeared throughout the building's walls would be its escape. Already some of the deadly thick green liquid had come into contact with electrical outlets and lighting fixtures, producing sparks that began igniting and rapidly spreading, travelling through the hallways. It already sensed the rest of the complex was compromised as heavy smoke billowed throughout. This prison would soon be reduced to rubble as well.

Petrino struggled to get back on his feet. Biting through the pain, he climbed the few steps into the *Big Boy*. This was his only escape.

Once inside with the door shut behind him, he navigated the large controls and pushed it forward out of the parking space. As the *Big Boy* was a stripped-down combat vehicle, creature comforts were non-existent, which was fine with him. He wouldn't be in this tin can for long.

"Time to find my property," he said. He had an hour yet so he figured he was still good on time even with his damaged leg that had slowed him down.

Inside the Poule reserve, Olivia cowered in fear. Large ominous cactus-like plants towered over her, blocking out the little light the planet offered. She looked up. The little she knew about her surroundings told her that this was a place of death. A natural survival instinct was all the girl had known since waking from her slumber.

She peered out, hoping for even a tiny glimpse of her protectors. She wasn't sure how she would manage for much longer, with those things out there and worse, the perverted doctor continuing to hunt her.

The ground beneath her felt unstable. She looked down and stomped her feet nervously. *What's under this?*

From a distance, she saw what appeared to be a pair of yellow lights piercing through the dust. Something was pulling out of the building and was now heading her way.

She began backing up instinctively and tripped over an exposed root from a nearby Poule plant, falling backwards and landing hard on her back. Olivia looked up at the looming plant, now shaking violently from the recent explosion. One of its thick arms above snapped and fell down toward her. She quickly rolled out of the way, bringing her arms to her face as the dead limb crashed beside her, exploding into tiny pieces and covering her in plant dust. She looked up and saw the rest of the plant splitting apart and about to come down.

Standing to her feet, she saw the lights in the distance growing closer. Instinctively, she knew it was her pursuer. The plant continued to crack down its center and was now falling to either side. She had to run or she would be crushed.

As if in a chain reaction, numerous dead Poule plants around her began splitting and shattering. She ran as fast as she could, turning her head to watch the falling plants behind her, then ahead to see the lights nearly upon her.

Black flakes from the plants spread outward as large pieces crashed around her. "Michael! Where are you? Help me!" she shouted in her helmet in desperation.

Michael, Sonia, and Elise moved as quickly as they could away from the Clone Living Quarters when they saw in the hazy distance a group of Poule plants begin to crumble. Behind them lie the Command Center's destruction, smoke pouring from the Clone Replication Facility, and the terrible sound of something shaking the door of the Clone Living Quarters. Ahead, they caught sight of the *Big Boy* moving across the desolate landscape toward the crumbling Poule plants.

A tiny voice crackled through their headsets. Barely audible. It was Olivia. Michael's eyes widened as he looked at his companions.

"She must be in the Poule plants! Petrino is nearly there!" Elise shouted. She aimed her Defender I and began firing toward the *Big Boy*, knowing it would do no damage at this distance but hoping to at least distract him.

Red laser fire streaked through the sky as Michael quickly joined in. At the very least, this would let the doctor know they were still in pursuit. They continued to fire and saw the *Big Boy* come to a stop.

Inside the armored moon rover, Petrino hit the brakes and looked on as beams of red fire shot toward him. Several made contact but merely pinged off the *Big Boy's* strong steel outer hull. He grinned and pushed forward toward the crumbling Poule plants in front of him until he saw his prey: the silhouette of a small person. Olivia.

"You'll come with me or I'll shoot you dead, girl! Give me back my fucking video recorder!" he shouted angrily as he quickly approached the small figure.

Laser fire from Michael's Defender II and Elise's Defender I continued to zip past him as he pushed forward at full speed, bearing down on the girl in front of him. Poule plants behind her crumbled to the ground, kicking up black debris.

He was nearly to her as he felt the ground below the *Big Boy* shake.

Elise watched with horror at the scene unfolding before them and exclaimed, "He's too close to the Poule plants! That moon rover is too heavy and those roots are dead!"

The three of them had made significant progress toward the girl. "Olivia, over here!" Michael yelled into his com.

Behind them, the door from the clones' living quarters building exploded outward, sending smoke pouring out. And something else.

"What the hell was that?" Sonia exclaimed, looking back at the horror they were trying to escape.

Get to the girl, save her, it is up to you! Michael was close enough that he now ran toward Olivia.

The *Big Boy* again came to a stop, one of its large tires sinking down into the crumbling ground. Inside, Petrino frantically attempted to dislodge himself from the hole. Moving forward, then hitting reverse. *Shit!* He looked out at the girl pulling away from him. The *Big Boy* shifted and another wheel sank. He was making it worse.

"Shit, shit!" Petrino yelled. He opened the door and leaned out with his Defender I, firing it in Olivia's direction.

The blasts zipped by her, nearly hitting the fleeing girl. Seeing the laser fire, Michael yelled into his com, "Olivia, drop to the ground, now!"

Roughly thirty yards away from Michael now, and in the other direction, thirty yards away from Petrino continuing to fire on her, she heard Michael's voice and did as he ordered.

Stopping in his tracks, Michael raised his Defender II, looking through the viewfinder with his finger on the trigger, lining up the shot.

Petrino fired aimlessly in frustration, quickly losing control of the situation. Olivia now lay flat on the ground between Petrino and Michael.

Michael put his finger on the trigger and squeezed.

Petrino saw a red streak of fire erupt behind Olivia, and then his chest burst inward. The laser blast seared through his heart and out other side, disappearing into the whirling dusty wind.

Immediately killed by the blast, Petrino spilled out of the *Big Boy* onto the ground.

"Olivia!" Michael called out, taking off toward her. She stood to her feet and met him, instinctively wrapping her arms tightly around his waist.

"Thank you, Michael!" Olivia cried, not releasing him. Her hero.

Before he could respond, a loud roar emanated from the clones' living quarters. They looked and saw the building was now clearly on fire, windows on all of the floors bursting and expelling plumes of black smoke.

But the fire was no longer their worst danger, it was the looming figure in the smoke that had exited through the opening.

CHAPTER 19

SOMETHING'S HEADING OUR WAY

"Something isn't right, sir," the tall, synthetic android pilot, aptly named Pilot 33, said gravely looking down at his scanners aboard the small spacecraft. Named after its designer, Sir. Victor Deimos, the ship was used by the Trorian military for stealth and reconnaissance missions.

A sleek looking vessel with a dark gray matte finish, the *Deimos* was nearly invisible to the naked eye when flying. The front point extended outward to two points on the very rear of the ship, making it essentially the shape of a triangle with an oval cockpit on top. As with nearly every transportation vehicle on Troria, the *Deimos* flew on Kernadium liquid powering its small but incredibly quick engine. It was a weapons-ready machine with a row of heavy laser disintegrators located under either wing.

"What's not right? We've been travelling from Mining Complex III for what feels like a full week. I'm tired of sitting in this damn thing. I want to make the pick-up and leave. We're gonna be stuck in this thing for another week at least getting back to Troria after this. All this for that damn doctor and his video recorder," Nic Mohr grumbled.

Mohr had been overseeing all ten of the Alnorix Mining facilities since their inception and was heavily involved in their creation, from development to completion. He was also overseeing the cloning process as well as their extermination, both after their year of service on the planets as well as any other injuries that were incurred.

The Rot epidemic that had swept through Moon 002 was quite disturbing, especially since there were nine other facilities still running. This had to be kept quiet and he was determined to do just that, regardless of the cost of clone or human life. And right now, a small handful of humans needed to be dealt with per Levon Gonidec's orders. Most importantly, Elise Bennet.

Elise had come to the company with the highest recommendations and qualifications, graduating top of her class. She was outgoing, attractive and strong- willed. Much later, they discovered she was involved with a faction on Troria determined to end not just the mining facilities off-world but also to overthrow the current regime. A faction that could be traced all the way to the planet Railara.

Mohr knew perfectly well the type of government that ran his home world: merciless, authoritarian, devoid of most things that made people good, noble and upright. But this was the only way AMO was able to do what they did. The company got richer as the government stayed in power, pushing its strict laws and regulations on the people to more and more extreme lengths. No longer was Troria a planet whose citizens could hold fair elections or were able to have any true voice of descension of any sort.

If Mohr intended to continue growing the Alnorix mining empire, he needed the government's approval and ongoing funding. It was a vicious cycle but one helped perpetuate and ensured him a spot in Gonidec's inner circle.

Those discovered taking part in this takedown attempt had simply vanished. Elise remained on Moon 002 even after she had been discovered as a traitor and informant to the resistance on Troria, but her fate was sealed. She wouldn't make it back home alive, per Gonidec's orders.

And then the Rot happened, further complicating things. Petrino, who had been instrumental in developing cloning technology, held all of Alnorix Mining's secrets, and with them, the secrets of the government that supported and funded their ongoing work. Work that involved slave labor, executions, and the harvesting of planets until completely used up of their natural resources.

Pilot 33, created to resemble a strong, athletic twenty-seven-year-old, glanced at the agitated, heavyset brute of a man sitting beside him. His orders were to accompany Mohr on this trip to Moon 002 and retrieve the video recorder and Dr. Petrino. "I'm getting multiple readings of explosions occurring on the planet. Looks like the good doctor has succeeded in knocking out the power there, but explosions mean the Kernadium storage facility could be compromised. There's still a lot of Kernadium in that warehouse. Enough that'll get us in trouble if it's lost."

Mohr glared at the man sitting beside him. He respected the strong fighter pilot, even if he was nothing more than an android, a robotic organism wrapped in synthetic flesh, which is why he was selected to fly this seemingly simple extraction mission with him.

Pilot 33 was one of fifty created at the start of Levon Gonidec's rise to power as a way to line his military with expendable yet powerful and extremely loyal androids.

However, the cost was high and mass production of the synthetic androids was far less sustainable than the cloning perfected by the AMO. Because of this, very few synthetic androids existed. And those that did served the higher-ups on Troria.

Running his hand over his slicked back brown hair now showing hints of gray at forty-nine, Mohr said, "If that doctor has fucked things up more for us, he's not making it off that moon alive. And I need to make sure we are both in agreement. Do I make myself clear?"

Nodding at his superior's harsh words, which his processing system and internal logic board were used to, he continued piloting the *Deimos*. Both hands on the helm, he looked down at the numerous readouts in front of him. They would arrive shortly. "Yes, sir. Video recorder comes with us. Same with the girl he designed. It's true her immune system is able to fight off the Rot disease?"

Nodding, Mohr replied back slightly less harsh, "Yes, indeed. With her DNA and the cure for Rot baked into it, we'll be able to create clones impervious to the disease. Which we now know could happen on any of the other nine mining facilities. I'm fine losing those buildings in exchange for the girl and the video recorder. The Kernadium, well, let's hope it stays safe. Or it's my ass."

"Yes sir," Pilot 33 responded emotionlessly as he pulled the helm to the right, flying past a small group of meteors. A beautiful purple and orange nebula sprawled out like a huge blanket in the distance, and in front of it, the small planet Treon III and its moons.

The four of them stood looking at the unmoving Petrino.

"He had it coming. I wanted to do the honor, but you earned it as well, Michael," Elise said grimly before adding, "I need his helmet."

Michael bent down and ripped the helmet off of the doctor's head. Dead eyes stared back at them.

"He won't be needing this any longer either," Sonia said as she bent down, picking up Petrino's Defender I.

They headed for the *Big Boy*, currently stuck in the ground.

"Think we can get that thing unstuck?" Michael asked. Olivia stood close beside him, even more bonded with this man born into chaos on this hostile world much like she was.

"We have to try. Now," Elise said urgently, looking over at the huge shape looming in the smoke, letting out another low roar.

The four of them bolted toward the *Big Boy*, Sonia taking Olivia while Michael helped Elise. "This is going to hurt, ready?" he said, slinging the Defender II over his shoulder and helping her up.

Michael hopped up into the vehicle last and scanned the layout, his mind processing and imprinting the fact that his job on Moon 002 had required him to operate this exact vehicle. He instantly knew how to operate it but hadn't yet begun to maneuver it when a loud explosion echoed from the Clone Living Quarters. They all looked out the windows of the moon rover as fire shot out of the building. Another explosion sounded and then it collapsed.

"Michael, go!" Sonia yelled from the rear passenger seat.

Hitting reverse, Michael began rocking the vehicle back and forth in an attempt to free it from the confines of the sink hole.

Another explosion, this time from the generator room. The fire had spread and once it hit the generator and server room, the machinery inside erupted. A huge fireball flew upwards as the building didn't just collapse, it exploded outward.

The Clone Replication Facility was hit with shrapnel from the destruction surrounding it, large chunks of steel flying through the air, smashing into it. The ground shook as the generator building split down the middle, concrete cracking, steel twisting, fire erupting as it too, collapsed to the surface.

The only building still standing at this point was the Kernadium facility. Set slightly out from the rest of the buildings with no linking tunnels, this didn't make it less compromised. Fire had spread throughout the mining complex. Burning debris floated in the air, landing in every direction including the Kernadium facility.

Poule planets crumbling to the ground, buildings collapsed, the entire area was in ruin. And somewhere, in the smoke, fire and destruction, another mutating creature lurked.

Near the collapsed buildings, the ground began to split open. The magnitude of the harvesting done on the moon's terrain had made much of the ground continually more unstable. The aggressive harvesting methods and collapsing buildings were the last in a long line of misjudgments and miscalculations in the poor and inexpensive design of the facility.

Still stuck in the *Big Boy* near the Poule plants, Sonia looked out her window at the ground around the generator building splitting open and shook her head in disbelief. "The ground is breaking apart!"

Shockwaves from what was essentially a quake shot through the ground, hitting the *Big Boy*—a tiny bit of good fortune. Michael hammered forward on the steering wheel, pushing it while stomping on the pedal below. The large six-wheeled machine finally broke free of its constraints below and jutted forward.

"Do you think whatever was inside that cloud of smoke is dead? Maybe it sunk into the ground like the buildings?" Olivia asked hopefully, looking at Sonia.

She looked at the girl as they attempted to flee the destruction unfolding around them, "I don't know, honey. I'm just glad we're all together. We need to figure out where this extraction point is that the doctor was so hell-bent on getting to. That's top priority, let's hope that thing doesn't follow us."

Olivia nodded and gave Sonia a small smile.

Tires spun in the loose dirt but found traction as Michael raced forward, attempting to get away from the quickly evaporating ground beneath them. Sonia and Olivia looked out at the rubble from the buildings slowly sinking as they passed by, now driving away from the destruction. The Kernadium facility alone remained intact, for now.

Elise opened her eyes from the back seat and mumbled, "The video recorder. We need to keep it safe. And you, Olivia. You are our top priority. We're expendable at this point."

Michael nodded grimly. Sonia opened her eyes wide. "Well, speak for yourself. I don't want to die here!"

"None of us do, Sonia, but clones are being murdered, have been for years across the quadrant. This whole outfit is corrupt. In it for nothing but wealth and power. Alnorix is a puppet and Gonidec's regime is pulling the strings. That's why I'm here. To take them down," Elise said gravely.

"What? What do you mean?" Sonia fired back.

"I mean…I've been here all along to gather intel on this place. Everything that goes on here. The executions of worn out and injured clones. What the clones are fed. The harvesting and killing of this planet's resources!"

"What the clones are fed?" Olivia chimed in.

"You don't want to know, Olivia," Elise said quietly.

Sonia shuddered. She had heard rumors about the repurposing of clones. Ground up and fed to the healthy ones. She had pushed it out of her mind, thinking to herself on numerous occasions, *They're livestock, just livestock. Keep thinking of your mom back home. She needs you! Stick with this and her surgery is ensured.*

"So, it is true. All of it. There had been talk of resistance fighters trying to infiltrate all ten of the mining facilities across the solar system. I had my suspicions," Sonia said, nodding to herself.

"And that is why I said *we* are expendable. The recorder and the girl. They both must survive and, more importantly, not fall into the hands of Gonidec's inner circle."

"We don't have much oxygen left in these tanks. Does this vehicle have oxygen?" Michael asked, searching his now extensive implanted memory for information about the oxygen functions in the *Big Boy.*

"Yes. But just like these tanks on our backs, it runs out. Good idea, we need to conserve it. See that button up there on the left-hand side of the steering wheel? Hit it. That'll open up the oxygen valves," Elise answered.

Michael hit the button and a soft hiss emanated from several vents inside the *Big Boy.* After a short time, a green light lit up above the button.

"Okay, helmets off, the cabin's been pressurized," Elise said then gritted her teeth at the pain in her abdomen.

"You okay?" Sonia asked, noticing Elise's sudden discomfort.

"I'm fine. Just dealing with the wound. I'll be fine, glad I have the extra helmet, though I'm surprised this hunk of junk lasted this long with the crack in the visor," Elise said as she shook her head slightly after taking the damaged helmet off, tossing it aside.

Sonia clicked her own helmet to unlock it, worried about Elise's cut and her makeshift sealing of it.

Michael and Olivia followed suit, breathing in the somewhat fresh air and glad to be out of the claustrophobic confines of an oxygen tank and helmet.

Accessing maps and locations inside his head, Michael couldn't get a read on their destination. "What's the location? My implants only go so far."

"The burn pit. Where they take used-up clones," Elise responded solemnly.

"Dear lord, that's actually real? I've heard whispers about it," Sonia said, her mind immediately thinking of her mother's warnings about this, which she had brushed off. *Nonsense! They wouldn't be that cruel! Besides, they're just clones, Mom!*

Silence fell as they all thought the same horrific thing.

"That way," Elise pointed, once more grimacing at the sharp pain as Michael quietly steered the *Big Boy* further away from the mining complex.

Olivia looked up at the sky above through the thick glass roof. She could see stars and distant planets past the moon's glowing atmosphere. Then she noticed something else. Something moving.

"Hey, I think there's something flying up there, it looks like it's heading this way," Olivia said, pointing up.

CHAPTER 20

THE ROT CREATURE

The creature moved slowly at first, examining its surroundings outside of the building it was created in. Made up of small pieces and parts of over forty clones, the entity soon realized it must move or be swallowed up by the quickly deteriorating ground beneath its appendages.

It registered the vehicle pulling away from the fallen Poule planets as the ground shifted and shook. A man lay on the ground past the vehicle. *Another one for my collection* it thought, stomping forward, creating more cracks on the moon's surface directly behind it.

Once at the fallen man, the clone Rot creature lowered its arm, a series of tendons and veins and muscle tissue, and opened its mucus-covered hand, grabbing the deceased Petrino from the ground and lifting the lifeless, bloody body to its head, inspecting it.

The creature resembled a human in form, having had more time to assimilate all of the clones, minus its outer flesh. Exposed organs and bone structure, it had assembled itself and quickly evolved after ingesting numerous clones. Their DNA ran through its veins. It expanded and grew exponentially into one enormous, mutated clone, its facial features ever-changing, taking on various deceased clones at will, accessing their memories.

It opened its large mouth and placed Petrino inside, then chewed, swallowed, and assimilated all of him and his memories into itself. Shaking its head, its facial features once more shifted.

White eyes laced with green veins blinked and surveyed the destruction its lifeblood had wrought over Mining Station VI. Exposed teeth formed a twisted grin as the massive mutant looked out toward the *Big Boy* in the far distance.

More warm bodies. Attempting to escape. Must eat them. Assimilate and grow.

The *Big Boy* continued onward toward the burn pit with Elise weakly pointing the way. They had all looked up at the tiny light in the sky and concluded a ship was heading toward the planet.

"That thing up there is our ticket out of here. If it was coming for the doctor, it's not going to be friendly to us, so we're not out of this just yet," Michael commented.

"Each of us is armed. Olivia, you're responsible for keeping that video recorder safe, got it?" Sonia said, reaching forward, putting her hand on the girl's shoulder.

"It won't leave me. Promise!" Olivia said confidently.

Sonia smiled then noticed blood on Olivia's head. "What happened here?" she asked, gently putting her hand on the girl's head to inspect it closer.

"That bad man hit me with his gun. It really hurt but I'll be alright."

Seeing the blood shook Sonia to her core. The girl felt pain just like she did. This beautiful child was not *livestock* or property. "I'm sorry, Olivia. I'm sorry you were hurt. He won't hurt you again."

Michael looked into the rear-view mirror above, watching Sonia tenderly touch Olivia's injured head, showing kindness and compassion, his mind working. *Get these people to safety. Protect the child.*

"Elise, are we getting closer to this burn pit? Probably a good idea to prepare Olivia," Sonia said quietly in the backseat, looking over at her injured commander, whose eyes were closed.

Her question was met with silence.

"Elise?" She nudged her shoulder and got no response. Sonia looked down and saw her mining suit had a damp red circle on it. "Michael, stop the vehicle!"

The *Big Boy* came to a stop, the mining complex far away in the rear-view mirror, and surrounding them were more dead Poule planets, dirt, and rocks.

Turning in his seat along with Olivia, Michael asked, "What's wrong?"

They all looked at Elise, eyes closed, the red circle growing larger across her abdomen.

"Oh, no, no, no! Elise, come on! Don't you die on us!" Sonia exclaimed. "I don't have any of my equipment with me! I have to get this mining suit off of her." She quickly unzipped the mining suit and gently pulled it down.

Elise's shirt was almost entirely covered in her blood. Fresh blood. Her wound had opened. She opened her eyes slightly and tried to speak but no words came out.

Olivia teared up as her bottom lip quivered. She couldn't watch. She turned back around to stare out front and screamed, "Michael! Look out!"

Michael turned and saw in front of them a huge, growing sink hole moving toward the *Big Boy*. He quickly hit reverse and began moving the moon rover away from the rapidly deteriorating surface.

A loud thud landed behind them. The clone Rot creature stomped its foot, cracking the ground beneath it.

Michael hit the brakes, staring at the large open cliff ahead that appeared to be impassable, then looked behind them at yet another monstrosity. "Shit!" he shouted in frustration.

The creature lifted its massive fists in the air, preparing to bring them down on top of the *Big Boy*, just as Michael floored the vehicle in an attempt to navigate around the sink hole.

The creature took chase, its massive feet smashing onto the ground, shaking it as it ran forward. It roared in anger at the fleeing vehicle, its face had contorted into something that now resembled Petrino, who, being the freshest human victim, once assimilated took over the hive mind of the massive organism.

The faster Michael pushed the moon rover, the closer the Petrino clone mutation got. He could feel the ground beneath the vehicle begin to give out, so he yanked the wheel to the right to avoid potentially dropping into the chasm.

The creature, however, wasn't as lucky. The ground gave way, causing the Petrino clone mutation to plummet into the abyss below.

Commander Mohr and his android pilot were still high above the planet. "What have we got?" Mohr asked, peering down at the scanner in front of him.

Pilot 33 ran his hands through his life-like, synthetic hair and sat back in his pilot's seat, frustrated at what he was seeing. "Well, from the looks of it, four of the five buildings are demolished, though the Kernadium storage facility is still standing. For how long, I don't know. I do not have the proper data until we arrive and inspect further."

"We're not breaking radio silence just yet. Take us down to the extraction point. It's nearly three AM. What a complete and utter fucking nightmare. I should have never put my faith in that washed up, chain-smoking doctor," Mohr said grimly.

Pilot 33 pushed forward on the helm and the *Deimos* rocketed forward, beginning its descent on Moon 002 with a course plotted for the burn pit.

Michael raced forward, relieved at losing the pursuing Rot creature, at least for now, and determined to get to what he hoped was the extraction point.

Sonia did what she could for Elise in the backseat. She was bleeding out, and while this would be an easy fix if she had the proper tools in a controlled environment, they weren't so lucky at the moment. She felt helpless.

Sitting in the front seat, Olivia did her best to stay quiet and not cry while they traversed over the rough terrain. The ship above appeared larger and would soon land.

Elise opened her eyes slightly, looking out the front windshield at their destination. "There," she mumbled and lifted her finger, pointing out at an approaching crater.

"Hang in there, Elise. Maybe someone on that ship approaching can help," Sonia said calmly, trying to console her friend.

This made Elise grin slightly before coughing up a bit more blood. Almost whispering her words, she said, "The girl. Please take care of the girl, Sonia, if I don't make it, promise?"

Sonia shook her head. "No, you hang on, damnit! Don't die on me! Michael carried you out of that burning room and I fixed you up for a reason, you hear me?"

Elise fell quiet once more as Sonia forced back the tears welling up in her eyes. She gently wiped the blood from Elise's mouth then looked forward to Michael. "That crater, that's got to be the pick-up spot," she said.

He nodded, but no one said anything else as they approached the crater in front of them. The ground inside of it was black with caked on ash and ground up bones from the numerous clone liquidations over the years.

Michael stopped the moon rover and put it in park, looking up at the sky above as the triangular ship began its descent toward them.

"We have to be prepared for anything at this point," Michael said ominously. "Whoever is onboard is likely not here to help us. They're here for Petrino, Olivia and the recorder. Olivia, you stay here with Elise until we get back, okay?"

"I don't want to wait here by myself!" Olivia cried out.

"Hey, I need someone to talk to, and who better than someone as kind and pretty as you?" Elise said faintly from the rear seat.

Olivia sniffed and nodded. She knew she needed to be strong now and could no longer break down and cry. They were all in grave danger and she had to help as best she could.

"I'll cheer you up, Elise!" Olivia said, forcing a smile, turning toward the back seat.

"I know you will, Olivia. You're a big girl, and you're a brave girl, don't ever forget that," Elise said quietly, glancing up at the spitting image of herself so many years ago.

"Come on, Sonia, let's gear up and meet our new ride out of here, one way or another. Follow my lead, I've got a plan," Michael said firmly, glancing back at her.

Trust this clone. No, trust this man! He's going to help get us off this rock! She nodded in reply, clicking her helmet back on and picking up her Defender I.

Michael clicked in his own helmet and gave her a thumbs up as they both exited the Big Boy. Sonia put her hand on Olivia's shoulder and gave it a gentle squeeze then shut the door behind her.

Olivia quickly climbed into the back of the moon rover and looked at her older twin, now slumped over with eyes closed. She wished there was a way to help Elise, looking behind her to the rear of the *Big Boy* which was large with room for storage.

Desperately, Olivia decided to explore in the hopes that something back there could be of use in this dire situation. She saw a box marked with what looked like a medical symbol and crawled into the back to check it out, periodically looking out the front windshield to see Michael and Sonia standing at the crest of the crater as the ship continued to lower to the surface of the planet.

Olivia climbed back over the seat with the box and gently shook Elise. "Elise, wake up, I found something, it might help you!"

Opening her eyes, Elise looked at the girl then down to the box in front of her. A medical kit, likely forgotten by one of the doctors on a previous burn pit run.

"Can you try to find something to take the pain away?" Elise asked softly.

Olivia held up a bottle of pills, looking it over. "Clone Stimulants? Would this work?"

"Yes, they numb pain somewhat for the clones. Works on humans as well. Take two tablets out and if you can, put them into my mouth," Elise said weaky.

Without hesitating, Olivia did as she was told. "I'm sorry Elise, I'm so sorry!" Olivia exclaimed as she could see that even this small act was hurting Elise.

Elise chewed up the pills and swallowed them, then fell silent, hoping they would take hold quickly.

CHAPTER 21

NIGHTLY ROUND-UP

Corinna Bonnel sat in her small apartment in the outskirts of the capital city on Troria, Paladine, listening to large tank-like vehicles outside causing her windows to shake. Her home was on the smaller side of small, but it had been enough for her and her daughter. Especially since for most of Sonia's life it had just been the two of them.

Now, with a bad heart that would kill her if surgery wasn't performed within the year, she was alone as sheer madness took over the city. She had heard the military was on the move, rounding up any citizen that had a history of being outspoken against the current regime in power, even looking at voting records and communications between family members and close friends. Anyone discovered was *taken.*

A fist pounded on the front door of her apartment sandwiched between several larger buildings. You would miss it if you blinked, but that wasn't the case on this cold evening.

Answer the door Corinna, or they'll break it down and you'll be taken away for sure. She held her hands to her mouth, afraid her breathing could be heard. Why was she afraid? What was she guilty of? At this point on Troria, "simply existing" seemed to be the logical answer.

She silently rushed over to the door and put on a pleasant face, not wanting to draw any unwanted attention. She knew how she had voted, and her daughter too, which could very well have sealed her fate. She unlocked the deadbolt, put her hand on the door handle and opened the old, squeaky door.

Two men dressed in black with Gonidec's Trorian military insignia on their breastplates stood looking at her, both armed with Defender rifles and clubs at their sides. They wore helmets but the visors were up so she could see the faces staring at her and into her quaint apartment.

The taller of the two had a large scar running across his cheek, she guessed from a run-in with someone willing to fight back.

"Yes, gentlemen, how may I help you tonight?" Corinna asked in as neutral a voice as she could muster.

"Ma'am, there's been talk of treasonous activity going on in this neighborhood. For the safety of all citizens, we're going door to door checking to see if anyone has heard anything. We are also spot-checking particular houses that may have links to terrorist organizations that could be a threat to our sovereign nation," the taller one said in a deep, low voice. The words he uttered sounded staged and rehearsed, as if he'd said them countless times, across countless streets in this city alone.

She knew instantly this was a ruse. A shakedown. With as much confidence as she could fake, she replied, "I don't know what you're talking about. I'm a sixty-five-year-old single woman in dire need of heart surgery. I have no time for things like spying on the government."

Two buildings up there was a ruckus, and she turned to see a military man pull a couple, Mr. and Mrs. Soyer, from their home. In their late forties, they were nice people that kept to themselves and had an eighteen-year-old daughter, Frankie.

"You too! Out!" another man yelled from inside the Soyer's apartment as Frankie spilled out onto the street. From Corinna's vantage point, it looked as though the girl had blood on her face and was crying.

Her father attempted to help her, breaking free from the first soldier's grip, rushing to Frankie. The soldier raised his Defender and shot the man in the back of his head, instantly killing him. He landed with a thud beside his now screaming daughter who leapt on top of his lifeless corpse, hugging him.

Frankie's mother went limp and was quickly thrown into the back of the armored transport, nearly identical to the *Big Boy* up on Moon 002. Frankie was quickly dragged to the back of the same vehicle along with what looked like several other individuals.

Corinna looked on in horror as the dead body of Leonard Soyer was pulled from the sidewalk, leaving a pool of blood behind, and thrown into the back of the vehicle. Screams sounded from the vehicle until the door slammed shut and an eerie silence fell over the street. She was sure others had seen what had just transpired close to her home.

Compose yourself, keep it together, Corinna. Do it for your daughter. "Well, sir, I have nothing to hide. Like I said, I am rather ill."

"Yes, you told me that already. I'm going to pull up your voting history," the man responded.

Thinking quickly, Corinna replied as calmly as she could, "Oh, no need. Don't waste your time on an old lady like me. Did I mention my daughter Sonia Bonnel? She's a doctor's assistant. She works for the AMO up on Mining Complex..."

She was cut off by the shorter military man, "Excuse me, did you say she's an employee of the Alnorix Mining Organization and is currently stationed at one of the mining complexes?"

"Yes, sir. That is correct. She's been up there for, oh my, over three years now. It will pay for my heart surgery, you see. I'm very proud of her," Corinna replied.

The soldiers looked at each other before the shorter one said, "Come on, let's go. We've bagged enough citizens for tonight. Plus, her girl works for AMO. That counts for something, I suppose."

Nodding, the taller and more intimidating military man looked at Corinna, his eyes filled with hate. She could tell he enjoyed this. Rounding up innocent people for murder. Quite literally, for pleasure and enjoyment.

"Today's your lucky day, ma'am. If we're ever called to do another sweep of this block, I'll be running a voting history on you. I don't give a shit how old or sick you are. If you're not for Levon Gonidec, you're against him. And if you're against him, you're against Troria. That makes you a traitor and worse, a terrorist. You've been warned. Good night, ma'am."

She managed a smile and closed the door, leaning against it and breathing heavy. She heard the soldiers outside that had just murdered Leonard laughing and calling out to the others down the street as they climbed into their own armored transport. "Nice shot, you dropped that shitbag like a rock!"

The other soldier laughed and replied menacingly, "When will these brainless morons learn, don't run! Hell, I think those clones up there are smarter than most of the Trorian population. Anyway, wait till you see what I do to the daughter. You see the rack on that fine piece of..."

The front of the armored vehicles doors slammed shut.

Corinna's bottom lip trembled. Burying her hands in her face, she wept. Wept for Leonard Soyer, his soon-to-be-murdered widow Judith, and Frankie, the young woman she had watched grow up on her street. She knew the horrors that awaited the young woman back inside Levon Gonidec's fortress overlooking the city. Her mind went to her own daughter and she shuddered.

Please, Sonia, please take care of yourself and stay far, far away from Troria.

CHAPTER 22

DOWN INTO THE ABYSS

Michael and Sonia stood close to each other on the rim of the crater looking out at what had been the dumping ground of countless clones, sentenced to death for the most minor of infractions. A badly injured foot, a broken arm that would take too long to heal. A bad cloning job that had resulted in a birth defect. And, of course, when their time was up. This was their final resting place, their ashes destined to swirl about Moon 002 for all eternity.

The triangular ship's landing gear extended as it came to rest on top of the black ashen covered landscape and after a minute, the rear boosters powered down. Inside the *Deimos*, Commander Nic Mohr and Pilot 33 peered out the front viewscreen at the two figures on top of the crater's entrance.

"What do you think? Is that Petrino and the girl?" Pilot 33 asked.

"Dr. Petrino, this is Commander Nic Mohr, come in."

The tall figure in the mining suit with a Defender II slung over his shoulder looked at the person standing beside him, then pointed to his helmet, shook his head, and raised both arms.

"I'm not detecting any com link malfunction, sir. However, that doesn't mean there isn't some other issue I am unable to detect considering the high amount of damage across the entire mining complex," Pilot 33 said.

"You think I don't know that?" Mohr shot back impatiently, glancing over at his android pilot.

"How would you like to proceed, sir? I am unable to get a facial lock unless the individuals remove their helmets."

"Shit! That could be anybody. Or it could be Petrino and the girl. Olivia, so I'm told," Mohr answered, continuing to stare out at the figures in front of them.

The com clicked on. "Hello, this is Olivia. Dr. Petrino's com is acting up. Please help us! The mining complex is compromised, we need out of here!" Sonia said, glancing over at Michael.

Come on, please buy it, please buy it! Michael thought as he continued to stare at the closed hatch on the sleek, triangular ship in front of them.

There was a hiss and a hatch underneath the ship near the landing gear slid open and downward, revealing a set of stairs that led into the ship's inner hull. Two figures descended holding weapons. The shorter, heavier-set individual carried what appeared to be a Defender I while the taller man, not wearing a helmet, carried a Defender II. Both of their spacesuits appeared to be of significantly higher quality than those worn on Moon 002.

Dressed in white with an upgraded oxygen tank attached to a sleek helmet, the heavier man moved past the tall one, walking toward who hoped was Dr. Petrino and Olivia. Both men had their weapons raised.

"Don't either of you move. Petrino, if that's who you are, lay your weapon on the ground until I can get a better look at you up close. Nod if you can understand me," Mohr said cautiously.

Michael nodded and lowered his Defender II to the ground and glanced over at Sonia, whose Defender I was latched onto the rear of her mining suit, hidden from the advancing men. Sonia kept her hands raised but was ready to take hold of her gun when things went south, which, she figured, was about to happen in seconds.

"Now, let's get a look at you," Commander Mohr said as he reached Michael.

The *Big Boy's* headlights clicked on, their bright lights illuminating the area and the engine roaring to life. Commander Mohr and Pilot 33 turned their surprised attention to the vehicle behind Michael and Sonia, which was all the time Sonia needed to reach behind her and draw her Defender I at the man closest to her, Pilot 33.

"Drop your weapons, now. Android included," Sonia said firmly.

"What the..." Commander Mohr shouted defiantly.

Michael swooped down and grabbed his Defender II off the ground and brought it up to eye level, but not before commander Mohr began firing, narrowly missing Michael's head as laser fire erupted around him into the dirt below.

Sonia saw Pilot 33 raise his gun, pointing it at her. She didn't hesitate, pulling the trigger. The blast hit the android, connecting with the outstretched hand holding the weapon, causing it to explode at the close-range laser fire. He dropped to the ground, sparks shooting from the open wrist cavity where his robotic hand had been.

Commander Mohr continued shooting wildly at Michael then over toward Sonia, laser fire zigzagging back and forth inside the crater.

"What the hell is this? Who the hell are you people!?" Mohr shouted angrily, continuing to shoot.

The android, whose weapon was destroyed by Sonia's laser fire, continued to pursue her. She continued blasting, hitting him in the chest and then knee which finally dropped him. Unable to run, the android came to a stop and, with its built-in self-preservation feature, shut down completely until repairs to its circuitry could be made.

Mohr wasn't able to get back to the *Deimos*. It was now two against one and he was losing. The *Big Boy* sat idling with its lights on and he ran toward it in hopes of making it inside, not knowing who, if anyone, occupied it.

He was nearing the driver's side door when it abruptly opened, smashing him in the face and knocking him to the ground. The extra few seconds was all it took for Michael and

Sonia to arrive, guns aimed. Mohr looked up at Elise Bennet glaring down at him.

"You," he spat inside his helmet, attempting to reach for his Defender I as two guns entered his line of sight. Michael and Sonia stood over him, fingers on their triggers.

"Don't," Michael said coldly, kicking his weapon out of reach.

Commander Mohr sighed and resigned to his capture.

Sonia quickly jumped into the *Big Boy* following Mohr's capture and surrender. He was hoisted up and held at gunpoint by Michael while she rummaged through the rear compartment of the vehicle to retrieve restraints to tie his hands.

"How did you get up there?" she asked, seeing Elise had moved to the front seat.

Elise, quite woozy, responded, "Clone Stimulants. I'm feeling a bit better now."

"Oh shit. Elise, that's not good," Sonia responded gravely, looking at her commanding officer in the eye.

Holding her gaze, she responded, "Sonia, listen to me. I don't know if I'm getting out of this."

The words shook her to her core. What if Elise, her commanding officer and superior, didn't pull through this? Then what? *Be brave, Sonia. You've come this far.* Shaking her head, Sonia replied, "Elise, come on, you will pull through this! The android, we can use it!"

She had learned in medical school that the androids of Troria had numerous programs built into their hard drives, one of which was that of a battlefield medic, able to stitch up mortally wounded soldiers.

"Don't die on me, Elise. Olivia, keep her awake," Sonia said, exiting out of the rear of the *Big Boy's* hatch.

"Hurry back, Sonia!" Olivia shouted back as the hatch closed.

Be strong, Sonia! If not you, then who? Sonia ran over to where commander Mohr stood silently, glaring at Michael who still had his Defender II trained on him. "You've got two options. One, you help take your wounded android over to our moon rover and load him into the back with Michael's help."

"And?" he responded angrily.

"Two, I tie your hands behind your back, we take your ship and leave you here. Not sure if your oxygen will last until the last Kernadium transport shuttle gets here. Maybe it will, maybe it won't," she shot back.

"Fuck you, lady," he mumbled into his com.

"Option two it is," Sonia said stoically as she walked over to him with the metal restraints, surprised at the ease with which she was able to stand up to one of Gonidec and AMO's goons.

She glanced at Michael and could see inside his helmet he was grinning at how she was not intimidated by the large, brutish man who had, minutes earlier, tried to kill them both.

"Wait, wait! Okay? Wait, damnit!" Commander Mohr responded with a hint of resignation in his voice, seeing how limited his options were. He sighed then nodded and looked over to the damaged android laying in the dirt. "Lead the way, whoever you actually are."

"The name's Michael Astier. A clone. Sentenced to death a year from now. Let's go," he said grimly, turning and walking toward the android.

Commander Mohr stared at the man, then followed after him with Sonia directly behind, her gun aimed at his back.

Approaching Pilot 33, Michael slung his Defender II over his shoulder before warning, "No funny games. All of us are out of time. You're going to help us out of here or I'll be happy to oblige Sonia's first option, understand?"

"Sure. Whatever. You won't get away with this, you know," the commander said cynically.

"And neither will you," Sonia said from behind. "Now, pick up the android by the legs, we need to get him to Elise."

Both men picked up Pilot 33 and slowly began carrying him over to the *Big Boy.*

"Why are we doing this? Why this waste of time and where the hell is Dr. Petrino?" Mohr shot out as he hefted up the heavy android.

"He's dead. I shot him," Michael stated, lifting the other end of the android.

"And this android here is going to help us fix up Elise, who was stabbed by your illustrious doctor earlier," Sonia added.

"Hmm, so the good doctor is with us no more. Well, that's tragic now, isn't it? My leader, and yours, for that matter, will be most interested in this turn of events. Yes, Mr. Gonidec will certainly want to hear all about it. The girl? What of her?" Mohr responded curiously without looking at either of his two captors.

"Just help Michael with the android!" Sonia shot back.

The clone horde that had assimilated into one large being, now mixed with Dr. Petrino's DNA, had fallen into the large chasm opened on the moon's surface by the crumbling mining buildings and Poule plants.

It had plummeted nearly a mile below the moon's crust until slamming against a large, jagged stone inside the great void, impaling it through its side. Howling in anger, the green Rot-covered entity flailed and struggled to free itself. Large quantities of thick green slime oozed out onto the sharp rock it was impaled onto.

Buzzing sounds emanated from far below. Deep within this moon, other creatures lived, tunneling through the hard silicate minerals with sharp pincers. These beings had resided deep in the moon's core for millions of years. For some time now, they sensed their home world being depleted far above and burrowed deeper into the core. Now that core was exposed.

Nearly one hundred miles farther below, a glowing ball of heat shot fire upwards through the split caused by the destruction of Mining Complex VI. Strange creatures zipped back and forth angrily in the opened split that had invaded their home.

The Rot mutation pulled itself off of the sharp rock it was impaled on and though badly injured by the fall, began slowly climbing up the side of the rocky cliffside to the top. The creature's face had changed to resemble an abomination of Dr. Petrino and numerous unnamed dead clones, constantly changing its facial features but always scowling. Filled with rage.

It peered down at the buzzing insects much farther beneath the moon's surface and wasn't sure what these beings were capable of. Not yet. As it climbed, it noticed the buzzing below it growing louder and more intense. Whatever was down there was also making their way up to the surface.

The Rot-infested creature extended its right arm toward the top of the chasm, its veins and tendons stretching, snapping, and pulling from its deformed bones and making it able to grab hold of the edge of the open gap that would lead it top side. Green Rot oozed out of the exposed veins. The creature roared in pain and anger.

Then it pulled itself up to the dusty surface.

Commander Mohr and Michael carefully lifted the disabled android into the back of the *Big Boy* after Sonia opened the hatch.

"Get in, now," Michael ordered, pointing inside the moon rover.

Glaring back at him, Commander Mohr entered, sliding in to make room for him and Sonia, both of their guns still trained on him.

Sonia quickly moved forward, saying, "Raise your left hand."

"What? Why the hell would I want," he began.

Sonia's Defender I inched forward slowly, clicking against the glass on his helmet, the barrel looking him squarely in the eye.

Sighing, he raised his left arm as Sonia took the metal restraint, clicking it to his wrist, and connected it to a steel ring above him. He wasn't going anywhere.

Michael grabbed his helmet and took it off, setting it beside him, then looked over at Sonia and nodded.

"Now, you're going to help us get this android back up and running and access its medical records. He's going to perform a quick and dirty surgery, got it?" Sonia said firmly, glaring at him.

"On who? What is this?" he shot back.

Elise slowly turned in her seat to meet his eyes.

"On me, that's who. You aren't getting rid of me that easy. Not yet at least. Your stooge is dead, and we've got his video recorder," Elise answered, still in pain but considerably less now that the Clone Stimulants were coursing through her body.

Mohr was stunned that Elise Bennet was sitting in the same vehicle as he was. He hated this traitor. This spy. This *resistance fighter.*

"You…" he hissed.

She didn't reply, trying to save what little energy she had left.

He looked over to see another figure in the vehicle with them as well. She turned to look at him and he smirked. "You look just like her."

"Thanks to your doctor, she is me," Elise said angrily. She turned to the girl who looked back at her and smiled, adding, "You're special, Olivia. And we're going to get you out of here, trust me on that."

"Time to revive the android. What do you call him?" Sonia said, taking charge.

Mohr looked over at her, wanting to tell her to figure it out on her own but thought better of it. Sonia thus far appeared to be someone who took no shit. He respected that.

"He goes by Pilot 33," Mohr mumbled.

"Turn Pilot 33 back on," Sonia ordered.

Commander Mohr leaned forward with his free hand and pulled the skin on the back of Pilot 33's neck back, revealing a series of wires and circuitry as well as several small buttons. He pushed the top button and reset the android.

A low hum emanated throughout the cabin of the *Big Boy* as the android began to reboot its system, its humanoid eyes coming back to life and opening.

CHAPTER 23

BATTLEFIELD SURGERY

"Pilot 33 returning to active duty. Please select specific service needed," the android said in a garbled tone due to its damaged internal voice replication processor.

"Looks like his voice replication unit is damaged from the shots he took from your Defender there, Sonia. That's on you," Mohr said snidely.

"His voice doesn't matter to any of us. His medical skills do. Access his battlefield medic program," Sonia shot back then glanced over at Michael who was looking down at the android with a furrowed brow. "What are you thinking, Michael?"

"I'm thinking...he's no more or less real than I am. Than Olivia is." He looked up at Olivia then to Sonia with confused eyes.

"Look," Mohr said, "I don't care one way or another about you damn clones. You wouldn't even exist without our technology! So, you gonna stare at each other or are we going to finish this? I'm sick of this shi—"

He was cut off by a solid right-hand fist connecting with his jaw. Sonia shook her fist after the punch, responding almost glibly, "They're more human than you'll ever be, *commander.*"

Elise coughed then grinned in the front seat. "Impressive, Sonia."

"I didn't think I had it in me, but this guy seems to be bringing out the worst in me—in an already shit situation," Sonia replied coldly.

Mohr rubbed his chin and, shaking his head, returned to Pilot 33's access hub on his opened neck.

After a series of buttons were pushed, the android said once more in a garbled tone, "Battlefield medic selected and activated. How may I be of help, Commander Mohr? Good to see you again, sir."

"Yeah, yeah. So, who needs the medic?" Mohr asked gruffly.

"Elise does, and your android is going to help," Sonia replied, glaring at Mohr.

"What happened to her?"

"She was stabbed by your doctor," Sonia replied coldly. She expected a snarky comeback from the commander, but none came. Mohr remained quiet, sealing up the back of Pilot 33's neck.

The android sat up, inspecting its missing hand, then the hole in its chest and finally the blast it had taken to its left kneecap. "I believe you did this, did you not?" it said calmly, looking over at Sonia.

"You were coming after me. I had no choice. And now you have no choice. We need you to perform surgery on one of our own," Sonia retorted.

The part of the android's programming that mimicked human emotion had been heavily damaged with the laser blast to his chest. He now moved much more robotically, swiveling his head sharply from Sonia to Mohr then scanning the rest of the passengers inside the *Big Boy*.

"Injury detected. Laceration of the abdomen. Small puncture wound located in liver. Medical assistance needed from heavy blood loss. Need to perform surgery. Need blood donor. Awaiting further commands." Pilot 33 fell silent.

"Do it, now," Sonia came back.

"Elise, we need to get you back here," Michael called out but was met with silence.

"Her eyes are closed again!" Olivia said frantically, looking back from the front seat.

"Screw it, I'll get her," Michael said, reaching over the seat in a crouched position.

"Awaiting further commands," repeated Pilot 33.

Michael gently lifted the unconscious Elise back to the rear of the *Big Boy* then laid her down in front of the android, lifting her blood-soaked shirt.

"She's already got meds in her. Do what needs to be done," he said, looking at Pilot 33.

He glanced over at Mohr who grimaced at the bloody mess.

Pilot 33 shifted its gaze down to its missing hand, where exposed wires and gears leaked trickles of brown greasy liquid from wounds inflicted earlier. Eventually, without repairs, it would cease to function properly. Already its systems were heavily compromised.

The android turned its head toward the bleeding woman in front of it then up to both Sonia and Michael before speaking. "I have one functional appendage. I will attempt to perform what is required to save this woman's life. Due to my heavily damaged internal processing system, I cannot do a full scan of this woman's body to see the full extent of her wounds. However, I can perform a basic sealant on the wound. She will need blood from a suitable donor. Are there any present at this time that are able to assist?"

"I'll do it. She has my blood and I have hers," Olivia said, raising her hand slightly while sitting in between Michael and Sonia now.

Sonia smiled at her. "Brave girl, just like your mother. Thank you, Olivia. Get to it then," she said to the android.

With its one functioning hand, it began to work on Elise. The fingers on its working hand retracted, replaced by surgical tools of various shapes and sizes.

"She will feel discomfort," Pilot 33 stated. Sonia nodded and it began its task. "I will need someone to hold the wound open. My other hand would have served this task, but it has been removed."

Setting his Defender II beside him, Michael leaned forward and placed both of his hands on the wound then pulled it apart as fresh blood rushed forward.

Elise remained unconscious from the heavy loss of blood, near death and not feeling the immense pain shooting through her body.

Pilot 33 bent over her and inserted a surgical tool into the open wound. As it worked, small amounts of water shot out of the center of its wrist, washing away the steady flow of blood from the deep cut.

A dull whirring sound began, from inside Elise's wound.

"What's happening?" Michael asked.

"He's sealing her liver up from the inside," Sonia responded. "I've seen this type of work before. It's quick and dirty but much more effective than the Surface Sealer we used back in my apartment. Time isn't on our side, but this is her last, best, and only chance."

"That is accurate, Sonia Bonnel. It is imperative this human receives blood immediately following the surgical procedure," the android responded in its heavily damaged robotic voice that was getting more and more indecipherable.

Mohr looked on in silence as Pilot 33 continued with the operation. When the worst of it seemed to be over, he cleared his throat and spoke. "So, what happens next?"

"Is there a way to reverse the one-year life span on clones?" Michael asked, shooting a glance at Mohr.

Mohr chuckled before responding, "You'd like that wouldn't you?"

Sonia didn't respond to his bait, she simply pointed her Defender once more at his head while remaining stone-faced.

"Fine. Fine. Yes, there is life extensions for our best clones. The one-year limiting lifespans are baked into your DNA but it can be overwritten and removed if need be. You essentially have human parts through and through. A procedure back on Troria can eliminate the one-year limit. Dr. Petrino was able to do it, she's proof, but it sounds like he's no longer among the living, is he?"

"Then we finish up with Elise, get her aboard your ship, and head back to Troria," Sonia replied.

"Fat chance. You really think you'll be granted access back home after all of this? None of you were supposed to make it off this rock in the first place. They'll shoot us down—me included—if they detect more than just my android and me aboard. The clone girl too, I suppose."

"Her name is Olivia, and they'll get her over my dead body. What about Railara? We could go there. I bet they'd love to get their hands on that video recorder, and you as well," Sonia said icily as she leaned forward toward Mohr.

Mohr squinted his hate-filled eyes at her. "Your dead body can certainly be arranged. AMO will not idly stand by while you steal their property. They're in the business of making a profit. You've succeeded in destroying most of Mining Complex VI and taken me hostage. So, you're going to have a whole lot of people from my government and this facility that you really don't want on your bad side hunting you and the girl down. She is, after all, just manufactured property. Like you, Michael."

Do not take this man's taunts. Show restraint in front of Sonia and Olivia. Be the bigger man. Leaning forward, Michael spoke in a tone just above a whisper, "I may be man-made, but I am the property of no man, understood?"

Mohr stared back at him, unsure how to respond. Michael was a big clone. Muscular and quite obviously, strong. Mohr had never in his life been spoken to like this from a clone and it stung even more than Sonia's punch to the face earlier.

Sonia looked over at Michael who shot her a quick glance. At that moment, she utterly respected the man, not clone. Cool and calm but no push-over. Even in this nearly unwinnable situation, she found his confidence and his continued kindness and selflessness toward her, Elise, and Olivia incredibly…attractive.

"Your ship's got a tracking system that can be turned off. I know those ships, so wherever we go, we can do so quietly and undetected," Sonia came back defiantly.

Hearing this, Mohr, sat back and looked away, falling silent.

"Please remove your hands from her wound, Michael Astier. I am about to seal up the flesh wound," Pilot 33 said, his monotone, robotic voice breaking the sudden silence.

Michael did as he was told. Elise was still unconscious as a steady trickle of water from the android continued to wash away the blood from her wound.

"Why do you do these things? Why do you hurt people like this?" Olivia asked in her eleven-year-old soft voice, looking sadly over at Mohr, her green eyes piercing his dark and anger-filled eyes.

They all looked over at her, the clone that shouldn't be. A carbon copy of Elise Bennet that had survived so much in less than a day.

"Well?" Sonia said, staring daggers into him.

Mohr shrugged. "Honestly? For the Marks. This is a huge business. And big business requires strong leadership. Which is what we have on Troria."

"It's all about Marks and power. Forget human decency. Forget empathy, right?" Sonia retorted.

"Hey, I don't make the rules, lady. I just follow them," Mohr replied glibly.

"Famous last words there," Sonia retorted.

They all fell silent once more as Pilot 33 finished sealing up Elise's cut and prepared for the blood transfusion.

The Rot-infected creature climbed out of the large split in the ground that led nearly all the way down to Moon 002's core. It pulled itself up, tendons and veins pulling back into and around its exposed organs, green liquid Rot working its way around the creature's body and giving it life. Or, the imitation of life. Its one goal was to assimilate and grow further.

It looked at its surroundings. The buildings were all decimated, except for one, the Kernadium storage building. A small part of the creature that had once been Dr. Anthony Petrino remembered it. The *Big Boy* had been inside, he had piloted the moon rover to retrieve the girl, the clone of Elise he had created for himself.

Dr. Petrino, its latest assimilation, took over and held sway on the decisions the creature made. The small part of Petrino that shared the monster's consciousness with the other clones recalled an attempt to leave this planet, near the place where the used-up clones were destroyed. That was where the man that had killed him had gone. *Him and the girl. And that bitch woman!*

All of them had done Petrino wrong. He had been treated unfairly, unjustly. They had talked about him, made fun of him, and ultimately, intended to kill him and take the girl. *Yes!* That's what they were doing. Taking the blond girl away. She belonged to it. It would assimilate her and they would be together forever, their minds linked. The creator and its offspring.

It would dispose of the rest of them. Rip their limbs from their bodies. *They will not make it off this planet. I will make sure of that.*

It began making its way to the burn pit where so many of its clone brethren had been taken and destroyed through the years. The pit's usefulness wasn't over just yet.

CHAPTER 24

PETRINO RETURNS

Back inside the *Big Boy*, the surgery was finished. Now, Elise needed blood. She had lost far too much since being stabbed in the Command Center earlier.

"The surgery is complete, although I cannot guarantee her survival. She has lost too much blood," Pilot 33 announced.

"How long will it take? We have a ship sitting here and the longer we wait, the better the chances we'll run into more problems," Sonia said.

"I can complete the transfusion quickly. It must be done," Pilot 33 responded with its significantly damaged vocal processor.

Michael and Sonia looked over at Olivia who once more signaled she was willing.

Putting his hand on her shoulder, Michael said calmly, "You ready? This isn't going to take long."

Olivia nodded and Pilot 33 raised his left hand. Out of his index and middle fingers now extended needles that would perform the procedure. Olivia lay down beside the still unconscious Elise. A small spray of water from Pilot 33 cleaned the arms of both and then the needles were inserted and blood began syphoning from Olivia and directly into Elise.

Olivia grimaced at the sharp prick of pain. Sonia put her hand on top of the girl's head. The human touch helped calm her down, slightly.

Everyone in the back of the *Big Boy* watched in silence until Mohr broke it, sharply. "So, this plan of yours. Steal my ship, pilot it to Railara and hand over classified video that belongs to the Trorian government as well as the AMO. You realize this is punishable by death, right?"

"Yeah. Pretty much, I suppose we aren't going back to Troria," Sonia replied glibly, staring on at the makeshift blood transfusion taking place.

"And who are you going to get to pilot that ship out there? Because I seriously doubt Elise will be in any shape. You? I'm pretty sure you can't fly that thing," Mohr said, looking at Sonia.

"I'm going to fly it," Michael replied firmly as he shot a glance over at Mohr who was stewing in anger. "Hopefully with the help of this android here. If not, I'll figure it out on my own. My implant gave me some pretty detailed flight training. So, I guess thanks are in order to AMO, right?"

Mohr remained silent at this, realizing it would more than likely succeed, much to his dismay.

"If I were you, *Nicholas*, I'd be wondering about how I'm going to survive here for another day with no oxygen before the last transport comes to collect its precious fuel. Have you thought of that?" Sonia said.

"Blood transfusion complete," Pilot 33 stated, breaking the growing tension inside the cabin of the *Big Boy.*

The chasm close to the mining facility had widened, breaching moon's core and causing molten lava to bubble upwards. With it, the creatures that had lived deep under the planet's crust also moved up toward the surface. Their bodies the size of a large human being, with four separate wings continually in motion on their thick backs, they relied on the sparse plants of Moon 002 and sensed their food source drying up.

Ranging in brightness, all of them had a metallic silver and black outer shell, with long pointed stingers sticking out past their backsides and heads slightly triangular in shape. They had no visible facial features other than a thin line that, when opened, revealed several rows of sharp and powerful teeth used to tunnel their way through the rocky interior of the moon. Six thin, black feelers on their underside were used to crawl through the tunnels they made, look for food, and sense vibrations under the rocky soil.

These insectoids were almost robotic in how they moved and acted, making sudden and quick jerking motions as they scuttled about through their tunnels deep underground. But they were very much a living, breathing species, one that now sensed imminent danger inside and above the place they called home.

The hive's buzzing grew louder and more intense as they neared the opened surface created by the mining facility's destruction.

Olivia sat up, rubbed her arm, and said cheerily, "Nothing to it!"

"Brave girl," Sonia responded with a smile. The girl showed bravery and a willingness to do what was needed to survive, much like her mother, whose life she had just saved, if only temporarily.

"We're leaving this place, and we're going in that ship," Michael said matter-of-factly, making sure to look over at Mohr.

"Pilot 33, are you able to help pilot the ship?" Sonia asked.

"Yes, even missing one appendage, I am still able to perform piloting duties aboard the *Deimos* with the help of another trained pilot, if one is present," the android replied.

"*Deimos*. Got it, let's go," Michael said, then added, "Sonia, don't let our guest try anything funny."

Stone-faced as she stared at Mohr, Sonia replied back, "He won't."

Mohr didn't reply but kept his face down, avoiding eye contact, lost in his own thoughts as to what his next move might be.

Michael climbed back into the driver's seat. He fired up the *Big Boy* and pushed forward toward the *Deimos.* Once close enough, he backed up until the tail end of the *Big Boy* lined up to the opened hull of the *Deimos* and hit the brakes.

"Everyone, put on your helmets. It's time to move!" Michael ordered as he grabbed his own mining mask.

Sonia helped pull Elise's suit on. She was starting to come to, shaking her head with her eyes beginning to flutter open. Looking over at Olivia, she said politely but urgently, "Come on, honey, time to go."

Olivia nodded and got her helmet, clicking it into place.

"What about me? You just going to leave me here?" Mohr retorted angerly.

Sonia glared at him then tossed his helmet over. He caught it with his free hand and clicked it into place.

Suddenly, the top of the *Big Boy's* roof shook violently as the Petrino clone mutation leapt on top of it. The thick, tempered glass instantly shattered on all sides from the devastating impact. It opened its wide mouth and bellowed loudly, partly yearning for the warm-blooded beings inside, partly seeking revenge and destruction. Combined, they made a nearly indestructible being.

It jumped off of the *Big Boy's* hood, landing beside it with a heavy thud onto the charred ashes of its countless murdered brothers. It lowered its head, peering into smashed hull of the moon rover.

Inside the heavily damaged vehicle, the stunned occupants attempted to get their bearings.

"What's going on?" Elise said shakily through her helmet's com system.

"It's that thing that busted out of the clones' living quarters!" Sonia yelled, looking out at the huge face beside the *Big Boy*, peering in at them. Sonia's eyes widened in horror at what looked like the face of one recently deceased Anthony Petrino.

"We've got to keep that thing away from the *Deimos!*" Michael yelled.

Olivia grabbed hold of Elise, trying to help her up, "Elise we have to go!"

Sonia, in a panic, looked over at Pilot 33, its head now caved in. The android had the misfortune of being positioned in the very back of the *Big Boy*, directly below where the mutation had landed, smashing the roof down and destroying the android. Sparks fizzled from its smashed-in head. Humanoid eyes hung from exposed metal sockets. Brown oil-based liquid was oozing out of numerous openings and destroyed areas of the flattened head.

"The android is gone!" Sonia exclaimed, staring at the ghastly sight of Pilot 33's interior circuitry.

In the chaos, none of them realized Mohr's restraint had disconnected from the roof of the *Big Boy.*

The nearly twelve-foot-tall clone mutation opened its wide mouth and roared as it peered in at the occupants of the smashed rover. It raised its fists and brought them both down on top of the *Big Boy*, its massive arms pulsating with the Rot and DNA of numerous clone miners.

The interior of the vehicle shook violently at the impact to the already crushed roof. The rear of the moon rover buckled under the pressure and busted open. "We've got to get out of here!" Sonia yelled.

Olivia helped a groggy Elise into an upright position while Michael slammed the vehicle into drive and pushed forward. Gears ground and smoke poured out from underneath the hood. The *Big Boy* was nearly to the Deimos when the clone mutation, chasing after them, brought its fists down on the hood, smashing the engine.

The moon rover stalled in its final resting place, no longer able to go any farther, fire and smoke wafting out from under the hood.

Mohr made his move, leaping over and onto the distracted Sonia, swinging his fist with the flailing restraint still attached. The metal connected with her chest and knocked the wind out of her, sending her backwards and smashing into the interior side of the now dead *Big Boy.*

In her surprise at Mohr's attack, she dropped her Defender onto the floor which he quickly scooped up and lunged out toward Olivia, grabbing her by the wrist. "You're coming with me!" he shouted and harshly pulled her out of the *Big Boy* with him.

Elise grabbed at his leg, but he was faster than she was, easily slipping away. Michael, meanwhile, didn't have a clean shot from the driver's seat.

Sonia struggled to get her breath back, staring out in horror at Mohr, now outside the vehicle, dragging a screaming Olivia with him toward the waiting *Deimos*.

Michael's door was stuck from the blow to the hood of the *Big Boy*, so he quickly climbed over the seat, scrambling to the rear exit. Elise, crawling on hands and knees, also attempted to make her way out of the destroyed vehicle.

He grabbed her arm, slung it over his neck and pulled her forward. Sonia exited from the rear as she regained her breathing.

"Come on, both of you, before he makes it to his ship!" Michael yelled in his com.

The creature brought both fists down over and over onto the nearly crushed vehicle as Michael, Sonia, and Elise spilled out of it onto the rocky surface of the moon. With a few more hard blows, it flattened to its wheelbase.

Michael raised his Defender II at the creature and, clicking over to the blow torch option, unleashed a wave of flames at the monstrosity before him.

Sonia grabbed Elise, pulling her up as both headed toward the *Deimos* and the fleeing Mohr. Olivia fought back stubbornly against the much larger man, digging her feet into the rocky ground beneath and pulling at his hand that tightly grasped hold of her small arm.

Michael's fire sent the Petrino-clone mutation reeling back slightly but due to its massive size did very little damage. Quickly, Michael changed his tactic when he noticed a large pool of liquid under the *Big Boy*. He repositioned his Defender II, aiming the fire at the rear of the *Big Boy*, toward the leaking Kernadium.

The *Big Boy* exploded, shooting up into the air and slamming into the creature standing over it, igniting it immediately into a massive wall of flames. It screamed in pain and anger as it flailed its burning arms, causing the fire to spread faster.

The explosion knocked everyone forward to the ground, including Mohr and Olivia just outside the entrance to the *Deimos*. Significantly lighter and more agile than the heavyset Mohr, Olivia leapt up, seeing her opportunity, and bolted away, back toward her companions roughly fifty feet away from her.

"Get back here, you little bitch!" Mohr yelled, bringing the Defender up to eye level as he stood to his feet. He pulled the trigger but didn't have a clear shot. The laser fire missing her head by several inches.

Michael raised his Defender II and aimed, then stopped in his tracks, staring upwards into the sky as Mohr was snatched and lifted by a large, flying silver and black insectoid creature. All six of the sharp pincers on its underside clung to the flailing man tightly as it launched upwards, its four wings buzzing at such fast speeds as to make them nearly invisible to the naked eye. The thin mouth on the front of its triangular head opened and sharp, pointed rows of teeth bit down onto the head of a screaming Mohr as he blindly fired his Defender into the air.

The laser fire lit up the smoke-filled sky as dozens of the bugs, roughly six feet in length and over three feet wide, zigzagged in circles around the burn pit. Several flew toward the laser fire, clamping onto Mohr's exposed arms, and in one quick motion, pulled the man apart, devouring him completely in several large bites.

The insectoids flew away, wings buzzing loudly as they zipped upwards. Through the smoke, the numerous flying bugs continued to swarm, now much higher around the burn pit, the explosion making them even more agitated.

The Petrino clone mutation was fully engulfed in flames now, screaming as green Rot liquid caught fire inside its exposed veins, bursting outward. Streams of fire exploded from the giant, landing near the survivors.

Michael shouted, "Get inside that ship, now!"

The traces of Kernadium that pumped through the clone mutation's veins ignited and the green monstrosity began turning orange and red, pulsating as the fire spread inside its organs.

Near the front of the ship, several shiny silver and black insectoids swooped down in an attempt to snatch the fleeing survivors, much like they had Mohr a minute earlier.

One narrowly missed Olivia who screamed as it swooshed by her, nearly grazing her back as she leapt out of the way.

Sonia looked over at Olivia while still holding onto Elise as one of the bugs pincers grabbed both of the women and began pulling them into the sky. They had barely made it off the ground when the insectoid's head exploded from a precision shot from Michael's Defender II, dropping them to the ground, the bug landing beside them.

"Come on, run!" Elise said, struggling to her to her feet first, pulling up a stunned Sonia whose head had landed hard on the rocky ground below.

"My oxygen tank is busted!" Sonia said groggily. "I can't breathe!"

Elise guided Sonia as quickly as she could to the Deimos while bugs continued to swell and zig zag above them.

The four survivors climbed into the *Deimos*, immediately closing the hatch once they were all aboard. Michael, finding two seats directly in front of the viewscreen, immediately sat down and ordered, "Find a seat and strap in, we've got to leave now!"

Sonia gasped for air as she took her helmet off, putting her hands to her throat trying to find oxygen that wasn't there.

"Michael! Find the cabin pressurization switch, now!" Elise called out.

Looking over the instrument panel, Michael tried to remain calm. He needed to make some educated guesses here, based on what information had been implanted in his brain about space travel.

"Got it!" he shouted and hit a small switch to his right aptly marked *oxygen pressurization*.

A whoosh of air began circulating through the Deimos. Sonia gulped for the much-needed air, drinking it in. She slumped over, breathing heavily, then put her hand to the back of her head. When she pulled it away several small drops of blood smeared her fingers.

"I'm feeling lightheaded from the lack of oxygen and that hit to my head, I might pass out here," Sonia said woozily.

"Hang in there, Sonia, I'll get something to bandage up your head," Elise replied, herself weak and feeling the pain of the surgery and her fall to the rocky surface minutes earlier, even with the drugs still in her system.

"I was hit hard on the head too, by the mean doctor, and I'm alright now. You will be too!" Olivia tried to sound reassuring.

Sonia smiled through the pain at her friends' attempt to help.

"Brace yourselves, that creature out there is going to explode!" Michael shouted, removing his helmet as well.

Outside, the Petrino clone mutation had turned dark red and expanded, Rot dripping from its engulfed body, flames shooting out in every direction. It tried to scream but only a dull moan escaped its gaping mouth. It was dying and felt its end coming soon.

While chaos raged on Moon 002, back on Troria, Levon Gonidec wasted no time in his decision to go to war with virtually all of the planets in quadrant 8304. His generals were busy preparing their massive fleet of battleships, known as *Paladine Fighters*, small, oval-shaped ships with a cockpit that sat above the dark-grey saucer. Well equipped with four heavy laser disintegrators, they were fast and deadly.

The first wave would be led by a host of larger bomber ships similar in shape and size to their smaller counterparts, simply known as *Paladine Bombers*. Following these would be a host of the smaller *Paladine Fighters*. The goal was to surprise and overwhelm the enemy.

Slow and steady would most certainly not win the race in this instance, Gonidec had warned his top inner circle in the preparation of the war. Any reservations they had shown were soon squelched, silencing them quickly. The same applied to a growing number of men, women, and children. More were being rounded up daily across Troria, Gonidec's fire awaiting them all. Only the strongest and fittest were to live on Troria moving forward. Save the precious resources for those that actually deserved it and had earned it.

The plans were laid out, the coordinates entered, the ships powered up, and then, row by row, they began launching upwards, quickly leaving Troria's atmosphere to join the large fleet already in a holding pattern above Troria's atmosphere. Each ship's navigation system had a detailed layout of the attack route, all ending at Railara.

It would be swift and brutal. Levon Gonidec had prepared for this day years ago. He stood atop his fortress, looking up at the ascending fleet, heading out to conquer. War was coming to all of quadrant 8304.

CHAPTER 25

INSECTOID FEEDING

The swarm was growing as more of the large insects flew out of the open chasm near the mining facility. Farther down into the abyss, another creature lay in wait, this one significantly larger than the rest, protected by the hive with their lives—their queen.

It had come from deep space after travelling for an unknown amount of time before finding this particular moon and burrowing itself near the heated core. There it had created its hive, undetected and left alone for eons, even after the mining complex had been built. Until now.

This celestial creature was nearly one thousand feet long and, unlike its offspring, completely silver and wingless. On its steel-plated exterior and oval body, the queen's head was filled enormous, jagged teeth used to tunnel through rock far underneath the surface. Two long feelers jutted out atop the fangs to guide its way underground, and rows of pincers lined the bottom of its vast underside.

It had been growing larger for centuries, producing more offspring, and now its home had been invaded. The queen rose from the deepest recesses of the chasm, fire from the moon's core merely bouncing off its thick, rock-hard outer shell.

More of its offspring swarmed around it as it breached the surface and surveyed its surroundings. Smoke and rubble clouded the area, its feelers moving about the destruction. Its enormous head turned in the direction of the burn pit several miles away, staring, waiting, sensing activity and more fire as it began making its way quickly to the site.

"I need to figure out this ship's helm—and fast," Michael said staring at the instrument panel in front of him, hoping to get the ship airborne before it was too late.

Sonia rubbed her injured and now bandaged head with Elise looking her over. "I don't think you have a concussion, just a little banged up. You'll be okay. So will I, I hope. Thanks to this brave girl here," Elise said kindly, looking over at Olivia who returned the smile.

A large insectoid landed on the front viewscreen of the Deimos, making them all jump in surprise, most of all Michael. It crawled across the viewscreen, as though looking for an entrance into the ship. Michael glanced over at the gigantic assimilation of Petrino and numerous dead clones now reduced to a large, pulsating gelatinous blob that had turned a shade of red similar to molten lava.

"I think that we sh—" Michael began but was cut off.

Deep in the recesses of the hive mind mutation, Petrino knew his end had come. Staring at the ship in front of it, it let out one more bellow of pain, defeat, and anger just before, much like the mutated clone beast inside the Command Center building, it exploded. Globs of thick burning Rot and dead clones shot in every direction, a violent display of mutated, virus-infected bloodshed.

The insect crawling on the viewscreen was hit squarely by a flying fiery chunk of the clone mutation, engulfing it in flames and knocking it to the ground.

"Nope," Michael said, firing up the engines on the *Deimos*. Flames ignited out of its exhaust ports. Pieces of the Petrino-clone mutation landed on top of the triangular shaped ship but had little effect on its thick, outer shell.

"You got this?" Elise called out groggily, taking her seat near Olivia.

"We're gonna find out, right…about…now," Michael responded with what he hoped sounded like confidence, pulling back on the helm. The ship began lifting off of the ground with insectoids buzzing around it at a fever pitch.

The *Deimos* stopped in mid-air as something latched onto it. Michael quickly pulled up the ship's scanners. On a screen in front of him a rear view of the ship appeared. "This isn't good," he said, glancing back at his traveling companions.

"What is it?" Sonia and Elise asked at nearly the same time.

Olivia, sitting closest to Michael shouted out, "Another flying thingy, but way bigger!"

The queen's long tongue was curled around the rear of the ship, dwarfing it in comparison to its huge size. It pulled back, the Deimos's rear exhausts having little effect on the enormous queen's tongue, and drew the ship into its open mouth.

Olivia screamed in terror as the mouth closed in on them, surrounding them in darkness.

Elise quickly took a seat beside Michael. "I know a bit about this ship's schematics, I'll help."

The ship tipped backwards, shooting down the throat cavity inside the huge queen insect.

"Hang on!" Elise shouted and hit the exterior lights. Warm orange light flooded their direct surroundings as fluids swirled outside, visible on the viewscreen.

"I think I'm going to be sick!" Sonia said miserably as the ship tossed and turned inside the creature's stomach. Various half-digested alien organisms floated by the viewscreen. The internal fluids of the queen stuck to the side of the ship, slowing its descent into the stomach.

Elise grabbed the laser disintegrator controls. "Not sure what's going to happen, but here goes nothing!"

Four streams of bright white laser blasts erupted from either wing of the *Deimos* into the creature's stomach, sinking into the thick red stomach lining, creating tiny tears. At this act of defiance, pink, fleshy tentacles quickly ejected out from the stomach walls, slapping onto the ship and sticking tightly before wrapping around the *Deimos*, completely engulfing it.

"Weapons inoperable! If we try that again, I fear the lasers won't break through whatever we're wrapped in and we'll self-detonate," Elise said as she looked over the readout on the screen in front of her.

The *Deimos* lay still. Michael switched the engines to stand-by mode in order to save fuel as well as life support functions.

Sonia joined Michael and Elise up front, peering out the viewscreen examining the seeming death grip the tentacles had on the *Deimos's* outer hull. "What are our options?"

Michael glanced sideways at Sonia, her close presence making his heart beat a bit faster. He cleared his throat, trying to mask the growing attraction he felt toward her. "From my limited knowledge of insects, my immediate concern is that this thing's internal makeup could eventually destroy this ship. Acidic secretion would be my hunch." he said, staring once more out the viewscreen in front of him.

"That or it continues to squeeze and crushes the ship. Take your pick, both are unpleasant outcomes," Elise said gravely, rubbing her abdomen.

The queen insect slowly moved from the burn pit, back toward the chasm it had crawled out of. Insectoids of various sizes swarmed around the gigantic creature, protecting their queen as it moved back toward the destruction of Mining Complex VI, its large pincers slamming down onto the rocky surface of Moon 002.

It felt the ship humming inside; it had what it wanted now, invaders of its home world, soon to be crushed by its powerful internal organs.

As tentacles continued to squeeze the *Deimos,* causing it to creak and moan, inside, Michael looked behind him to where an extra spacesuit and helmet hung on the far wall. He got up and headed toward the rear bulkhead, discovering a small area with what appeared to be food and beverages. "Hey guys, come back here."

Olivia jumped out of her seat first and moved to the rear of the shiny steel inner hull, followed by Sonia then Elise, continuing to rub her stomach as she walked.

"You sure you're okay?" Sonia asked.

"Yeah, I think so, I could use some water," Elise responded unconvincingly.

Olivia immediately grabbed something that resembled a candy bar in a wrapper with the words "Sobler Bar" written on the front, ripped it open, and took a bite of the light blue bar inside. Sonia reached past her, picking out some food and a bottle of what she hoped was water. Michael found what appeared to be a sandwich and offered it to Elise, noticing how pale she looked.

"Just a water?" she asked and grimaced. She took it from him, opened the lid, and took a gulp. The water bottle dropped from her hand as she quickly doubled over in pain.

Sonia caught her as she began falling to the ground, lowering her to the floor.

"What's the matter, Elise? Talk to me," she said worriedly, looking down at her fallen commander.

"My hands, they hurt. And my stomach is on fire. I don't think it's from the surgery. Maybe it is but this feels...different," Elise said through gritted teeth.

Crouching down to look her over, Michael said, "Elise, I'm going to take your gloves off, okay? Let's see what's going on."

Nodding her approval, Elise rested her head to the floor and closer her eyes.

Michael and Sonia carefully removed the right-hand glove from Elise's mining suit. Sonia eyes widened at what she saw.

Eyes closed, Elise asked, "What is it? What do you see?"

"Olivia, go to your seat please," Michael said calmly, looking down at Elise's hand.

"What is it?" the girl asked, curiously peering over Michael's shoulder.

"Olivia, please, go, it's best you don't see this right now," he responded more firmly, glancing up at the now visibly frightened girl.

She obeyed his command, moving past them and sat in her seat, crossing her arms before taking another bite of the candy bar.

Elise raised her hand to inspect what had caught them off guard. Underneath her fingernails, thin lines of green liquid were forming. She turned her hand over and saw the veins had darkened slightly, giving off a hint of green. Elise shook her head then lowered it back down to the floor.

"Put my glove back on," she said quietly.

Sonia did so, looking into Elise's eyes. "You've been through so much, Elise. I'm so sorry."

"It's okay. The girl is safe, the video recorder is safe. It's not so bad. Now I have a clear vision on what we need to do," she said, still grimacing. She lay still and closed her eyes, as though shutting out the horrible reality of her dire situation for a moment.

Michael and Sonia quietly moved a few feet away. "Why do you think her stomach hurts?" he said softly.

"My hunch is that the Rot has found its way to the freshly stitched wound, and it's working its way through her body," Sonia whispered, not wanting Olivia to hear the dire news. She shook her head and added, "It's spreading too rapidly, she'll turn soon. Possibly hours, but no more than a day. Then she'll likely turn violent."

"But isn't Olivia immune to the virus? And yet Elise still got it?" Michael said, frustrated.

"She must have gotten this before the transfusion inside the Big Boy. Plus, she still has a lot of her own blood flowing through her body. Not her clone's, which was designed to be asymptomatic to the disease."

The two of them moved over to Elise's side again, crouching down. "Do you have any idea how you were in contact?" Sonia asked gently.

"When I shot an infected clone in the generator room that Carley let in. Some of the Rot got on my helmet and my glove," Elise answered.

"But Sonia and I both got your blood on us after you were stabbed by Petrino!" Michael said, trying to keep his voice down, refusing to believe this was happening to Elise.

"Too soon," Sonia said grimly, pulling Michael away from Elise again. "Her blood hadn't yet been contaminated by the small trace of Rot. The time varies from person to person once infected. She had no signs that early on. With all the trauma her body has been through, it sped things up significantly. And here we are."

"Here we are indeed," Michael said sadly, looking back at Elise as she continued rolling her head back and forth in pain.

"Elise, what did you mean when you said you have a clear vision of what we need to do?" Sonia asked, glancing up at Olivia who had turned around in her seat to look back at them talking.

"I know how we're getting out of this creature's stomach, that's what," Elise retorted.

CHAPTER 26

ONE WAY OUT

What had once been Leah Lowe was now nothing more than a mass of green, thick, jelly-like substance. A form that could have once been human still existed but little else.

The human eyes had long since been replaced with white orbs inside a malformed skull that continued to deteriorate, sinking in on itself. In less than an hour she would be no more than a puddle of liquid splashed about on the warehouse floor—the end result of extended Rot infection unless the body was completely destroyed.

She was all that remained of those infected with the deadly virus. The rest had been decimated in either the destruction of the buildings or the massive clone mutation that was now nothing more than burnt ash floating away from Moon 002.

She recalled being tasked with an assignment: oxygen tanks, warehouse, ignite. Images flashed across the foggy intelligence that remained of a once perky, upbeat, and generally pleasant young woman. Forcing herself to stand on legs whose bones were fast beginning to snap apart, she stumbled over to the pile of oxygen tanks she had gathered earlier while she was still somewhat mobile. The fog of her rapidly diminishing brain wondered how she would ignite both the barrels and the tanks.

Instinctively, she opened the hole on her face that was once a mouth and expelled a torrent of thick green mucus onto the oxygen tanks below. The contaminated liquid had traces of Kernadium in it, as all Rot did, and the oxygen tanks started to hiss as the bile slowly ate away at the cheaply constructed material.

One more task, then it will all be over.

She moved clumsily over to the closest drum of Kernadium sitting on a nearby pallet, one of forty remaining drums for final extraction by the AMO before the site was completely abandoned. On top of it sat a long, metal crowbar-like tool used to latch and unlatch the tops of the barrels. Her green mucus-covered hand reached out and picked it up.

Elise got to her feet and, although shaky, was able to stand, for now. She propped herself up on a nearby ledge against the inner hull of the ship.

Olivia jumped up and stood beside her. "Elise, are you okay? I thought the surgery and my blood fixed you," she said innocently.

She looked at the beautiful young girl, a spitting image of herself at that age, and smiled. "The surgery did work. And your blood has kept me alive for this long. Long enough to do what has to be done in order for you three to live and get that video recorder and what's inside your brain to the right people. People that can help."

Sonia and Michael looked over at her. "What do you have in mind?" Sonia asked, curious.

"I'm taking this ship's stash of explosive neutron charges stored in the bulkhead. Ship's log shows there's six total. I'm going to put on that spare suit, with the significantly better helmet than the garbage back at the mining complex, then go out there into this thing's guts and set them off," Elise said as firmly as she could in spite of the increasing pain she was feeling.

"No. No, you're not. That's suicide. There's no way you can get back here in time. Those have, what, a ninety second timer? Max?" Sonia responded angrily, glaring at Elise.

Shaking her head, Elise replied, "I'm dead. And so are you and Michael if I don't get out of here. I feel it working its way through my body. I was dead when that shit got on my gloves and helmet back in the generator room. You know it and I know it. I've survived this long for this moment. After this, it will be up to you and Michael to get the hell out of here." She paused and winced at the pain that slowly crept up her arm.

Olivia began to cry softly, catching Elise's eye, who was quick to console the child. "It's gonna be okay. Look, you are my future, honey. You. You have the opportunity to right the wrongs that have been going on across all of the mining complexes in the solar system. All of you. The mass executions of the clones. The cannibalization. The mass corruption being perpetrated by Levon Gonidec's regime and the AMO. The war that bastard plans on waging if something isn't done. You three are going to bring them all to their knees, understand? So, you *must* live!"

Silence fell inside the *Deimos*. Michael was about the speak then thought better of it. His implants couldn't explain how to best to handle this very human situation they found themselves in. They couldn't explain Elise's self-sacrifice. In his short life, Michael knew hate. He hated the man named Levon Gonidec and his murderous thugs who flippantly created and took life at will. *If I can, I will bring hell to you, Mr. Gonidec, someday, somehow.*

Sonia looked toward the viewscreen up front. The tentacles were pulsating, squeezing, while the ship made creaking sounds that were not normal for such a well-built, highly advanced spacecraft. She understood why Elise was doing this and, if she was being honest with herself, she would do the same thing in Elise's position.

Sonia nodded at Elise. "Okay. I'm not sure how much time we have left, so if this is going to happen it needs to happen now. However, I think we should use this video recorder one more time. And I think it should come from you." She paused, staring at Elise to gauge her response.

"I don't think we have the time," Elise began.

"Please. You need to, Elise," Sonia said firmly.

Olivia took the video recorder out and held it up, "Ready," she said softly.

Elise cleared her throat and then spoke. "This is Elise Bennet. I've been stationed at Moon 002 for one year. I don't have much time left. I'm infected with the Rot virus, and I was stabbed by Dr. Anthony Petrino who was also stationed on Moon 002. Here is my story."

She proceeded to give all pertinent information that indeed confirmed and collaborated much of what Petrino had stated in his own video footage. About the corruption of AMO with its slow destruction of every planet where mining was taking place as well as the countless murders of the clones they produced at their facilities. About the human rot of authoritarian dictatorship under the false leadership of Levon Gonidec that had wrapped itself into a neat bow disguised as "Pro-Troria."

Elise concluded with a short message to Jake Riley. "Jake, I hope this message finds you well. Sorry I'm not going to be around to personally say thank you for listening and believing. It's up to you and my friends here. Do what needs to be done. Take them all down. Elise Bennet, commander of Mining Complex VI, out."

She looked down as Olivia turned the video recorder off, her face filled with sadness. Everyone mirrored her grim look. Then she put her helmet on, locking it in place.

"Let's get this done," Sonia said, breaking the silence just as another loud creak echoed throughout the hull of the *Deimos*.

They all looked up and around the interior of the ship. "Michael, can you get the explosive neutron charges in the bulkhead?" Elise said quietly, as even speaking now hurt her whole body.

Michael pulled the sliding compartment open revealing six neutron chargers located securely within. Used in heavy combat, each one had a wide destructive blast radius of one hundred fifty feet. He looked them over, each one no bigger than a baseball, and pulled out the case they were in and handed it to Elise. "How are you going to ignite all of them at the same time? In that mess out there?" he asked.

"I'm going to set one. I'll have ninety seconds. You two be ready to get the hell out of here when it happens. The explosion will make a big enough wound inside this fucker that you should have enough time to fly out. But you've got to punch it!" She grimaced at the growing pain overtaking her body.

Michael handed her the charges and his Defender II. "You'll need this to make some room through those things out there." He glanced at the tentacles that continued to wiggle and writhe around the outer hull of the ship.

Elise attempted a small smile and replied, "Good luck, Michael. I hope someone, somewhere, can undo that age restrictor on you. They certainly produced not just a fighter but a good man with you."

She turned to Sonia. "Take care of yourself, and thanks for saving my life and getting me this far. I'm paying that debt back to you three now."

Sonia gently hugged her friend and commanding officer then backed away with tears in her eyes.

Finally looking at the girl she barely knew but who felt like her own child, she said, "Olivia, you may have come from my DNA, but you are your own unique person. Make the rest of your life count, okay, honey?"

Olivia hugged her mother tightly as Elise whispered in her ear for only her to hear, "You gave your blood to save me, now I shall do the same."

Elise pulled away from the crying girl. The time had come. She stood up carefully, the pain vibrating through her legs and up her spine, then turned and walked to the rear of the ship where a small decompression chamber would lead her out of the rear cargo hold and into the belly of the beast.

Elise didn't turn around to see the door slide shut behind her.

Sonia wiped her eyes as she and Michael took their seats up front with Olivia quietly sitting behind them, securely locking herself in tight. Michael began firing the engines up.

In the decontamination area Elise hit the "arm" button on one of the explosive neutron charges as a small screen displayed "90" and began counting down. She hit the exit hatch on the underside rear of the ship and it slid open as Elise lifted the Defender II up and began firing into the tentacles that spilled into the decontamination room.

Immediately, they recoiled at the sharp blasts that pierced the soft mucus-like texture.

This was the opportunity Elise had hoped for. Fighting the immense pain, she ran forward into the now exposed stomach of the enormous creature, jumping through the door and hitting the "close" button on the way out.

She began pushing her way through the thick jelly, continuing to pull the trigger on the Defender II which sliced through the fluid, allowing her to continue onward, away from the *Deimos* and its crew of three.

The timer read forty-five seconds. Once the first neutron charge exploded, the rest would follow suit. She just hoped the blast wouldn't damage the ship. "Forty-five seconds, Michael," she said into her com.

No response came back, but the engines were now fired up, tentacles swirling around it as if attempting to pull it apart. Elise pushed forward as fast as she could, trying to ignore the constant pain running through her body. It would all be over soon.

Thirty seconds until detonation.

She felt as though she were swimming inside jelly, she could move but it was slow going. The Defender no longer had any effect on the inner workings of the large beast, so she let go of it. The gun appeared to remain in suspended animation where she had released it.

"Come on, Elise, keep going!" she said, pushing through the thick slime.

Fifteen seconds until detonation.

Keep pushing forward.

Five, Four, three, two…

Elise closed her eyes.

Inside the *Deimos* the explosion shook the entire ship, making it feel as though it were about to explode itself. The tentacles wrapped tightly around the ship, blowing fragments throughout the stomach. The stomach lining of the creature burned up instantly as all six of the neutron charges ignited, one after the other in a chain reaction, leaving a huge hole in the creature's belly.

Elise felt nothing. One second she closed her eyes and the next she was gone.

The explosion, which originated behind the ship, pushed the *Deimos* forward up through the creature's alien anatomy. Michael punched it immediately, rocketing the ship forward once the tentacles were destroyed. Sonia was now able to use the onboard weapons, firing at will as they travelled up through the creature on their way to its mouth.

Leah Lowe had managed to pry the nearest cannister of Kernadium open. The liquid sloshed around inside as she pulled on the barrel, attempting to knock it over onto the smoldering oxygen tanks. As she pulled, her left arm tore off, dropping to the floor. With only one arm left, she pulled with her whole body—what was left of it. The barrel tilted, then collapsed on top of her, engulfing her with the flammable liquid, instantly crushing her jelly-like body under its weight.

The Kernadium splashed out and rushed forward onto the floor toward the oxygen tanks.

Within seconds, the storage facility erupted in a catastrophic explosion, decimating the building and what remained of the entire site, leaving a mushroom cloud in the sky where the warehouse once stood. Fire engulfed everything; the Poule plants quickly turned to dust, blowing backwards, away from the blast. Swarms of insectoids sizzled and fried to death in the air.

The monstrous silver insectoid creature, reeling from its internal injuries, was about to leap into the deep chasm from which it came. Thick brown liquid spilled from holes in its underbelly from the six bombs disintegrated inside its stomach.

Before it could climb down, the Kernadium storage facility exploded. The explosion was catastrophic, decimating the building as well as what remained of the entire site. A mushroom cloud formed in the sky where the large warehouse once stood. Fire quickly engulfed everything, the Poule plants instantly turned dust, blowing backwards, away from the blast. Swarms of insectoids sizzled and fried to death in the air before even making it to the ground.

The queen was immediately engulfed in flames, its outer shell cracking open, the long feelers on its head burning, its multitude of legs snapping off as fire burned through them.

Flailing back and forth in an attempt to escape the fire, it opened its mouth at the sudden intense pain hitting its teeth: the *Deimos'* heavy laser disintegrators pulverized its now opened jaws. The small triangular ship shot out of its mouth into the mining complex area, now little more than a fiery wasteland of destruction.

As the *Deimos* and her crew escaped its large jaws, the enormous silver queen let out a staggeringly loud death screech, looking upward to the sky above.

"Hang on!" Michael yelled out as Sonia and Olivia both gripped their seats and winced at the piercing noise that reverberated through the ship. The *Deimos* rocketed forward as behind them, the open-mouthed queen shook its head then collapsed, dead, the fire cooking its outer shell.

The *Deimos* continued its trajectory upward, quickly leaving Moon 002's fire-engulfed wasteland behind. Soon, the viewscreen in front of them filled with twinkling stars and distant planets in quadrant 8304.

Inside the ship Sonia sat back in her seat, emotionally, physically, and mentally exhausted. She sighed heavily and glancing over at Michael, said, "I can't believe what just happened." Her mind went to Elise, after all her commanding officer and more importantly, *friend* had been through to end up sacrificing herself for them all.

"I haven't been around long, but I know courage when I see it. Now it's up to us to make sure her death was not in vain," Michael replied, staring ahead at the vastness of outer space.

They flew in a straight line for a few moments in silence, all playing back the events of the past day before Olivia piped up behind them. "Where are we going? That planet to deliver the video recorder?"

"Yes, Railara. I'm not sure what to expect there but I'm pretty sure we'll be safe," Sonia answered as she glanced back, then after a quick scan of the controls in front of her, turned off the tracking system and all communications to and from Troria.

"Plotting a course for planet Railara now," Michael said, punching in the proper coordinates.

"The last Kernadium transport ship is going to be in for quite the surprise here soon," Sonia added as the horrors of Moon 002 grew smaller in the rear-view monitor in from of them.

From behind them Olivia said sadly, "I don't have a mom or dad. What will they do with me? I don't want to go back to a scary dark room and be alone again."

Sonia, her heart breaking for the girl, glanced back and said warmly, "Not a chance, sweetheart."

Michael thought of his own birth inside the pitch-black room, understanding the young girl's fear well. He looked back at Olivia. "Agreed, not happening, ever. We're sticking together."

The ship continued on its plotted course toward Railara.

CHAPTER 27

SIDETRACKED

Olivia was being chased by an unseen entity, most likely, an infected Rot clone. The hallway was long and dark and seemingly endless, closing in on her. The faster she ran, the closer whatever was pursuing her got. It seemed to go on for hours. Running, out of breath, looking back to see a shadowy figure close behind. Just out of reach, barely.

She tried to scream but no sound came out. Her mouth was open, trying to catch her breath as she continually ran. She desperately wanted Elise, Michael, Sonia, but they were nowhere to be found. It was just her and her unseen assailant.

Her feet seemed to move in slow motion as a sinister voice behind her whispered in her ear, "Olivia, I made you and you belong to me. You always will belong to me."

Turning her head, she saw Dr. Petrino, covered in green Rot. It was pouring out of his mouth. His eyes had turned white and he had a large hole in his chest. With his outstretched boney hands, he grabbed her by the throat, pulling her toward his open, gaping mouth.

Opening her eyes, Olivia screamed, sitting bolt upright in her seat behind Sonia and Michael.

Sonia jumped out of her seat. "Olivia, honey, what is it? Bad dream?" she said, brushing the girl's blond hair out of her sweaty face.

Nodding, Olivia tried to catch her breath. Her eyes darted back and forth, falling on Sonia in front of her. Instinctively, she lunged forward, wrapping her arms around Sonia and squeezing her tightly.

Not sure what to do at this sudden outpouring of love, Sonia wrapped her arms around Olivia and suddenly felt a lump in her throat.

Sonia wasn't used to the affection of a child, or anyone but her mother, for that matter. An only child, raised by a single mom in a small apartment complex back on Troria, her upbringing had been rough and lonely. Always the ugly duckling in grade school and high school, she'd had nobody to truly confide in. And even through the nightmare of her time at Mining Complex VI on Moon 002, she had mostly been alone in a sea of ever-changing security guards, administrators, clones, and doctors' assistants.

And now, here she was, receiving such kindness from an innocent girl, and she, reciprocating that love. She quickly got to her feet and wiped her eyes; she had kept it together. She smiled at the girl who seemed to be regaining her composure after the bad dream. "It's gonna be a long flight to Railara, why don't you go get us all something to eat?"

Olivia nodded and headed to the back to look over the rest of the food supply as Sonia turned and took her seat beside Michael once more. She undid the bandages on her head, her brown curly hair once more falling into her face. Her head still hurt, but she was sure it wasn't a concussion as she had feared earlier and was beginning to feel better.

Michael glanced over at her, noticing her pull her hair back, something he had watched her do instinctively numerous times now. It was obviously one of her quirks and he liked it. The way she nervously glanced around as she did it, self-consciously, was endearing.

They sat in silence for a period, hearing Olivia rustling around in the rear of the hull for food. Michael grinned. He liked the kid, a lot. And he liked this woman who had shown him kindness and bravery through seemingly impossible odds ever since meeting her in the Command Center of the ill-fated Mining Complex VI. She had been awkward at first, slowly coming out of her bubble and proving herself invaluable to the success of their escape from Moon 002.

Sonia glanced over at him and their eyes locked. "What are you thinking?" she asked gently.

Tilting back in his seat as he turned to stare out the front viewscreen into space, he sighed heavily and ran his hands through his hair as he contemplated their next move. His mind was active. He knew how to pilot a ship relatively well thus far, but this was new territory for him. His specific implants could only take him so far, he was discovering. He knew the planets his father had travelled to, but this was real. He sensed that the memories had come to a stop, and from here on he was learning as he went.

"Sonia, I have to be honest here. This is all new territory for me. My implants, I'm still trying to grasp..."

Sonia cut him off, "Michael, it's okay. Together we'll figure this out."

Nodding his thanks, Michael added, "Railara seems to be our only option from the limited information I have. I think I've got the hang of this ship, so with your help I think we have a legitimate chance of making it there."

Sonia nodded then said softly, "We need to figure out how to get that one-year life span reversed on you. From what Mohr said, it can be done. Just as it was done with Olivia."

"We shall see. I just want to make sure you and Olivia are safe. We've all been through a whole hell of a lot in a very short period of time. I just hope the worst is behind us."

Instinctively, Sonia reached over and patted the top of Michael's hand, which he turned palm up then took hers and squeezed it affectionately. She blushed, but smiled and returned the loving gesture.

Michael took a deep breath and exhaled slowly. They had been through so much and had managed to make it this far. His programming hadn't factored in all of this but he felt as though facing it together, all of them, had made him more human. He was having to make decisions with the limited knowledge he had, and then hope for the best. Nothing about his life so far felt like simply "doing his time" before a certain death. He felt alive. Olivia and Sonia, and Elise, had a lot to do with that and he was grateful.

Olivia joined them up front and they quicky released hands. Cheerily, she showed them the snacks she had discovered in one of the lower drawers and they each took what looked like bags of salted nuts, thanking her as she took her seat.

The *Deimos* and its crew continued gliding through space. Past nebula, past stray asteroids and meteors, Michael and Olivia taking it all in for the first time. Sonia, for the first time in a long time, felt at peace. Her thoughts drifted to Elise and Chris. To Leah and Carley. Even Dex. All gone. Thanks to Anthony Petrino. She hated him, and thinking of his face brought her back to her current situation. She was alive. Unlike him.

"Michael, if you don't mind, I'm going to rest my eyes for a bit. I'm not sure when I actually slept last!" Sonia looked over at the man who, now that they were relatively out of danger, she noticed was even more handsome. Chiseled facial features, muscular chest, kind yet determined eyes.

"Of course! I'm good to go. At least, I think so. I assume I have to sleep at some point?" Michael asked.

Smiling, Sonia nodded and replied, "If you're like the other clones, they typically got seven to eight hours of sleep per day so they could be well rested for mining. So, yes, your body needs sleep just like a…" she paused. She was quickly not liking thinking of him and Olivia as *different*.

Michael sensed what she was about to say and circled back to the original topic. "Take all the time you need. Looks like we're roughly a day's travel time away from Railara and, if these calculations are correct, about the same distance from Troria now if we took a different flight path." He paused. "Forgive me for asking, but why work for them, Sonia? Why work for the Alnorix Mining Organization?"

Sonia thought about this for a minute. "I've got my ear to the ground, so to speak, though not as much as Elise, who was part of the resistance, it seems. Me? I'm just a girl trying to make her way through life. Gotta pay my dues. My mom's old. She's in pain and she's dying. Money is tight and with my education, well, this was what I was eligible for. Call it blood money, call it selling my soul, but I love my mama."

She paused as her mind went to the frail woman back in the apartment she grew up in.

"My payout for the job on Moon 002 was going to get her the much needed and expensive heart surgery she had been hoping and praying for. Now? Forget that. We're literally fugitives. I'm honestly surprised we haven't been tracked yet. If we haven't been, we most likely will be as soon as that last transport arrives and sees the destruction back there."

Michael contemplated this before responding. "I'm truly sorry to hear about your mom, what's her name?"

Sonia sat upright in her seat at the question. "That's the first time anyone has ever asked me that. Or shown the slightest interest in my mother's and my situation," she responded shakily as she felt tears starting to well up at this sudden display of kindness, thinking of her ailing mother back on Troria, alone.

"Her name is Corinna Bonnel. She's sixty-five and has had a rough life, and a bad heart that gets worse each year. I need to take care of her, which is what I was doing until…" she trailed off.

Nodding, Michael glanced back at Olivia who had once again dozed off, then back to Sonia. Her curly dark hair, a smattering of freckles on her cheeks, eyes that were sad yet had an untapped sparkle to them. He had seen her take charge back on Moon 002, determined to survive. In her vulnerability and openness, he found her incredibly beautiful. This was a new feeling—attraction to the opposite sex.

"Thanks for sharing that, Sonia. We'll see what we can do for Corinna Bonnel, okay? Why don't you try to get some sleep now."

Sonia glanced back at the sleeping Olivia, immediately making her droopy-eyed. She nodded in response, tilted her chair back slightly, and rested her weary head, closing her eyes.

Sleep came quickly, overtaking Sonia like a warm blanket. Much like Olivia, her dreams were unpleasant. In them, she found herself locked back inside the Command Center. Cigarette smoke lingered in the room. A man covered in shadow, always just out of reach, blowing smoke continually. Out the large window overlooking Moon 002, swarms of insectoid creatures buzzed and flew past, as if trying to get inside. From the sky, another insect creature flew toward her, nearly as big as the silver queen insect that had swallowed their ship earlier.

She recognized the shape of it.

"Sonia, wake up! We've got company!" Michael shouted, startling Sonia out of her dream.

She nearly fell out of her seat as the *Deimos* veered sharply to the left, waking up Olivia as well, who let out a small shriek at the abrupt awakening. Michael, wide-eyed and pulling back sharply on the helm, rocketed the ship upwards. Sonia looked out at what was in front of them.

Another silver being floated in space, similar to the insect that swallowed their ship whole back on Moon 002. Thin and nearly seven hundred feet in length, shorter but significantly wider than the queen they had destroyed earlier, its insect-like wings were outstretched and tilted upright in what appeared to be an attack formation. Two large, jagged pincers on its head slammed together as it dove toward them.

Michael swerved again, this time to the right. The silver insect-being nearly missed their ship, blasting past them and quickly turning around for another attack.

Olivia screamed in terror at the sight of another enormous creature similar to what they had encountered earlier.

Wasting no time, Sonia looked over the instrument panel, finding the weapons controls. "Not sure how I'll do with these, I've only had a bit of weapons training back on Troria and that was almost four years ago!"

Michael glanced over at her in the co-pilot's seat. "I suggest you point, aim, and fire!"

She prepared to fire all four of the heavy laser disintegrators when the creature was within firing range and not behind them.

"Why do I feel like this thing came knocking after hearing its cousin, or mate, whatever it was, dying back on the moon?" Michael said, swerving back and forth with the enormous insect-like being in close pursuit.

The creature's exterior had turned a brighter silver as it opened its mouth wide, spitting out a stream of thick ice, nearly hitting the *Deimos*, crackling around the ship's outer hull. Michael pushed down on the helm and took a steep descent while the being sailed past them.

Following Michael's simple instructions coupled with her basic spacecraft weapons system knowledge, Sonia laid on the laser disintegrators, hitting the creature in its mid-section. While not doing any damage, it was a much-needed distraction. Its mouth closed and the ice stopped flowing out as it swerved away from the laser blasts.

This gave Michael the time he needed to gather his wits about him. Nearby, a grouping of nearly one thousand asteroids floated by. The *Deimos* headed toward them as Michael hollered out, "Hang on, it's gonna get bumpy!"

Olivia clicked into the safety restraints and sat quietly, gripping her seat. Sonia ceased firing, letting Michael pilot the ship into the oncoming asteroids ranging from small space rocks to gigantic boulders, some large enough to land a ship on.

Weaving in and out of the smaller ones, Michael attempted to stick close to several large ones in the hopes of losing the pursuing creature.

The colossal flying insectoid attempted entering the asteroid field, once more opening its mouth and expelling torrents of thick ice, smashing into every asteroid it made contact with, creating thousands of new smaller space rocks and ice particles in the process, further expanding the debris field Michael was navigating.

"On my mark, fire those laser disintegrators, Sonia!" he shouted.

Sonia's hands gripped the weapons as she nervously awaited the command, feeling way out of her element. *You can do this, Sonia, keep going! Protect the ship, protect Olivia, protect Michael!*

Michael, meanwhile, circled around a medium-sized rock, easily maneuvering the Deimos and shooting out around the other side, placing the ship's guns within firing range of the pursuing creature.

They stared down the front of the floating beast, heading straight for its head where electricity was building once more inside its opened mouth. Above it, a large asteroid floated by.

"Now, Sonia! The asteroid above it!" Michael called out as they continued toward the space beast.

Grimacing as she attempted to aim the guns upward, Sonia opened fire, missing the mark with the first few blasts but then making direct contact with the asteroid. It shattered into semi-large chucks and smashed into the creature just as torrents of ice once more shot forth.

Michael cut the ships trajectory quickly to the left of the creature and the falling debris as he shot past it. Space rocks rained down on the creature's tough exterior as its own ice shards hit several other asteroids nearby, making it more challenging for Michael to avoid being hit.

The *Deimos* swerved back and forth, narrowly avoiding the seemingly continuous onslaught of asteroids.

Olivia flinched and whimpered as several small rocks bounced off of the ship's outer hull, knocking the ship violently back and forth.

"Hang on, Olivia, we're almost out of this!" Sonia hollered back to the frightened girl.

An undetected asteroid underneath their hull slammed into the ship, sending it spiraling upwards. Emergency alarms rang out inside the ship as smoke began kicking up in the rear, close to its dual engines.

Michael pulled back hard on the helm, trying to regain control before they hit another rock which could breach their hull and destroy the ship completely. The *Deimos* blasted out of the asteroid field damaged but still in one piece. He was glad this much knowledge of spacecraft flight was implanted; it had become invaluable to their survival.

The creature, meanwhile, had temporarily lost its sense of direction as asteroids smashed into it from all sides. Brown and bright silver blood leaked out of several wounds around the creature's sternum.

Inside the *Deimos*, Michael regained control of the ship, slowing it enough for Sonia to unbuckle from her seat and run to the back, Olivia joining her on the way.

Michael turned off the alarm while assessing the damage from his pilot station. Looking over the ship's diagnostics, he yelled back to Sonia, "Once you put any small fires out, we need to check for any leaks around the engine coils. You'll have to remove the panel to access it, from what I'm seeing on this readout up here!"

"Got it!" Sonia replied as she retrieved a small extinguisher against the side wall and began spraying the fire that had started when they were hit on their underside. The liquid from the extinguisher quickly took care of the fire, smothering it in a coating of white foam.

Olivia moved forward to help Sonia remove the panel. She had found a tool kit earlier when digging around for food which she now opened, looking down at the assortment of foreign instruments.

Sonia examined the tools until finding what she needed to open the panel, then pulled the shiny metal instrument out and removed the screws before opening up the panel to get a better look at what they were up against.

Immediately, smoke flowed into the main hull of the *Deimos*.

"Shit!" Sonia hollered out as both she and Olivia began coughing and waving their hands across their faces.

"What's it look like in there?" Michael called out, glancing back.

Putting her hands on her hips and squinting into the opened hatch, Sonia replied back, "Not good. I don't have much experience in this type of repair work so I'm kind of just going by what my eyes see here."

Sonia glanced over to see Olivia innocently imitating her, peering inside with her hands on her hips and squinting. She was quickly falling in love with this precious creation. Possibly the only good thing Petrino had ever done in his pathetic life.

A shrill alarm sounded, echoing throughout the *Deimos*. A computerized voice spoke through the cabin: "Warning, warning. Hull breach detected. Complete loss of air pressure in T-minus thirty minutes, warning, warning."

Michael hit the autopilot and leapt up, running back to where Sonia and Olivia stood. Olivia held her hands over her ears as smoke wafted from the rear compartment.

Michael peered inside the opened hatch. *Come on implants, help me out here. Give me some background knowledge.*

The engine was sparse but incredibly versatile. The Trorian military had crafted their fleet to be low maintenance, high productivity. This ship had a particularly well-designed, large square engine with visible gears and other fairly straightforward mechanical components.

"Looks like a few gears here were jarred loose, but for that to cause total loss of air in thirty minutes and a hull breach?" Michael shouted over the alarm. He continued frantically looking inside then stopped.

"What? What is it?" Sonia shouted back, sensing Michael found something else.

"There," Michael yelled, pointing past the engine onto the floor where a panel had come loose and was vibrating from the hum of the engine.

"Hand me one of those screws you took out!" Michael exclaimed.

Olivia, who had been holding them for Sonia, dropped a screw into his palm.

He placed it between his index finger and thumb, then tossed it into the air. The screw quickly flew forward, landing against the vibrating floor panel and staying there as if being pulled forward, trying to get outside.

"Not good! We have an outer hull breach! That panel is going to break free if we don't do something. We're going to lose cabin pressure and the ship will likely fall apart, starting with this engine here being ripped right out of the ship. The thin panel is possibly the only thing keeping this ship from imploding!"

"Oh no, oh no, no, no!" Sonia exclaimed.

"What are we gonna do?" Olivia said urgently, still covering her ears at the alarm continuing to echo throughout the inner hull of the *Deimos*.

Michael looked at them both and exclaimed, "I'm going out there to fix it!"

CHAPTER 28

RUMINATIONS AND REPAIRS

The creature was wounded but had freed itself from the heavy barrage of asteroids. It searched its surroundings for the mysterious triangular shape that had evaded it and caused it harm. The ship was nowhere to be seen.

The creature turned its attention back to its original destination, the location from which it had earlier heard one of its kind crying out in pain.

This being was one of many that had roamed the solar systems, galaxies, and ultimately, entire universe for billions of years. Few remained as the more aggressive beings had killed each other off through the ages in a show of dominance, so now, when one called out, others came. It was the one to come forward, quickly travelling a great distance from where it had been quietly exploring.

The celestial entity resumed its journey to the planet where the signal had originated, now sensing many signals. Not just the one that had originally drawn it and, at this point, it could no longer detect. Descendants of the being were calling to it, beckoning it through the solar system. Its offspring needed its help. Something it hadn't experienced in many centuries.

Taking off, it drew closer to the planet Treon III and, more importantly, one of its orbiting moons, 002.

Sonia looked at Michael worriedly. "No! Michael, no! You can't go out there!"

She had turned the alarm off inside the cabin so they could think more clearly.

"What are our options? See for yourself," he responded as calmly as he could despite his nervousness, pointing at the screen readout in front of them continually flashing in red at the piloting station.

"Hull breach imminent, land or repair spacecraft Deimos immediately."

Sonia and Olivia both moved in closer to Michael. They were a team looking out for each other, scared for each other. This bit of comradery helped Michael, even though his nerves were frazzled at the thought of what must be done.

Clearing his throat, Michael looked over at Olivia. "I'm going to need a tool, a welding device to be exact. Have you seen anything like that back there?"

Glad to be of help, Olivia said, "In the cabinet where all the tools are stored, I think I saw something that had the word 'welder' on its side! Hold on, I'll go get it for you!" She made her way to the rear of the hull.

Turning to Sonia, he said quietly, "I need you to take control of the ship. Keep it steady. My hunch, and this is a hunch, is that creature was heading to the mining station, not backtracking to find us. Judging from its appearance, I think we may have killed its mate with the neutron charges Elise set off. If that thing's still there when the last transport shows up, they're gonna have their hands full."

Sonia nodded, moving slightly closer to him, several strands of brown curly hair falling over her eyes. She reached up to brush them away, but Michael beat her to it, lightly pulling her hair back into place. She blushed as he smiled at her.

"You are a brave woman, Sonia Bonnel. And we're going to fix this ship, get to Railara, and find a way to get your mom the surgery she needs. But time is not on our side, I've got to patch that piece immediately."

There was a slight pause. Both of them felt something spark between them as their eyes met.

"Found it!" Olivia came running back up to the front holding a pistol-shaped device with the words *Trolarus 300 Laser Welder* etched on the handle. She held the instrument out for Michael to inspect.

He took it and looked it over before switching it on. A bright blue flame emitted from the barrel. As he gently squeezed the trigger, the flame became more intense until he released it.

"Good find. This is what I needed. Time to suit up," Michael said, then walked to the back and retrieved the second Trorian Pilot spacesuit and hastily put it on. He grabbed the corresponding helmet and stopped and turned toward them. "If this doesn't work," he began, but was quickly cut off by Sonia.

"It's going to work," Sonia said with as much confidence as she could muster. "I don't like this one bit, but you can do it. See this? It's a retractable cord, latch it on to one of the hooks outside the ship. You'll see them, all space travel ships from Troria have them, I learned that back in school, seemed like useless information back then. Anyway, it's your lifeline. Please don't go floating off into outer space. I'm going to power the ship down now. We have twenty minutes." Her mind wandered back to Elise leaving the ship for the last time.

Michael took a deep breath and quickly put the helmet on, latching it in place. Then, with the *Trolarus 300 Laser Welder* in hand, he headed toward the back hatch and stepped into the small decompression chamber, turned and nodded to Sonia and Olivia as the hatch slid shut. Olivia raised her hand to wave goodbye as the hatch was closing and Michael caught the small, kind gesture.

Turning around to face the hatch that would open to outer space, he felt his heart begin to race faster. *Come on, Michael, you can do this. With everything else you've been through, you've got this. They'll die if you don't succeed!*

The small decompression room still had remnants of the creature whose belly they had been trapped in when Elise was there. She didn't make it back, and he knew his chances weren't much better.

He quit pondering what might happen and pushed the button next to the outer hatch and the door slid open. In front of him loomed the vast emptiness of outer space peering back ominously.

Michael's com crackled to life with Sonia on the other end. "Michael, your oxygen is currently at well over four hours. You've got plenty of air."

"Roger that," Michael came back. He peered over the edge of the opened outer hatch, trying to find something to connect the tether to. Sure enough, there was a latch close to the door. Carefully, he reached out with his free hand holding the tether, feeling around the side of the *Deimos* until the metal connector at the end of his flexible steel wire rope hit the latch, clicking into it securely.

"Got it clicked in. I'm heading out," Michael said into his com. "I'm going to keep the outer hatch open. I feel safer knowing it'll be an easy entrance back in."

Gripping the welder tightly in his right hand, he stepped off of the ledge of the *Deimos*' rear hatch into outer space, immediately floating down, away from the ship.

He controlled his breathing as the weightlessness of space took hold until the tether finally came to its end and he stopped. He was now looking up at the underside of the ship and could clearly see the damage the asteroid had done earlier.

His mind raced. He figured at this point in time he had less than fifteen minutes to get it sealed up or the ship would be destroyed and Sonia and Olivia along with it.

He saw the area he needed to work on. Near the rear of the outer hull was a significant dent, in the middle of which a small piece of the thick metal frame had been pulled back after being slammed into by the asteroid a short time ago.

Michael began retracting the tether connected to his suit by pushing a small button on his waist. The steel rope wire began winding back inside his suit as he made his way up toward the damage. Once close enough, he reached out and touched the outer hull, inching his way to a small ledge near the damage. It wasn't much, but he needed something to hold onto so he could begin the welding.

A small clicking noise sounded from his spacesuit, but he didn't hear it.

Inside the *Deimos,* Sonia and Olivia anxiously waited in the pilot and co-pilot seats. The ship didn't have an external camera at the location of the damage, so they were reliant on Michael to give them updates.

Sonia, not wanting to interrupt his concentration or think about the clock counting down the minutes until a full hull breach, focused her attention on Olivia. She had so recently lost what was essentially her mother and could tell by

Olivia's expression that the girl was terrified at the possibility of losing Michael too.

"Olivia, I want to tell you a story about the woman whose DNA gave you your life," Sonia said evenly, trying to control her nervousness at what was happening underneath the ship.

Olivia immediately sat upright, her full attention now on Sonia.

"There was a time, I forget exactly how long ago, shortly after she arrived on Moon 002, when Elise—er, your mom—was," Sonia began.

Olivia cut her off. "You can call her my mom. I like that. It makes me feel like I come from somewhere instead of just a lab."

Smiling at her kindness and innocence, Sonia continued. "She made friends quicky, not like me. I've always been shy, always ate by myself. And it didn't help when Petrino would make comments about my messy hair, or my freckles, which he called 'skin defects'".

She frowned at the memory, then continued. "So, one day, I was in the mess hall, and I had just gotten over a head cold, so I was looking a little ragged as I still had to pull my weight and work my shifts. I was exhausted. I was trying to get some bland soup down, and this woman walks over and asks if she can join me."

Sonia tried desperately to not think about Michael under the ship, risking his life to repair the damage. She shook her head, getting her mind back on the story.

"So, I was awkward, of course. I mean, this beautiful woman who seemed to make friends instantly decided to sit with the loner who was blowing her nose and sneezing. I remember nodded hello and she sat across the table, smiling. We both ate in silence for a bit then she started asking me about myself. How long I had been there, what my goals were, what my hobbies were. Never even giving me a chance to ask her about herself."

Sonia smiled at this nice memory on Moon 002, so few of them existed. She continued, "She was genuinely interested in getting to know me! I answered her questions, we joked about how our last names sounded oddly similar, about music, art, you name it. In a short amount of time, I got to know what a kind person she was. She even commented on my curly hair, something she said she wish she had instead of straight blond."

Sonia chuckled when Olivia gently raised her hand, like a schoolgirl wanting permission for something. "Yes?"

"What was she eating? I mean, it's not important, but what did my mom like?"

Glancing down at the still blinking warning light in front of her, Sonia replied, "Well, that day I remember it vividly. She was quite health conscious, usually eating mainly fruits and vegetables and healthy grains. She did, however, like sweets every now and again. Something she had that day."

"Oh, I love candy and pie too, I've discovered!" Olivia said excitedly.

Sonia chuckled again and replied, "Don't we all?"

The warning light was still blinking. Five minutes until things would go from bad to much worse inside the Deimos.

Focusing on Olivia, she continued, "She also asked me why I always sat by myself. I explained that making friends didn't come easy for me, and she said that was going to change. We started hanging out together in the lounge in the evenings, and she began slowly drawing me out of my shell. I started opening up a bit more. All because she made the effort to sit with a lonely and sick woman one gloomy day on Moon 002 when no one else would."

Sonia stopped, once more reminiscing about that kind gesture that now felt like a lifetime ago.

"Thank you for telling me that. It makes me glad to know my mom was a kind person to you. You and Michael are all I've got. I need both of you. You both seem to work good together. You should get married!" Olivia said, smiling at Sonia's surprised expression. "I know what that means. It must have been imprinted." Then she added, "He's so strong! You should have seen him take care of some of the infected people when we first met. He took care of me."

Sonia quickly looked away, trying not to cry at the girl's tender-hearted nature that was showing more and more. It amazed her that Olivia looked up to her. And that she referred to her beloved role model Michael and all of the other clones as people.

In the vast emptiness of space, an eleven-year-old girl managed to find the good in her fellow...*humans*. This young and quite innocent girl was softening her own heart toward a great number of things.

"Oh, and my mom wasn't lying. You have the most beautiful hair ever," Olivia added.

CHAPTER 29

SPACE WALK

Michael began inspecting the tear in the underside of the hull. It appeared to be roughly two feet in length and made a "V" shape. The welding would be a dangerous task. His right hand had found an area of the hull he was able to hang on to while his right hand, the one holding the *Trolarus 300 Laser Welder* would do the work.

Pressing the trigger, he saw a small blue flame erupt from the welding device then lifted it to the tear and held it to the metal hull. Sparks flew, startling Michael, his left hand almost slipping from its tight grasp against the ship. Concentrating, he continued holding the flame to the tear, slowly inching it forward, leaving behind a jagged, but functional weld. He felt nervous sweat crease his brow but continued to focus on the welding, not the tickling wet on his forehead.

Slow and steady, Michael. Take your time. I have to make this hold. He knew it was mere minutes before the air would be sucked from the hull and Sonia and Oliva would be unable to breathe.

The laser welder worked well, like cutting through warm butter. He moved the blue flame all the way up to the point in the "V" shaped tear then back down, impressed by the ease and speed with which the small device operated.

Flashing through his mind were images of his youth, teen years, adulthood. The skill set he had been continuously utilizing since awakening inside the dark room. Weapons training and operating land and sky-based machinery were two he was thankful for at the moment. He also had extensive knowledge about mining, just like his *father*, though he would never have to utilize that knowledge if it were up to him. All these traits were fabricated, of course, created in a lab, just as he was.

He thought of Sonia and young Olivia, relying on him. And how he, too, would need Sonia's help with a possible reversal on the one-year lifespan limiter he was sentenced to. The truth is, they all needed each other right now.

Sonia. A survivor and protector for young Olivia and… so beautiful. He had experience with women but only in as much as the memory implants allowed: faceless women in his teen years and through college. No real contact and non-sexual in nature. Sonia, though, was real. Even after knowing her for such a short time, he felt as if their paths were meant to cross.

He shook these thoughts out of his head, focusing on the task in front of him.

The burning blue flame had succeeded in completely sealing up the leak. He clicked it off once the seal appeared to hold and surveyed the battered underside of the *Deimos*. It was heavily damaged but other than the small tear appeared to be holding.

Now if we can just make it to Railara with no more issues, he thought as he reached for his com to alert Sonia that the breach was repaired.

Inside the *Deimos*, Sonia silently held her breath. One minute blinked on the now silent alarm. It may as well have been on, though, as she heard it blaring in her head. *Less than one minute and it's all over. We're dead. Must keep calm. Come on, Michael!*

As if sensing what Sonia was thinking, Olivia took her hand and said, "Michael's got this! We know he does!"

Sonia fought back tears and gripped Olivia's hand tightly. Thirty seconds until the ship would implode from the weight of outer space.

Ten, nine, eight, seven, six…

"Sonia, come in," Michael said, clicking his com back on.

Brief static followed by her excited voice. “You did it! The hull breach warning turned off! Three seconds until…” Sonia paused, out of breath.

“That’s the answer I was hoping for!” Michael said, relieved. “I want to be sure no air is still leaking, even a tiny amount. Can you head to the back and see if that floor panel is still rattling? If it’s not, we’re good to go. Otherwise, eventually the alarm will sound and we’re back to square one.” He continued to keep his grip tight against the hull.

“Will do, hang tight,” Sonia said, catching her breath.

“Was that a joke? Because it sounded like a joke,” Michael said lightly. He heard Olivia laugh which made him chuckle slightly. And then he waited.

He turned his head slightly to peer out at the vastness of outer space. Below him, a small green planet hung in space, thin rings of rocks looping around it. Just past its rings was a tiny moon, smaller than Moon 002 which orbited Treon III. Surrounding him were clusters of stars, millions upon millions of them in every direction he turned.

He wondered what else was out there. Which of those distant quadrants of space held life? Would he be able to one day explore them? He wondered if these thoughts had been baked into his DNA by those who had manufactured him or were they genuine ideas and ambitions he himself was developing on his own.

“Michael, we’re good. The rattling seems to have stopped. We won’t be completely sure until we fire the ship back up, so you need to get back inside. Good job!" Sonia called out into his com.

"Yeah, good job!" Olivia called out behind her happily.

He breathed a sigh of relief and smiled then responded, "Got it! I'm heading back."

The arduous task of making his way back to the decontamination room involved first letting go of the ledge he had been clinging to with his free hand. He slowly began drifting while quickly winding the tether back into his spacesuit, inching closer and closer to the opened hatch. In a minute or two he would be reach it and climb back in safely.

From inside his helmet, he heard something snap on his spacesuit. He stared out at the tether he was relying on to get him back aboard the *Deimos* just as a red light began blinking inside his helmet, followed by a computer voice speaking through his com, repeating over and over, "Tether Malfunction."

The creature that had attacked the *Deimos* in the asteroid field arrived at the hollowed-out wasteland of what had been Moon 002, its wings buzzing frantically as it made its descent to the surface. It had followed the smoke to the rubble of Mining Complex VI, now nothing more than a gigantic crater after the destruction of the Kernadium storage facility.

It landed beside the queen, its mate from a time long since passed. Around it buzzed several of its offspring, though most had burned to death in the explosion. The male insectoid inspected the dead queen, charred, her stomach ripped apart, her mouth still open from her last death shriek which it had heard far out in space.

And now it was here, and it was angry. Several smaller insectoids crawled on the ground, their hard-shell exteriors in flames. The enormous bug opened its jaws and blew out freezing liquid, quickly extinguishing the flames of its offspring until all that still lived were safe from the flames.

And then it waited.

The "Tether Malfunction" warning continued to blink inside Michael's helmet. Frozen with fear, he quickly came to his senses and tried not to panic. Panic could mean certain death if he wasn't careful.

He clicked on his com again. "Sonia, something's wrong with my tether, I'm getting a malfunction warning."

She responded but he didn't hear it. His tether was no longer winding. In fact, just the opposite. He was floating away from the ship.

His mind raced. Eventually, it would reach its end then he would stop. *But what if it's broken?*

Attempting to grab hold of it with both hands, he clipped the welding tool to his side and reached for the flexible steel rope. It wasn't working. The tether slid forward as he tried to grasp it and he was unable to hold it tight enough to stop drifting away from the ship. Again, he felt himself start to panic.

"Michael! Come in!" Sonia's voice brought him back to the moment.

"Sonia!" Michael shouted back, unable to hide his panic.

"I ran a quick scan of your suit, it's showing that the tether snapped. Are you drifting?"

"Yes, but right now the tether is still attached, I haven't reached the end yet. I can't stop the descent thus far. The steel rope is sliding through my gloves!" Michael watched the *Deimos* floating further and further away.

"Shit!" Sonia responded, frustrated.

Michael continued grabbing at the tether, but it was too thin. He heard a zipping sound in his suit and glanced down to see the end of the steel rope popping out from the opening on his suit. He was seconds away from drifting off into space.

With his right hand, he attempted wrapping the flexible metal rope around his gloves. His descent stopped with under a foot remaining before the tear.

Breathing a sigh of relief, Michael called out to Sonia once more, "I wrapped the tether around my right hand. Got it stopped but not sure for how long. I've reached the end of the tether where it snapped off."

"How far are you from the ship?" Sonia quickly replied.

Michael looked up and over at his surroundings. "I'm guessing around fifty feet. I'm going to try pulling myself in."

Inside the *Deimos*, Sonia glanced over at a worried Olivia. "He needs our help, so I'm going to put my helmet on and try to pull him up myself. You stay put."

Olivia began protesting but it was too late, Sonia had clicked her helmet on, latching it in place then heading to the decontamination room.

She looked out the small window, remembering Michael had said he was keeping the hatch open for a quick re-entry. It was indeed still open.

"No!" she yelled as she backed up, taking her helmet off.

"What?" Olivia exclaimed.

"The outer hatch is opened. If I open the inner hatch, we'll be sucked out immediately. We're stuck in here and he's stuck out there unless he can get back into that room and close the outer hatch!"

"Michael, the outer hatch is open. I can't depressurize and pull you up without sucking all of the oxygen and us right out of the ship. Talk to me, can you pull yourself up?"

"Working on it," was the reply back.

Sonia ran her hands through her curly hair in frustration and pushed her glasses up on her nose. "What am I missing? What other options are there?"

"I wish the spacesuits could fly, then he could just land inside the decompression room," Olivia said almost to herself.

Sonia froze in place then quickly looked over at Olivia, her eyes wide.

Michael felt his grip on the steel rope once again slipping. The gloves simply couldn't get a tight enough grip and eventually he would either lose oxygen or grow too tired to continue this arduous process.

Not giving up hope, he continued on, inching his way up. He reached his left hand out, attempted to take hold, and it slipped. His body went end over end, spiraling downward until he hit the makeshift knot at the end of the break in the steel rope. This time, it didn't hold. The torn end of the tether sliced through his glove as it silently slipped through his gloves and he began floating in empty space, drifting away from the *Deimos*. He held up his hand, watching as air began slipping out from the tear on the palm of the glove.

"Michael, I have an idea," Sonia said through the com.

"Better be a good one. I'm floating. The broken tether slipped through my glove and ripped it open. I'm leaking oxygen now," Michael came back grimly.

He was breathing heavy. Too fast. Using up precious oxygen that he might need later. If there was a later. *Maybe I should just open my helmet up? Quick and easy. Spare Sonia and Olivia from having to watch me float away, and at least they'll be safe, for now.* Michael looked at the *Deimos* now growing smaller in his peripheral vision.

"This will require you to let go anyway, so step one complete," Sonia shot back.

"I'm all ears. Better make it quick," Michael responded, no longer struggling as that seemed to push him further away from the ship and push more oxygen out of his suit.

"Release your oxygen; it will push you forward. I'll line up the rear of the ship and you sail into the cargo room then seal the door behind you," Sonia came back.

They were both silent for a few seconds before Michael responded. "Alright. But it's a longshot. If I overshoot or miss the mark, that's it. I won't have enough oxygen for a redo. If it fails, you take Olivia and get to Railara. Got it?"

"I believe in you Michael. I'm going to power the ship up and get it into position. When I give you the go-ahead, blow the tank once you're lined up."

The com went silent. Michael waited and watched while the engines on the Deimos fired up, the ship now no larger than one of his fingers when he held up his hand to his face.

He looked at his oxygen level, already down to fifty percent and leaking faster than he first thought. *I'm barely going to have one try, this is going to be close.* Michael attempted to push himself forward slightly, so his head was facing the Deimos, hoping his positioning would launch him toward the opened outer hatch. One in a million chance, and quickly dwindling.

The Deimos moved forward and began making a circle, keeping a wide enough berth from Michael, flying past him before coming to a stop significantly closer to him than before. The exhaust ports dimmed as Sonia slowed down to a standstill.

Michael looked at his oxygen level, now forty percent. He held out his hand once more, watching the air escape. His heart raced in his chest. *Come on, Michael, you can do this. You've gotten this far. One more challenge. Come on!*

Sonia's voice came through the com, "Okay, this is the best I can do. What's your oxygen level?"

Looking at the readout inside his helmet, he shook the cold sweat from his face and replied, "Thirty-five percent. I don't know if I have enough to make it to the hatch!"

"You're going to try, damnit! *You are going to try!* Now, go!" Sonia shouted into the com.

Michael took a deep breath of air and held it tightly in his lungs. With his right hand, he felt around the lower half of his oxygen tank strapped to the back of his spacesuit. His memory implants had trained him on the basic mechanics of things like this and he instinctively knew where the oxygen release was. A small, curved tube on the bottom of the tank, once pulled free, would instantly release all of the oxygen in the tank from the newly opened hole.

The *Deimos* was roughly one hundred feet away now.

Thirty percent oxygen left.

Michael's heart suddenly ached with what he could only guess was love for the two people in the awaiting ship. *What does that even mean—to love? Have I been pre-programed for this? I'm guessing not. To hell with my data. To hell with those who created me. I'm my own person, and I am choosing to fight for these people who need me, right this instant!*

"Michael, now!" Sonia exclaimed through the com.

He heard the anxious voice of Olivia say, "I know you can do it!"

Staring straight ahead determinedly at the opened hatch, to life and survival, he pulled the tube on the back of the oxygen tank and felt an immediate surge as air escaped through the opened hole on the oxygen tank.

Michael's body lunged forward, his eyes widening at the abrupt rush, headfirst, toward the open hatch. He pushed his arms back against his body, hoping to propel himself forward even quicker as his oxygen level plummeted. Twenty-five, twenty, fifteen, ten. The *Warning Low Oxygen* alarm began sounding in Michael's helmet.

The hatch rushed forward toward him. Down to five perfect oxygen as Michael's body slammed against the bottom of the hatch headfirst, cracking his helmet visor but not breaking it open. Arms flailing, hands grasping for a ledge, anything to save him from floating away again as he felt the air in his lungs growing hot while he continued holding his breath.

Zero percent oxygen. Red text displayed in front of his visor: *Oxygen levels depleted. Please remove helmet immediately.*

Frantically grabbing, he clenched the edge of the hatch opening and pulled himself in, his helmet cracking further. Any second now, he would no longer be able to hold his breath or worse, his visor would bust and he would freeze instantly.

He flailed wildly inside the small room, trying to find the button to close the outer hatch. His hand hit the red button beside the opening and the hatch slid shut just as his visor broke open, sending thick glass floating into the room that had not yet been pressurized.

He let out the air in his lungs but there was no air to replace it. "I...need...air," he choked out as darkness began to wash over him.

A whoosh of oxygen swept through the small room as pieces of glass from the broken helmet, and Michael himself, fell to the floor. He lay still, unconscious, no longer breathing.

Olivia ran into the room with Sonia following closely behind. Both nearly slid onto the floor reaching Michael while Sonia took charge, rolling him onto his back. His face was pale, his eyes closed, and she quickly deduced he wasn't breathing.

Sonia immediately removed his busted helmet, throwing it out of the way, and tilted his head back, opening his mouth slightly and pressing her lips against his, filling his lungs with her oxygen. She released, took a breath and began pumping his chest with her hands clenched.

Administering CPR was something she had been trained in thoroughly in school but it had never been needed on Moon 002. A sick or injured clone was basically a dead clone, deemed unworthy of being saved. Furthermore, they had much easier methods of resuscitation, if necessary, not this archaic breathing and chest compression method only used in the direst of circumstances when no other option was available. Yet here she was, desperate to save this man's life. Never once thinking he wasn't worth the effort, that he was less than human. Willing to do anything to ensure he survived. K*eep calm, you can do this. Bring this man back!*

She came up for air. "Come on Michael, breathe for me, you can do it!"

Olivia watched on, her bottom lip trembling. She was trying to stay strong for her friends, but tears welled up in her eyes and spilled down her cheeks. Her fragile, fresh mind tried to understand the chaotic universe she had been born into, filled with such uncertainty and death. *Why? Why do people we love have to die? Let Michael live, please…let Michael live!* She lifted her hands to her mouth, covering it, while Sonia continued to administer CPR to their fallen friend.

Several more long breaths filled Michael's lungs, but it wasn't working. In her frustration, Sonia slammed her fists against his chest once more. "No! You made it this far, damnit! You are not going to die! Do you hear me?!"

Tears flowed from her eyes as hopelessness began to take over. Elise, gone. Chris, gone. Not Michael! Not him. *Please, not him!*

She put her lips on his again, trying to blow more air into his lungs but she had none left. Out of air, lips trembling against his, she did the last and only thing she could think to do. She kissed him with all the growing passion and love she felt for him in this moment.

Michael opened his eyes and moved his head, startling Sonia so much she sat up, eyes wide. He shook his head and looked over to see Olivia crying, then Sonia with tears running down her face.

He sat up as they both shouted, "Michael!" simultaneously.

Olivia immediately threw her arms around him, squeezing him tightly. He returned the hug while looking over at

Sonia, her hand to her mouth, trying but not succeeding in holding her emotions in. He held out his free arm and she quickly fell into it as tears of frustration and sadness turned to overwhelming tears of happiness.

Olivia's head burrowed into Michael's strong chest, her eyes closed, Sonia's wet cheek against his as she squeezed him tightly. The three of them clung to one another. Survivors.

"You saved me," he said softly into Sonia's ear.

She pulled back slightly, their lips an inch from each other. "I only did what I thought—"

Michael stopped her, gently kissing her lips. She closed her eyes and kissed him back.

CHAPTER 30

AMTF-24 UNDER ATTACK

The last Kernadium transport ship from Troria, Alnorix Mining Transport Freighter 24 or, AMTF-24 was about to arrive on Moon 002. It had reached Treon III and was plotting its initial descent onto the barren moon below.

The ship was a large rectangular vessel, big enough to store every barrel of Kernadium located inside the moon's storage facility if necessary. The transport freighter was nearly nine hundred feet long and while it didn't have much in the way of onboard weaponry or creature comforts, it was top of its class when it came to transporting expensive components in large quantities due to its thick, well-constructed walls.

The dark grey vessel slowed its exhaust ports down as it approached the moon below.

"Lieutenant, I'm not detecting any buildings down there," a young pilot named Travis Axwall said, looking back at his commanding officer, Lieutenant Omar Botto.

"What? What do you mean no buildings? I know communications were cut off, but the Rot infection was under control. Check again," Botto replied harshly.

Botto had come along on this final trek to Moon 002 to oversee the final Kernadium extraction. He would also see to it that no one remaining on the planet would be leaving alive, something the AMO didn't want to take part in, liquidating humans. So, the job fell to one of Levon Gonidec's top brass.

"See if Mohr is still down there. He was supposed to pick up that doctor and his mutant girlfriend or kid, whatever she was. And while you're at it, scan for any other life-signs at all. No one left alive makes it off that rock! My records indicate that along with that Petrino character there should be three other humans."

The ship's Command Center was staffed with five people, including Lieutenant Botto. More staff were spread out throughout the large freighter to ensure the drums were properly stored and secured. Most were from the AMO, but due to the close relationship the company had with Gonidec, these ships often had military on board to ensure safe passage to Troria.

It was well known through all of Troria along with the rest of the planets in quadrant 8304 that Gonidec had funded the cloning research for the sole purpose of mining the Poule plants across the solar system. Because of that, the AMO and the Gonidec regime were connected at the hip with nearly every aspect of cloning and mining.

Gonidec had been in the planning stages of an all-out invasion of Railara and, true to his word, had unleashed his military might. Conquering and toppling their government would ensure a puppet regime on a planet whose military was vast. The entire quadrant of space would be under Gonidec's control, and with it, unlimited funds and resources from numerous smaller and far less stable governing planets.

The mining of Kernadium would be, in the long term, unsustainable. Eventually, they would have to find another fuel source. There had been talk of a blue liquid able to power magnetic propulsion drives on certain ships, but that would require redesigning all of the fleets on Troria as well as the entire quadrant. Plus, the planet where it was located was much too far to pursue at this point in time. Still, it was an option Gonidec considered and had shelved for the time being.

And now, at the final pick-up on one of Treon III's dead moons, Lieutenant Botto stood up, adjusted his well-groomed black military attire and walked to the front viewscreen looking out at the approaching moon. Even from this distance, a patch of smoke could be seen on the tiny planet. Something had indeed gone wrong. This was not good. Not for Botto and not for Gonidec.

Lieutenant Botto clicked on the com system. "Commander Nic Mohr. Do you copy?"

Silence filled the Command Center as no response came back.

"Who the hell was he flying with? An android, right?" Botto barked at both of the pilots in front of him.

Travis looked at his co-pilot, Joseph May, a relatively new employee of AMO, and pointed at the information panel in front of him. "Look it up, come on!"

"I asked a question, pilot," Botto said coldly, looking at the visibly nervous Joseph May.

"Um, let's see here," May responded, flustered as he pressed several buttons, attempting to access the Deimos's schematics and crew that left Troria earlier.

"You have got to be fucking kidding me!" Lieutenant Botto shouted, making his way over to the nervous co-pilot.

"Wait, here it is. Yes. He was flying with Pilot 33. Just those two," May said, nearly tripping over his words to get them out quickly enough so as not to incur the wrath of Omar Botto, master of the many methods of pain tolerance back home.

Botto stopped short of the young man and stood upright. "Hmm, Pilot 33 and Mohr. Try the Command Center and take us down while you're at it. Let's go!"

"This is pilot Travis Axwall, come in Complex VI."

Silence on the other end.

Lieutenant Botto continued to stare out the viewscreen at the cloud of smoke growing larger and larger.

"Enhance image," he commanded.

Joseph immediately blew the image on the screen up. "Something certainly appears amiss down there. Also, sir, it looks like something is lying there, close to the Kernadium plants near a large opening in the ground that wasn't there before."

"I can see that," Botto shot back, immediately silencing co-pilot May.

The transport freighter AMTF-24 lowered further, breaching the desolate landscape below toward the open clearing where all transport freighters landed when picking up their large hauls of Kernadium. The large, heavy circular landing gear slowly withdrew and unfolded from the bottom of the ship.

"They're gone. All of them, and that crater is their exact location. *Was*, I guess is more like it," a voice from behind Botto observed.

Botto turned to face the woman typically in charge on this run from Troria to Moon 002, until he decided to come along and assert his authority. Captain Edith Hitzig, a tall, assertive, thirty-four-year-old employee of the AMO for over five years, ran this vessel back and forth to the various moons and planets where her employer had set up their facilities.

Botto fell silent, wanting to reprimed her but stopping just short of it. He respected Edith, the black-haired, stern-faced woman who stood up for herself even to him. One of the few people he knew who would be that bold. He, however, was still in command when on board any of the vessels ultimately owned by the government on Troria, and the woman he had taken to bed numerous times knew that as well.

Everyone on the bridge of the ship stared out at the wasteland that had once been Mining Complex VI. All five buildings had been wiped off the moon's surface. The landing spot was also gone. In its place was part of the crater where all of the buildings had once stood.

"So, what the hell happened here? And what is that thing outside this crater?" Botto said quietly, staring out at the destruction around them all.

Joseph May cleared his throat, nervous to say anything at all.

Travis Axwall spoke. "It's some sort of insect, from what my scanners are showing. It's burnt up, likely from the explosion that happened here."

Silence fell over the bridge. No one wanted to infuriate the Lieutenant further. Except Edith. "We need to let HQ know about this, immediately. Lieutenant? Do you concur?"

Finally breaking his silence, Botto cleared his throat, nodded to himself and spoke once more. "Yes, contact headquarters. Let them know what happened. Mining Complex VI is gone. Dr. Petrino isn't responding either."

Joseph May nodded. "Yes, sir, right away, sir."

"Sir, there's something else you should see," Axwall said nervously.

"What? What is it?" Botto barked back as Captain Hitzig joined him, standing at his side.

"Sensors are picking up activity outside the crater, around that, that bug."

"We didn't see anything when we were landing. What did we miss?" Botto replied, looking out the viewscreen then down to Travis's sensors that were blinking red and showing numerous dots floating around the screen.

Joseph May began communicating the dire situation back to the Alnorix Headquarters when something from above flew down, landing hard on the viewscreen.

Everyone, Botto and the usually unshakable Edith Hitzig included, jumped when the insectoid creature slammed against the viewscreen. It stuck to the window as if peering in, its outer shell charred and still sizzling.

"What the hell..." Travis said when another large insect landed on the other side of the large viewscreen. Directly above and around the ship, the flying silver and black bugs began swarming, primarily coming out of the large crack in the surface of the moon near the crater, attacking the vessel.

Captain Hitzig quickly took charge, not waiting on Lieutenant Botto. "We need to get out of here, now! Axwall, May, take us out."

Botto spun around to stare at the hardened assertive face of Hitzig, but she was no longer standing beside him. She had moved back to her command post. He was about to object to her giving the departure order but stopped, realizing something else was moving in toward them. Something much larger than their ship.

Climbing out of the top of the crater, an enormous silver bug was emerging, its many legs smashing down onto the rocky, burnt soil, its head moving back and forth as if surveying the area. Around it swarmed more of the smaller insectoid creatures that resembled it.

Quicky putting the pieces together, Captain Hitzig shouted out, "I think we're looking at the mate to whatever that huge dead thing is out there. And these are its offspring! I assume it's none too pleased to see us!"

The AMTF-24 had already begun lifting off of the surface of Moon 002 when Lieutenant Botto shouted to the pilots, "Come on, come on! Quicker!"

"Sir, if we move any quicker the ship could stall! This thing is heavy even without a load of Kernadium barrels onboard," Axwall responded.

Botto was about to protest but Captain Hitzig cut him off. "He's right. We need to let this play out. Joseph, if that thing gets any closer, start firing our Pulsar Cannons at it. They probably won't do much, but it might scare it off."

"Damnit!" Botto shot back, disliking their situation more with every passing second. Mining Complex VI was gone, the last haul of Kernadium was gone, and Dr. Anthony Petrino was gone.

The enormous creature stomped toward the AMTF-24 as it continued lifting up off the rocky wasteland below. It opened its jaws. A silver substance filled its mouth while it reared back slightly before launching a tirade of liquid that froze when exiting its gaping mouth.

"Brace for impact!" Captain Hitzig shouted, watching the oncoming stream of freezing liquid streak across the crater toward their ship.

Joseph May had opened fire on the insect, but the orange beams of laser light seemed to do little but bounce off of the creature's thick outer shell harmlessly.

Botto grabbed hold of a control panel in front of him as the pilots did the same.

The liquid smashed into the side of the AMTF-24, now just over three hundred feet off of the moon's surface, knocking it sideways and violently shaking everyone inside.

Joseph and Travis tried to correct the large freighter, now knocked off-course and, due to its large and heavy structure, had to be done precisely. The ship was nearly on its side with the thrusters on its underside blowing them further sideways.

"Course correct this thing or we're going to crash, you fools!" Botto shouted angrily, pulling himself up off the floor.

"He's right, we need to straighten this ship out immediately!" Captain Hitzig called out to her pilots.

From behind them, a crew member shouted, "We've got structural hull damage from that blast! I'm trying to assess how bad it is!"

The ship was starting to even out, thanks to the piloting skills of May and Axwall, as it continued upwards, still at a slight angle.

Beneath them, the creature moved forward into the crater, peering up at the ship now a mere seven hundred feet above it.

"We're not out of this yet," Captain Hitzig shouted, staring at the monitor showing the creature below, appearing to rear itself back for another blast of the freezing liquid.

"Give us more power, Axwall! We can't get hit by whatever that thing is shooting. Try to burn it!" she ordered, glancing over at a visibly worried Omar Botto, an expression she rarely, if ever saw on him.

Travis obliged, pushing the thrusters further than normal this close to the surface of a planet. Fire shot down from the exhausts on the bottom of the AMTF-24, scorching the top of the silver creature below. This bought the crew precious seconds to continue their ascent as the massive insect couldn't exhale its freezing liquid.

"Keep it up! It's working!" Lieutenant Botto yelled to the pilots.

The Kernadium-fueled fire rained down on top of the creature and propelled the ship further upwards. The creature's offspring flew around the larger bug, scattering away from the fire that was engulfing it.

"We're receiving a transmission from home base. Shall I patch them through?" Joseph May exclaimed, glancing back at both Botto and Hitzig.

Before either could answer, the creature from the surface below launched itself upwards into the sky, sailing past the ship, its outer shell now on fire. The crew inside the Command Center stared out at the monstrosity now facing them, keeping pace with the AMTF-24, both breaching the moon's atmosphere. Buzzing back and forth, both the creature and the ship it stalked soared into outer space.

"It's toying with us," Botto exclaimed, watching anxiously at the insectoid hovering.

Co-pilot May opened fire again but the creature easily swerved away from the oncoming Pulsar Cannon blasts.

Captain Hitzig clicked on the com and spoke to both the crew and the Alnorix Mining leadership back on Troria, "This is Captain Edith Hitzig. Mining Colony VI is lost, including the last pick-up of Kernadium. We've encountered a creature of unknown origin on the moon's surface that has followed us into space, and we aren't sure how to..."

She was cut off by a blast from the creature's open jaws, sending a thick stream of freezing liquid smashing against the front outer hull of the AMTF-24. The massive insect flew around the ship, continuing to blast it with the liquid that immediately froze solid against the slow-moving vessel. At the rear of the ship, it blew out more of the instantly freezing liquid against the rear exhaust ports, quickly covering them with thick layers of ice, extinguishing the flames. Soon, the ship was cocooned inside a massive chunk of floating ice.

Communications had ceased as soon as power was lost throughout the ship. The Command Center crew looked horrified at each other, no one knowing what to do next, Botto and Hitzig included.

"Power is down across the entire ship," a crewmember announced gravely but no one acknowledged him. They all knew their situation was dire.

Travis and Joseph sat back in their seats, staring out at the ice that had glazed over the viewscreen. A distorted image of the creature could be seen as it flew around the ship.

"Fifteen crew, counting us," Hitzig said grimly, glancing over at Botto who continued to stare out furiously at the ice on the viewscreen.

"We're not done yet," he said, gritting his teeth.

The silver insect, no long aflame, moved to the top of the ship and dug its numerous sharp claws into the ice that engulfed its prey. It slowly moved away with its catch, off into space, leaving the charred ruins of Moon 002 and its small, swarming offspring behind.

CHAPTER 31

SPACE STATION INFINITUM

Sonia, Michael, and Olivia resumed their charted course toward Railara without any more incidents. The torn outer hull that Michael had nearly lost his life repairing held for the duration of the flight.

Little was said for a short period after Michael had been revived, all lost in their own thoughts of the many near-death experiences they had shared over the last several days. They thought of Elise who gave her life for them to live on, her legacy now resting on the young girl with the bright blond hair.

Approaching the highly advanced planet Railara from space, the planet cast an almost neon blue hue, much of it from the numerous city lights that illuminated the planet, as well as the blue water masses spread throughout its surface.

Between them and the small planet beyond floated a large disc-shaped silver metallic construction, its numerous ports lining the flat circle. Rows of windows were visible from space, wrapping their way around the impressively large structure.

"Approaching vessel, please state your business," a man's voice cracked through the com inside the *Deimos*.

Michael and Sonia stared out at the planet they were approaching then glanced at each other nervously before Michael clicked on their com and responded.

"Hello, this is Michael Astier along with Sonia Bonnel and Olivia Petrino of the starship *Deimos* from the planet Troria. We're coming from Moon 002 near Treon III. Two of us are clones and one of us is a doctor's assistant. We have valuable information about not just Mining Complex VI but the entire AMO as well as Levon Gonidec's regime back on Troria. Requesting permission to land."

He stopped talking and Olivia whispered to him, "I want to change my last name. Can I do that?"

Sonia smiled and replied, "I would bet that could be done. And I don't blame you a bit, honey."

Olivia smiled and leaned back in her seat. "Awesome!"

"You said there are clones with you?" the voice came back with a sense of urgency.

"Yes. You're speaking to one of them. The other one is a girl, eleven years old," Michael answered.

Olivia chimed in, "Hi, nice to meet you! What's your name?"

The com clicked on again. "Well, I suppose it's nice to meet you too, young lady. My name is Connor Brook, communications officer here on the Space Station *Infinitum*. You're the girl, Olivia?"

"Yep, I was created by a very bad man. He's gone now. But I have his video recorder with a lot of notes about a lot of bad things. My mom left a message at the very end. Her name is Elise Bennet. She's dead but she was a good person, and I was created from her." Olivia stopped and took a breath.

"Hmm, Elise Bennet, you say? Hang on, let me put you on a brief hold. I'm scanning your ship, and it looks like it is equipped with four heavy laser disintegrators. We would like you to temporarily power down your vessel for now and disable your weapons. We have a tractor beam lock on you and if access is granted, we'll bring you in to one of our space docks. Please acknowledge," communications officer Brook said firmly while still keeping a friendly tone, knowing a child was aboard the incoming vessel.

Michael looked over at Sonia. "What do you think?"

"With everything we've been through over the last several days, trust is a hard thing to come by. But we've got to trust these people. Elise would have wanted it," Sonia replied assuredly.

"Trorian spacecraft *Deimos*, do you comply?" Brook said again, this time a bit firmer.

"Yes, we comply. Powering down now," Michael responded, trying to mask his displeasure at the request.

Officer Brook came through the com once more. "This is standard protocol for all off-world vessels. Especially one from Troria. I'll be in touch soon."

And with that, the com went silent. Michael nodded to himself and powered the *Deimos* down. The booster flames extinguished, and the ship remained stationary due to the invisible magnetic tractor beam now holding it in place.

"Did you notice his response when Olivia mentioned Elise's name? He's heard of her. That's a good thing," Sonia said as Olivia hopped up from her seat and stood in the middle of the Command Center between Michael and Sonia. All three gazed upon the beautiful neon blue planet and the large silver disc in front of them. Several other spacecrafts were docked in various random ports, some significantly larger than the *Deimos*, some so small they could only seat one passenger.

"This here is what I call the last stop. And yet, I can't stop thinking of my mother right now, back on Troria, all alone. Who knows what they'll do to her if they find out I'm alive and in Railarian space?" Sonia said sorrowfully.

"I'm going to do everything I can to help your mom. I promise," Michael said as he placed his hand on top of Sonia's. She looked down at his strong hand and gripped it tightly into her own.

Olivia, wanting to be a part of Michael's promise, placed her own hand on theirs and exclaimed happily, "All three of us! Rescue mission for Sonia's mama!"

Michael chuckled lightly but Sonia bit her bottom lip, trying not to shed more tears. She was finding it hard to imagine life without either of these two people who had been with her such a short time. It was as if they had been imprinted into her in real time, much like the clones were imprinted on by their makers.

After several long minutes, the com clicked back on with Brook on the other end. "Sorry about that. I had to go through several channels before finding the right person, but I found him. I'm going to have you speak briefly with Mr. Riley. He needs to confirm you are who you say you are."

"Mr. Riley? Surely, he doesn't mean," Sonia began.

"Sonia? Is that you? Sonia Bonnel?"

"Jake! What are you doing here? Didn't you leave Moon 002 on a transport back to Troria?" Sonia exclaimed excitedly, staring out at the looming Space Station *Infinitum* directly in front of them.

"Sonia, it's so good to hear your voice! We have much to discuss. Sonia, there's a girl with you? She said Elise is dead?" Jake asked nervously.

The com went silent. She wasn't sure how to respond and looked over at Michael.

"Jake Riley, this is Michael Astier. I'm a clone, Number 572. Developed on Moon 002 by Dr. Anthony Petrino. We really need to speak with you," he said calmly but firmly.

They were met with silence once more on the com. Then, slowly, the Deimos was pulled in toward Space Station *Infinitum*.

"One step closer," Sonia said, watching the space station now growing larger in their viewscreen.

Docking was an easy process. Once the *Deimos* was connected, Officer Brook came back on the com. "You three are cleared for entry. If you have any weapons on you, leave them on your ship, got it?"

"Got it," Michael replied back, happy to be able to get off the battered spacecraft.

"After you disembark, we request that you all go through our decontamination and showering room. We understand your need for privacy, but we also need to make sure the disease that has taken over the moon where you travelled from hasn't followed you here," Brook said firmly.

"We understand completely," Sonia replied, glad she would be able to get the stench and dread of the last two days off of her and the child.

"I'll personally meet you outside in the hallway once you're cleared. See you in a bit," Brook said then clicked off the com.

Olivia was the first to exit through the hatch door. Michael and Sonia walked closely together behind into the hallway of the *Infinitum*.

"Woah, this place is really neat!" Olivia exclaimed, looking around at the inviting and comfortable walkway leading out of the docking bays toward an open area where people were mingling in what looked like a waiting area and large bar and restaurant.

They were met by a woman wearing a yellow suit and a face mask, and while not the most inviting of sights, they realized the importance of keeping the space station sanitary considering the hellish virus they had been exposed to. She quietly directed them to the decontamination and shower room.

They all took turns in the decontamination tubes which were similar to many of the space ports located throughout the galaxy. Olivia giggled as the white mist sprayed her. Only when it hit her head did she grimace slightly at the sting, recalling the blow to the head Dr. Petrino had given her back on Moon 002.

All three took long showers in their own stalls then put on fresh clothes that had been given to them, compliments of the "hard working staff here at Space Station *Infinitum*" as the card placed on each of their sets of new clothes read.

Olivia was the last out as she had taken the longest, enjoying her first official shower and one of her first truly enjoyable experiences since she escaped the Clone Replication Facility. She bounded over to Sonia who was inspecting Michael's attire rather closely.

"What do you think? They gave me a dress to wear! Do you like it?" Olivia said happily while she did a quick spin in her white dress, showing herself off.

"You look absolutely beautiful, young lady," Sonia said smiling.

"Agreed. But not sure about this shirt on me, I think I need one size larger," Michael said grinning, looking down at a black, form-fitting T-shirt with the Railara planet emblem in its center. The shirt showed off his toned chest and arms a bit more than he would have liked.

"Geez, I knew you were strong but look at those muscles!" Olivia exclaimed, patting him on the chest.

Sonia glanced up into Michael's eyes and said softly, "The shirt looks good on you."

Michael grinned at what he deduced was a subtle flirtatious comment.

Sonia wore the standard issue women's clothing on the space station, a white shirt that also had the planet's emblem, a simple neon blue planet with the words, "One World, One People" embossed under it.

Down the hallway a tall man in a navy-blue uniform holding a long laser rifle similar to the Defender II stood waiting for them. The man had short blond hair and was fair skinned. He looked imposing and strong. Michael, Sonia, and Olivia headed down to meet Officer Brook.

"Welcome to Space Station *Infinitum*. I'm Connor Brook. Looks like you three got cleaned up. Did the accommodations meet your needs?" He shook all three hands, smiling at Olivia who shook his hand extra hard.

They all nodded a hello.

"No signs of infection, by the way, clean bill of health. Other than a few bumps and scrapes. Ah, you must be Olivia. How would you like some Plucress Berry Cake now that the three of you cleaned up?"

"Whatever that is, it sounds great!" Olivia exclaimed, glancing at Michael and Sonia for their approval.

"Well, as long as we stay together," Sonia said glancing over to Michael who nodded in agreement.

"We figured you would all like some food while we wait to see Mr. Riley and our chancellor Mya Brant who is currently enroute to our space station. Seems as though the three of you are already quite popular. The girl is safe here with us, all three of you are. You have my word on it," Brook assured them.

"I suppose some food would be good," Michael said, glancing at his surroundings, numerous people mingling about the large restaurant.

They took a seat and soon were eating various foods from the planet beyond the space station.

"This meat is fantastic, better than literally anything back on Troria," Sonia said, taking another bite of a pinkish well-cooked meat.

"It's actually not meat. Protein-based and manufactured on our home world with the highest levels of quality control," Brook said, glad they were enjoying their food.

Olivia was quietly eating and quite enjoying her Plucress Berry Cake after finishing the "healthy" food. Sonia and Michael were beginning to take on a parenting role with the girl, she desperately needed after the first several chaotic days of her young life.

The food they ate, while delicious, took Sonia back to Moon 002 and the "food" that the clones had unwittingly eaten year after year—recycled and repurposed expired clones. If anything could sum up the corruption of the AMO and its puppet master, the dastardly Levon Gonidec's regime, it was that. Making sentient beings eat each other. She shuddered wondering if she and the rest of the staff had also on occasion, unwittingly eaten clone meat.

She tried to refocus on their immediate situation: getting the video recorder into the right hands and stopping the madness that was the AMO and Levon Gonidec's military from the destruction it was continually perpetrating across the quadrant.

"Ahem, Sonia, that really you?" a voice from behind their table asked evenly.

Sonia quickly turned around in her seat to see Jake Riley, arms behind his back, shoulder length brown hair combed back, looking just like he had on Moon 002. His brown eyes were kind yet determined as he stared down at the three guests in front of him.

"Jake Riley! How did you end up here? I still wasn't sure if that really was you on the com back in our ship!" Sonia said, standing to her feet. It was an odd moment for both of them—the shy introvert facing the good-looking, extroverted "popular" guy from their Moon 002 days. Sonia knew she needed to fill him in on what happened to Elise, and she felt terrible about being the bearer of such bad news.

Jake gave her a hug, which she returned, bringing back a rush of memories of Elise and their experience at the mining complex. Jake was glad to see his quiet friend of the past several years alive and well, but he sensed something different about her now. He had gotten used to her personality back on Moon 002—quiet, timid and ultimately, depressed—and this new Sonia seemed to have more warmth and confidence. He liked it.

"Jake, I mean, Commander, this is Michael Astier, a clone that...survived. Actually, scratch that. A *person*, like me, that survived," Sonia said giving Michael a slight nod, then added. "Without his leadership and selflessness, we wouldn't be standing here in front of you right now."

Saying the words out loud and seeing the brave man in front of her, Sonia felt ashamed of how she had once, not long ago, thought of clones as *lesser than*. Her mom was right those many years ago and she had been wrong. She knew that now. These clones were very much equals, if not, in some regards, even more advanced than humans, demonstrating higher levels of empathy, kindness, self-sacrifice and bravery. Traits that many of her fellow brethren would shy away from, herself included.

Michael held out his hand to Jake who took it, shaking it firmly. "Michael, it's a pleasure to make your acquaintance. I'm glad you made it out of there alive. We have much to discuss."

"We do," Michael said coolly, quickly pulling the note from his pocket he had kept with him from one of the dead clones back at the Replication Facility. He opened it and handed it to Jake.

Looking down at the letter, Jake took it from him and read it aloud. "Clone #206: Subject named *Seth* shows extreme signs of malnutrition from the infection. Feeding tube not taking well to the host's stomach due to internal alien growth. Several more green rotting lesions spotted on lower intestines.

Recommend ceasing incubation before more resources are spent. Body to be incinerated. Signed Dr. Anthony Petrino."

"Did you know this was going on? Before you left?" Michael asked pointedly, wanting to gauge the previous commander's reaction.

Jake frowned and met his eyes, studying the man that had somehow safely left Moon 002 in one piece with two other survivors. "Yes. As a matter of fact, Michael, I did know. All too well. That's why I'm here, it's why I risked my life escaping to Railara. Come with me, there's someone I need you to meet. But before that, who is this young woman sitting before us with a mouthful of cake?" He looked down smiling at Olivia who met his gaze.

She hopped to her feet, wiping her mouth, then held out her hand. Jake moved forward, taking it into his own. "Olivia? You said you had a mom, and her name was Elise?"

Looking into his eyes with her own piercing green eyes, she nodded yes. "It's all here in this video recorder. Notes that a bad man name Dr. Anthony Petrino made. A very bad man. He tried to kill me and had a hand in killing my mom. That disease got to her."

Jake got to one knee, looking into Olivia's eyes. *Just like her mother's.*

"Olivia, I'm sorry to hear about your mother not making it. She was a special woman. A very special woman," he sighed and hung his head, suddenly feeling tears begin to well up in his eyes.

"She died saving our lives after we attempted to leave in the Trorian ship," Sonia said grimly. "Elise was stabbed by Dr. Petrino and later infected with the…" she trailed off. "It's been a hell of a time there since you left."

Jake looked solemnly toward Sonia and Michael. Getting back to his feet, he said, "I can only imagine what you all went through there, and I desperately wish I could have helped. I was re-assigned by the AMO. And I was being watched, they knew something was up with the level of resistance activity being intercepted on Troria. My name came up on their *lists* but hadn't been confirmed. Rest assured, if I hadn't escaped, I would be dead right now. Elise felt it best that I go. In fact, she forced me to. She was to follow once the skeleton crew was relieved. With the help of the Railarian government, who we've been in continual contact with now for several years, I was given safe passage here. They worked out the details, I can tell you more about that later, it isn't important."

He motioned for them all to follow him, turning to Officer Brook. "Thanks for helping out, officer," he said, giving the tall man a nod.

"It was a pleasure meeting you all. If there is anything we can do to make your stay as pleasant as possible here aboard the space station *Infinitum* please do not hesitate to ask," the officer said smiling at them all.

"More cake!" Olivia called out as she turned to follow Michael, Sonia, and Jake who had turned to leave.

The four of them walked out of the restaurant to an elevator where they paused and waited for the doors to open.

Jake looked at Michael and Sonia and said, "Chancellor Brandt doesn't fly up from Railara on a whim. She wants to meet with you both. And you too, Olivia. War, it seems, has begun."

Sonia and Michael looked gravely at each other as the elevator doors opened; a hushed silence came over them on the ride up to the top floor of the *Infinitum*.

Jake led them to a set of closed doors marked *Conference* Room A. The four of them entered a room at what appeared to be the top of the space station, complete with a glass ceiling displaying incredible views of a distant Nebula in outer space as well as large swaths of stars and planets.

A woman stood in the center of the room filled with tables and chairs clearly set up for speaking engagements and important meetings. She turned to greet her guests. In her forties and wearing rather elegant clothes befitting her status—a slate gray pantsuit that fit perfectly around her athletic build—she looked to be in good health, even with her brown hair showing significant signs of graying, which she wore in a bun at the back of her head. Everything about Chancellor Mya Brant said *leader*.

"Michael, Sonia, Olivia, I would like you all to meet Chancellor Mya Brant, second in line to the monarchy on planet Railara. She was instrumental in my escape from the transport shuttle from Moon 002 to Troria. I've been working with her for quite some time now but only up to a certain point. I don't have what you seem to be in possession of currently." Jake turned to look at young Olivia, still holding onto the video recorder.

"He's right," Chancellor Brant said, assertively making her way across the room and holding out her hand, first to Sonia, then Michael and finally, Olivia. After shaking their hands, she stood upright, putting her hands behind her back and speaking authoritatively.

"Everyone, please take a seat!" the Chancellor exclaimed, motioning with her eyes toward the chairs wrapped around the large table in the meeting room. She waited for the new arrivals to comply then continued, "I'm not going to mince words here, our peaceful planet is on the brink of war. A war we desperately need help to win from other nearby planets in our quadrant. A war that will decide the future of cloning and mining planets of their valuable resources. A war that could cost us everything, or, free this entire quadrant of a vile regime hell-bent on plundering and conquering by force as far and wide as their resources and the resources of those they conquer can carry them. Your home world, Sonia. And I suppose yours as well, Michael and Olivia."

Silence fell across the room, all eyes on the woman in the gray pantsuit. She began pacing back and forth then spoke again. "Gideon Novare is our leader on Railara. He admits to having dragged his feet on this impending war far too long. Mining colonies continue being developed by the AMO which are essentially concentration death camps for literally every single clone. They, you, actually…are considered property, nothing more." Her eyes fell on Michael as she paused for a moment. "But I'm guessing you know that already."

She continued, "They'd been good at hiding their atrocities until Elise and Jake here came to us with a long-term plan which is in the process of being implemented now." She paused again then looked at Olivia. "I hear there is a video recorder with information on Trorian military installations that could be of use, is this correct?"

Olivia held out the video recorder. "Here, I knew I needed to keep it for a reason. My mama is on there too," she said in a hushed, almost reverent tone to the elegant but authoritative woman standing in front of her.

Chancellor Mya Brant's stern exterior melted as she looked down at the beautiful, spitting image of an eleven-year-old Elise Bennet. She smiled at the girl then took the video recorder from her, looking it over. "I would like to view the contents to confirm its authenticity, as it could potentially be our last and best way to rally the troops, so to speak. Otherwise, we fear our planet will be invaded by Gonidec's massive military. All for our Kernadium, which we have in abundance because using it sparingly, in small doses, works. Harvesting the plants too quickly results in their death and the death of the planets from which they're harvested. It's foolish, greedy and shortsighted. Something Mr. Gonidec excels in, I'm afraid."

"I snagged a piece of paper from one of the rooms back on Moon 002, it confirms some of what is on the video recorder," Michael said, digging into his pocket and handing the paper over to the Chancellor who took it and read over it.

"More proof of the murder that was and still is taking place across the quadrant, and spreading," she responded grimly.

"Jake, I'm still surprised you actually escaped," Sonia said.

Inhaling deeply, Jake responded, "Elise and I had it planned out. We'd known each other for quite some time. I loved her."

He paused, looking over at Olivia, then continued. "We met back in our training on Troria and quickly found similar interests. Mainly, the corrupt government we both wanted to have a hand in taking down. There's a major underground communication network back on our planet that put us in touch with the Railarians. We've been feeding them information for years now on all of the countless atrocities perpetrated by Gonidec's regime. It was incredibly difficult while at Mining Complex VI due to the tight security from the AMO, but seeing it firsthand was important and ultimately, we decided, worth the risk. It was imperative that we find a smoking gun to get others onboard, not just rumors and hearsay. Then I was called back to Troria, that's when my escape plan had to begin."

He fell silent. Chancellor Brant accessed the video recorder, setting it on a table in front of her and patching it through to a large screen descending from the ceiling behind her.

The five of them watched the video clips of Dr. Anthony Petrino. They listened to the horrors of what went on at Mining Complex VI and other Alnorix mining facilities across the galaxy. The feeding of clones their own dead. The dangerous and often times fatal working conditions along with the burn pits. The Rot spread and what could very likely happen on other mining facilities if left unchecked. And then of Olivia and how she came to be. What he had planned to do with her and vital information he had stored deep in her memories as a safeguard for him and his safety.

"We didn't watch all of this," Sonia said when new video clips popped up detailing Gonidec's military complexes, primarily, entrance into his own private bunker. Information that could potentially bring them to their knees. Information regarding weak points on their fleets. Weak points in the security inside Gonidec's own bunker and other numerous high profile military targets. He referenced Olivia at times, exclaiming that more detailed information was stored inside her brain. All of which would be handed over upon assurance of him being taken well care of.

"How in the bloody hell did he come across all of this seemingly top-secret information?" Sonia asked, truly impressed with the vast wealth of information found on the video recorder.

"We think he had been planning this ever since being assigned to Moon 002," Jake responded. "While still on Troria. Say what you will about the man, but he had connections deep inside the Gonidec government that trickled over into the AMO. Money talks. Rumors are, and these are just rumors, mind you, Petrino was quietly creating clones for special individuals. Servants, in the worst way possible, if you catch my drift." He was careful to not get into too many ugly details in front of the young girl.

Sonia shuddered at the thought of possible clone sex slaves made by the same creepy individual that created Olivia. All to service the vile humanity that infested Gonidec's military.

"All about leverage," Chancellor Brant said, quiet enough for Olivia not to hear. "The man was thinking he was setting himself up quite nicely. Good chance he would have been executed. Along with the girl, just having this information will get you a quick gunshot to the head there."

Jake nodded in agreement silently.

They skipped to the end and watched the clip of Elise saying her goodbyes. All were silent in the room. Jake hung his head. It was tough to see the beautiful Elise, seconds away from her death, captured on this screen. He thought back to their last night together on the hellish landscape that was Moon 002. A night of lovemaking and goodbyes. Now he knew they were indeed, permanent goodbyes.

Michael and Sonia went on to tell of what had happened over the course of the last several days. From Michael's awakening and finding Olivia to Elise ultimately giving her life for her crew, and their perilous journey through space and finally arriving at Railara.

"Her death will not be in vain. She saved you three and this video recorder. Railara is indebted to her, and you four. Jake, I know how difficult it was for you to slip through the cracks. They assume you're dead," Chancellor Brant said looking in his direction.

"Long story, that one. Let's just say for now that we made my transport shuttle accident look quite fatal, and I guess for one of their androids, it was," he replied, noticing Michael and Sonia looking over at him.

"That's enough for today. Rest. Space Station *Infinitum* is yours to relax in. Olivia, sometime soon, with your permission, we may need to do a scan on you. It won't hurt, but it could give us vital information on the organization that perpetrated the numerous crimes you were witness to," Chancellor Brant said softly.

"As long as Michael and Sonia say it's okay, it's okay with me. I want to help," Olivia responded.

"You're a good girl, it sounds like you take after your mother a lot," Brant replied with a smile.

They said their goodbyes to the Chancellor and left the conference room on the top floor of the space station. Jake was assigned the duty of making copies of the video recorder's contents that would be sent out to surrounding planets in the coming days. The contents would certainly raise eyebrows and hopefully lead to their ultimate goal—the takedown of Gonidec's regime once and for all.

"Look, I know this is a ton of stuff to process, but I'm here to help. I'll show you to your rooms tonight then we can reconvene tomorrow, sound good?" Jake said while the elevator made its way to a lower level where sleeping accommodations were provided.

"I didn't want to say anything up there, but Michael has only a one-year lifespan, Jake. And from what I've heard, that could be reversed. Do you know anything about this?" Sonia asked.

Nodding, Jake replied, "It's true. It can indeed be reversed. Michael should be able to live out his life to the full, barring any unforeseen ailments. I can't promise anything, that's not my area of expertise, but it's a process that can only be reversed back on Troria."

Sonia grimaced and looked over at Michael who was playing a hand gesture game with Olivia, something implanted from his childhood. She looked back at Jake, bitterness in her eyes.

"I see how you look at him, Sonia," he said quietly, so only she could hear. "Of course, you know how things like that are looked upon back on Troria."

She nodded, "Oh I know. And it's sick. In the nightmare we managed to survive, I've come to the realization that they are people. Just like you and me. People with their own thoughts, hopes, dreams."

"You're right, of course. We have to stop this authoritarian regime. If we do nothing, evil will assuredly win. This is why I was willing to do anything I could, going so far as to work on Moon 002 for as long as I did. Seeing first-hand what happens in the hopes that I can do something. The same was true of Elise," Jake said sadly.

"I never thought I'd be a fighter. That's not me. But I will, I'll fight for my mom back on Troria and for each and every clone destined to a short life of servitude. And for free planets like Railara."

Michael and Olivia stopped playing their game and moved in beside her. She looked at them both, adding, "For my friends." Michael took her hand into his as Olivia leaned her head against Sonia's shoulder.

The resistance was underway.

CHAPTER 32

WISE WORDS FROM GIDEON NOVARE

The following day, the three of them travelled to Railara with Jake Riley in a small shuttle craft specifically made for running guests back and forth from the space stations around the planet. They marveled at the beauty of Railara with its busy cities and large swaths of peaceful countryside.

The planet was a technical marvel. The infrastructure was wonderful and while there was crime on the planet, it was substantially less than on a planet such as Troria. Railara's people were peaceful and worked hard at bettering themselves and those around them. All were looked upon as equals, regardless of what area of land or what settlement they resided in.

The shuttle craft took the four of them to a hospital that specialized in advanced biotechnology where Michael received a thorough scan to determine if indeed a one-year life-cycle inhibitor had been programmed into him by the AMO.

Sonia waited with him to hear the results along with Olivia.

"How long will I live, doctor?" Michael asked the elderly doctor who greeted them in the waiting area.

The doctor took a seat across from the group and cleared his throat. "You might be a 'clone'—I hate that word, by the way—but you are made up of everything any of us in this building are made up of. However, in your current state, you have a lifespan of only one year, I'm sorry to say. Olivia, though, could live to be one hundred if she takes care of herself." He paused to let the news sink in before continuing. "We do not clone here, for obvious reasons. Therefore, the method to reverse the one-year limiter is beyond our capabilities. The Trorian government, such as it is, has the technology to reverse it. But that's on Troria, I'm sorry."

Upon hearing this, Sonia's mind went to the countless clones that had been euthanized after one year of hard labor, to quickly be replaced by another and turned into food or simply burned in a large unnamed and unmarked pit.

Michael looked over at her, and she felt as if he knew what she was thinking. She felt dirty for being a small cog in the Alnorix death machine, even if she had attempted numerous times to throw a wrench in the wheels of death on Moon 002. He gave her a reassuring smile, instantly pulling her back to the moment.

"We'll figure something out, Sonia," Michael said hopefully.

Sonia looked away, tears welling up in her eyes once more, ashamed for not doing more when she had the chance, willfully being a part of the cloning industry for years. She tried to hide her emotions in front of Olivia.

The doctor looked directly at Michael and said, "I'm not sure you are aware of what clones go through at the one-year mark, Michael, but I think you should know so you're prepared."

Michael shook his head, replying, "I'll pass, doctor. I have one year, and I intend to live it to the fullest. In the meantime, I'm confident I will find a way to reverse the lifespan limiter."

Nodding and smiling briefly, the doctor replied, "As you wish. I truly wish you all the best and hope everything works out."

They thanked the doctor and made their way, once more with Jake, back to the transport shuttle and on to another building, a skyscraper whose peak crested the beautiful neon blue clouds in the sky.

Olivia, her child-like mind easily leaping from the heaviness of the doctor's visit to their new surroundings, commented excitedly, "Wow, these buildings almost reach outer space, don't they?"

"Maybe not quite that far, but close, I suppose," Jake replied chuckling as he explained to them the marvelous infrastructure in the cities of Railara.

Sonia stood near Michael as the shuttle docked and they were led to a facility that would quickly and painlessly extract the information Petrino had stored inside Olivia's mind. Her own mind continually went back to what she had already known but was confirmed by the doctor hours earlier. Michael Astier would cease to exist in one year. His body functions would cease, and he would die. She couldn't fathom the horror of it.

"Will this hurt? I think I can take it. I donated blood to my mom," Olivia said bravely.

The doctor, a woman in her mid-thirties named Hannah Rowe, assured her it would be painless.

Seeing Olivia's nervousness, Sonia quickly walked over to the girl, bent down slightly and whispered in her ear, "It'll be okay. We're right here in the same room. We aren't leaving you. Do you trust me?"

Looking up with her piercing green eyes, identical to her mother's, she nodded and gave Sonia a hug then went with the doctor to lie down on a soft mat, waiting for the machine to power up.

"I wish she wouldn't have to do this," Sonia said quietly to Michael and Jake, her arms crossed and a concerned look on her face, still trying to shake off her sadness over Michael's news.

Instinctively, Michael put his arm around her shoulder and she immediately leaned in, accepting his affection.

Noticing this, Jake spoke, quiet enough as to not disrupt the procedure about to take place. "Have you two thought about what you'll do with the girl?"

Michael and Sonia looked at each other, then at Jake. Michael said, "She stays with us. We were brought together for a reason back on Mining Complex VI and we've been through more than most people should have to deal with their entire lives."

"And, what about this?" Jake said, acknowledging the budding relationship in front of him, one they all knew would be cut short in less than a year.

Sonia and Michael looked at one another again, smiling. Neither responded.

The machine hummed to life as a red glow emanated from the top down onto Olivia. Numbers and data appeared on a screen in front of Doctor Hannah Rowe as she scanned over them then checked on Olivia.

The process was completed in less than five minutes.

"That wasn't so bad now, was it?" the kind doctor asked.

Olivia nodded and smiled as she rushed over to Sonia and Michael. "Did I do okay?"

Michael gently put his hand on the back of her head affectionately, and said softly, "You're the bravest girl on Railara. And I mean that. I don't think anyone else here has done the incredibly courageous things you have in such a short time, am I right?"

"Right!" Olivia exclaimed.

"Well, it's all here," Doctor Rowe said. "I don't know how this Petrino guy did it, but there are details laying out future attacks on virtually every planet here in quadrant 8304. I see financial records that could literally bring the AMO and Gonidec's regime to their knees. Here you go." She handed Jake the file, stored safely on a small thin metallic square ejected from her monitor.

"Thank you, doctor. Follow me," Jake said to the others with a hint of urgency, turning and leaving the room. In the long hallway leading out to the transport shuttle, he said, "It's time for you three to meet the leader of Railara, Gideon Novare."

They flew to a large circular building in the center of the city, landing on top of the massive steel structure where they were greeted by two guards dressed in uniform. A large Railara planet flag flew in the warm breeze.

"This way," Jake said as the guards parted ways, letting them pass. They entered the building and quickly made their way through a beautifully decorated walkway to a pair of closed double doors.

The tall, handsome leader shook their hands as they entered, stopping at Olivia. "Young lady, you have done more than you can imagine. The people of Railara and our allies are all indebted to you."

Olivia smiled wide, and said politely, "Thank you, sir."

Gideon Novare then looked up at the adults in the room, motioned for them to take a seat, and his tone grew more serious. "We've detected heavy movement in Trorian space, he's amassing his fleet as we speak. Things are moving quickly. We've sent all of the information you three have provided up to our allies across the quadrant far and wide. This gives them all a significant advantage and puts us in a great spot for a quick ceasefire—pending the removal of Levon Gonidec, of course," he said, running a hand through his well-groomed wavy and graying head of hair.

"Sir, if I may, who takes over if you *can* get rid of him?" Sonia asked. "From the information gathered on the video recorder, it appears his security is nearly impenetrable. Won't it be hard to remove him?" She knew all too well the horrors that man had wrought across all of Troria. Leading with fear had its advantages. His people were terrified of him and what he was capable of doing.

The room grew quiet. Gideon Novare looked over at Jake Riley.

"Jake? You would take over Troria?" Sonia exclaimed, surprised at this revelation. But on further reflection, she realized it made sense. She had heard from several of the other doctors' assistants, while stationed back on Mining Complex VI, of Jake Riley's numerous achievements back on Troria. He was well liked by not only his fellow trainees but also his superiors, taking charge and getting things done quickly while still showing an overt sense of empathy. Many that knew him believed he could have a future in politics.

"Temporarily," Jake said. "What Troria needs now is stability. Then a free and fair democratic election. No games. One person, one vote, down the line across the planet."

"We have many people inside the Gonidec regime ready to move," Gideon Novare said. "His own people reached out to us for help. Some of whom were discovered and quickly executed. But those that remain are ready and waiting. We've got to cut off the head of the snake. A great number of his military are ready to fold, and this bit of good fortune by way of the video recorder and Olivia herself will help save lives, all over the quadrant. I understand this came at a high price and am so very sorry to hear about the tragic loss of Elise Bennet. She was an incredible woman, and her memory lives on through you, child." He looked at Olivia with compassion.

"If war comes to Troria, innocent civilians will perish," Sonia said sadly. "I made a promise to my mother I would be back. Back with the proper resources to give her the heart surgery she desperately needs but can't afford."

Jake spoke up at this. "We are hoping for little ground combat. This war will be fought primarily in the sky. And if my mission is a success, even less chance of boots on the ground urban warfare."

Sensing Sonia's unease, Gideon Novare added, "Sonia, I feel for your mother. For all people on Troria, held captive by a dictator. This quadrant of the galaxy will soon fall to ruin if nothing is done. I take personal responsibility for how far this has gone. Too many planets have been stripped of their resources by the AMO. Even now, Gonidec has plans to move farther past the quadrant if he is successful in his attacks. He intends for the top five percent to own and rule over the ninety-five, and mark my words, he will succeed if we fail."

Sonia nodded slowly. She knew he was right. She had seen this day coming for years. Once Levon Gonidec had assumed power on Troria, things went downhill. The health and wellbeing of the people plummeted and mistrust sprang up. There was no more honest information available to the people, all news was filtered through the Gonidec regime. Most people began living off of scraps while the wealthy and powerful gained more wealth and power. And then came the clone slaves and with them, Rot on Moon 002.

"Olivia, I know you gave your very own blood to your mother," Novare said gently. "I hate to ask this one more favor of you, but I must. Back when we extracted the data from you, we took a blood sample. May we use it? Dr. Petrino was a bad man but he purposely created you devoid and immune of the Rot virus. This same virus has been detected on several other planets now where Kernadium is being harvested. We must have a vaccine to counteract another breakout. It cost the lives of nearly all of Mining Complex VI. I hate to think what it could do if it spread on other worlds where Alnorix has set up their slave camps. Once we defeat them, these concentration work camps will immediately cease and every clone will be freed."

Olivia didn't hesitate, "Of course! I'm a pro at giving blood! If blood saves lives I will give it all!"

Sonia and Michael smiled warmly at Olivia's selflessness.

Her childlike innocence caused Gideon to chuckle. "Well, we won't need it all, but thank you for offering. You are a brave girl, Olivia. All of you in this room are brave."

There was a knock at the door. "Come in," Gideon said quickly.

A young woman peeked her head in the door. "It's time for your presidential address, sir."

Gideon nodded, "I'll be right there, thank you, Claire."

She shut the door behind her and silence once more fell over the room.

After a moment, Michael said, "What about me, sir? I'm ready, willing, and able to do what needs to be done."

Sonia and Olivia snapped to attention at his comment.

"Michael, that is for you to decide," Gideon replied. "You three have been through so much. I'm not asking you for anything other than you enjoy your life on our planet for as long as you like. There are plenty of jobs that would suit you perfectly. Same for you, Sonia. And you, Olivia, we have the very best schools in the quadrant." He smiled warmly, nodded, then with his head held high, headed out to address his people.

"I know what you're thinking, Michael. Please, no," Sonia said quietly. Her eyes pleaded with him not to do what she knew he was thinking of doing—joining the fight.

"Come on, let me show you to where we have you set up. You'll love your apartments," Jake interrupted.

Sonia continued to stare into Michael's eyes, the first man in as long as she could remember that she had genuine feelings for. Her mind went to the kiss they shared on board the *Deimos*. Her heart broke for this man who had been dropped into her life with a death sentence hanging over his head. Less than twelve months and counting.

Sensing her unease, he glanced over at her, gave her a quick smile then took her hand and walked out with her, Olivia, and Jake, back to the transport shuttle and on to their temporary apartments.

All three of them asked Jake questions about Railara on their journey. About the delicious and sustainable food sources, life on the planet, and the Kernadium buried deep under their soil that Gonidec so desperately wanted to mine for his own gain. Jake, in turn, told them what he knew of these things, and of a new resource he and other scientists were excited about.

"I'm convinced that a liquid some have named *synth* is the future. It's been located on several worlds moons already and can be extracted without disrupting the ecosystems of the moons, if there are any. It replenishes itself and, while it is highly flammable, would bring about a new age in space travel. Magnetic propulsion. It's in the early stages of development and we're already in contact with several planets in other quadrants monitoring how sustainable it really is. Time will tell. We could be many years away from it, we simply don't know. But Kernadium harvesting is archaic. And extremely dangerous. As you all know by now."

They flew past other transport shuttles, all varying in shape and size, many of which were hauling people to and from work and school. This was the main means of transportation on Railara, Jake told them.

After a short flight from the Capital building, they landed on a grassy patch near several small building complexes. Outside, people were mingling in the street or working in their own private yards, mowing the grass, tending to gardens, and doing other small chores.

"We're here. I made sure you three got a large condo. Two stories, three bedrooms, two bathrooms. Cozy. Temporary, of course. It's crowded here in the capital. If you decide to stay here, there are some stunning locations spread out across the planet with much more room to well, spread out. For now, consider this home. You're in apartment number eight. Right over there." Jake pointed to the two-story apartment in front of them.

It looked similar to the others in the neighborhood which was just fine with Michael and Sonia. They wanted to blend in and not draw any unneeded attention, not after everything they had been through.

"A bit of rest will do us all good," Sonia said looking up at the sky. Swirling clouds had given way to dusk. It had been a long day of doctors and meetings and they were weary. Olivia was already inching her way impatiently toward the apartment Jake had pointed to.

"Food and drinks in the kitchen. You'll find all the creature comforts you want." Jake paused and glanced quickly at Michael. "Not sure how long I'll be around. My time on Railara ends soon, my destination is Troria."

Michael immediately sensed Sonia's eyes on him. He cleared his throat and held out his hand for Jake to take. "Goodnight, Jake. Thanks again for everything."

Jake smiled and took Michael's hand into his. A strong hand. T*his man is a fighter.*

"Goodnight, Sonia," Jake said and turned to leave.

"Hey, Jake, one quick thing," Sonia said.

"Yes?"

"Remember when Petrino was drunk and acting inappropriately toward Elise? We were all in the rec room hanging out together," Sonia said quietly so Olivia was sure to not hear more talk of Petrino.

"I do. How could I forget it?"

"Well, thanks for sticking up for her and not flying off the handle at Petrino. I loathed that man, truly. But he was still a person. You made every effort to be kind to him, you were the only one to do so, and I think he respected you for that in his own way. I guess what I'm really trying to say is, I wish Elise were here for you," Sonia said sadly.

Jake nodded slowly, touched by her words. "So do I, Sonia. Petrino though, well, every person has the opportunity to do the right thing and he had many. I'm not sure where things went wrong with that man, but his legacy isn't all bad. He may well have helped us win the war just as it's ramping up."

"And he gave us her," Sonia said lovingly, looking over at Olivia who had grabbed Michael's hand, pulling him toward the awaiting apartment number eight.

"Indeed, goodnight, Sonia." He glanced at Michael then at her, smiled and turned away, walking back toward his transport shuttle.

CHAPTER 33

GAME PLAN

The three of them made themselves at home that evening in their new apartment. It was quaint and roomy, especially in a city as populated as Aphus, the capital of Railara nearly three million people called home on a planet of just under one billion.

They soon noticed the apartment was not only stocked with food but clothes as well. The day was fast approaching its end, so Olivia showered, put on fresh pajamas and headed to bed for the night.

Sonia peeked her head into Olivia's room and asked, "How are you holding up?"

Olivia motioned for her to come into her room which Sonia obliged, sitting beside her nestled under her covers yawning. She ran a hand through Olivia's straight blond hair, identical to Elise's.

"What's going to happen to us? I mean, we're just visitors here, right? Where is home?" Olivia said with a hint of sadness.

Contemplating this a moment, Sonia responded, "Well, honey, this can be home, if you want it to be. The schools here are great from what we were told. Right? And it's beautiful here, even a large city like this is just so, clean."

"I guess so," Olivia responded hesitantly, looking away.

"What is it, honey? What's on your mind?" Sonia asked quietly, still running her hand through the girl's hair.

"Well, it's just, I don't have a mom. Or a dad. I don't have anyone. I don't know anyone. What if you and Michael leave me? I've tried to be strong, but I'm scared, Sonia! I keep having thoughts of the mean man that created me. Holding a gun to me and hitting me over the head with it. Trying to kill me! And those monsters that were chasing Michael and me, and the one that ate our ship. So many scary things I try to push out of my mind, but they keep coming back. The scariest thing though is the thought of being alone. Michael only has one year to…" Olivia stopped speaking, her bottom lip trembling and her eyes tearing up.

Sonia never stopped running her hand through the girl's hair affectionately, and never broke her gaze with Olivia's green eyes, now brimming with tears.

"Now, Olivia, I want you to listen to me. Okay?" she said softly but firmly. "I will never, ever leave you. Do you understand? Where I go, you go. Where you go, I go. This is my promise to you. Those monsters we escaped from? They're gone. We defeated them, in a sense, we defeated the whole planet. As for Michael, well, we keep fighting, okay?" She paused, fighting back tears of her own. In a sense, they were all faced with the question of *what next?*

Olivia's tears now flowed freely. "Yes, but what about Michael? He escaped but really, he didn't! I saw the way that Jake guy looked at him. He wants him to go along with him to Troria, I can tell! I don't want him to die! You and Michael are all I have!"

Sonia was at a loss for words; she agreed with Olivia. She didn't want him to leave either, but that was a conversation for another time. She leaned forward and kissed the girl on her forehead then wiped away her tears. "Do you trust me, Olivia?"

Olivia nodded yes quickly.

"Then you get some sleep. You know where my room is. You're brave, the bravest girl I know. Just remember, where you go, I go, where I go, you go."

"Where you go, I go, where I go, you go," Olivia repeated, sniffling and wiping her eyes.

Sonia began to stand and Olivia quickly pulled herself up, wrapping her hands around Sonia tightly and squeezing her. "I love you," the girl whispered.

Sonia's heart broke all over again for the girl she held tightly. "I love you too, honey."

Olivia laid back down on her bed, staring up at Sonia, her green eyes filled with love.

After closing the door behind her, Sonia made her way down the hallway. Michael was up one floor and she saw his light was on in his room. She turned from the stairs so she wouldn't have to look in that direction. *What the hell are we going to do? One year! Michael has one year to live! And my mom less, much less!*

She stood in the hallway as her mind once more went to the brief kiss they shared aboard the *Deimos*. She yearned for another. To be close to him. "Please don't leave us, Michael," she said quietly, turning to go to her own room.

"Sill up?" Michael said quietly as came down the stairs and saw her standing in the hallway unmoving.

Caught off guard, Sonia jumped. "You scared me," she said, more curtly than she was intending.

"Sorry, I just saw you standing down here so I..."

She cut him off, trying to whisper so as not to wake Olivia. "Michael, you just, you just cannot leave Olivia! She needs you! I saw the look Jake gave you. He's a good man but he's going to convince you to go to war with him and you can't, Michael! You've done your time!" The words rolled off her tongue. She wasn't even entirely aware of all that she was saying.

Michael, caught off guard, stared into Sonia's eyes. She wasn't wearing her glasses and it made her eyes look all the more beautiful. He reached out, took her by the waist and pulled her into him. Their lips locked as she put her hands on the back of his neck, pulling him in tighter.

They quietly bumped up against the wall, not breaking their embrace. Michael's hands moved over her back, feeling her warm body tight against his. Their feet moved, almost in unison, toward Sonia's bedroom door.

Michael gently closed it behind them, continuing their passionate embrace. A small light illuminated the room, leading them to the bed. Sonia took off Michael's T-shirt, taking in how good he smelled from his recent shower. Her whole body was warm to his touch as they fell onto the bed, their clothes quickly thrown on the floor behind them.

Later, they both fell asleep soundly in each other's arms and slept the whole night through.

Sonia opened her eyes and stretched. She was still in bed, but light was shining through the window on the far side of the room. Sitting up in bed, she immediately felt her nakedness and stood up, wrapping the blanket around her. Michael wasn't in the room, but the door was closed. She heard talking from somewhere else in the apartment.

Her mind went to the previous night of lovemaking and Sonia blushed, running her hands through her hair and out of her face. She grabbed her glasses then slipped the blanket off and got cleaned up.

Once showered, she put on fresh clothes provided by the good people of Railara and headed out to see Michael cooking Olivia breakfast while she sat at the small bar in the kitchen talking his ear off. A warm smile spread across her face at the sight in front of her.

She strolled into the kitchen, catching both Michael and Sonia's attention. Michael, it appeared had worked out early and was still in warm-up pants and a tight tank top while Olivia wore a white night gown.

"Hey there, sleepy head!" Olivia said as she made her way into the cooking space to see what Michael was making.

"Pancakes and sausage links is what's on the menu, if you're interested," Michael said happily.

"Mmm! That smells delicious!" Sonia replied, looking down at the grouping of perfectly round cakes and sizzling links beside them on the stove top.

"Mine has added sprinkles in them, I requested them specifically," Olivia said happily, reaching over the bar top and pointing to little multi-colored pieces of sugar on top of two of the cakes.

"So, what if I want them? Huh?" Sonia teased.

"Well, then you'll have to just wait, right Mike?" Olivia retorted back.

"Mike? I'm not on a shortened name basis?"

"For now," Olivia said back smiling.

"Well, Mike agrees with her. You'll have to wait your turn for a custom order," Michael said.

Sonia once more smiled warmly, watching Michael cook for them. He glanced over at her while Olivia focused on the pancakes and Sonia leaned in and gave him a quick kiss on the lips.

He smiled at her then looked back at the pancakes shouting, "Order up!"

They ate together cheerfully, chatting about random, insignificant topics while enjoying each other's company. Their own little family unit taking shape.

Over the next few days, they explored the sights of the city, one day going to an aquarium to see all of the alien creatures that populated the seas of Railara and staying up late watching movies on the holographic display in their small living room. Comedies were Olivia's favorite.

Michael and Sonia walked hand in hand when they were all together, something Olivia noticed and adored. Whenever she caught them holding hands, she quickly parked herself on the other side of Michael and took his free hand into hers.

In between the fun, more serious conversations took place. Jake and Michael talked in depth about his strategy for taking down Levon Gonidec. Jake discovered Michael was incredibly intelligent when it came to strategizing and coordinating against the enemy. He marveled that this man, this *living being*, had the DNA that made him a true asset to Railara and the free planets in quadrant 8304.

Sonia didn't bring up his meetings with Jake. She knew what they were about and wanted to focus on their time together in the present moment.

Less than a week later, the three of them were called to a meeting with President Gideon Novare and Chancellor Mya Brant in the capital building in Aphus.

Jake had picked up Michael, Sonia, and Olivia in the morning and on the brief flight over, hinted that Olivia and Sonia could opt to stay out of the meeting if they chose to.

Sonia agreed that Olivia should not be a part of it, but she was determined to sit in on it.

"I've earned a spot at the table for this meeting!" she said.

Begrudgingly, Jake agreed.

Inside the president's office, they all sat around a table, including Officer Brook who had expressed interest in helping out and had taken a liking to the three survivors of Moon 002.

When all six of them were settled around the circular table, Chancellor Brant spoke first. "New details are coming in from our people on Troria. Gonidec is holding executions across numerous cities. His military has been rounding up anyone deemed an *enemy of the state*. This includes not just those who have been outspoken against the regime, but even minor infractions, like their voting history. He's going so far as to imprison the sick, elderly, and those with severe disabilities. And by imprison, well, we all know what that means. They're being liquidated."

Sonia's eyes widened at the horrific news, her mind immediately going to her poor mother. She looked at Jake, hoping he would say it was only rumor.

He shook his head. "We have video proof of these things taking place. Thinning the herd, so to speak. You don't want to see it, trust me," was Jake's grim response. The room fell silent, everyone pondering what they had just been told.

President Novare cleared his throat and spoke. "So, here's the plan. Jake is going to Troria tomorrow morning, first thing. He's taking the *Deimos*, which has been fully repaired. Its navigation logs are wiped and new coordinates have been entered, indicating it's been to Moon 002 then got hung up with a damaged com and nav system and got mixed up with some pirates in their *Executor* ships."

He paused and looked around the table before continuing.

"Levon Gonidec has launched an all-out assault on the nearest planets around Troria, which are already reporting heavy casualties, I'm sorry to say. However, this heightened activity will help us quietly slip onto Troria at nighttime, drawing as little attention as possible. We have voice recognition devices programmed onboard to mimic Nicholas Mohr's voice, who went missing on Moon 002 and no one knows what happened to him. Once Jake's in, a small group of Gonidec's inner circle will be waiting and at his command. He will then make his way into and through Gonidec's bunker, get to him and take him out."

"They're going to know Mohr isn't on the ship the second the hatch opens, you realize that right?" Sonia blurted out, stating what she believed was the obvious.

Brant nodded, acknowledging the remark. "We don't participate in cloning here on Railara, but we are able to create life-like facial masks with the use of the subject's DNA, which we found on the *Deimos*—hair strands, to be exact. It won't be perfect, but it'll get Jake in. It's as close as we get to cloning. The similarities from mask to individual are uncanny. They're nearly perfect matches. The skin is synthetic, and a quick scan show it to be actual living human tissue."

Sonia's mind went to how Olivia was created back on Moon 002, with strands of Elise's hair and blood samples from the waste basket in her room. She was glad this same technology would be used to take down an evil man this time. "And by *take him out,* you mean execute him? Even if he surrenders willingly?" she asked, keeping her voice level this time.

"He won't go willingly," Novare replied grimly. "The man has a neutron charge strapped to himself at all times. He will without question take everyone in the room out if he senses his options have run out. The wristwatch he wears is the detonator. His index finger touches it, and it's all over. For everyone. And he will use it."

Small gasps around the table registered this awful detail before Novare went on.

"Even with the few from his inner circle helping us in this attempt, there are still many obviously willing and ready to die for him. And they will be around him at all times. Jake has a plan for the right time to get to him, I'll leave the details for him to explain later."

President Novare paused, trying to avoid eye contact with Sonia but quickly glancing over at her. "What you're all here for is, well, I don't know the best way to ask this."

Jake took over. "We need a team of three. Myself, Connor Brook here, and,"

"No. Please, no! Not Michael!" Sonia all but shouted, standing to her feet. She had expected this but hearing it firsthand was still a punch to the gut.

"Sonia, please, hear them out," Michael said softly, standing to his feet, resting his hand on her shoulder.

She glared at everyone around the table then at Michael, her eyes filled with anger and hurt and then tears. She nodded curtly and sat down with Michael.

"Jake is going to wear the mask. Mohr flew with an android; Connor Brook will play that role. That's easy, Gonidec's guards won't question them. That leaves Michael, our pilot. He knows his way around the *Deimos*, his DNA is tailor made for a high-level task like this," Gideon said firmly, then waited a moment before delivering his final point. "And once this mission is over and they succeed, Michael will get the one-year life limiter removed by a trained professional on Troria capable of the procedure."

Sonia turned this over in her mind. He would be on the one planet capable of giving him a full life. Still, it was so dangerous. "So, who is he supposed to be? There was only two of them when they came down to get Petrino and Olivia," she shot back.

"He's Michael, a clone that survived Mining Complex VI," Chancellor Brant said confidently. "They'll be able to confirm it. He'll have the video recorder, which we have no need of any longer. Olivia and Petrino didn't make it, but this clone did. Taken due to his extensive knowledge of what transpired on Moon 002. They still don't know we have all the information we do, thanks to you three."

"This is quite literally a suicide mission if there ever was one," Sonia said, shaking her head.

Michael raised his hand to get everyone's attention. "My one-year clock is ticking, and the cure for this death sentence is on that planet if we succeed. There's payback coming for the countless clones that have perished at the hands of the AMO. For the nameless innocents back on Troria and other mining complexes across the quadrant that now, as we sit here talking, are being murdered. Burn pits, we're thrown into burn pits. Shot first in the head if there is no resistance. Resistance fighters being thrown in alive! I've watched the videos coming out of Troria."

Sonia's heart ached for Michael. She knew he was right but fear for his safety threated to overtake her. She sighed, looking down at her hands. "My mom, how can we save my mom? Corinna Bonnel is her name."

"We can't get detailed accounts of individuals there. Unfortunately, with her heart condition, she will not survive if we don't do something immediately. If she's still alive…" Chancellor Brant replied bleakly.

"The choice falls on you, Michael. You, Sonia, and Olivia are welcome to stay here and live out your lives. But we could use your help right now," President Novare said steadily.

Michael reached his hand over to Sonia under the table and took her hand in his. She clenched it tightly, nodding her approval and fighting back bitter tears. In her thirty-two years, she had never felt this way about anyone. She was already dreading telling Olivia.

"The pieces are falling into place. Good luck to you three. Once the mission is completed, Michael, you are to fly back to Railara. Sonia and Olivia will be here if they so choose, that's between the three of you. Meeting adjourned," President Gideon said, standing to his feet.

The rest of the room followed suit. The president and chancellor spoke briefly to Connor and Jake while Sonia and Michael spoke quietly to each other.

She placed both of her hands on his chest, leaning into him. "We need to tell Olivia together."

CHAPTER 34

THE DOGS OF WAR

They would be leaving in less than a day. Sonia tried to process this as Jake took the three of them back to their apartment after several more meetings prepping Michael for the upcoming mission. Olivia, oblivious to the news she would receive later, chattered on like a normal eleven-year-old.

In the afternoon, Michael took Olivia out of the city to visit a nearby waterfall, something she hadn't seen before, and she marveled at the beauty of the huge falls. Afterward, they got a chocolate-flavored treat similar to ice cream as she talked on about how she was going to paint a picture of the waterfall. After their sweet snack, he took her shopping for some new art supplies, impressed with how she was quickly becoming her own unique person with distinct interests all her own.

Back at the apartment, Sonia was equally busy, and grateful it got her mind off of Michael leaving. Supper was to be their last meal together before his departure early the next morning and she had enjoyed putting together a simple meal for them to share.

As they ate together, Olivia was the first to broach the topic. "There are so many cool things here on Railara! I can't wait to go to school, I'm sure I'll make some good friends. At least I think I will. What about you, Michael, what will you do first?"

Michael took another bite of his pasta before wiping his mouth and clearing his throat. "Olivia, that's a very good question. I have a job. And, well, it starts tomorrow morning."

He looked at Sonia whose head was down, looking at the uneaten food in front of her, while Olivia stared at them both as if beginning to suspect something was amiss.

"What? What's the job? Tell me! Maybe flying around in one of those shuttles transporting people? Oh! Maybe, maybe, a bodyguard for the president! Or helping out that nice man up on the space station, Connor!" She stopped when Sonia looked up, her face shrouded in sadness. "Well?" Olivia asked, this time with growing unease, setting her fork down onto her plate.

Michael put his fork down as well. "Olivia, I'm not sure how to best tell you this so I'm just going to say it. The man that had a part in creating you worked for a very bad man, Levon Gonidec. You know he is being truly terrible to a lot of people and intends to bring a war to this planet. But Jake Riley and I, along with Officer Brook, have an opportunity to remove him from power and save lives. Potentially billions."

He paused, looking at the young girl's serious expression as she listened to him. "Jake Riley is going to become the leader of Troria, your mom's home planet. At least, temporarily. He needs me to fly that ship we came here on, the *Deimos*, and help him get rid of the bad guys. Once we're done, I'm going to be able to have the one-year life limiter removed from my DNA, then I'll come home. But I need to go to the other side of this quadrant of space, tomorrow morning. I'm not sure how long I will be gone. But you need to know, it could be a while, depending on how the mission goes."

A silence pierced the kitchen. No one was eating anymore. "Wait. We just got here after all of us nearly died…and… and…my mom died. *You* nearly died in space fixing the ship! And now you're leaving us?" Olivia's voice was rising with each word. She was getting angry.

"Olivia, wait, I will come back," Michael said weakly, knowing how awful this news must sound to her young ears.

"No! How do I know you won't die this time? Then what?" Olivia said, glaring at him, tears already spilling down her face.

"Listen, if I don't go, I *will* die in one year!" Michael replied more firmly.

"Maybe I'm being selfish, but I need you! We need you! You can't go! Your one year could be cut down to just a few days if you go!" Olivia's voice grew to a panic level.

Michael was about to say something more, but Olivia jumped up from her chair, sobbing, and ran to her room, slamming the door behind her as she went.

Michael sighed heavily as he sat back in his chair, his appetite completely gone now. He looked up at Sonia who, as he had figured, was crying too. "Well, that went worse than I expected."

"I understand, Michael, I do. Too much is at stake here, I just wish it wasn't you. I have gone through every possible scenario but at the end of the day, you're the man. And I know you can do it. If Gonidec's security check the records, and they probably will, your data should show up as the only surviving clone from Moon 002. I hate that word. *Clone*." She hung her head.

He didn't know the difference anymore. Clone or human, he never imagined he could feel all of these emotions, including this deep need to protect Sonia and Olivia. It was why he ultimately had to accept the mission laid out in front of him earlier. Regardless of whether the life-limiter was removed.

They cleared the table in silence after reaching out to Olivia, who refused to come out.

Michael knew he needed as good a night's sleep as he could muster. He showered early and after trying Olivia's room once more to no response, he went to his room. Sonia stood in the doorway with a blanket wrapped around her. She opened it as he stepped into the room, closing the door behind him.

After their lovemaking, Sonia laid her head against Michael's bare chest. Neither spoke. Michael softly ran his hand through her curly hair. She loved his touch, his smell, everything about him.

Sonia broke the bittersweet silence of the moment. "I'm not good at this, I've never been one to share my emotions. And I wasn't expecting this—us, and her. That girl down there absolutely adores you, Michael. And, for what it's worth, so do I. I told her earlier that where she goes, I go and where I go, she goes. And now you're leaving."

She paused, her head rising slightly against his chest with every breath he took. Her hand brushed against his muscular stomach.

"I feel the same, Sonia, I have vivid memories of things that never happened, but this, this here is real. I'm not sure if a clone can love. Was that programmed into my mind? I don't know. All I know is I've learned on my own, from you and Olivia, what it means to love and be loved. We were all brought together for a reason, I'm convinced. And nothing in this entire universe is going to pull us apart. Jake, Connor, and I are going to stop this man. Mark my words. The three of us are going to be reunited, and I'm going to have a lifetime, a full lifetime, to love you."

Morning came far too quickly. Michael got up early and slipped out of bed. Olivia's door was still closed, and he was sure she had fallen asleep early and hoped she would sleep in. It was going to be difficult enough leaving. He loved her like his own daughter. He quietly ate his breakfast in the solitude of their small apartment that had quickly became a home, complete with drawings Olivia had painted and hung up.

He thought of the confusion he had felt when he woke up on Moon 002 in the pitch-black room. About finding her, alone, scared and confused. Of the many near misses that they experienced together.

And now he was leaving. The odds for this mission succeeding were fifty-fifty, and even that was wishful thinking. He shuddered at the thought of the many dangers that awaited them, but he had to do this. The entire galaxy may very well hinge on the success of this mission, and he knew it. He had become a leader and a fighter. It may not have been how he was originally designed and implanted, but he had adapted, evolved, exceeded far beyond what those that created him would have ever thought possible.

He finished his breakfast, cleaned up, and checked his watch. Jake would arrive any minute in the transport shuttle that would take them to space station *Infinitum* and from there, they would begin the trek to Trorian space. He wished he knew how long he'd be gone, but no one could be certain.

From one end of the solar system, known as quadrant 8304, to the other where Troria was located was quite a far distance. The system was large and consisted of ten planets that were life sustaining and contained AMO mining complexes, and another ten planets without life.

They hoped for a quick takedown, but Gonidec wouldn't be going down easily. Obstacles could arise on their voyage to Troria, especially since war had been waged across the quadrant. There would be no contact with Railara until the deed was done and Jake Riley had assumed provisional leadership and Gonidec's military had ceased fire. It might be quick and dirty or a long, drawn-out mission. Time would tell.

His packed bags sat beside him on a bench outside the apartment as the sun slowly began to rise in the distance. It was still quite dark outside, but Michael could see a pair of lights in the sky heading in his direction. A lump formed in his throat.

Behind him, Sonia came out and wrapped her arms around his chest, squeezing him tightly. He turned to face her, beautiful as she always was, even first thing in the morning. He loved her curly hair, the way she pushed her glasses up almost habitually, her trim figure, the little freckles on her cheeks. He stared into her eyes, hoping this wouldn't be the last time they would hold each other. Their future felt as uncertain as the day they met back in the Command Center on Moon 002.

The transport shuttle landed in front of the apartment and the hatch slid open. Connor Brook stood peering out, ready for him.

Sonia kissed him hard, not wanting to end this moment even as the hum of the transport shuttle rumbled nearby. She knew it was time for him to go. She pulled back and took his hands into hers. "You come back to us. Take Gonidec out, get the one-year life limiter removed. We'll be waiting. And save my mama."

"I love you, Sonia Bonnel," Michael said above the sound of the ship.

He looked toward the apartment, hoping to see Olivia once more, but she wasn't there so he picked up his bags and headed to the ship.

He was about to climb aboard when Connor Brook, with his hand outstretched to take one of Michael's bags, looked up past him. Glancing back, Michael saw Olivia running toward him, still in her pajamas.

He knelt down to one knee to meet her as she flew into his arms, squeezing him tightly. He felt her wet tears on his cheek and held onto her.

Over the dull drone of the shuttle, Olivia choked out the words, "I'm sorry I got angry! But I don't have a mom and dad and you're all I have! I love you!"

"I love you too. And you do have a mom and dad, honey. I'm coming back. Take care of your mama, okay?" Michael said, looking into the young girl's green eyes.

He stood to his feet as Olivia handed him a picture she had drawn of the three of them in front of a house, standing side by side and holding hands. He took it and said, "Beautiful, just like you."

He climbed aboard the transport shuttle as Brook waved at Olivia who had run back to join Sonia. The hatch slid shut.

Sonia put her arm around Olivia as the transport shuttle lifted up slowly and then shot up out of Railara's atmosphere toward the outline of space station *Infinitum* above the horizon, still visible in the semi-dark sky.

"Please tell me he's coming back?" was all Olivia could muster through choked tears.

Sonia nodded, peering up at the tiny light that vanished into the breaking dawn. "Yes, honey, we will be reunited with him again. I'm sure of it. Where you go, I go, where I go, you go." A promise she meant to keep.

The sun continued lifting into the morning sky, drowning out the darkness as the shape of the space station *Infinitum* disappeared from view.

CHAPTER 35

THE WAR BEINGS

Weeks had passed since Levon Gonidec had unleashed his *Paladine Fighters* and bombers into the solar system and declared war on quadrant 8304. Many battles had already been fought and more lives had been lost on the planets closest to Troria, which were hit the hardest as his fleet of death dealers continued pushing outward toward their eventual target, Railara itself.

Gonidec had become significantly more paranoid after the initial wave of surprise attacks, but as the battles raged on with no major victories and his enemies ramped up their defenses, he was downright rattled. He hadn't expected so much resistance on each of the planets they invaded, many of them pushing back to the point that his takeover operations ceased. Too many pilots were being lost to this resistance, a fact which made Gonidec even more unhinged since coming to power. Much of what had previously brought him fame had vanished, his charisma fading in a haze of sex and alcohol.

Weaknesses in the Trorian fleet had been discovered and used to his enemy's advantage; information that had travelled from Moon 002 to Railara, then out to the united planets in quadrant 8304, causing his fleet to dwindle all the more. Revolts had also been heard to have taken place on numerous mining complexes across the quadrant as news of the Rot infestation on Mining Complex VI had spread. Clones on the mining complexes were made aware of their situations and had formed their own pockets of resistance. Many were executed but the damage was done. Staff were abandoning posts, heading anywhere but Troria, seeking asylum. Sabotage was occurring at many of the complexes, including Mining Complex II, which was destroyed after a disgruntled staff member caused an explosion similar to the one on Mining Complex VI, killing everyone, clones included, instantly.

These incidents had left Levon Gonidec even more suspicious of everyone around him. Sensing a battle that he was losing and his power grip on Troria slipping, he had doubled his efforts to execute anyone he felt wasn't sympathetic to his cause. Daily executions now took place across the planet by virtually any means necessary. Any soldier that failed in his duty was executed along with the innocent people that had been rounded up by his or her commanding officer.

Chaos seemed to have nearly taken over the planet. Rebels did their best to fight back but were woefully undernourished without proper weaponry to fight and defend themselves. Still, they pressed on and slowed the advancing death machine that was Gonidec's military force. The head of the snake needed to be cut off, though, for the horrors to truly end.

Towns were razed in a brazen show of force. Burned to the ground on Gonidec's orders, his loyalists enacting his most violent tendencies, almost enjoying the killing. These upper ranking militia had free rein to kill at will, something they had taken great pleasure in at the beginning of the purging of the Trorian population, but even they were growing weary of the daily violence and destruction.

Gonidec heard his staff talking in hushed tones, but silence fell across the room when he entered. He had even heard whispers of a possible assassination attempt underway but dismissed it as more gossip nonsense. But not before threatening the staff members with their families' lives if he heard anything like that again. And he meant it.

CHAPTER 36

VOYAGE TO TRORIA

"Captain, I've got something on my radar here. Looks like three bogies approaching about one thousand miles out. We'll be in range in several minutes. They're going to spot us as well any second now," Officer Connor Brook said over his shoulder to Jake Riley who was sitting behind him and pilot Michael Astier.

Leaning forward in his seat, Jake peered at Connor's screen in front of him, running a hand through his short, well-groomed beard. "This could well be our first encounter with some *Paladine Fighters.* They're pretty far out from Troria, though. What's the closest planet?"

Connor accessed the star map at his station. "Looks like we're nearing Veaphus. We've already made our way past Druthea, and no enemy craft was detected. Gonidec's fleet haven't made their way that far yet. Honestly, I'll be surprised if these are his military fighters. Not yet."

Nodding, Jake looked at Michael. "I don't want to draw unnecessary attention. Slow us down, I'd like to get a look at what's heading our way, but I don't want to engage. Not yet."

"Got it. I'm going to circle back a bit, buy us a few minutes and park us on that large asteroid over our right side. Should give us a clear view of whatever's passing by. Plus, we can power down and go undetected," Michael responded, glancing back to get Jake's approval.

"Good plan, get on it," Jake replied, sitting back in his captain's seat.

At Jake's command, Michael pulled back on the helm, slowing the *Deimos* down and banked the ship hard right.

The three bogies were still pinging on Connor's radar. "T-minus sixty seconds until whatever those three ships are out there come into contact with us. Then forget about hiding. In fact, that'll do nothing but draw more attention," he said decisively.

"Working on it," Michael responded, squinting at the front viewscreen at the upcoming asteroid, big enough for numerous craters to blanket its oblong round exterior. He saw a particularly large crater with a lip on its outer rim to further shield them from the oncoming ships. The *Deimos* hovered over it as Michael lined up the descent then pushed the helm down.

"Thirty seconds," Connor said quietly.

Michael, knowing time was running out, dropped the *Deimos* quicker, nearly hitting the bottom of the crater but stopping just in time to gently rest the landing gear on the rocky surface below. The ship came to a jolting halt, engines still firing.

"Ten seconds," Connor announced, trying to mask his nervousness. Though nervous by nature, it actually made him an asset to the team because he was good at scoping out obstacles, one reason he had been stationed on Space Station *Infinitum*. He questioned each and every ship that docked there, more so than any other communications officer. His insistence on strictly following the rules had gained him unwanted nicknames and jeers from his work associates, but also numerous accolades from his superiors, eventually leading him to higher profile rolls in protecting Gideon Novare and Mya Brant.

He would die for his planet and die for its freedom from tyrannical leaders such as Levon Gonidec. He had essentially become a sort of *Secret Service* while stationed both on Space Station *Infinitum* and the presidential building in the city of Aphus. He knew the inherent risks of this mission, the success of which fell on this small rag-tag crew and the few waiting resistance fighters on Troria.

The *Deimos* powered down with a hiss as the seconds ran out. Michael and Connor both breathed a sigh of relief, sitting back in their respective seats in the cockpit. All was quiet as the three ships approaching in their flight path continued to move forward, not diverting in any way. The *Deimos* and her crew hadn't been detected.

"I sure wish we could take those Trorian Defender pistols along with us inside the bunker," Connor said, breaking the silence while waiting for the ships to pass.

Jake nodded. "I hear you, but it's simply too risky. Once we're inside his bunker it won't matter. We aren't stationed there, and it'll look suspicious. My plan is to take the guards by surprise once we hit the elevator leading up to Gonidec's room. That's where we'll be arming ourselves. Getting there in the middle of the night should ensure us a skeleton crew down that long hallway. Two guards, if we're lucky. If we're found out at any time leading up to that elevator ride to his room, game over. Surprise attack is essential. The reinforcement cavalry should be stationed and ready once we're on top level."

"I've gone over the plan plenty and it's safe to say it's burned into my brain," Connor said. "If there's a way in, we're gonna do it, I'm confident the mask and voice concealer will get us pretty far, though I'm concerned about playing the role of android."

The command center of the *Deimos* once more fell silent, all lost in their own thoughts, working through the difficult job that lay ahead. All three sensed they likely would not make it out alive.

"Michael, I haven't had a chance to tell you thanks. Thanks for what you did back on Moon 002. For helping out Elise and getting her daughter, I guess that's what we can call her, and Sonia out of there. I just wish she could have been here, or back on Railara. What an asset she would be to the mission," Jake said quietly from behind the pilot's station.

Contemplating this, Michael nodded. "I didn't know her for long, but that woman was a fighter. She kept going until the very end."

"I always knew she would go out in a blaze of glory but I never imagined she'd be detonating six neutron charges inside the belly of a gigantic space insect. Damn, I miss her," Jake responded quietly.

"That move saved us, got us all to this point in time. With the video recorder and the knowledge inside Olivia's mind. Without it, I don't know if this war would be winnable. Not with the massive fleet it sounds like Gonidec has. I'm looking forward to meeting him, by the way," Michael said grimly.

Nodding, Jake added, "Aren't we all?"

"Game time, here they come. They're still on course. They might just be Veaphus patrol ships, but I don't want to break cover, not even for our allies," Connor said, watching the red dots on his radar now nearly on top of them.

"Bring it up on the viewscreen, let's see what we're dealing with," Jake ordered, leaning forward in his captain's seat.

The camera system onboard the *Deimos* was equipped for magnifying images, which Jake and his crew figured would be a huge asset on this particular mission. A large image appeared in between Michael and Connor: stars filled the viewscreen as three ships flying in formation could be seen gliding through the cosmos.

"What do we have here? They don't look like any ships from the planet nearest us, Veaphus. Hell, they don't look familiar to me at all," Jake said, puzzled at the foreign objects approaching.

They continued watching. "What's their status, Connor?" Jake asked.

"Looks like they're three hundred miles and closing fast. They're going to fly by any minute," Connor responded.

The small ships were black and pointed in the front with round rocket boosters on sides that extended out into long wings. Their rear tails were short, almost cut off.

"Oh, shit. Those are *Executors!* Stuto pirates fly those things! That's what I was afraid of," Connor said, grabbing hold of his navigator seat's arm rests.

"I'm not familiar with them but their ships look, fast," Jake replied tensely.

"They are. They'll outrun this thing, even with some of the modifications done to it. Their ships have one pulse cannon located under the bottom hull, engines on either side, and one pilot per ship. Here they come," Connor said shakily, staring out the front viewscreen.

The three *Executor* ships flew past the large asteroid where the *Deimos* was parked silently. Several smaller asteroids surrounding them helped to keep them better concealed.

"What's their story?" Michael asked, watching the ships in the distance fly past.

"They're scum, like gangsters in space. I'm surprised there aren't more than three of them. They live primarily on the space ports that litter not just our solar system but surrounding systems. My guess? These three are scouting for unsuspecting space travelers fleeing the war zones closer to Troria. They'll stop ships with their death threats, board and rob them blind. The rear hulls are typically filled with stolen goods taken to space ports to sell. Bastards, the lot of them," Connor said bitterly.

"We don't have time for this shit," Jake said, watching on.

"Well, we've got to give them time to move past," Connor answered. "A ship like this, they'll come after for sure. A well-built Troria stealth fighter would go for a high number of Marks. Those little *Executors* are bad news, their tracking systems are quite good, depending on whether they pick up any stray fuel partials we left behind before powering down."

Sighing, Jake sat back in his seat and drummed his fingers on his arm rests, itching to go.

Glancing back at Jake, Michael said, "Give me the word and we're gone."

"Hang on!" Connor shot back.

Michael liked these men, each of them brought their own unique talents to this dangerous mission. Jake was destined for leadership and had done much to make this mission a reality. Michael was determined to see that it was, indeed, a success even if it cost him his life.

"Oh shit, it didn't work, they're circling back!" Connor exclaimed.

"Damnit! Michael, punch it!" Jake shouted.

Michael wasted no time, firing up the engines and lifting the *Deimos* up off of the asteroid. Once at a safe distance from the floating space rock, the Kernadium-fueled engines pushed forward, blasting the ship out of the small asteroid field.

The three *Executors* rocketed toward the *Deimos'* location, faster than the *Deimos* and much more agile. Their weapons, however, were not as lethal.

"Michael, time to see what you can do. Connor, on guns, get ready," Jake commanded.

Both men responded with a firm, "Yes, sir."

"Buckle up," Michael added.

Swerving the *Deimos* hard right, they avoided the first barrage of green laser fire from all three ships. Michael flipped the ship end over end as the green lasers continued to blast, missing them by mere feet.

Punching the helm forward and up, the *Deimos* launched straight up then made a complete loop. The faster pirate ships weren't expecting this sudden move and flew past, all three breaking formation now that the *Deimos* was behind them.

Connor wasted no time, opening fire on the nearest *Executor* in the middle of the pack. All four heavy laser disintegrators erupted from the wings of the Deimos, three of them missing their target. One did not.

The middle *Executor* exploded in a brilliant display of fire and destruction leaving only tiny pieces of the ship pushing outward from the sheer force of the blast.

The last two *Executors* both shot into opposite directions, communicating with each other. Circling back, they would soon be behind the vulnerable *Deimos* once more.

Michael chose the ship to the right. Better to go after one than have them both on their tail. Connor hadn't let up on the firing. A barrage of jagged red laser beams blasted through space. This pilot, however, was ready and sped up, avoiding their shots.

The Deimos rocked from the sudden jolt of the *Executors* green laser fire. They had been hit. "The Deimos has a strong outer hull but it can only withstand so many of those shots!" Connor shouted.

"Keep on target, Connor!" Jake shouted back, pointing at the fleeing Executor.

Another hit shook the Deimos and a warning alarm sounded inside the Command Center.

"Get this son of a bitch off us!" Michael shouted.

From his command seat, Jake accessed the decoy drones and hit "release."

From the bottom of the ship, three small round decoy orbs ejected and began flying in random circles.

It worked. The laser fire from the pursuing *Executors* single cannon was drawn to them, one of which exploded after being hit, buying the *Deimos* and its crew valuable seconds.

Michael once more, punched the controls forward. "Five seconds and he's yours, Connor!"

"Make it quick!" Jake interrupted.

The fleeing *Executor* was targeted as another decoy exploded. Green laser fire erupted around them.

"Fire!" Jake yelled to Connor.

The second *Executor* exploded, finally unable to outfly Michael.

The last decoy was now destroyed. One *Executor* left and they weren't shaking this one. Michael continued maneuvering the *Deimos* away from the laser fire, but this could only last so long.

"Wait, sir! I'm seeing multiple incoming ships. Not good! Not good!" Connor shouted.

"Shit! We aren't giving up!" Jake commanded.

The *Deimos* took another hit, this one much more jarring than the last two. More warning lights, more alarms, when suddenly, the last *Executor* behind them was vaporized by a stream of white laser fire.

"Whoa! What the hell!" Connor hollered.

Two saucer-shaped crafts shot forward, one on either side of the *Deimos*.

"Capibor fighter ships, from the planet Veaphus!" Jake said in amazement.

The ships continued to fly in formation beside the Deimos before breaking radio silence.

"Jake Riley, that you?"

Breathing a sigh of relief, Jake replied, "I recognize that voice. Zaman Berker! Man, are we glad to see you!"

Connor and Michael sat back in their seats, both breathing a sigh of relief, glancing at each other with exhausted looks.

"That's me. Man, it's been, what? Three years? You were stationed at Mining Complex VI last we spoke. I knew you were going to be passing through here in that Trorian stealth shuttle but wasn't sure when. We've been patrolling this sector for the first signs of any *Paladine Fighters* making their way to Railara. Or any other planet in this section of quadrant 8304. Bastards have already hit their neighboring planet, Husdone, quite hard. Word throughout the quadrant is that Solla V is next. They're gonna get pummeled. They don't have the resources to fend off Gonidec's massive fleet." Zaman spoke in a dialect Michael was unfamiliar with that must have been native to his planet.

Jake thought on this then replied, "Well, that why we're here. To help."

"I assume you can't tell me the details of the mission? All I know is what my commanding officer tells me, which isn't a hell of lot," Zaman replied.

"You would be correct. Hang tight, is all I can say. By the way, looks like your Capibor ships got a pretty major upgrade since I last saw one in person. Upgraded weaponry, I assume?" Jake wanted to change the subject. He trusted Zaman Berker, but he didn't know who was in the other ship, and regardless, this was top secret stuff and not to be discussed with anyone. Though it was nice to know that there was some help flying around out here in deep space.

"Yep, good eye. We've suspected war was imminent since that bastard took over on Troria. All of our ships got major upgrades to the weaponry and significant reinforcements to the exterior build quality. Anyway, we must be moving on, we got word there's a few more pirates in those damn *Executors* attempting to transport a significant haul of our small arms weapons from Veaphus to the nearest space port. Rotten fuckers, the lot of them. We'll get em," Zaman said.

"I'm sure you will. You Veaphus military are not ones to mess with. If the Trorian military make it here, they're in for a right proper Veaphus beat down, am I right? Anyway, thanks for the hand, you saved our asses!" Jake replied.

"Hell yeah, you know it! Our pleasure to help you out. Keep your eyes peeled for more of those Stuto Pirates. Rat bastards. Anyway, safe travels. Take care of what needs taken care of. Berker out."

The two Veaphus Capibor fighter ships moved forward, away from the *Deimos*, then shot out of sight quickly, leaving a trail of vapor in their wake.

"Well, that was…intense," Michael said, shaking his head and taking control of the helm once more.

Nodding in agreement, Connor added, "Those guys are not to be messed with. Capibor ships are badass."

"Let's hope the Trorian military doesn't get this far out into the quadrant for them to find out. There are more planets before Troria and Veaphus that aren't as well protected. We need to keep moving," Jake said grimly.

Michael nodded, taking that as an order, and pushed forward on the helm.

As the ship rocketed onward, moving through the stars, Jake shared stories of people like Zaman Berker, who was part of the widespread resistance throughout the quadrant, and he knew most of them. The tales he told made Michael and Connor see they were a part of something much larger than the small ship they were traversing in through the solar system. All alone.

For all the stories that Jake told of bravery in the face of tyranny from a great number of fellow resistance fighters, all three men knew that ultimately, the fate of quadrant 8304 rested firmly on their shoulders and their nearly suicidal mission.

The *Deimos* and its crew continued on their course for Troria's capital and to Gonidec himself after what had already seemed like an eternity of perilous space travel.

CHAPTER 37

TIME'S UP

It was one o'clock in the morning as Levon Gonidec stood on his balcony overlooking the capital city of Paladine, a green drink in his hand rattling with ice. Lifting the strong alcoholic beverage to his lips, he took it down, burning through his throat into his stomach. He set the empty glass of ice down on the ledge and took a puff of his cigar, blowing it into the wind before dropping it into the glass and heading into his sprawling, luxurious bedroom. A house of horrors in which numerous crimes against humans and clones alike had been perpetrated through the years.

Many nights he had women or men, or both, joining him for his ritual of meaningless sex, but not tonight. Tonight was his "alone" night which always fell on the first day of the new week when he liked to be solitary with his drink and his cigar.

Moderately confident that his military would be victorious after suffering heavy losses and several outright defeats, his mind went to the sparse selection of androids he had hoped to use as military soldiers. Maybe when he had infinitely more resources, he would start that failed project back up once more. So many things to accomplish but never enough resources. That would change, he told himself. *We will push forward! This war must be victorious!*

There was a knock at his door and immediately he grabbed his Defender I. He wasn't wearing his neutron charger nor his watch that remotely activated it, not when he was in his room, but it was nearby. Any assassination attempt would kill them all. He secretly wanted to go out in this fashion, on his own terms and no one else's, getting the last laugh by killing those attempting to gain the upper hand.

"Who is it?" he hollered out.

"Sir, Nicholas Mohr is about to land and would like to speak to you," the woman's voice said from behind the door.

"Shit. That's right, he's back. Does he check out?"

"Yes, the facial recognition was good. He has his android and a clone with him. The android was going to take the clone to get checked out. Might be of use to us. Lone surviving clone of Mining Complex VI that doesn't appear to be infected with the Rot. He might have information on Alnorix Mining Transport 24 before or after their S.O.S. transmission, claims he has a video recorder from one Dr. Anthony Petrino," his personal secretary Kimberly Ludz stated.

"About fucking time. Put the clone into interrogation room five, Nic can wait until morning. I'm half drunk and tired," he said groggily.

"Of course, sir. Have a good night, sir," Kimberly replied.

"Yeah, yeah. Fuck off," he mumbled to the faceless woman he had bedded numerous times before eventually growing tired of her. He flopped down onto his large bed.

Silence fell throughout the leader of Troria's lavish bedroom. Sleep washed over him.

The *Deimos* checked out and they were granted access to land in a nearby military complex. Slowing their trajectory, Michael carefully lined it up with the landing platform below and took the ship down.

"This is it, gentlemen, this is what it's all about. What we do tonight will dictate the trajectory of the war moving forward. We'll either end it or prolong it indefinitely. Possibly even lose it. If Gonidec detonates that neutron charge inside the bunker it will surely kill him, but it'll kill us as well as the resistance soldiers. Someone needs to take charge immediately. So, we can't fail. Do I make myself clear?" Jake said with authority.

"Yes sir," both Michael and Connor responded gravely.

After touching down and upon inspection, they were given clearance to the Gonidec compound by a fellow member of the resistance who had been strategically stationed in the terminal once their flight was confirmed to land at around one o'clock AM.

The man, Lieutenant Filip Marsa, looking stoic in his Trorian military uniform, shot Jake the quickest of glances as they walked past. Behind the artificial Nic Mohr mask, he knew, was the future hope of the planet. He was leading a clone in shackles, and a tall, fair-skinned man walked beside them. Claiming to be an android, he wasn't checked by security per Filip's orders.

"I'll personally see to it that Mr. Gonidec is made aware of their arrival, thank you officer," Marsa told the guard at the checkpoint leading to Gonidec's compound. The guard nodded and let Marsa and the visitors pass.

The four of them sat quietly in the small oval shuttle that was to take them to the compound where Levon Gonidec's private bunker was located. Marsa reached up and switched off the com system inside the shuttle now coasting silently toward the large, imposing metal fortress.

"Gentlemen, I would ask how your trek through the quadrant was, but time is not on our side. You made it, and that's all that matters. Sir, it's an honor to help you." He reached over to Jake in the synthetic facial mask and extended his hand.

Jake reached out and shook it. "Good to see you, Filip. Michael, Connor, meet the man responsible for our gaining access into Gonidec's bunker."

Marsa, a man of few words, glanced back at the two men sitting behind them and nodded hello.

"Nice to meet you," Connor said. From what he had been told, the white-haired, grizzled lieutenant had played the long game in the planning and hopeful execution of taking down Levon Gonidec. His brother, a high-ranking lieutenant himself, had been executed several years earlier at Gonidec's command for conspiracy to commit treason.

Filip didn't respond to Connor, instead focusing on the masked Jake Riley. "You look just like that bastard. Glad to hear he's no longer among the living, couldn't have happened to a worse human being. Anyway, Gonidec is in his room, drunk again. We're going to meet with resistance inside, but I've got someone there to help. I trust her," Marsa said grimly while he piloted the shuttle closer to the looming bunker that reigned tall over the city.

Connor looked at Michael, whom he had gotten to know on the long journey across the solar system to Troria, and trusted him implicitly. Thus far, everything was going according to plan, but time was running out. Once daybreak hit and Gonidec was up from his drunken stupor, he would be far less vulnerable and likely surrounded by loyalists inside the bunker, or worse, at his military outpost where they landed. Once there, it would be pointless to attempt any kind of takeover.

Once at the bunker, armed guards greeted them, saluting both Marsa and whom they assumed was Mohr. They looked warily at the prisoner Michael, who kept his head hung low. Little attention was paid to the 'android' Connor Brook, as androids still in operation had numerous human faces. As long as Mohr was back and he checked out just fine, along with Marsa—two of the highest-ranking officials in the Gonidec regime—even at this late hour, their arrival was welcome and didn't raise eyebrows.

They entered the large bunker that was more like a palace than a fortress. Huge paintings adorned the walls, many of which portrayed Gonidec in some sort of regal or militant stance. Every luxury imaginable could be found inside these walls as Gonidec had spared no expense to pleasure himself. He was beyond wealthy, riding on the backs of slave clones as well as his impoverished planet and its people.

"Think the alarms are disabled?" Connor whispered to Jake.

Hearing his question, Marsa answered, "We're going to find out soon if things go south."

Michael looked at Connor and Jake with a grim look. This was it. They knew it was now down to a lot of things falling into place planned literally years in advance since the humble resistance began.

After several more checkpoints where Marsa and "Mohr" flashed their credentials, Filip Marsa led the three men to the final checkpoint inside the bunker at the end of a long hallway where armed guards stood watch.

"Lieutenant, we were informed that the clone would need to be taken to interrogation room five," the guard with an ugly scar on his face stated.

"And Mr. Gonidec informed us that he was to receive no visitors until the morning," the other chimed in, adding, "You both should know that better than anyone."

"Are you insinuating that I am stupid?" Marsa replied harshly, the way most officers addressed lower-ranking military, and guards especially. The tall, ugly man lowered his head slightly at this humiliation as Marsa continued authoritatively, "They've flown from Mining Complex VI and have important news to share with Mr. Gonidec. We're going to need to see him, now."

The guards looked at each other then at the three men waiting to be cleared for entrance into the elevator that would lead up to Gonidec's top floor suite.

"What news?" the scar-faced guard asked.

"How dare you speak to me, you insolent little piss-ant! Do you know who I am? You think we don't know Mr. Gonidec doesn't take visitors at this hour unless it's of the utmost importance?" Jake Riley exploded at the guard, then held out Petrino's video recorder.

Silence fell. The guard in question looked sheepish and uncomfortable.

Jake continued, his voice rising in anger. "We're going to pass. And you aren't going to give us any more shit! I've been stuck inside a spaceship for god knows how long with an android and a worthless clone and now I'm being told to wait?! We're getting in that elevator and we're going to see Gonidec. And if we aren't permitted to pass, you can most assuredly kiss your families for the last time when your shift ends. You do realize this man in front of you, Lieutenant Filip Marsa, has carried out numerous executions. Do I make myself perfectly clear?"

"Yes, sir," both guards exclaimed at nearly the same time, hanging their heads at the curt reprimand.

Marsa noted two other guards stationed at the entrance to the long, dimly lit, cold hallway adorned with more pictures of a victorious looking, regal Levon Gonidec in various poses. Four guards total, none of which were part of the resistance, he surmised, looking each one over.

The hallway had a scanning system, which they were prepared for, but at this hour, there were typically only two guards stationed, not the four currently on duty. Gonidec had grown more paranoid. And rightly so, as many wanted him dead throughout the quadrant, even some of his own military at this point.

The first security guard said shakily, "We're going to have to do a scan on your android here. Just to confirm that it is indeed an android. You don't have a problem with that, right?"

Silence fell across the hallway. This was the only way in or out of Gonidec's private quarters. They had gotten this far with the help of Marsa's rank and Jake's masterful disguise, moving through the landing complex and now the bunker with relative ease, even with the tedious checkpoints along the way. But here they were, seemingly stuck. One elevator from the mission objective.

Each was equipped with thick combat suits that were blast resistant and armed with a Defender sidearm and a Defender II rifle slung over their right shoulders. The only armed member of the small resistance here was Lieutenant Filip Marsa, who had one sidearm, no match for four trained guards. They would need to be dealt with using hand-to-hand combat. And Connor wasn't going through that scanner. If he did, their gig was up.

Noticing the brief pause, the guard repeated his command. "Sir? The android? We need to scan him then you'll be given..."

"Well, you see, that's going to be a problem..." Jake cut him off.

Michael and Connor took their cue and rushed the guards, each slamming into their respective opponents and driving them to the ground, stunned.

Immediately, the two guards in the rear of the hallway grabbed their rifles and ran forward.

"Go, this is your chance!" Marsa yelled to Jake.

Jake saw this was their opportunity before the situation became worse, but he couldn't leave his fellow crew mates.

The approaching guards in the rear of the hallway were about to open fire when Marsa lunged at them, clotheslining them with his large arms before they had a chance to react to his surprise aggressive attack. Michael and Connor struggled with the two guards closest to the elevator, Connor choking one and Michael getting punched in the face by the second.

Connor rendered his man unconscious and leapt on top of the guard that continued to punch Michael, not seeing that Michael had pulled the scarred man's knife from his belt. Michael slammed the knife into the guard's neck and sliced it open, hot blood spilling down onto his face.

The guard fell limp as Connor pulled him off of Michael and grabbed the Defender I from the dead guard's waist, tossing it toward Jake, who caught it in midair then turned and got into the elevator as the doors were sliding open.

Connor grabbed the dead guard's Defender II while Michael grabbed the other's Defender I pistol and ran to help Marsa, wiping blood from his face as he went.

A laser blast echoed through the hallway and Marsa went down, shot through the chest, a hole blasted through where his heart once had been. He collapsed dead onto the floor, close to a stunned and angry Jake.

"Filip!" he hollered, then trained his Defender on the pursuing guards.

The guards both raised their guns on Connor and Michael, but not fast enough; both were able to get off their own shots at point blank range. Michael's shot hit the guard in the forehead, causing the nearly headless man to fall forward, dead. Connor's shot connected with his guard's stomach, who was able to get a shot into Connor's stomach as well. Both dropped to the ground.

Jake took care of the remaining guard with a quick shot to his head, another immediate kill shot, dropping the man to the ground, a pool of blood surrounding his lifeless body.

Looking over at Connor, Jake saw he was likely mortally wounded from the large hole the guard's Defender had made in his stomach. "Connor! No!"

Connor sputtered, "It's been a pleasure..." but was cut off by a shot to his neck. The last guard had regained consciousness after being choked, and with his remaining Defender, got a shot off. Blood spat from Connor's wound. He was killed instantly, eyes wide open in a death stare.

"No!" Michael yelled, raising his Defender, shooting the guard in the chest several times. He fell over dead, eyes wide at the stunning last kill shot.

The room was a bloody mess. Six dead bodies littered the floor.

Michael ran to the elevator and hit the button while still clasping his own Defender I, Jake following close behind. Time was running out.

Gonidec opened his eyes, the alcoholic haze still washing over him. He glanced over at the clock. Three AM.

"Huh, what the?" he muttered, rubbing his eyes and reaching for the light at his bedside. Shots, he heard shots.

He immediately awakened and leapt out of bed, grabbing a large, custom-made laser pistol from the holster around his bed post. With his other hand, he grabbed the lone neutron charge that he had on his person—his insurance that if he goes, everyone goes.

With both of his defenses in hand, he rushed out of the room hollering for his armed guards and personal assistant, Kimberly Ludz.

It was dark in his hallway. *Where the hell are my guards? Where the hell is Kimberly?* "Hello? Where are my lights, damnit!?" he shouted into the empty room. "Main floor lights, on!" he commanded but the system would not comply.

"Sir, get down!" one of his two guards yelled.

Laser fire shot through the large room, illuminating the floor where his second guard lay dead in a pool of blood, his throat slashed wide open. Beside him lay Kimberly Lutz, two blast holes in her chest, a small bloody knife in her right hand, blood trickling out of her mouth.

His heart slamming in his chest, Gonidec made his way through darkness to where his personal guard had hollered out. "What the *fuck* is happening!?" he called out to his remaining guard who had his Defender II drawn.

"Your assistant, Kim..." the guard called out but was cut off, a shot to his face. Most of his head exploded, covering Gonidec in blood and pieces of brain before he slumped over, dead.

Gonidec wasted no time is opening fire. Bright red shards of laser light shrieked through the room randomly. A chair exploded from the impact of his gun, several fresh holes appeared in the walls. But the room appeared to be empty.

"Who's there? I've got a neutron charge on me!" he hollered out at his unseen assailant.

Michael peered down at the murdered woman then over at Jake. He realized this was their other person on the inside—Kimberly Lutz, used and abused for years serving under Gonidec. Assaulted numerous times and beaten mercilessly, constantly threatened with execution, her family was imprisoned after her husband faced execution for simply voicing an opposing view on Gonidec's handling of water filtration issues that plagued the city. Knowing it would cost her life, she had communicated with the resistance for over a year, planning this very night with full knowledge that she would likely die.

Reaching up, Jake peeled off his Mohr disguise so the dying woman could see his face. He threw the mask to the ground, staring at Kimberly whose nearly dead eyes widened.

"Jake," Kimberly struggled to speak. "I tried. Alarms are disabled, help is on the way. Others should be here soon. You've got to take him out. I did the best I could…save our planet…find my girls and my parents. Please make sure…" she fell quiet, a gurgling sound emanating from her throat, a stream of blood flowing out of her lifeless mouth.

Jake hung his head, her sad story fueling his rage even more. He looked up into the darkness, about to lunge out in anger, but was stopped by Michael.

Michael, who continued to calculate and assess their situation, becoming a better fighter and thinker, surpassing and evolving beyond clone programmers' expectations, was now his creator Gonidec's biggest threat.

"We need to use our heads. It's down to the two of us and he's got a bomb strapped to himself," he said urgently in a whisper.

More blasts of laser fire erupted around them. Furniture exploded from Gonidec's high powered laser pistol. One hit would bring about instant death.

"I knew her. Filip. Elise and countless others," Jake said bitterly.

More laser fire exploded around them.

"Okay, let's kill this son of a bitch," Michael said firmly.

In the distance, laser fire could be heard. Resistance versus Gonidec's loyalists. If they reached the elevator and made it up to the top floor, all would be lost. The resistance had to hold firm until Gonidec was no more.

Michael made his way around the side of the dark room as Jake headed in the other direction. Both crouching low, guns raised.

"You're going to come out of hiding you rat-fuck! If you think I'm scared of destroying this whole compound, you're mistaken! Whoever you are, you won't win! No one beats me!" Gonidec shouted.

Moving forward quietly, Michael and Jake had now cornered him. Michael ached to be the one to take the shot. He hated this man. *Keep your wits about you!*

"Come out! Or one push of the button..." Gonidec began as his right arm flew from his body from a laser blast shot through the room from Jake's Defender I.

Gonidec screamed. His pistol, still connected to his lifeless hand, now lay nearby.

Michael rose from his hiding spot behind a nearby desk, revealing himself, gun raised.

Gonidec looked at him with fury-filled eyes. "Who are you?"

Behind him, Jake rose, Defender raised.

More laser fire below. The ping of the elevator. Someone below had hit the button. Friend or foe? Resistance or Loyalist guards?

"I said, who are you?" Gonidec shouted, his left hand gripping the neutron charge.

"I'm the clone that survived Mining Complex VI. And I'm here to take you out. For crimes against the solar system and against your fellow man, clones included," Michael said grimly.

Gonidec looked at him, then back at Jake. "You," he said, recognizing the commanding officer from Mining Complex VI that had slipped through his fingers and was thought dead. A traitor.

"Your time is up," Jake replied.

"Fuck…you…both, this planet belongs to me! Mark my words, if I go this whole building goes," he said through grinding teeth, blood pouring out of the stump where his right arm used to be. He pushed the button on his neutron charge and the countdown began. Fifteen seconds.

The elevator whirled to life.

Jakes eyes widened. The timer was ticking. Ten seconds.

Gonidec laughed while more blood poured from his stump.

Michael didn't hesitate, he ran forward, wrapping himself around Gonidec's body, scooping him up, heading toward the window behind Gonidec and raising his Defender, shattering the window.

Five seconds.

"Michael! No!" Jake shouted, rushing forward.

The elevator door slid open.

Off the top floor of the compound, Michael and Gonidec flew, falling forward, Michael pushing the screaming tyrant from him once they were airborne. His mind went to his beautiful Sonia. His beautiful Olivia. Waiting back on Railara.

Water from Gonidec's personal swimming pool shimmered below. Could he make it in time?

Gonidec exploded into tiny pieces, floating to the ground. The compound shook from the explosion, causing severe damage to its exterior. But it held.

The elevator door slid open and several guards spilled out into the plush living space with weapons drawn. Jake swirled around, Defender I outstretched.

Silence fell over the room. All weapons drawn.

Shrouded in darkness, the first figure uttered, "Sir? Jake Riley? Is that you? Are you okay?

CHAPTER 38

FREEDOM

Olivia sat in the small kitchen of Sonia and Michael's apartment, eating an after-school snack while Sonia put groceries away from a recent run to the nearby store. Michael had been gone almost six months and Sonia and Olivia felt every day of it.

The city of Aphus was bustling every day by eight AM. People going to work, kids going to school. The city came alive. Olivia had gone to school shortly after she and Sonia took up permanent residence at the apartment they had been assigned when they first arrived to Railara nearly six months ago. She entered the fifth grade and immediately fit in, making friends and catching up on studies she had missed out on for the first nearly eleven years of her life.

None of the students looked oddly at the young clone girl but accepted her and made her feel at home in their school, something the principal and teachers focused on.

During their time on Railara, Sonia had learned more about the Kernadium on the planet and how it had been used sparingly while scientists on the planet continued to find safer and more sustainable ways of travel. The war that had been waged had moved all forward progress to the backburner as the people and their government had busily prepared for the worst while hoping for some sort of resolution to the unfolding conflict.

Finishing up putting several jars away, Sonia closed the cupboard full of food and stared at the holographic images of news footage currently being displayed just outside the kitchen, close to where Olivia sat eating her snack.

"And so, it does seem that Trorian leader Levon Gonidec, shown here addressing his planet from his bunker in an old video clip, has fallen. First reports from Troria's neighboring planet, Husdone, show vital images of fleets of *Paladine Fighters* and *Paladine Bombers,* named after the city of Paladine, the location of Gonidec's regime, ending their aerial assault after the ceasefire was called by now acting president, Jake Riley, a native of Troria and former commanding officer on Moon 002's Mining Complex VI."

Sonia dropped a bag of vegetables to the floor at the stunning events unfolding. After nearly six months of silence, the top-secret mission Jake, Connor, and Michael had embarked on paid off.

"When speaking with the new acting leader of Troria, this is what President Jake Riley had to say," Mia Kirst from Aphus News at Noon said as the holographic image cut to a bearded Jake Riley sitting behind a desk previously occupied by Levon Gonidec.

Olivia, seeing her mom bring her hands to her mouth as tears began welling up, hopped off her barstool and ran over to her, wrapping her arm around her as they both continued to watch the breaking news unfolding.

"My name is Jake Riley. Nearly one year ago, we received vital information on a quadrant-wide military push underway from Levon Gonidec's regime. It was unanimously decided between all of the free planets of quadrant 8304 that the time for peace had ended and a time of war was, unfortunately, at all of our doors."

Olivia and Sonia clung to one another, hardly breathing.

"We fought back, all of us. We resisted the opposing forces of tyranny and while many lives were lost, both in the air and on land, we, the free planets of quadrant 8304, prevailed. I have myself lost people in this war, friends and even a crewmember, who wanted what this war was fought over, freedom. Those losses will haunt me for the rest of my years. But we are a strong, resilient quadrant where all planets will now strive to live in peace."

"What does he mean, Mom? Lost a crewmember? Who? Not my dad, right?" Olivia said, panicked, looking up at Sonia.

The young girl had quickly begun referring to Michael as her father after he had left on his mission with Jake and Connor. It made her feel good to know that somewhere out there beyond the stars her father was fighting for her and her mom. She loved Michael dearly, as did Sonia. She had vowed that she would urge him to adopt her as soon as he returned, just as her mother had, signing binding documents months earlier making the girl her own. She was now Olivia Bonnel.

"I don't know, honey. I don't know what Jake Riley meant. But we're going to continue to hope, right?"

Looking up at her mother, Olivia nodded, unconvinced. They both looked on, listening to the new acting president continue his formal address to all of Troria as well as the other nine planets spread throughout the solar system.

Clearing his throat, the new President Riley spoke. "My first order of business, apart from the ceasefire, is that all Alnorix Mining Organization facilities will cease operations across the solar system. Those responsible for the continual perpetrating of crimes against our species, which includes clone enslavement and murder, will be brought to justice." Jake paused for added dramatic effect.

"We will be working with Railarian leaders Gideon Novare and Mya Grant in setting up a new governing body here, one ruled by peaceful elections throughout the planet. In the meantime, I will be acting president. I must stress this, Levon Gonidec is gone. Any attempt by those sympathetic to his cause on the lives of any free Trorian will be harshly dealt with. The age of authoritarianism on this planet is over. Now."

The news reporter came back on the holographic imagine in Sonia's living room. "And there you have it, new President Jake Riley of Troria speaking out in opposition of war and a call to immediate ceasefire. It seems as if, for now, his commands are being honored as multiple reports are coming in of large fleets of *Paladine Fighters* and *Paladine Bombers* ceasing operations and making their way back to Troria. We'll keep you posted here on any and all further developments on this breaking news. Again, I repeat, Levon Gonidec has been removed along with several other members of his inner circle. We don't have full details on whether he is still alive but will continue bringing updates to you as we get them in. This is Mia Kirst from Aphus News at Noon, a truly good day out there, fellow Railarian, stay safe."

The image of the dark-skinned news anchor vanished and in her place, the animated show, *The Further Adventures of Breckett and Zaid* featuring several strange alien animals chasing each other around a building returned.

Olivia stared at the images that seemed as though they were chasing each other inside the apartment.

Sonia continued staring at the holographic images in front of her. Even Olivia, always one to love a good cartoon comedy once her homework was completed, was stunned into silence at this most important news that would surely change their lives moving forward.

Olivia quietly walked over and turned the holographic image system off and returned to Sonia, staring up into her mother's eyes. "Mama, do you think…?" She fell silent.

Sonia's thoughts drifted to Michael. It sounded like the mission was a success. But did Jake mean Michael or Connor when he mentioned a fallen crewmate?

She knew what they were up against as the days, weeks, and months had ticked by. She had played out the scenario in her mind over and over while tossing and turning in her bed. She yearned for Michael to be by her side, but she knew he was the right man for the mission. And it would be fitting, when he succeeded, that a clone produced as disposable labor by the government would be the one to take them down.

Reliving the images that had just appeared in her living room, Sonia's mind went to her mother, who's only hope had rested on the daring mission that the three men—including her Michael—had attempted.

"I think he's alive," Olivia said, breaking Sonia's concentration.

Sonia looked over at the girl, dressed in white shorts and a pink tank top, her straight blond hair naturally falling into place. She smiled, trying to keep a positive attitude, replying back, "So do I. If anyone would have succeeded, it would be him. Am I right?"

Smiling widely, Olivia replied, with hope in her voice, "Right! But I do miss him. It feels like forever ago that he was leaving us. When will we find out if he's okay?"

"We're going to find out as soon as we can honey," Sonia responded, collecting her thoughts and wondering the very same thing. She hoped she would be contacted by the evening.

Olivia blurted out, "My favorite times were when us three would hold hands. It made me feel…normal. Those little moments where I felt normal, I miss that."

Sonia put her arm around Olivia, squeezing her tightly, knowing it was her responsibility to ease the girl's mind. "Everyone is unique in their own little way. And you know what? Why be normal? I used to be normal. It was boring. So please, Olivia, don't be normal, that's an order! Okay, enough of that holographic stuff, let's get outside. I feel like a stroll to the park and then back to your homework."

They both hopped up as Sonia pulled her curly hair back into a ponytail. She hit the lights, taking a glance around the apartment before closing the door behind her.

Olivia's art was plastered on the freezer box in the kitchen and several other places around the living room she felt the need to display her artwork. She had insisted that Sonia put Michael's picture in a frame in the living room so they wouldn't forget him. They chose a picture with all three of them, laughing and squeezing each other, taken at the local aquarium before he had left on his mission nearly six months ago.

She sighed, standing in the doorway, contemplating the momentous news and what it would mean for their little "family." She and Olivia had come so far. Her reclusiveness had been broken by Michael and the young Olivia. Her paranoia was still there and would rear its ugly head from time to time, but knowing someone was relying on her, trusting her, and most importantly, loving her unconditionally had changed Sonia. Much like their daring escape from Moon 002 had made her stronger, Michael and Olivia had softened the heart of a woman that at one time hated her life. A woman who figured she would never fall in love, much less have a child of her own. Now, Sonia Bonnel had purpose.

Likewise, the scared girl that had awakened inside a dark room back on Mining Complex VI had changed and blossomed. And along with it, her love for life, love for people, and finding the good in everything and every circumstance if possible. She always seemed to have a kind word for Sonia. About how much she liked her cooking, the curly hair that fell into her eyes, how she smelled when she put on perfume. How she wished she would grow up to be just like her mom.

She closed the door and turned to join Olivia. Outside, the street bustled with activity. People stood outside their apartments talking with each other, most assuredly about the breaking news. Sonia didn't want to interact with anyone. She wanted to be alone with Olivia. Continually trying to push the thought of Michael no longer being alive from her mind made each step more difficult. *Be strong for the girl* she thought, making her way out of the neighborhood.

Her communicator vibrated in her pocket. She reached into her pants pocket, producing a small rectangular device, and pushed *On*. A small hologram appeared above the flat surface. Acting President Jake Riley himself projected in front of her, stopping Olivia and Sonia in their tracks.

CHAPTER 39

WELCOME HOME

"Sonia, Olivia, how are you?" Jake Riley asked.

"We're fine, Jake. Michael, where is Michael?" Sonia blurted out.

Jake sighed. "Sonia, this was a hard-fought battle every step of the way. But we did it. First, your mom, she's alive and doing well. She's going to get that surgery she needs. I promise she will."

Sonia's tears welled up, streaming down her cheeks. Olivia clung to her mother, looking and listening to the now acting president of Troria. "Where's my dad?" she asked meekly.

"Olivia, it's been so long. I actually think you've grown a bit!" Jake responded gently.

Sonia and Olivia both fell silent. W*hat was he not telling them? Why was he avoiding answering about their Michael?*

Jake sighed. "So, here's the deal. Michael took a fall, along with Gonidec himself who set off a neutron charge. He saved my life and put the final nail in Gonidec's coffin so to speak," he said reverently.

"And?" Sonia responded curtly, her heart slamming in her chest.

"And...luckily, he landed in the bunker's private swimming pool. Gonidec's lavish excess broke Michael's fall. Connor didn't make it. A lot of people didn't make it," Jake said sadly.

Now Olivia was crying. So far, all the news to her still developing brain seemed bad.

"Is Michael alive?" Sonia said, holding her breath.

"Yes, he is alive. But Sonia, he's in bad shape. The fall was high. We're still trying to figure out the extent of the internal injuries he sustained. Thus far, he's non-responsive. We don't know if there's substantial brain damage or if he's paralyzed. We'll have more information soon. I have the best doctors here on Troria already working on him now." Jake hung his head at having to be the bearer of such bad news.

Sobbing, terrified, Sonia forced herself to be strong. Strong for her daughter who needed her right now more than ever.

"Okay. So, what now? What do we do?" she asked shakily, pulling herself together.

"Hang tight. I'll keep you posted," Jake replied, his heart heavy for them, and for the entire region he was now charged with leading. There was still much to do. People enslaved. Factions of Gonidec's regime hunkered down for a fight. The Alnorix Mining Organization was a whole other mess he was going to have to work through.

"No," Sonia said quickly, wiping her eyes. "We aren't going to sit here and wait. We're coming to Troria. For Michael. For my mom. We've made Railara home, for now. But home is wherever you're loved ones are. And that's not here."

The holographic image of Jake Riley fell silent, staring at a determined Sonia and her daughter. He looked off-screen at someone talking to him. "Okay, yes, I'll be right there."

He looked back at Sonia and sighed. "There is one bit of good news, potentially. We can't perform it in the shape he's in, but if there is any improvement whatsoever, we can indeed do the life-limiter reversal. I won't get into the logistics of it, not now. But if he survives..." Jake paused.

"If he survives," was all Sonia could respond. The lump in her throat stopped her from saying more.

"Look, we can talk about this later. He's a good man. A fighter. And we'll do everything we can on our end, that's the best I can do right now. Olivia, he kept that picture you gave him on the morning he left in his pocket. He loves you. He loves both of you. I'll be in touch. Jake out."

The holographic image vanished as Sonia and Olivia stood in silence, contemplating the news they had just received.

"What now, Mama?"

"What now? We go to him, that's what," Sonia replied, turning to hold Olivia in her arms.

"Where I go, you go. Where you go, I go," they both said to each other.

In the weeks following Gonidec's death and his military's defeat, the leaders of every planet in the quadrant met to discuss the next steps for maintaining peace throughout the solar system. Kernadium and Poule plant harvesting were primary topics of discussion, the very reason Gonidec had started the war in the first place.

Gideon Novare spoke at length about Railara's experimentation with magnetic propulsion fueled by a liquid called synth, the use of which meant travel time from one side of the solar system to the other was cut in half. A small fleet of experimental space travel vehicles had been developed and were exceeding all expectations. This would lead to the near complete ceasing of Poule plant harvesting, saving numerous planets from their ultimate destruction and thus saving the planets they were being harvested on.

Cloning for means of profit was banned immediately across the quadrant. The AMO and some of its leaders, including all of its board of directors went into hiding off-world once Gonidec's authoritarian government was dismantled in the weeks after Jake Riley became the acting president. Most, however, were quickly captured and extradited back to Troria to stand trial later. Mercy was shown to the remorseful that surrendered willingly, but all were held accountable.

Those Gonidec sympathizers who had committed war crimes fled Troria in their *Paladine Fighters* but with nowhere to go, were quickly captured and brought to justice. None of the planets in quadrant 8304 allowed any ship from Troria to enter their airspace without approval from its new, free government.

The remaining mining facilities were shut down temporarily until it was decided what to do with them. Building back each planet and moon's ecosystem from the AMO's destructive practices was top priority—a huge undertaking, but one that the now united planets of quadrant 8304 all agreed to take part in. The infrastructure was already there so a bit of tweaking and the mining facilities would become planet rehabilitation stations.

Moon 002, however, was a lost cause. The Rot was still there and had potentially gone airborne, if initial reports and scans of the surface were to be trusted. The large insectoid creatures that had surfaced from the deep core of the moon after the mining complex's destruction remained for a period then retreated back down into their cavernous dwelling places. Moon 002 was deemed 'off limits' across the quadrant. The hope was for the planet to eventually heal itself, though top scientists across the quadrant estimated it could take hundreds, if not thousands, of years.

Memorials were held across the planet for the countless dead, murdered at the hands of Gonidec and his kill squads, as well as for the countless clones, burned to ashes for minor infractions or slight defects, or simply after one year of service. And for all of those who gave their lives fighting against tyranny, including Elise Bennet, Kimberly Lutz, Filip Marsa, Connor Brook and the numerous members of the resistance.

No mention was made however, of one Dr. Anthony Petrino. His information was indeed vital to the success of the war that had been waged, but for his crimes against both humans and clones, he was to be forgotten. And he quickly was.

Candidates were soon selected on Troria, and a free election was to be held within a year's time. One person, one vote. Absolutely no voter intimidation. Jake entertained the thought of running, but thought it best for the planet to start fresh. He would go where he was needed. And for the first year of a new Troria, he would fill the shoes of president until the planet was stabilized.

No one ever discovered what had happened to Alnorix Mining Transport 24. It was surmised that the creature that took the ship kept it as a souvenir. Once, a year after its disappearance, a distant and barely audible transmission came through to Trorian airspace controls. Garbled and brief, the most observant of officials reported it sounded like the voice of one Omar Botto, a high-ranking lieutenant in Gonidec's regime wanted for numerous war crimes. A single word could be made out in the static. "Help."

No one knew how to track the transmission, when it was sent, or if it was indeed Botto. Regardless, his arrest warrant remained active throughout the quadrant, *just in case.*

The large celestial being that had frozen the AMT-24 was never seen again in quadrant 8304. Much talk was made on all of the planets about what it might have been. The only evidence of its existence was Michael, Sonia, and Olivia's eyewitness account of their run-in with it. That, and the queen's carcass back on Moon 002, most of which no longer existed. But it remained proof that enormous celestial beings once roamed the universe.

A sleek, shiny orb glided through the solar system. Its occupants, one Sonia Bonnel and her daughter, Olivia Bonnel. Their current destination, Troria. The ship utilized new technology shared from a highly advanced planet in a nearby quadrant of space. It had been discovered that one of the moons orbiting the planet Druthea, the planet closest to Railara, was flowing with the bright blue liquid known as synth which powered the new technology Railara had created.

Sonia piloted it, having been granted access to it personally by not only Gideon Novare but also the acting president of Troria, Jake Riley. After several weeks of back and forth, constantly being met with "It's too dangerous," she finally got the only answer she would accept: "Yes, you have clearance."

Once granted, it was a win-win for Railara as well as Troria. The spacecraft's technology was to be shared throughout the quadrant and in a show of good will, Railara wanted Troria to have it first. The prototype was named *The Elise*.

With the magnetic engines fueled by the synth, the small shiny silver craft could achieve significantly faster speeds than even the greatest ships in the Railarian fleet. Or any other ship in the quadrant, for that matter.

All planets' governments were made aware of the mission and instructed to lend a hand, if needed. While the quadrant was free from the Gonidec war machine, there were still pirates that flew their *Executor* fighters, jumping from space port to space port and scouring the solar system for a quick payday. New tech such as the *Elise* would be highly sought after.

Once Sonia was quickly trained on the relatively simple operations of the *Elise*, they were on their way. She was now grateful for the small bit of training she had received on piloting space vehicles when she attended Otheania University years earlier.

The *Elise*, while small in size, had bedding and a washroom and the flight had been pleasant, fun even, with Olivia constantly looking out the viewscreen at the wonders of outer space. There was even a holographic viewer to entertain Olivia, along with her drawings. One of which was similar to the one she had given Michael the morning he left on his mission, though now significantly better in quality.

On numerous occasions during their trip, they were greeted by ships patrolling the planets they passed. Olivia loved this and gave each individual ship its own unique name, making up her own stories of their daring adventures across the solar system while Sonia piloted the ship and listened to the wild and inventive stories, sometimes joining in on the storytelling.

When they arrived at their destination, President Jake Riley was too busy to meet them at the landing port, but they were given a warm welcome by several of his top aides who quickly took them to the Trorian hospital Mercy Medical, located in the heart of Paladine City where Jake had made sure to have Sonia's mother transferred.

The sky was blue and the star that lit this end of the quadrant shined down on the city bustling with activity—once home to Sonia. Now she was back, though she was not sure for how long. She had grown fond of Railara, but much hinged on the status of her mother and the man she loved, both of whom were waiting for her inside.

She and Olivia stared up at the tall, old, and somewhat imposing hospital in need of renovating, something she was sure would happen now that funds were freed up on Troria. Jake Riley's aides had to get back to their duties in the capital building but gave Sonia a card that was good for an unlimited stay in the closest hotel to the hospital until she figured out what her next step was. Though far removed from the technically advanced Railarian city of Aphus, Paladine City was looking significantly better than the last time she had been here, attending the university.

Olivia sensed her hesitation and took her hand. "Come on, Mama, he's waiting for us," she said, sounding surprisingly grownup in that instant.

Sonia smiled down at her daughter who wore a white sundress that always made her bright green eyes and vibrant blond hair stand out. It was her favorite outfit; she wanted to look her best when she saw Michael for the first time in over seven months.

This young girl constantly gave Sonia a newfound appreciation for life, showing her that each day was a gift not to be wasted but to be treasured. To make wherever you are better than if you weren't there. Olivia had made Sonia a better person and Sonia treasured every day she was blessed to have this young girl in her life. Her daughter, whom she now loved more than life itself.

They walked into the hospital and were greeted by several friendly staff members who were expecting them. Upon arrival, they checked in, showing the proper credentials and were directed to the recovery ward where Sonia's mother was waiting for them.

"Mom!" Sonia exclaimed, opening the double doors leading into the large recovery ward. She ran forward with Olivia, wrapping her arms around her mom who stood to her feet and returned the embrace.

"How are you, Sonia?" Corinna asked, teary-eyed.

"You're out of bed!" Sonia exclaimed, pulling back to look at her.

"Surgery went great, full recovery. Thanks to your friend and our current president, Jake Riley!" Corinna exclaimed.

The woman had aged drastically since Sonia had last seen her. Gray-haired and frail, but alive and happy.

"And you, you must be Olivia," Corinna bent down to look at the young blond girl.

"Pleased to meet you," Olivia replied, shaking Corinna's hand.

"Honey, you don't know me, and I don't know you, yet. But if you wouldn't mind, I would sure like to try out one of those famous hugs your mom's told me about," Corinna said.

Olivia didn't hesitate, throwing her arms around the elderly woman, being careful not to squeeze too tightly, knowing she had surgery recently.

Corinna pulled back, her eyes wet with fresh tears.

"So, can I call you grandma, or should I call you Cor..." Olivia began.

"Grandma. Grandma would be just perfect, sweety," Corinna said warmly, wiping her eyes.

Corinna filled them in on her successful surgery and discharge from the hospital, and their short discussion came to a close with a plan for getting together the next evening to share a meal. Corinna insisted they come over to her place.

"Okay, Mom, it's a date. Do you have a ride back to your place?" Sonia asked.

"Oh, don't you worry about me, honey. I've got connections with the president of Troria. I've got a ride ready and waiting," Corinna responded laughing.

Corinna became serious, moving in closer to her daughter so Olivia wouldn't hear what she was about to say. "Sonia, the things that I have witnessed since you've been gone. Awful things. Neighbors raped and murdered, people starved to death, torture, destruction. I didn't want to go on. I wanted to die. But knowing you were somewhere up there in the stars doing what you could to save me, it's what kept me going."

She paused, a tear rolling down her cheek.

Sonia rested a hand on her mother's shoulder. "Mom, I'm sorry I left you for so long. That I didn't heed your words about cloning and working for as corrupt a company as the AMO. I will live with that the rest of my life. You've been so good to me. And I intend to make your golden years the best of your life, and to do my best to count each day as the blessing that it is."

Corinna wept softly again at her daughter's dramatic change. She was staring at a new person, one now filled with hope. She sniffed and said calmly, "Go to him. It's time."

Sonia immediately felt a lump in her throat and her heart began racing.

They said their goodbyes, gave one more hug, which Corinna gave Olivia a big thumbs-up for, making the girl giggle, then parted ways.

The elevator ride up to the intensive care unit felt endless. Even Olivia fell silent. Once at the top floor, they checked in and a staff member led them to his room. Room 406.

The door was closed but the nurse told them they were free to enter whenever they wanted. Sonia and Olivia stood outside the door. "Olivia, honey, I've been given updates regularly on his status. But you know he was severely injured," Sonia said shakily.

"I know, Mama. I just want to see him, he's my hero you know?" Olivia said simply.

Sonia quickly looked away; she felt the tears coming once more. The innocence and love that emanated from this child on a seemingly daily basis amazed her. Composing herself, she opened the door and, holding Olivia's hand, walked through.

The room was well lit, a window against the back wall revealed tall buildings and periodic transport shuttles zipping by. A vase filled with multi-colored flowers sat at the bedside. Pings and beeps softly emanated inside the room from the various life saving and life-preserving machinery set up throughout.

Michael lay on his bed, his eyes closed. Seeing him, Olivia broke free from Sonia's grasp and ran to him, throwing her arms around the sleeping man, her left hand clasping the picture she drew for him on the flight in from Railara.

Joining Olivia, Sonia looked down at Michael, thankful he looked as good as he did, considering what he had been through and the injuries he had sustained, including numerous broken bones, a collapsed lung, minor brain trauma and a spinal injury. After multiple surgeries, the brain and spinal trauma were no longer life threatening.

However, she had been told by the doctors earlier that he had regained consciousness but only intermittently. And although the one-year life-limiter had been removed, per Jake Riley's request, he would need to fully regain consciousness and begin recovering from his injuries in order for the procedure to take effect. As it was now, he was asleep more often than he was awake, and when he was awake, he was non-responsive. Thus far, he hadn't uttered a word since the fall into the pool.

Sonia had remained strong through the news. She had to, for Olivia. But now, seeing the broken man lying in front of them, willing to give his life for the good of all the planets in the solar system, for the two of them who loved him so much…it was all so overwhelming, Sonia didn't know how she was going to keep from coming undone.

Olivia wouldn't let go. She clung to him tightly, her small body almost lying on top of Michael. Resting her ear on his chest, she felt his slow, shallow breathing. Hot tears streamed from her green eyes onto Michael's white sheets.

Sonia gently stroked his hair, running her hands through it, her own tears falling to the floor. With her free hand, she reached over and took his limp hand into her own. It was warm. She squeezed it gently.

"Oh, Michael. We've so missed you, but we're here now," she whispered.

Neither her nor Olivia said anything for a brief period, the three of them breathing together in the quiet room.

Olivia moved up to his ear and whispered in her childlike voice, "Mom and I came across the solar system to be with you. I love you and want you back. Can you hear me? Please? I need you, we both need you! You're the only dad I have, the only one I want, forever! Please!"

Sonia bent down, ready to gently pull the weeping child off of Michael, afraid it might hurt him, but she stopped. His hand softly squeezed hers. Wide-eyed, she looked up at him. His free hand was moving, wrapping around the girl, holding her, as the hand that Sonia held pulled her in.

Olivia felt his embrace and buried her face against his chest.

Michael's eyes opened, feeling the warmth and the love that surrounded him for the first time in months. His hoarse voice whispered, "Sonia? Olivia?"

Through her tears, Olivia whispered back, "Where you go, we all go."

And all was well on Troria and across quadrant 8304.

ABOUT THE AUTHOR

Eugene Weaver was born on August 8, 1974 in Millersburg, Ohio. He and his wife Joani have been married for 20 years and have two boys. They currently live in North Canton, Ohio.

Eugene has been an avid lover of movies, music, and the arts nearly all his life. At 12 years old, he wrote his first novel, *Pivoron Mountain* in longhand cursive. With the persuasion of his boys, he has decided after 36 years to take another trip to that magical world he created in his childhood home where all he had was his imagination, a pencil, and some paper. The basement has been replaced with a home of his own and the pencil and paper are now his laptop. His first novel, *Thunder Stone Realm,* was published in 2023. *Battle for Quadrant 8304* is his fourth novel.

Printed in the USA
CPSIA information can be obtained
at www.ICGtesting.com
CBHW071921090924
14064CB00009B/132